DECREE

TRICIA MINGERINK

DECREE

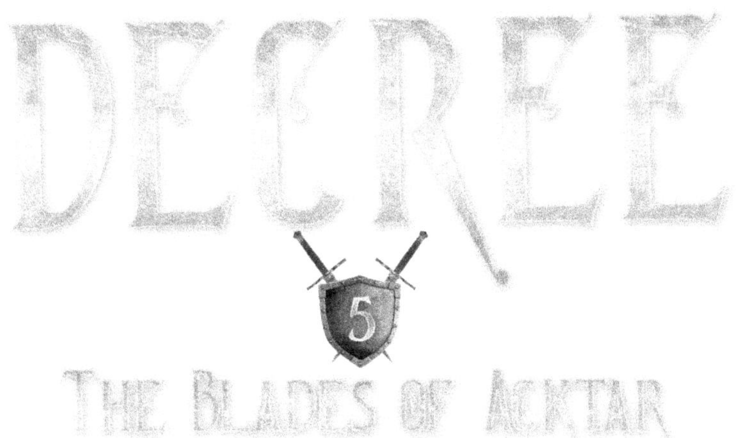

THE BLADES OF ACKTAR

DECREE

The Blades of Acktar Book 5

Copyright © 2018 by Tricia Mingerink

Published by Sword & Cross Publishing

Grand Rapids, MI

Cover Art by Jesus Da Silva on Fiverr

Typography by Get Covers and Sword & Cross Publishing

Map by Md Shah Alam on Fiverr

Character Illustrations by H.S.J. Williams

To God, my King and Father. Soli Deo Gloria

LCCN: 2019907325

ISBN: 978-1-943442-07-2

So he fed them according to the integrity of his heart; and guided them by the skilfulness of his hands.
\- Psalm 78:72

Before I was afflicted I went astray: but now have I kept thy word...It is good for me that I have been afflicted; that I might learn thy statutes.
\- Psalm 119:67,71

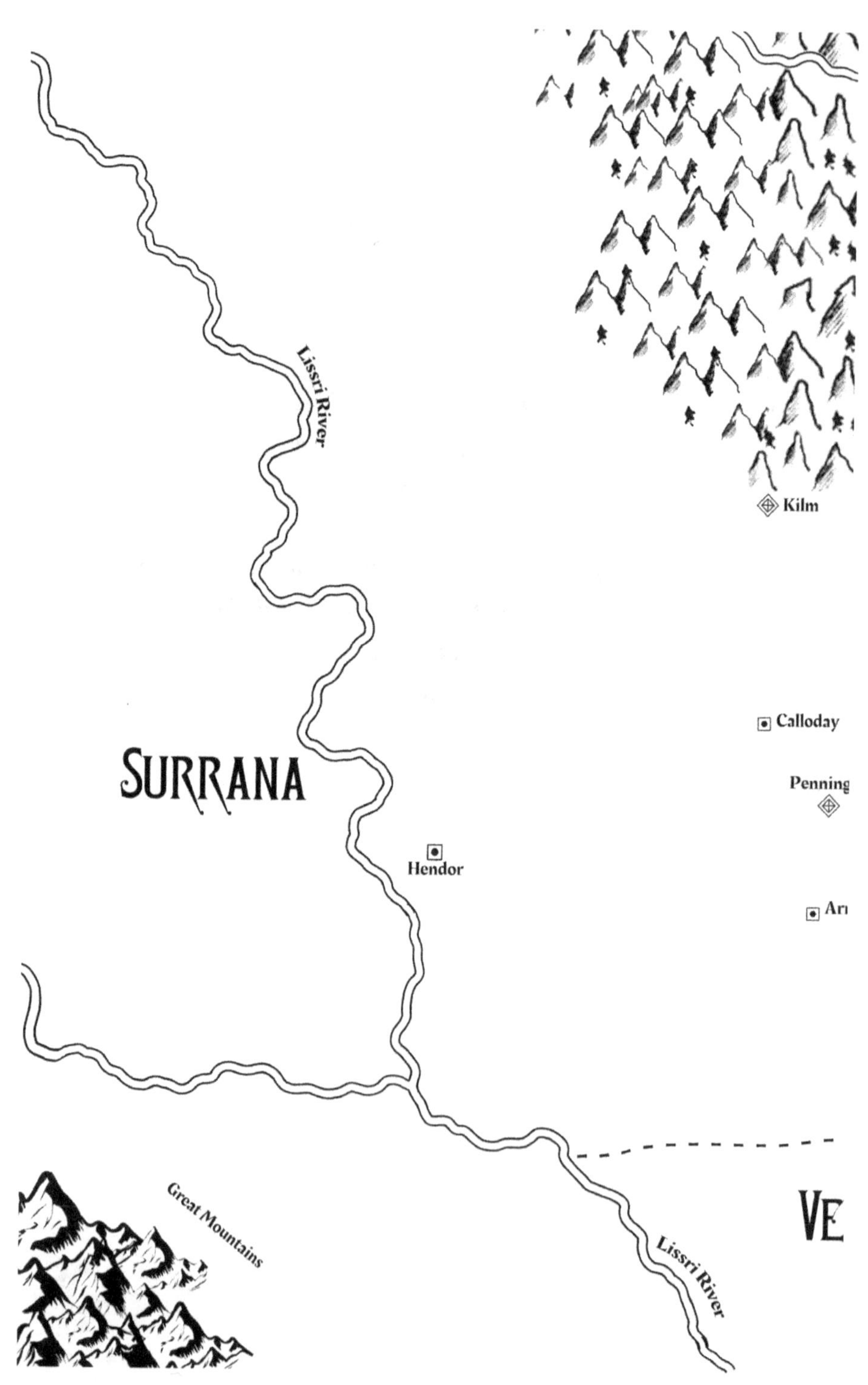

Lissri River
Kilm
Calloday
Penning
SURRANA
Hendor
Ari
Great Mountains
Lissri River
VE

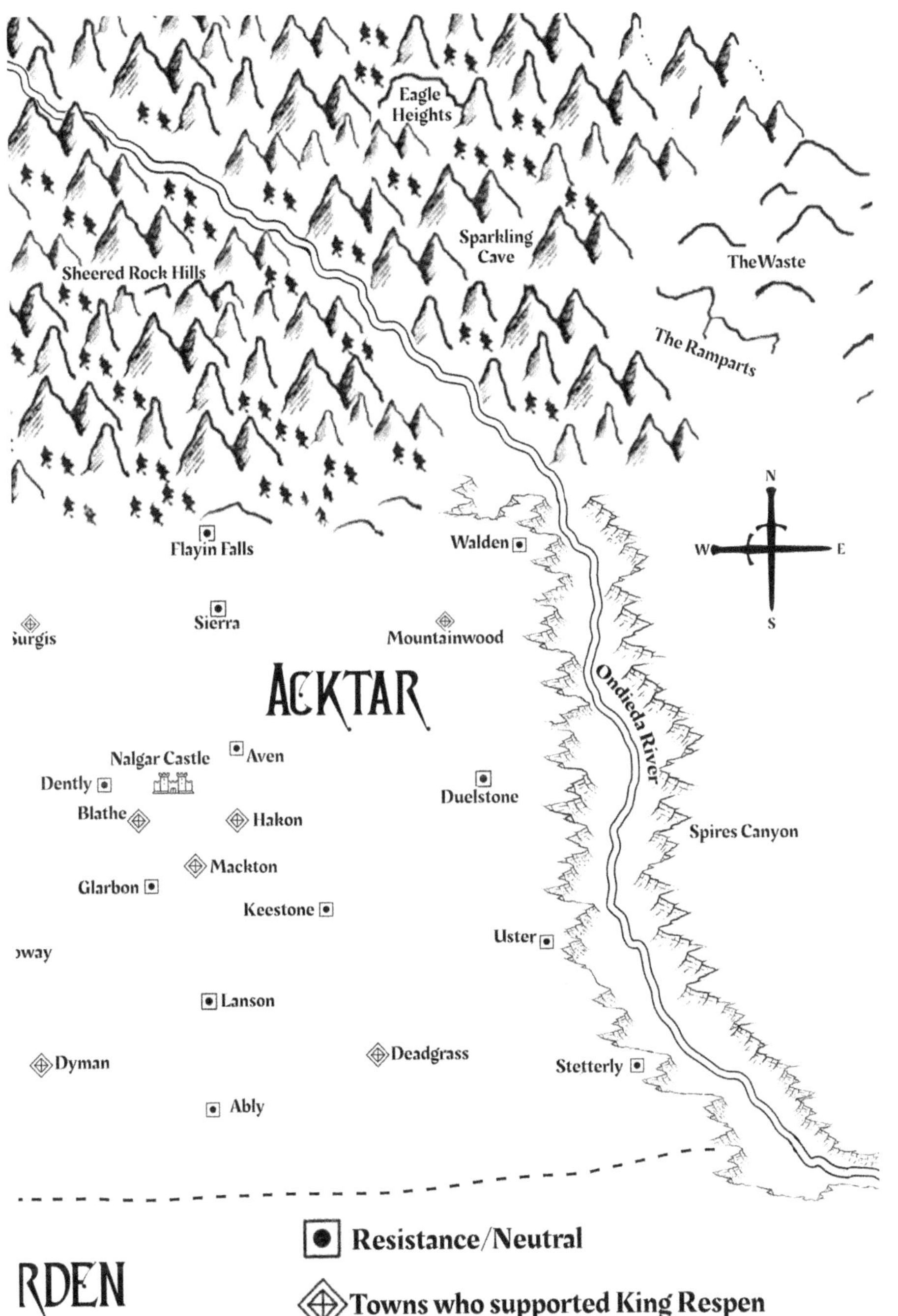

Eagle Heights
Sparkling Cave
The Waste
The Ramparts
Sheered Rock Hills
N
W
E
S
Flayin Falls
Walden
Sierra
Surgis
Mountainwood
Ondieda River
ACKTAR
Nalgar Castle
Aven
Dently
Duelstone
Blathe
Hakon
Spires Canyon
Mackton
Glarbon
Keestone
Uster
oway
Lanson
Dyman
Deadgrass
Stetterly
Ably
RDEN
Resistance/Neutral
Towns who supported King Respen

MEETING MARTYN

Martyn's stomach ached. It had given up on rumbling two, almost three, days ago now. He curled up on the thin blanket on the floor, trying not to shiver at the cold in the church's sanctuary in the town of Blathe.

His nine-year-old brother Owen curled next to him, his lips chapped and white with the cold and hunger, mumbling his prayers before bed.

Martyn probably should be saying his own prayers, but what good would it do? Why wasn't God listening?

Papa knelt beside them and gripped first Owen's shoulder, then Martyn's. There was something in his grip. Something strong, despite the lack of food turning his hands into nothing but jutting bones and tendons. When he spoke, his voice had an odd, choked sound to it. "Did you boys say your prayers?"

"Yep." Owen said, shifting closer to Martyn. Huddling together for warmth.

Martyn nodded. A lie, even if he didn't say it out loud.

When Papa looked down at him, his dark brown eyes—just like Martyn's and Owen's—had an extra sheen to them.

Martyn had seen that look before, every time Papa had to tell the family he'd lost everything and they'd have to move. Again.

What was wrong now? Martyn's stomach clenched even tighter, stabbing pain through his middle all the way to his back.

Mama knelt beside Papa and stroked Owen's hair. "Goodnight, Owen. Get some sleep."

Her hand moved to Martyn's hair, and he didn't remind her that he was eleven years old and far too old to have his mama tucking him into bed each night.

"Sleep tight, Martyn." Her voice broke, and her fingers lingered in his curls. She bent and kissed his forehead. Something wet and warm splashed against his cheek.

When he looked up at her, Papa was helping her to her feet and held her, whispering something to her too quietly for Martyn to hear.

Something was wrong. Or perhaps it was the three days without food. Maybe Mama and Papa feared they wouldn't be able to get food tomorrow either.

How long did it take a person to starve to death? He wasn't sure he wanted to know the answer. All they'd had for the past three days had been handfuls of snow. Even he knew they couldn't live forever on just snow.

The Bible said stealing was wrong, but God wasn't giving them food and Martyn no longer cared. Tomorrow he would slip away and take food. He wasn't going to let Owen go another day without something to eat.

With that decided and the winter wind howling through the church's rafters, Martyn drifted off to sleep.

He woke cold. He rolled over, patting the spot where Owen had been last night.

Empty. Not even a blanket lay on the cold, wooden floor.

Martyn opened his eyes and bolted upright. "Owen?"

No one answered.

"Papa? Mama?"

Still no answer.

The sound of shuffling feet came from the main aisle. Martyn clambered to his feet, peering over the pews.

The minister strode toward him, his face pinched with a scowl. His gaze scanned the sanctuary before landing on Martyn. The scowl deepened. "They aren't here, boy."

"What?" Martyn glanced at the stained glass windows. The colored glass made it hard to see, but the outside light had the dark gray of early morning.

"They left in the middle of the night. Asked me to look after you." The minister's mouth curled. "Riffraff couldn't even be bothered to look after their own children. Think I'd let their brat dirty my church?"

Gone? Martyn stared. Why had they left him behind? "Where did they go?"

"Don't you get it, boy? They skipped town. Couldn't be bothered with feeding you." The minister marched up to Martyn and grabbed his shoulder. The minister's fingers dug in like a dog bite. Martyn squirmed, trying to get free, but the man's grip only tightened. "As if I would allow you to spend one more minute infesting this building."

Martyn couldn't resist as he was propelled down the aisle and out the main doors. The minister gave him a shove, and Martyn slipped on the icy steps. He fell, striking his elbow, his hip, his shin, before he cracked the side of his head against the ice and cobblestones of the road.

Behind him, the church doors slammed shut.

Martyn staggered to his feet, pain lancing from his head down through his arms and legs.

They'd left him. That's what the tears and the choked voices were about last night. This wasn't an accident. His parents had purposely left him behind.

The town of Blathe spread before him, coated in a layer of ice and snow. Heavy flakes drifted down from the solid gray sky. Bundled shapes of people hurried up and down the street. Strangers. Strangers who, if they were anything like the minister and the others his parents had begged for help in the past, would only kick at Martyn and turn him away.

"Papa! Mama!" Martyn cupped his hands around his mouth and shouted. He knew there would be no answer, but the empty wind still tore through him.

Alone. Abandoned.

The world tilted and swayed. Hunger. The pain in his head. He sank onto the church's steps, hugging himself to try to stay warm. Tears pricked at the corners of his eyes. Why had they left him alone? Would they be back? Or had they left him for good because he was one mouth too many to feed?

"Mama!"

Of course there was no answer.

A single tear leaked from his eye, and he shoved it away before it could freeze on his cheeks. No, he wasn't going to cry. He was far too old to cry.

The faint whiff of baking bread wafted on the next gust of wind.

Food.

Papa and Mama weren't here. No one was here who would care if he stole as much food as he wanted. And the more he thought about it, the more strength surged back into his fingers.

He was on his own. And if that meant stealing to survive, then fine. That's exactly what he'd do. He'd steal, and he wouldn't care if Papa and Mama said it was wrong.

If they'd wanted him to be a good boy, then they shouldn't have abandoned him.

Twelve-year-old Martyn pushed his legs to go faster, pumping his arms, a loaf of bread still gripped in his hand. He didn't look back. That would only slow him down.

Instead, he darted into an alley, turned up another tiny alley along the back of the crumbling houses, and worked his way deeper into the maze that was the oldest section of Blathe. The ground sloped underneath him, making his calves hurt and the air hitch in his chest.

He turned a corner and skidded to a halt. A group of six boys, all older from fourteen to seventeen, leaned against the walls of the buildings and a crumbling, four-foot-high stone wall that cut through this part of the town.

Martyn tightened his grip on the bread. Only a few more

yards, and he could've bolted into the hole none of the bigger boys could squirm into anymore. But, no, this gang had to intercept him. And on a day that he'd managed to steal a freshly baked loaf, not just a burned crust.

He wasn't going to hand over his rightfully stolen bread without a fight. Perhaps, if he made a dash for it, he could get past them.

The oldest boy sidled forward. "Hand it over."

Instead of replying, Martyn ducked his head and charged forward. He rammed a shoulder into one of the smaller boys, opening a gap.

Only a few feet farther. If only he could get past them. Just a little faster. A little farther.

An arm entered his line of vision, swinging toward him. He didn't even have time to slow before it slammed into his stomach.

Pain. Martyn's knees hit the cobblestones.

The oldest boy was standing in front of Martyn. The boy swung a foot back, preparing for a kick.

It was either take the beating or fight back.

Martyn stuffed as much of the loaf as he could in his mouth and lunged. He tackled the boy, landing on top.

A short victory. The other boys piled on top, and it was all Martyn could do to lash out. A fist there. A kick there. But he was taking more than he was giving, and in another moment, his face smashed into the cobblestones.

Another lost meal. Another beating. Martyn struggled, but too many hands and knees pressed him down. Still he fought.

Then a weight lifted from his back. The hand shoving his face into the ground released him.

Martyn raised his head and found himself looking at a pair of large hooves only a few inches away. He followed the hooves up to brown hair and knobby horse knees before he couldn't crane his neck any farther.

He scrambled to his feet. A man sat astride the horse dressed in a fine, dark blue shirt with black trousers and knee-high black boots. His hair and neatly trimmed beard were also black.

Martyn had only seen him at a distance before, but he recognized him.

Lord Respen Felix, lord of Blathe.

This couldn't be good. Martyn glanced around for a means to escape, but Lord Felix's guards hemmed him in. The other boys had disappeared or were huddled on the ground cowering before the guards.

A slow smile crossed Lord Felix's face, and he nodded, as if in some decision. He pointed at Martyn. "Take him with us."

Martyn didn't fight the two guards who pushed him down the hallway in Blathe Manor, not with Lord Respen Felix's words still ringing in his ears. Loyalty. Obedience. All Lord Felix asked. In return, Martyn would always have a roof over his head, food in his stomach, and clothes on his back. More than his parents had managed to provide for him.

Freshly bathed and clothed in a set of new, black clothes, Martyn hugged the stack of books he'd been given, his stomach filled for the first time in nearly a year since he'd been abandoned on Blathe's streets.

Would his parents come back for him? Surely if they intended to return, they would've done so by now. Lord Felix had promised he would send men to look for them, but it would do little good. Martyn's parents had abandoned him, and that was that. No explanation. No goodbye. No warning. Just gone.

The guards halted in front of a door near the end of the hallway, and one of them took out a key and unlocked the door. The second guard shoved Martyn inside and slammed the door behind him. The back of Martyn's neck prickled at the sound of the key turning in the lock once again.

He swept a glance around the room in front of him. Bunk beds stuck out from the walls on either side of the door, leaving a long aisle down the center.

Boys, dressed in black like he was, lounged on several of the bunk beds, some with books spread out before them, others just sprawled.

Martyn tensed, the instincts he'd gained from a year on the streets pinging inside his head. There was something in the eyes that swung his way, a look he recognized from the gangs of street boys that banded together, the kind that punished those who didn't bow to their demands.

Seven of the boys were clustered in the bunks close to the door on the right side. That was the gang in this room. In the back of the room on the left, an eighth, dark-haired boy sat in the corner on the top bunk, a book open before him. That one had refused to join the others. A loner.

The boy on the bunk nearest to the door swung to his feet. He was over half a foot taller than Martyn with sandy-colored hair and pale blue eyes. Probably sixteen years old or more with the bulkier muscles of a teen rather than the stringy, lanky build that Martyn still had at twelve.

Trouble.

Two of the other boys swung to their feet as well, flanking the first boy.

Lots of trouble. Martyn braced himself, gripping the stack of school books to his chest as if a few books were going to stop these older boys from giving him a beating. If he'd been on the streets, he would've been looking for the nearest alley to bolt. No such escape here.

Would the guards come back if they heard trouble? Or was this pack of boys left to fight it out?

The pale-eyed boy halted in front of Martyn and crossed his arms. "What's your name, street rat?"

Martyn lifted his chin. The worst thing he could do now was show fear. "Martyn Hamish."

"Well, Hamish. I'm Harrison Vane. I run things here. You do what I say. If I want a portion of your meal, you give it to me. If I want you to do my mathematics work for me, you do it. Understand?"

Martyn hadn't put up with the bullies on the street. He wasn't about to squirm for this one now. "And if I don't?"

Harrison Vane uncrossed his arms, letting his clenched fists lower to his sides. "Then you're going to spend tonight with bruises. And when you fail your training tomorrow, you'll have to deal with Lord Felix's punishment too."

Martyn shot a quick glance at the boy still sitting in the far left corner. The boy's head remained bent over his book, a pen in his hand as he scratched an answer to a problem. Still, Martyn had the impression that the boy was aware of everything going on near the front of the room.

There had to be a way to avoid joining. Vane and his gang were leaving that one alone.

But, if the boy was anything like Martyn had learned to be on the streets, there would be no help for Martyn from that direction.

When Martyn focused on Vane again, Vane's eyes were narrowed, a scowl on his face.

Martyn dropped the books. They hit the wooden floor with a ringing smack, and several of the boys behind Vane jumped. With no escape, there was only one option left with bullies like this.

Fight.

Clenching his fists, Martyn faced Vane. "I'm going to keep my own food and do my own work. Not yours."

Before Vane could attack, Martyn dove at Vane's legs, tackling him. Together, they crashed to the floor. Martyn sprang to his feet and tried to skip away, but then the other boys were on him. Two of them gripped his arms.

He tried to shake them off, but they were bigger. Better fed. Stronger.

Vane approached. His eyes were the ice-blue of a winter sky, but there was a spark in them, like he enjoyed this.

Martyn ducked his chin. Not in surrender, but to protect himself from the coming blow. If he couldn't escape, then he would take this beating the best he could.

Vane's fist blurred toward Martyn's face. Before it connected, another boy was there, a blur of dark hair and black clothes.

The boy grabbed Vane's arm, yanking it back as he planted a foot behind Vane's knee and smashed the heel of his palm into Vane's face.

Vane stumbled back, hands to his face. Only the boys behind him kept him from crashing to the floor.

The boy spun, kicked a heel into the knee of one of the boys holding Martyn. With one of his arms freed, Martyn shoved the second boy away from him.

Vane straightened, dabbing at a trickle of blood from a split lower lip. "Torren. You don't want to step into this. You can't win."

The black-haired boy crouched in front of Martyn, every muscle in his body tensed for action. "No. But I will make it hurt. And you don't want that. Not if you want to keep your perfect record with Lord Felix."

Vane eyed the boy, then swept a glare up to Martyn.

Martyn did his best to glare back. Whatever it was about this boy that was making Vane back off, Martyn wanted to help as much as he could.

"Fine." Vane stepped back, half turning as if the two of them were so far beneath his notice they didn't deserve his attention. "Keep the street rat if you want. Useless thing that he is, he won't last a year."

Vane sprawled onto his bunk as if backing down was all his own idea. The other boys trailed him, some spitting at Martyn as they passed.

Martyn turned to thank the boy who'd forced Vane to back off, but the boy was already stalking back to his bunk in the far corner. After grabbing his books from the floor, Martyn hurried after him. It was either that or stay alone near Vane and his pack of bullies.

The boy—Torren, as Vane had called him—swung onto the top bunk, placing his back to the corner once again. His eyes flicked up briefly, too quickly for Martyn to get much of an impression besides that they were some light color and nearly as hard and cold as Vane's.

Martyn halted. Should he claim the other far corner and try to stick it out here alone as he had on the streets? In a large town like Blathe with plenty of alleys and abandoned homes to provide hideaways and escape routes, surviving by oneself worked.

But here, in this one room, there was no place to run. Vane and his bullies could do whatever they wanted to Martyn the moment he tried to sleep. He could either give in and join them or he could try to convince Torren that sticking together was their best option.

Was Torren any better option than Vane? He was just as cold. Just as dangerous.

But he had saved Martyn from a beating and risked a beating of his own to do it. That was something.

Martyn pointed to the lower bunk. "Mind if I take that one?"

This time, Torren's gaze lifted and stayed on Martyn. There was something in his eyes—something beyond the cold—that struck Martyn. Almost like...

Owen. Martyn swallowed. Was his brother all right? Or had his parents abandoned him, as they had Martyn? Surely not. Surely, if they'd taken Owen along, then they'd chosen to keep him. He had to be happy. Cared for.

While Martyn was here. Locked in this room with a bunch of boys that seemed one wrong word away from killing each other.

"Why?" Torren's voice was short. Sharp.

Martyn didn't look away. "Because I would rather join

you than them. And we'll be stronger together than each of us on our own."

"How do I know I can trust you?"

What kind of life had Martyn stumbled into? Strangely enough, the question was reassuring. Loving his family and attempting to cling to the faith of his parents had required trust, trust too easily broken. Perhaps this trust—one based on their shared need for survival—was the kind of trust that could actually work.

"You can't, just as I don't know I can trust you." Martyn did his best to appear as fierce as possible. "But I promise that as long as you guard my back, I'll guard yours."

Torren's green eyes studied him. Then the boy gave a sharp nod. "It's a deal. I'm Leith."

"Martyn." Martyn set his books down on the bottom bunk. It seemed right claiming that bunk, just like he'd always had the bottom bunk at home.

Home. With Owen and Mama and Papa.

No. He wouldn't think about them anymore. They had abandoned him. They'd chosen to keep Owen and leave Martyn to fend for himself. This was Martyn's home now. This life—whatever kind of life it was—would be his, and he would be good at it.

Martyn sat on the mattress and opened the mathematics page to the one he'd been assigned to finish before tomorrow. It had been a while since he'd been in school, but a few minutes of staring at the page brought back some of his distant memories. "Does Lord Felix know Vane bullies everyone else? Why doesn't he stop it?"

The bunk creaked as Leith shifted in the bunk above him. "As long as we don't kill each other, he doesn't care.

Toughens us up. Do your duty, and you'll survive. He's training us for something. I'm not sure what."

"At least it's better than living on the streets." Martyn muttered as he scribbled the answer to one of the problems. As dangerous as these boys in this room seemed, Lord Felix had been generous. He'd fed Martyn. Given him nice clothes. Intended to make sure he had schooling.

More than Martyn's parents had managed to do.

Leith's head appeared in his line of sight, hanging upside down with his black hair standing out around his head. "How are you at long division?"

"I haven't been in school for a year, so I'm still trying to remember. Why?" Martyn braced himself. Would Leith expect Martyn to do his work for him, just like Vane?

"Just wondering if you could help show me how. I don't quite get it yet." Leith shook his head, which looked odd hanging over the edge of the bunk bed as he was. "You really went to school? What was it like? I always wanted to go to school, but I wasn't...well I didn't have much for schooling until Lord Felix took me in."

Martyn relaxed. No, Leith apparently wanted a friend, not someone he could boss around. "I don't have much for regular schooling either. My family moved around a lot. I'm twelve, so I probably wouldn't have stayed in school much longer anyway."

"I'm twelve too." Leith did some sort of swinging, flipping thing and landed on his feet on the floor. "Maybe we have the same lesson. Then we can work on it together, and it will make more sense to both of us."

There was such an eagerness in the voice and eyes, eyes

that were no longer hard and cold, that Martyn couldn't help but grin.

When Leith grinned back, that's when Martyn knew this wasn't going to be just a cold, protect each other's backs sort of thing. This might even turn into a friendship.

A BLIZZARD FOR BRANDI

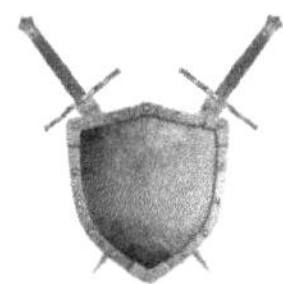

Being fifteen didn't feel all that different from fourteen.

It really ought to. Fourteen had been nice, but fifteen was practically grown up.

Brandi opened her eyes and stretched, staring at the wood rafters and slatted ceiling of her loft bedroom. Light streamed in from the small, square windows on either end of the attic space. She drew in a deep breath of the air filled with the salty scent of ham and the new woodsy smell of the cabin.

A year ago, she'd celebrated her birthday at Walden with Uncle Abel and Aunt Mara. It had been the last full day she and Renna had with them before...

Brandi sat upright and pushed aside the blankets. She wouldn't think about last year, not with the lump that always came into her throat at the thought of Uncle Abel and Aunt Mara. Someday, maybe, she would be able to look back on her fourteenth birthday as the happy day it had been without also bringing up the painful memories of what had happened only a few short weeks later.

She didn't want to be sad today. She was done with sadness. Absolutely done with it. Life was too good, too beautiful right now to spoil it with sadness.

Someday she'd probably be sad again. She'd lost too much not to know that. But God had brought her through those times of sadness, and He would bring her through future hard times. Right now He'd given her happiness, so happy was exactly what she'd be.

She dressed in one of her few shirts that still fit and a pair of trousers she'd "borrowed" from Jamie when he'd outgrown them. Thanks to all the growing she'd done in the past year, especially in the past few months, she barely had any clothes that fit. A bother, really.

After buckling on her short sword, she hurried down the steep stairs from her loft bedroom to the main floor of the cabin.

Renna, of course, was already bustling around the kitchen, laying out ingredients for baking. Not a trace of the breakfast dishes remained, probably already washed and put away by either Jamie, Ranson, or Leith, whoever had taken their turn in helping Renna that morning.

"Happy birthday." Renna pulled a plate from the back of the counter and plucked off the covering towel. "I saved you breakfast. Do you need it reheated?"

"No, I'll just eat it on my way out." Brandi wasn't going to make her sister go through all that extra trouble, not when it was Brandi's fault she always slept so much later than the others.

Well, kind of her fault, anyway. It wasn't her fault that

everyone else seemed to be such annoyingly early risers. Brandi couldn't understand what the appeal was in waking up before the sun. Hardly seemed worth it.

But in a cabin full of former Blades, she should've expected it. They all got up, ran an absurd amount of miles, ate breakfast, then settled into at least an hour of weapons practice. All before they started what they actually planned to do that day.

After grabbing the slice of bread and lukewarm slice of ham from the plate, Brandi headed out the door. Although it was only a short hike from the cabin to the spot to the north where Leith and the others practiced each morning, she had most of her breakfast either eaten or in her mouth by the time she crested the hill and approached them.

Kayleigh and Owen were sparring slowly while Jamie and Ranson watched, probably a demonstration of some kind. As Kayleigh had been raised by her guardsman father and Owen had trained as a guard in Surgis, they knew more about fighting with swords than anyone else in Stetterly.

Off to one side, Leith faced Martyn, and whatever sort of drill they were attempting wasn't going well. As she got closer, Martyn's coughs were harsh and raspy as he bent over his shaking knees.

"...be in bed." Leith was saying.

"I've been stuck in bed for the past month and a half. We leave for the Gathering in a little over a week. I can't..." Martyn coughed again and straightened, lifting his knives. "I have to regain my strength."

Brandi swallowed the last bite of ham, and it turned into a hard lump on the way down. The Gathering. The one where her cousin Keevan would announce his plan to form a new Blades sort of law enforcement thing, with Leith, Shad, and Martyn as its first three members and leaders.

If effort had any merit, then Leith and Martyn had certainly been putting enough into studying Acktar's laws and history to pass the test Keevan planned to give them. Knowing Keevan, it would be an extremely challenging test.

Would the Gathering agree to Keevan's plan? No matter how much Leith and Martyn studied, no matter how qualified they were, it all came down to whether the nobles would agree.

And nobles being the stuffy, uncooperative lot they were, with a few exceptions, the Gathering was going to get interesting.

Kayleigh halted her sword practice and glared at Martyn. "You aren't going to regain your strength by pushing yourself past what your body can handle. You've only barely recovered from the walking and staying up all night you did for Leith and Renna's wedding."

"I'm fine." Martyn's jaw was knotted as he faced Leith. "Let's run through it again."

Leith had his hands at his sides. "No. You aren't strong enough for a full-on practice fight yet. You should rest."

"I've done all the resting and studying laws and regulations and obscure history as I can stand." Martyn deepened his crouch, as if he was preparing to jump at Leith and force him into a fight.

This was going to get out of hand in a moment or two. Martyn was grumpy—as all former Blades seemed to get when they were wounded and stuck in bed for weeks on end —and grumpy people didn't think clearly. They just made other people grumpy along with them.

Brandi forced on a smile and walked forward with as much nonchalant bounce to her step as she could manage. She sent one of her best smiles Martyn's way. "It's my birthday. You don't want to be grumpy on my birthday, do you? When I left, it looked like Renna was baking maple sugar cookies, and she won't be giving maple sugar cookies to grumpy people."

Martyn scowled. "Are you trying to bribe me with cookies?"

"Yes." She tried to put even more brightness into her smile. Even a few months ago, she hadn't liked Martyn all that much. He seemed permanently grumpy, and he'd been responsible for capturing her and Renna, dragging them to Nalgar, forcing Leith to leave Renna behind during a failed rescue, and torturing Leith when he returned to rescue Renna.

But in the past month and a half, things had changed, somewhat. She would've been grumpy too if she'd been separated from her sister for as many years as Martyn had been separated from his brother.

She'd taken over looking after his horse, Wanderer, for him while he was stuck in bed, and he seemed—beneath all his gruff and bluster—to pay attention when she reported on Wanderer's wellbeing.

If Martyn had the good enough sense to court Kayleigh —who was about the amazingest person Brandi knew besides Renna and Leith and Jamie—then Martyn couldn't be all bad.

Besides, Martyn was practically Leith's brother, and Leith was her brother for sure now that he'd married Renna, so that made Martyn kind of sort of almost in a way her brother too. And he seemed like just the sort of brother who needed a little sister to work through his huffiness.

It worked on Leith and Jamie and Ranson. Surely her charm would work on Martyn too. Eventually.

Martyn huffed, sheathed one of his knives, and ran a hand through his hair. "Do I have much of a choice with all of you turning on me?"

From Martyn, that was the equivalent of giving in and saying he loved Renna's cookies. Which might be true. Renna had managed more of a brother-sister relationship with Martyn than Brandi had. Something about those weeks locked at Nalgar Castle with only Martyn and Respen for company created some sort of understanding between Renna and Martyn.

"Not really." Brandi kept her grin in place.

With another huff as if to make sure everyone knew he was doing this under protest, Martyn sheathed his other knife and thumped to the ground off to the side of the practice area.

Owen sheathed his sword, sat next to Martyn, and dug a fist-sized rock out of the sandy ground. "Your arms weren't burned. You could try a few basic strengthening exercises that you can do sitting down."

"Why didn't you suggest that in the first place?" Martyn dug around for another rock. "If you'd told me a sensible alternative like that instead of merely grousing at me, I would have listened."

Brandi was sure she wasn't the only one rolling her eyes at that. Of course Martyn would've listened. Just as he was listening to the sensible orders of the healers who told him to rest because it took a while for a body to recover from being nearly burned at the stake.

With Martyn now occupied and a little less grumpy, everyone else seemed to take that as the signal to resume their practice.

Leith gave Brandi a one-armed hug. "Happy birthday."

She hugged him back. Not that she needed much for celebration or presents. She'd already gotten the best birthday present two weeks ago when Leith married Renna and became Brandi's big brother officially.

Then a week ago she'd moved into the loft bedroom Leith had built for her just like he'd promised he would, and she'd finally been home in her very own bedroom for the first time in over a year.

It would be hard for any birthday celebration to top that.

That evening, Brandi leaned against the paddock fence, the Bible Renna had given her gripped in one arm. The breeze carried the scent of the cooling prairie and the faint smell of the river down below in the Spires Canyon. The taste of the three maple sugar cookies she'd eaten still lingered, and she nearly turned around to see if she could sneak one more.

But Blizzard was walking toward the fence, the limp from the injury he'd sustained last year nearly gone.

The goat Ginger trotted along behind Blizzard. Ginger had been found along with Uncle Abel's mule Stubborn wandering the prairie with a group of cattle months after Respen's attack on Stetterly. Stubborn enjoyed his new home with one of the widows to plow fields and be spoiled by her children, but Brandi kept Ginger.

After turning to keep the Bible out of Blizzard's reach, she ran her free hand over Blizzard's neck, finding one of his favorite itchy spots to scratch as he snuffled at the pockets of the new divided skirt she'd received from Renna. Blizzard blew a breath out his nose and stepped back, probably at the new fabric of the clothes she wore that didn't yet smell of her or horse or apples stuffed into her pockets.

"Well I like the new clothes Renna made for me even if you don't." Brandi held out her hand until Blizzard came back to the gate, probably having decided in his horse brain that it was worth braving the new items.

She gripped the Bible—her favorite of her birthday gifts—tighter. She didn't have to open it to picture the first page with her mother's handwriting scrawled across the paper. So like the one Brandi had, before Respen tossed it in his fireplace. Only Respen's strange fascination with Renna had saved this Bible from being burned as well.

Renna had her silver cross necklace given by their parents and Uncle Abel and Aunt Mara's Bible. Brandi had a Bible from their parents and the silver cross necklace from Uncle Abel and Aunt Mara. They both had their memories.

Footsteps crunched the grass, and Jamie halted next to her.

"Jamie. Perfect. You're just the person I wanted to talk to." Brandi turned as much as she could while petting Blizzard and protecting her new Bible. She really ought to have left it in the cabin, but she couldn't shake the feeling that something might happen to it the moment it was out of her sight.

"Really?" Jamie's voice squeaked a bit on the word.

Apparently boys' voices started doing that as they got older and their voices deepened. It must be terribly annoying to speak and not know if your voice would cooperate or if it would randomly jump into another octave.

And Jamie was growing. He was even a few inches taller than Brandi now.

"Yes. We apparently have only a week and a half to plan a birthday party for Ranson. I can't believe he didn't tell us about his birthday—or the day that he celebrates as his birthday. It must be so strange for him not to know when his actual birthday is."

It had taken a bit of prodding at dinner for everyone to say when their birthdays were so that Renna and Brandi could plan for them. Maybe they were all getting too old for things like fancy birthday parties, but to Brandi's way of thinking, they had a few birthday parties to make up for.

"What kind of cookie is his favorite? Do you know? Or do you think he would prefer a cake? What should we make him for a present? I have no idea what he'd want."

"Um, I don't know." Jamie stared at the ground, and the starlight reflected on the waves in his brown hair. "Are you disappointed I didn't get you a gift?"

After she'd told all of them not to get her anything? It wasn't like Brandi had even expected anything from Renna and Leith, considering they had just gotten married two weeks ago. They probably wouldn't have had anything for her except that they gave her a Bible Renna already had and Kayleigh had helped with sewing Brandi's new clothes.

"Of course not. After all, you were my birthday present last year. I think you are more than enough of a present for a couple years." Brandi grinned and kept grinning until Jamie grinned back. "When I was little, all I wanted was a horse of my own and a brother. I now have three brothers. Well, four if you count Martyn, and I think I will because then Kayleigh will eventually end up my sister."

"Kind of." Jamie's grin tilted until it wasn't quite a frown but wasn't a smile anymore either. "Just because you're Renna's sister and I'm Leith's brother doesn't make us brother and sister."

"Close enough." Brandi patted Blizzard's neck. What else could they be but one big family all crammed into the cabin as they were. Brandi, at least, got her own loft out of the deal. Ranson and Jamie had to share a room.

Jamie glanced toward the cabin. "I'll see if I can get Ranson to tell me what his favorite cookie or cake is. Do you want me to take your Bible inside for you?"

She hadn't wanted to let it out of her sight, but Jamie was a different story. He could be trusted. She held it out for him, and he took it carefully as if he understood how much it meant to her.

Maybe he did. As far as she knew, he didn't have anything of his family to remember them by. Nothing but memories that he didn't talk to even her about. Not yet, anyway.

Brandi drew in a breath of the silence and the cooling night air and rested her forehead against Blizzard's neck.

Only a faint crackle of grass, a whisper of cloth, warned Brandi before Leith appeared next to her and leaned on the fence on the other side of Blizzard's head. "Was it a good day today?"

She focused on Blizzard, scratching at the itchy spot in

his neck until Blizzard's upper lip stuck out and his head cocked.

Had it been a good day? Definitely. Lots of laughter and the joy of her new family and friends surrounding her. Yes, it still ached with the sadness of all those she was missing. Father. Mother. Uncle Abel and Aunt Mara. Her friend Ian who she'd barely gotten to know before he'd been killed in the war. "Yes, it was."

Leith ran a hand down Blizzard's neck. "It's not quite over yet. I still have a gift for you."

"You do?" Brandi leaned back to peer around Blizzard. What did Leith have to give her? Until he officially started his new job, Leith didn't exactly have any income.

When Leith patted Blizzard, there was something final in the gesture. He turned to her. "Blizzard's yours. I know he's been kind of yours ever since the war ended, and you've spent so much time working with him to help him recover from his injury, but I want you to know that he's yours all the way now."

"You mean that?" Brandi froze, unable to decide if she should hug Blizzard or Leith first. Blizzard solved her problem by nudging her with his nose, and she wrapped her arms around his neck for as long as the horse would tolerate before she turned and hugged Leith. "Thank you so, so, so much. I'll love him and take good care of him."

"I know you will." Leith patted her back.

A brother, a home, and a horse of her very own all in one month.

Yes, she was as happy as she possibly could be.

THE BLADES AS THEY SHOULD'VE BEEN

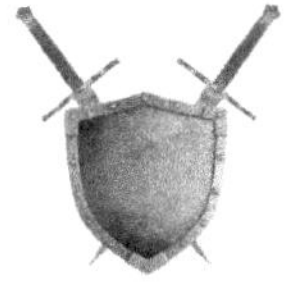

A Novella

1

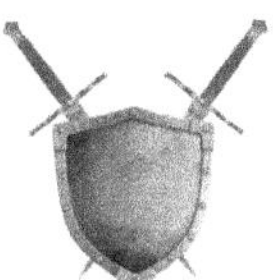

When the towers of Nalgar Castle crested the horizon, Leith sucked in a breath. Behind him, Renna stiffened, and her arms tightened around his waist. He patted her arms and nudged Valor back into a walk. The lead rope tied to the saddlehorn for their second horse tightened a moment before Big Brown caught up with Valor.

The rest of their group of Stetterly—Martyn, Kayleigh, Owen, Brandi, Jamie, and Ranson—followed behind them.

It had been nine months since they'd ridden out of those gates, and he wasn't sure he was ready to face this castle again. Yes, the castle would be different with King Keevan on the throne. But too much of Leith's past haunted that castle still.

"What set of laws did King Rorin I enact?"

Leith glanced over his shoulder to where Martyn sat straight and stiff on Wanderer. Even after two months, his burns weren't completely healed. "That's an easy one. He enacted the second half of the Decrees of Citizens and Sovereignty. The first ten were put in place by King Brian in his first year as king. I'll recite the second half if you go through the first half."

Martyn smirked and opened his mouth, but Kayleigh leaned over and swatted his arm. "What did Renna and I tell the two of you? No more studying tonight."

The weight of Renna's head rested against Leith's back between his shoulder blades. "At this point, I think *I* could pass that test."

"We all could, if we wanted to." On the other side of Martyn, Owen shook his head. "I've picked up more about Acktarian history than I ever learned in school."

Maybe Leith and Martyn had gotten a little carried away in their game of quizzing each other on the ride from Stetterly to Nalgar.

Leith waited, but Brandi didn't add anything to the conversation. He swiveled in the saddle as much as he could with Renna clinging to his waist.

Behind Martyn, Kayleigh, and Owen, Brandi's face had paled nearly white, her hands gripping the saddlehorn and her mouth pressed into a tight line. She swayed in time with Blizzard's gait. Jamie had positioned Buster close enough that he would be there in an instant if Brandi started to fall from her saddle. On Brandi's other side, Ranson kept glancing at her as if he too was prepared to catch her if she tumbled from Blizzard.

Renna turned as well and frowned. "Her headache is getting worse. Good thing we're nearly there."

Leith straightened in the saddle. The frequency of Brandi's headaches had decreased in the nine months since she'd been wounded in the Battle for Nalgar Castle, but she still got them occasionally, especially on a trip like this with the heat of early summer blazing down on them. She'd kept insisting she was fine.

When they entered the castle and halted their horses in the cobblestone courtyard, a herd of stablehands descended on them to take their horses, directed by a stocky man with curly brown hair.

Leith helped Brandi from Blizzard's back. She tried to stand straight but swayed. Leith pulled one of her arms over his shoulders. "You all right?"

"Just a whacking great headache." Brandi squeezed her eyes shut. "Rather annoying. I'm not even hungry right now."

It was a bad one, then. Leith steadied her as she leaned her head on his shoulder. "We'll get you to your room soon."

"Good."

King Keevan strode from the passageway between the cobblestone courtyard and Queen's Court. "Welcome. Good timing. A few of the other nobles have arrived early and it would be best if you didn't...mingle yet. They are distracted with supper at the moment." King Keevan glanced from Leith to the Great Hall.

Leith and Martyn were both far too recognizable to those lords and ladies who had supported Respen. And it wasn't time for that confrontation yet.

King Keevan turned to Renna. "It's good to see you again. Addie has supper waiting in our room, if you're hungry."

Renna hugged Keevan. "Thank you. Supper sounds wonderful, but I believe Brandi needs to lie down."

Keevan glanced over at Leith and Brandi. His frown

tightened his scar across his cheek. "I see. There's supper for everyone else in one of the other rooms. Follow me."

Leith helped Brandi and together they followed Keevan and Renna toward the passageway between courtyards. Martyn, Kayleigh, Owen, Ranson, and Jamie trailed behind them, Kayleigh and Martyn whispering back and forth too quietly for Leith to hear.

Leith expected Keevan to turn to the right up the stairs to what had once been King Respen's chambers, but Keevan continued all the way to the end of the passageway.

There, a guard held open the door to the long gallery that stretched alongside the Great Hall. The upper floor above the gallery housed the rooms reserved for the king's family.

Leith caught his breath, nearly halting at the threshold. Surely Keevan didn't want him here of all places.

But Brandi was swaying, her face white, her eyes closed. Leith couldn't hesitate when she needed to lie down before she passed out.

Stepping inside, Leith caught a glimpse of the gallery stretching into the distance, paintings of former kings and Acktar's history, as well as swords and other artifacts of historical significance, decorating places along the right wall. The left wall was filled with tall, broad windows overlooking the Queen's Court and the guest apartments on the far side.

But Keevan had already turned to the right and started up the flight of stairs, the others following him.

Brandi's fingers tightened on Leith's shoulder, her face going another shade of white.

Leith picked her up, huffing as her weight settled against

his arms. She sagged against him, burying her face against his shoulder.

He climbed the stairs, unable to see his feet while holding Brandi. After six steps, the staircase opened into a landing before turning and going the rest of the way to the second floor.

The staircase opened into a hallway as long as the gallery below, but far narrower and darker. To the left, doors marched along the hallway, each one opening to a set of rooms with broad windows overlooking the Queen's Court.

Leith had been in this part of the castle only once before on a moonlight night. Not much had changed in this corridor except for a new, oak door had been added at the top of the stairs. Fresh, light mortar stood out starkly against the aged gray of the stones, though some of the edges showed the fresh look of recent chiseling.

It must be one of the modifications Leith had heard Keevan was doing to the castle. Knowing the layout of the castle, that door must lead to what had once been the king's chambers.

By the time Leith reached the others, a brown-haired maid was informing Keevan that supper was ready for his guests in the farthest room down the hall.

"Thanks, Juliana." Keevan shot a glance toward Brandi and Leith. "Is Brandi's room ready?"

Juliana nodded and pointed. "It's that one over there. There are beds for her and Kayleigh Ainsley all set for them. Renna and Leith are across the hall, and everyone else has the biggest room at the end."

Brandi lifted her head and squirmed. "Let me down. I can get to my room by myself."

"Are you sure?" Leith eased her to her feet, but he kept a hand on her arm to steady her.

Even with her eyes narrowed in pain, Brandi still managed a huff and an eyeroll. "I'm not dying. It's just one of those annoying headaches. All I need is to lie down in peace and quiet, and the sooner you all leave for supper, the sooner I can get that."

"I'll look after her. I'll fetch a cold cloth for you. That always helps my mama when she gets a headache." The maid Juliana stepped forward and steadied Brandi. Pausing, Juliana cocked her head, her gaze focused on Leith. "My mother gave you food poisoning once."

Leith blinked, not quite sure what to make of that statement. The only time he remembered being that sick was shortly after Respen took over Nalgar.

Juliana didn't wait for him to comment. She turned and helped Brandi down the hall.

Renna stared after them, a wrinkle forming across her forehead. Leith moved to reassure her, but Keevan beat him to it.

"Juliana's my sister-in-law. She'll take good care of Brandi." Keevan opened the door next to him and waved. "Shall we?"

Renna smiled and entered, but Leith couldn't force himself to move. The rest of the castle was bad enough, but this place...this room...

Last time Leith had stepped inside, he'd pressed a hand to Keevan's mouth, looked into his eyes, and slit his throat.

Keevan was regarding him now, his face blank, his eyes cool. Leith swallowed. "You can't want me here."

"No, I don't. But then again, it isn't my choice, is it? You're the one who chose to marry my cousin." Keevan's tight expression didn't waver as he gestured at the door again. "The food is getting cold."

With a deep breath, Leith brushed past Keevan and stepped into the room.

A table with five chairs now occupied the space only a few feet into the room. A few overstuffed chairs pushed against the window and a folding screen divided this temporary sitting room from the rest of the bedchamber, concealing the bed where Leith had once tried to commit murder.

Renna was finishing a hug with Queen Adelaide and knelt to coo over the young Prince Duncan where he sat on a blanket on the floor. Adelaide scooped him up and held him out to Renna. "Would you like to hold him?"

Renna's face brightened, and she took the baby, balancing him on her hip. "He's getting heavy."

"He's eight months old already and scooting around on his stomach." Adelaide sank into a chair. "It won't be too much longer before he starts getting into everything."

Leith couldn't move. The look on Renna's face as she bounced Duncan...it twisted something deep inside him and it wasn't too hard to replace Duncan's brown curls with blond like Renna's. The thought brought a churning deep inside him.

The door clicked shut. "If you would care to have a seat." Keevan's rasp had a bite to it.

Leith managed to cross the few feet to the table. After holding out a chair for Renna, he sank into the one next to hers.

While Keevan moved the fifth chair that had been meant

for Brandi out of the way, Adelaide slipped into the chair across from Leith. "I'm sorry it's crowded, but the former king's chambers are under construction at the moment."

"We don't mind, do we?"

By the way Renna was smiling and looking at the baby in her lap, Leith wasn't sure if she was speaking to him or Duncan.

Keevan took the remaining seat, the one next to Leith. His gaze held a challenge. "Would you like to open with prayer?"

Leith wasn't sure he dared pray here, not in a place where he had to so starkly face the killer he'd been. Could he pray in the same room where he'd once intended to kill?

He didn't have much of a choice. Either he prayed or Keevan did. Killer or victim.

And, perhaps, that was precisely why the two of them had to sit at this table together, share this meal, and pray.

"Let's pray." Leith cleared his throat as the others around the table bowed their heads. "Father in Heaven, we are thankful that all of us are able to sit down at this table as a family and partake of the blessing of this food together. Amen."

When he opened his eyes, Leith didn't dare look at Keevan.

Adelaide sprang to her feet and lifted the covers of the serving platters, dishing out the steak, corn, and rolls. As she returned to her seat, she held out her hands. "Would you like me to take him back, Renna?"

"No, I've got him." Renna balanced Duncan on her knee and reached for her fork with the other. Duncan leaned forward, reaching for the potatoes.

Leith remained silent while Renna and Adelaide started a conversation about Duncan transitioning to eating some solid foods or something like that. Keevan didn't seem like he wanted to make small talk any more than Leith did. What could they talk about anyway? Especially in this room.

He waited until everyone else, including Keevan, had taken several bites before he dared eat anything. He didn't think Keevan would have his mother-in-law give Leith food poisoning again, but he couldn't be sure.

When they finished, Adelaide began stacking the plates and platters. Renna stood to help, but her hands were full with Duncan. She held Duncan out to Leith. "Would you like to hold him?"

There came a sharp intake of breath from Keevan. Adelaide froze, a plate in her hand. Renna halted, as if realizing what she'd said.

Leith stilled. "No...no, I'm fine. I don't..."

Adelaide drew in a deep breath and added the plate to her stack. "Keevan, he's family. It's all right."

Before Leith had a chance to protest, Renna dumped Duncan into his lap. Leith blinked down at the baby. Duncan stared back, a finger in his mouth, blue eyes regarding Leith as if he wasn't sure what to think.

Keevan had his arms crossed, his fingers clenched so tightly his hands shook. His wide eyes focused on Duncan.

The look in Keevan's eyes...it wasn't anger. It looked more like fear.

Leith couldn't blame him. How would Leith feel if Respen or Vane was holding his child? Because that's what Keevan felt now seeing Leith—his would-be killer—holding Duncan.

To be honest, if Leith had been in Keevan's place, he would've snatched his child away and drawn a knife for good measure.

But Keevan was a better man than Leith.

Small hands fisted in Leith's shirt. Duncan reached for the leather straps crossing Leith's chest, tugging on them. Thankfully Leith hadn't worn his knives. That would've sent Keevan over the cliff's edge.

After a few moments, Duncan let go of the leather straps and squirmed. Leith picked him up and held him out. "I don't think he likes me much."

"He has good taste." Keevan snatched him away from Leith and strode toward the screened off part of the room. "He probably needs a change anyway."

Leith straightened his shirt. If Keevan needed a moment to hold Duncan close and take a few deep breaths, Leith couldn't blame him. Not here.

Keevan had done more than could be expected already. Not everyone managed to sit down and eat a meal with the man who'd once tried to kill him. Leith couldn't ask more than that.

Especially since, in two days, Keevan would risk his crown and his reputation to defend Leith in front of the all the nobles in the Acktar.

And even that was more than Leith deserved.

2

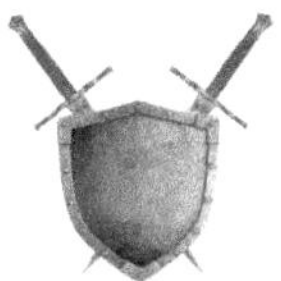

On the other side of the screen, Keevan held his son tight and sank to the floor beside the bed.

He was trying. No one could say he wasn't trying to be civil. A sit-down family meal with his cousin and her husband. Smiles and small talk.

Yet in that moment when Leith held Duncan...all Keevan could see was a flashing knife and gushing blood. But instead of himself, it was Duncan with the slashed throat, the baby choking...convulsing...

Keevan buried his face against his son's wispy blond hair. This was the hardest part of forgiveness. It would've been so much easier if Leith wasn't a Christian. If he—and Martyn—had been like the other Blades and even Respen who had never had a change of heart, then Keevan could let the guilt rest on them, forget, and move on.

But as much as Keevan would like to deny it, he knew Leith was sincere in his faith and his repentance for the things he'd done. And that meant Keevan had to forgive as

41

he should forgive a brother in Christ. With restoration to a place of fellowship and family.

And Keevan wasn't sure he was strong enough to do that. He'd been praying for strength for the past month, knowing he'd have to face this moment. Still, he was gutted and weak under the weight of the memories and the fears, even groundless fears, of the future.

This was about more than just Leith's attempted assassination. Leith's had been the only face Keevan had seen that night.

For nearly five years, even though Respen was the main concern and the other Blades had been responsible for the deaths of Keevan's family, it was Leith's face that Keevan connected to those murders. Leith was the one he'd blamed for everything.

Letting go of this final piece of blame meant letting go of his family for the last time.

Somehow, he had to figure out a way to do it if he was going to live in the here and now instead of the past. In two days, he would back the Marshals with Leith as their leader with everything he had. He had until then to work out the last of the animosity.

In his arms, Duncan squirmed and gurgled. A damp feeling touched Keevan's hand supporting his son.

With the practiced reflexes of eight months of fatherhood, he held Duncan away from him before the swiftly wetting diaper could soak through into Keevan's clothes. Duncan's mouth split in a wide grin.

Keevan grinned back. "I snatched you away too soon, didn't I? You had revenge for your papa all planned out, and I ruined it."

Leith, as inexperienced with children as he was, would not have recognized the dampness that warned of a soaking. That would've been worth pushing through the memories to see.

Keevan stood while holding Duncan away from him. Turned out his excuse to change Duncan was a reality. "Next time, I won't snatch you away before you've had your chance."

Duncan grinned and gurgled again. Something in Keevan softened at his son's smile, and the fact that the rasp in his voice didn't lessen that smile. He'd lost much over five years ago now, but he had been given so much in the years since. Addie. Her family. A couple of nieces and nephews on her side. Duncan.

And now, an expanding family on his side, if he could figure out how to be family to the cousins he'd tormented as children and the Blade he'd hated for so long.

After changing Duncan's diaper, Keevan strode back around the screen.

Renna and Addie were turned toward each other, talking with waving hands and smiles. Good to see Addie so comfortable with Renna. Back when they'd married, she'd feared she would never fit in with the little family Keevan had left. Life as queen could be lonely. Never knowing if the "friends" gathering around her were genuine or only there because of status. Renna would be one of the few with whom Addie wouldn't have to worry about pretense.

Leith sat to the side, arms crossed. Though the way his shoulders were hunched, his head tipped down, the crossed arms were a sign of discomfort more than defiance. By the stiffness in his back, he'd heard Keevan's footsteps and was trying hard not to look wary having a potential enemy at his back.

Keevan drew in a deep breath, strode toward the table, and deliberately plopped Duncan onto Leith's lap.

"What—" Leith startled, grasped Duncan under his arms as if by reflex, and glanced between Keevan and Duncan, mouth parted in an expression that would've been gaping on anyone else.

Keevan forced his hands to remain steady, his posture to remain relaxed, as he returned to his seat. He would not give in to the memories of knives and pain. Leith was family, and Keevan would—even if it killed him—treat Leith as family.

If Renna had married nearly anyone else, Keevan probably would've treated him as more a long-lost brother than a cousin.

Though, considering Renna had nearly married Respen, Leith wasn't the worst option.

Leith stared at Duncan, reminding Keevan of the first time Frank's wife Suzanna had handed their newborn to Samuel, the youngest of Keevan's brothers-in-law. Samuel had that same expression: part curiosity, part wariness, and part abject terror.

Leith was the same age as Samuel. On the night Leith had nearly killed Keevan, he'd been only a year older than Keevan's youngest brother. At Leith's age, Keevan had been fumbling his way through becoming the Leader in Eagle Heights. And yet Leith, despite being young, was married and ready to take on the leadership of the Marshals.

A little brother. A pesky, annoying little brother he was stuck with.

Keevan gritted his teeth and forced a smile. Perhaps it

was time to settle this once and for all in the manner of brothers everywhere. Either beat him up or get beat up by him and move on. "Meet me an hour before dawn tomorrow outside the castle walls. It's time for a rematch."

Leith's gaze snapped to Keevan, his muscles tensing. As if he heard in Keevan's rasp and saw in his expression that this would be more than a friendly chat. "Where?"

"You'll figure it out. Consider it a test of your tracking skills." Keevan crossed his arms and leaned backwards in his chair as far as he could without lifting the front legs from the floor.

Perhaps Leith would never feel like family, but as long as he became less the pain of a flashing knife in the dark and more the mild annoyance of a burr tangled in bootlaces, Keevan would be able to live with that.

AFTER SLIPPING OUT OF THE CASTLE AN HOUR AND A HALF before dawn, Keevan finally stopped over the crest of a hill out of sight of the castle. "This should work."

All four of his brothers-in-law halted with him. This morning, facing Leith and the memories of the night that had stolen his brothers, the solid presence of his new family surrounding him was more than he could've ever asked.

His oldest brother-in-law Frank glanced around at the hills surrounding them, his hand on the hilt of his sword. "Do you really think this is a good idea?"

Purposely setting up a fight with the former Blade who had once tried to kill him? Worse, planning to provoke him to fighting for real? Didn't sound like his most brilliant plan.

Yet, much as Keevan would like to continue to see Leith as the villain, Keevan knew Leith wouldn't kill him, no matter how much Keevan provoked him. Annoying when former Blades turned honorable.

Keevan tapped his sword's hilt. "Yes. I'll be fine. I trained for five years for this."

He wouldn't be denied this fight now because of small details like the fact that he was king, Leith was his cousin by marriage, and the Gathering of Nobles was tomorrow, and both of them would show up with unflattering bruises because of this.

Patrick flopped to the ground. "Do you think he'll find us out here? I know he's a Blade, but we stuck to the paved path, climbed over the wall, walked around the castle several times, and did everything we could to hide our trail. He'd have to have the nose of a bloodhound to track us out here."

"Or I could watch you sneak across the Queen's Court and follow you."

Samuel jumped a good six inches with a short, stifled sound. Patrick scrambled to his feet. Brennen reached for his sword while Frank whirled, sword in hand.

Leith strode from the darkness, his empty hands spread to show his knives remained in their sheaths. Dressed in black, wearing knives strapped across his chest, on his belt, in his boots, and probably a few places Keevan couldn't see, Leith looked more like the Blade he'd been on the night this had begun.

Keevan didn't jump or reach for his sword. "I guess you pass the tracking and sneaking part of the test."

"Good to know." Leith glanced around at Keevan's brothers-in-law. "I was under the impression this was the sort of fight where we were supposed to come alone, but maybe I should have brought back up?"

"I am king. Even when I recklessly sneak out before dawn, I still need my bodyguards along." Keevan shrugged. If only his rasp wasn't quite so noticeable this early in the morning. "These are also my brothers-in-law, Frank, Patrick, Brennen, and Samuel."

Leith's expression remained neutral as his gaze flicked between them. "I see."

He probably did.

Keevan drew his sword. "Last time, I had no warning and I was unprepared. This time will be different."

Leith sighed and drew two of his knives. "Will this help?"

Keevan nearly said it couldn't hurt, but that would've been a lie. This might hurt a great deal before they were done.

But he needed this. Maybe it wasn't the healthiest way to handle his anger. Probably not all that Christian. Yet, if he caused Leith pain, drew some blood, then perhaps he might be able to banish the flashing knife and memories of that night.

He didn't wait for more small talk. He lunged, drawing his dagger as he went.

Leith parried both his sword and dagger easily but stepped back, waiting with his knives at his side rather than moving in for a counterattack. It was the posture of a man refusing to fight any more than he had to.

Keevan tried three more strikes, and each time Leith merely sidestepped or shoved the blades aside with his own.

Why couldn't he oblige Keevan and at least try? This was

supposed to be a rematch of that night, this time between grown men instead of boys in an ambush.

Keevan chopped his sword at Leith's head. Leith swayed aside, giving another step of ground.

"Why won't you fight? You aren't even trying." Keevan glared, steadying his sword and dagger for the next strike.

Keevan's brothers-in-law remained in a wide circle around them, hands on their swords even though they didn't draw them.

"Of course I'm not. I don't want to kill you." Leith held his knives lowered at his sides, his stance less wary than it should have been. "Then again, you aren't trying either."

Bother. No, he wasn't. Keevan didn't want to kill Leith either. Not anymore. Maybe give him a bloody nose. Throw him in a cave for a few weeks. But not kill him.

Leith spread his hands out wide, still holding his knives but not in a defensive stance. "You're the one who wanted this fight. If you want it to be real, then you're going to have to be the one to provoke it because I don't hate you. I never did."

"Didn't you? Not even the night you tried to kill me?" Keevan stepped closer, hefting his sword.

"Not even then." Something in Leith's voice changed from the easy tone he'd had before to something lower. Almost dangerous. "I've truly hated only one man, and he was dead long before I had a chance to kill him. You were nothing but an order to me. I didn't hate you. I didn't hate any of those I killed."

And that, perhaps, made Leith the scariest sort of killer. One who didn't kill out of a blind rage or hatred or ideology or a host of other passions. He had killed merely for the cold reason of a mission. And he'd been good at it.

Even now, he fought with ice instead of Keevan's fury. He'd dared Keevan to provoke him, yet Keevan couldn't be sure that was even possible. Not without going lengths that Keevan would never go.

"And now, I'm loyal to you." Leith shook his head. "If you want this fight, then fine. But I don't want to fight you."

And that's when Keevan knew this fight would never truly become a fight if Keevan made it about the past. In Leith's mind, the past was over and done. That night hadn't been the life-shattering moment for him that it had been for Keevan. Leith had other nights and other nightmares, but that night was just one among many.

Keevan lowered his sword in relaxed readiness. He waved at his brothers-in-law with his other hand, still holding his dagger. "This is a test, remember. And if that's how this is going to be, then I guess we'll have to fail you."

That sparked a flare in Leith's eyes, a stiffening of his stance. "What do you mean?"

That was the way to get to Leith. Leith might not hate Keevan, but he hated to fail.

"As a Marshal, you're going to have to fight, and a lot of times, you might not want to. I understand you don't want to be the Blade you were. But if you continue to hesitate after the time for battle has come and gone, then I'm afraid my cousin will be widowed far too soon. Give them a chance to surrender peacefully, but you have to be willing to fight when needed without hesitation." Keevan forced his blood to run cold instead of the fury of before. "And right now, you're hesitating."

"Are you going to surrender?" The corners of Leith's mouth twitched in the hint of a smile.

"No." Keevan didn't wait for Leith to react but stepped forward and swept his sword up. No holding back this time. No aiming for just above Leith's head. This time, he swung for real.

Instead of blocking the blow, Leith caught the sword with one of his knives and guided the sword over his head as he pivoted underneath.

Keevan brought his dagger up to block, only to realize too late that Leith's attack came not with his other knife but with his elbow aimed at Keevan's stomach. Keevan tried to jump back but not quickly enough. Leith's elbow slammed into his stomach, knocking a gasp out of him.

Still, he brought both his sword and dagger up, reversing the grip on his sword to smash the hilt at Leith since Leith was too close to use the blade.

Leith grabbed Keevan's wrist, planted a foot, and hammered his elbow into Keevan's chest.

Keevan stumbled back, but something—Leith's boot— caught his foot. Next thing he knew, he was on his back, Leith's knee and hand pinning him down and a knife at his throat.

Again Keevan found himself looking at green eyes and a flashing knife. But this time, Keevan wouldn't freeze. He wasn't going to panic.

He let go of his sword, grabbed Leith's wrist, and twisted as he rolled, pinning Leith beneath him.

His victory was short lived as Leith managed to continue the roll and threw Keevan off him.

Keevan lost himself to the fight. The striking, parrying,

slicing, dodging. Blood and sweat. The whistle of a knife against the morning air. The satisfaction of a blow to his opponent.

As he staggered forward for yet another strike, Frank appeared before him and placed a hand on his shoulder. "That should be enough, I think."

Keevan peered past Frank's shoulder. Leith was breathing hard too, though he seemed steadier on his feet than Keevan was.

Leith raised his eyebrows and asked between panting breaths, "Is it enough?"

For a heartbeat, Keevan let that settle. Was it? He swiped at the sweat trickling down his forehead. His fingers met something thicker. Blood.

Across from him, Leith wiped at a similar line of blood making its way down his cheek.

Something about the sight caused a grin to tug at Keevan's mouth. "Yes. I think I've had more than enough."

The tightness in his chest had dulled. Perhaps now the memories would stay in the past and, when they lingered, the heat and pain wouldn't simmer. Leith was his cousin now and, if everything went well at the Gathering, they would have to work closely together as king and captain of the Marshals. There wasn't room in either of those roles for animosity, and maybe now the bitterness would remain gone.

Since his clothes were already grimy and blood spattered, Keevan wiped his sword and dagger clean on his shirt. "Who is the one person you hated? Respen?"

"You'd think so, but no." Leith remained almost too focused on cleaning his knives on a torn section of his shirt.

"My father. Even then, I never hated him because of my broken bones or bruises. No, I hated him for my mother's bruises."

There was still a depth of vehemence to those words, an ember that wasn't fully extinguished.

Leith sheathed his knives with a snap. "Did I pass?"

Time to let the topic drop. "I don't know. Did he?" Keevan stepped back to take in Patrick, Brennen, and Samuel, along with Frank.

Patrick snorted. "He could've killed you in the first two seconds if he'd wanted to."

"His pinning technique could use work. Maybe it worked when he was slitting throats, but now he needs to come up with something that leaves him less vulnerable to counterattack while making an arrest." Brennen shrugged as it was no big thing to critique a former First Blade.

Frank crossed his arms. "He's young yet."

Samuel spread his hands, eyes wide and mouth gaping. "I thought it was brilliant. If I could fight half as good as that...what was that move you did right at first? You had Keevan on the ground in seconds."

Leith shifted. "It's just getting a foot behind his."

Keevan eyed Leith one more time. He was tough, but he was still young with that unsettled look of a boy still figuring out who he was and where he belonged. Some of that was caused by all the changes and upheaval of the past year, but some was just...youth.

And Keevan planned to place a huge responsibility on his shoulders. Many would question giving such an important task to someone not yet twenty. But Leith would grow into the job, and the job would grow with him. With the seasoning of a few more years, Leith Torren would become one tough, capable man. And that was the person Keevan was appointing to this task almost more than the still uncertain young man before him.

He nodded to Leith. "You passed. Now let's return to the castle so we can hopefully get cleaned up before our wives see us like this."

Leith touched a split on his swelling lower lip. "Don't want to admit to your wife that you've been brawling?"

Patrick snorted and clapped Leith on the back hard enough to send him staggering. "Addie? She'll just roll her eyes and blame us for being a bad influence. She grew up with four brothers. She's used to it."

Keevan shook his head but winced when the movement caused a throbbing to pulse at his temple. "No, it's Renna I'm worried about. She will probably blame me for beating up on my younger cousins again and might not speak to me for another five years. I may need you to smooth things over."

"Possibly." Leith fell into step with them. "But at least I wasn't obsessively studying for the test like I promised I wouldn't do."

When Patrick chuckled and Frank snorted, Keevan didn't fight his grin. Someday, he might be able to tolerate this cousin-in-law of his after all.

3

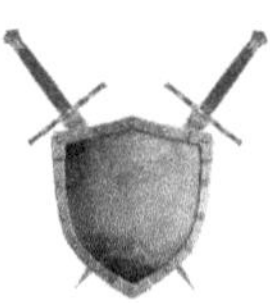

"When I told you not to spend the evening and morning studying, I didn't realize your version of preparing for a test was to get up before dawn to fight someone."

Sitting at the edge of the bed, Leith held still as Renna plastered a bandage over one of the deeper cuts across his ribs. "I didn't start it. And it wasn't a random fight. It was the fighting portion of the Marshals test."

Mostly. It was a bit more than a mere test, but that's how it would go down on paper.

Renna snorted and reached for another bandage. "Well I hope you finished the fight. Does Keevan at least look as bad as you do?"

"Actually, Keevan's bodyguard Frank finished it and, yes, I'm pretty sure Keevan has just as many cuts as I have." Leith dabbed at his lip with a cold, damp cloth. And possibly a black eye, though that hadn't shown up yet as they'd walked back to the castle.

He wasn't about to admit to Renna that the fight had been...thrilling. The best practice bout he'd had in months, what with Martyn still regaining his strength from the burns and Shad at Walden or Sierra.

Now if any of King Keevan's brothers-in-law-turned-bodyguards had joined the practice, that really would've made it interesting.

After a knock, the door opened, and Martyn strode inside. "Are you about...what happened to you?"

Leith set aside the damp cloth and reached for the clean, gray shirt Renna had placed next to him. "Had a practice fight with Keevan this morning."

Martyn crossed his arms. "I turn my back for one night and you start scrapping with the big kids. I thought you would've outgrown that bad habit by now."

"Apparently not." Leith started to stand.

Renna put a hand on his shoulder to stop him from getting up. "I still have one more to bandage."

"It's little more than a scratch. It doesn't need a bandage."

"If you were wearing a black shirt, then no, it probably wouldn't. But that light gray shirt will show blood soaking through." Renna huffed and mumbled something under her breath about "scratches" that could've used stitches.

Across the room, Martyn was smirking. Probably enjoying the sight of someone else being fussed over for a change. Two months of healing from his burns had turned Martyn rather grouchy about following a healer's orders.

Leith began to grin back, only to have the movement tug at his split lip. "At least I passed the assessment of my fighting abilities."

As the leader of the Marshals, only Leith needed to have

his skills assessed by someone else since he would evaluate the skills of those under his command. But Shad, Martyn, and Leith would all take the written test together that morning since Keevan had decided it would, hopefully, make the case for the Marshals with Leith as their captain and Shad as second-in-command more convincing.

Martyn swept a glance over Leith's injuries. "Makes me wonder what sort of written test King Keevan has come up with if his fighting assessment was that hard for you."

"I'm expecting plenty of trick questions." As Renna stepped back, Leith stood and pulled the shirt over his head. The bandages tugged at his skin as he moved and a few of his muscles ached with bruises, but all in all he wasn't bad off.

With a knock on the still open door, Shad popped his head inside the room. "No need to panic. Father and I arrived this morning in plenty of time before...Leith, what—"

Leith held up a hand. "I'm fine. Just a practice bout with King Keevan and his bodyguards."

"So you're the reason King Keevan had the beginning of a black eye when he greeted us a few minutes ago?"

Leith winced. Well, Keevan hadn't wanted him to hold back. "Um, yes. That was me."

Shad shook his head and stepped farther into the room. "King Keevan said to let you know they are ready when you are."

Tension curled through Leith's stomach. He was ready. He'd done his best to memorize the Acktarian laws and history in the books Keevan had loaned them. But if he didn't pass this test...

Renna kissed Leith's cheek. "You'll do fine."

He certainly hoped so.

LEITH, SHAD, AND MARTYN FILED THROUGH THE NEW DOOR into what had been the king's chambers. They had to climb a few stairs in a short corridor before reaching a space Leith should've recognized but didn't.

To his left and right, the timber frames of walls outlined two rooms while in front of him, short half walls further divided the large room.

The only way he even knew this had once been the king's chamber was the door that led to the stairs between the two courtyards and the window where Leith had once stood to watch Respen's execution. Beyond those two features, the rest of the room was stripped down to stone and bare wood with walls torn out, rearranged, and in a jumble of partial construction.

Keevan strode toward them with a young woman who looked similar to Queen Adelaide with dark brown, wavy hair, brown eyes, and a wide smile. She held a stack of papers. A rather thick wad of paper.

Two of Keevan's bodyguards trailed them while in the far corner, Lord Stewart, former Resistance general and now lord of Blathe, leaned against the wall with his arms crossed.

Keevan swept an arm at the room. "Far different than the last time you saw it."

"Good riddance." Martyn glanced from the window to the fireplace at the far end to the door. His jaw tightened.

Keevan nodded. "Too much death happened and was planned in this room. It needed a good clean start."

Leith could only imagine the trouble Keevan was having figuring out what to do with the former Blades' Tower. It had been built by King Brian, Acktar's first king, and for that history alone it wouldn't be demolished.

Yet now it was the symbol of the terror of the Blades. Perhaps it would revert to a prison tower as it had been under King Leon and his predecessor, though even that wasn't a perfect solution. As far as Leith knew, no one had suggested a better option.

Keevan gestured to the young woman with him. "This is my sister-in-law Penelope. She's also my personal clerk and will be assisting me this morning."

Penelope smiled and leafed through the paper in her arms. She grabbed a third of it and held it out to Shad. "Lord Shadrach, you're in the far corner of what will be the king's office. There's a temporary desk and pen and ink waiting there for you. Martyn Hamish, you're in the front corner of the new fancy dining room, and Leith Torren, you're in the front corner in what will be a clerk's office over there."

Leith accepted his stack of paper, a twinge of tension zipping down his back. This test was...intimidatingly long.

Penelope clasped her hands behind her back as she continued her instructions. "You won't be able to see each other, and no tapping, scraping, or other suspicious noises that could be construed as passing information back and forth will be tolerated. Each test has the same two hundred questions, but they aren't in the same order on each test. You'll have two and a half hours. Any questions?"

Shad raised his eyebrows and glanced at Leith and

Martyn. "Apparently the king doesn't trust us."

Martyn smirked. "How the trusted lord's son has fallen. Now you're just one of us untrustworthy rabble-rousers."

Keevan scowled. "I don't want there to be any question whatsoever that the three of you passed this test without cheating. That's also why he's here to provide a witness for the Gathering." Keevan waved toward Lord Stewart.

Leith eyed him. Lord Stewart was hardly impartial, given the depth of his loyalty toward Keevan, but he was one of the few nobles who knew about Martyn and Leith's past as Blades but didn't have a personal connection to any of them. Lord Alistair and Lady Lorraine were both related to Shad, Renna was Leith's wife, and Lord Conree of Surgis had Martyn's brother as one of his guardsmen.

Keevan turned to Penelope. "Ready."

She held up an hourglass. "You have a few seconds to find your desks, then I'm turning this over."

With a final glance at Martyn and Shad, Leith strode around the timber wall frames and stepped over stacks of wood until he reached the front corner. There, a wide board had been laid across two trestles with a quill and ink set neatly to one side. At least there was an actual, wooden chair set before the temporary desk instead of some random stack of boards.

He set the papers on the board and took his seat as Penelope called, "Begin."

After dipping the quill in the ink, he glanced at the first question. *Name the first five kings of Acktar.*

Some of the tension relaxed from his shoulders. Good. An easy question.

Perhaps he would pass this test after all.

4

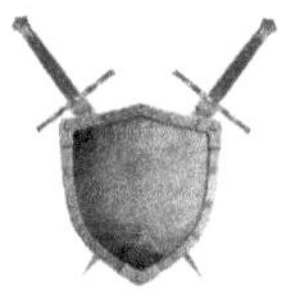

"I wish I was waiting here with you."

Leith smiled and caught Renna's hands before she could straighten his shirt's collar for the sixth time since they'd gathered in an alcove at the back of the Great Hall. Across the room, Ranson fidgeted while Jamie paced. Brandi bounced on her toes, chatting to both Ranson and Jamie, fully recovered after her headache. Owen leaned against the wall, quiet and still.

A few feet away, Kayleigh was fussing over Martyn, and, amazingly, Martyn was putting up with it.

Leith squeezed Renna's hands. "I'll be fine. And you look lovely."

Her light blue dress, the same one she'd worn for their wedding, shimmered when she moved. Her hair flowed across her shoulders, and all Leith could think of was running his fingers through the strands.

She tugged a hand free to straighten his collar again. "Are you going to be all right with this?"

Leith gave in and slid his fingers through her hair. "Yes."

He'd once told Keevan he'd confess what he'd done as a Blade. Back then, he thought he'd be confessing to Keevan and maybe his general.

But in a few minutes, Leith would reveal his past to every noble in Acktar, and from there, the whole country would find out. Not an easy truth to face, but it was time.

The door opened, and Keevan stepped inside, followed by Shad and Lord Alistair. "Everyone ready?"

Leith nodded and glanced between Martyn, Ranson, and Jamie. They all nodded too.

Keevan held out two pieces of paper to Martyn and Ranson. "Official pardons for the two of you. In case the nobles want to quibble about the difference between a pardon and clemency."

"Thank you." Martyn took the paper, staring at it as if he couldn't believe what he was seeing.

Kayleigh gripped his arm, stood on her tiptoes, and kissed his cheek. She whispered something in his ear that had him grinning.

Leith couldn't help but grin too. Martyn and Ranson should have their pasts wiped as clean as his.

Voices rose on the other side of the thin, wooden wall. Keevan turned to Renna. "Ready?"

Renna kissed Leith's cheek and gripped her skirt. "Yes. Let's go."

As she and Keevan disappeared out the door to the Great Hall, Lord Alistair lingered, glancing at Martyn before fixing his gaze on Leith. "In all the time I've known you, I've never asked about your past. In some ways, it didn't matter. But I have one question I need to ask before we are taken by surprise at the Gathering."

Leith braced himself. He thought he knew what the question was—one they had all been avoiding until they couldn't avoid it any longer.

Behind Lord Alistair, Shad's posture was stiff, his arms crossed.

Lord Alistair drew in a deep breath, the lines around his mouth and on his forehead deepening. "On the night Respen Felix took over the castle, did either of you kill my father Lord Farley Alistair or my father-in-law General Hannoran?"

Leith sucked in a breath, a knot twisting inside him. He hadn't, but—

The swear word Martyn blurted was so loud both Brandi and Jamie jumped. Martyn braced himself against the wall. When he raised his head, his mouth was tight. "I killed General Hannoran."

Lord Alistair's shoulders didn't relax, but some of the stiffness left. "Not an unexpected answer. We...guessed that might be the case. It doesn't take too much guesswork to count through the Blades and figure out you were the first of the Blades not assigned to a member of the royal family. The general in charge of the army would be the next logical target."

"I am sorry. If I could do things differently...well, there's a lot about my past I'd change." Martyn glanced between Shad and Lord Alistair, leaning against the wall as if he needed its support to stay upright. Kayleigh took his hand while Owen moved to stand on his other side.

Leith stayed where he was, knowing all too well the ache

of the guilt Martyn would be feeling. It was the same weight he'd felt that moment in Eagle Heights when he'd seen Keevan.

Their past—the blood on their hands—was hard enough to bear on most days, even with the knowledge that Christ's blood washed that guilt away. It was much heavier coming face to face with those they'd hurt, the families they'd torn apart, the ache no number of sincere apologies and confessions could erase.

The hardest part was knowing that nothing they did could ever heal what they'd done. They could bare their guilt for all to see with an honest admission of the truth. They could repent and beg forgiveness on their knees. They could live upstanding lives for the rest of their days. But nothing they did could ever heal the brokenness they'd caused.

Only God could work forgiveness in the broken hearts of others and heal what seemed unhealable. But even that was rarely immediate but instead a process God worked slowly.

"Neither of us killed Lord Farley Alistair." Small comfort at this point, but Leith was thankful he didn't have to look Lord Alistair in the eye and tell him his knife had taken his father's life, not when Lord Alistair was the closest thing Leith had ever had to a father. "The Seventh Blade killed him. Respen hadn't wanted him to survive long enough to rally any of the others."

"He would've been a threat to Respen, had he lived long enough." Lord Alistair's voice had a rough edge to it as he adjusted the sling supporting his crippled left arm. "As would my father-in-law."

"He died quickly. Not that it's a whole lot of comfort at

this point." Martyn grimaced and squeezed his eyes shut, as if he couldn't face Shad or Lord Alistair at that moment.

What else could they say? Leith remembered General Hannoran's body. The blood. The gash. So like the others he'd inflicted that night after joining Martyn in subduing the other army commanders after he thought he'd killed Keevan. Death had come for many that night. Some of it quick. Some of it long and painful. All of it bloody and brutal.

"You killed Walter Esroy too." Shad's voice was quiet as he stared at the floor. "He was the man leading Renna and Brandi to Eagle Heights when you ambushed them."

Martyn ran a hand through his hair and nodded. "A friend of yours?"

"Yes. A friend and a...mentor of sorts"

Leith hadn't known Walter Esroy was more than just a scout. No wonder Shad had been so affected when they'd found Esroy's body a year ago. There hadn't been much left of him after the wild animals got to him.

"No wonder you hated me." Martyn's face was pale, his shoulders hunched.

"It's forgiven and over now." Shad lightly punched Martyn's shoulder and grinned, though the grin was thin and tight as if somewhat forced. "Though I might never forgive you for getting a better score on that test than I did. It really wasn't fair that you had a whole month in bed with nothing to do but study while I was so busy I barely had time to think, much less study."

Martyn returned the grin. "If that were the case, then why did Leith get a better score than either of us?"

"Motivation." Leith shrugged. "Besides, I hardly think

scoring one or four points better on a two hundred question test is that big of a difference."

At least the attempts at humor dissipated some of the darkness of a few moments before. Not that the reprieve would last long. Once they started confessing to the whole Gathering, the whole of the bloody and shameful truth would be bared for the country to see.

Heading for the door, Lord Alistair nodded at Martyn and Leith as he passed. Then he left, back straight, head high.

Without another word, Kayleigh dug in her pocket and pulled out what looked like a bar of soap.

Martyn grimaced. "Can it wait until later? I really don't want to go through this whole Gathering tasting that."

"Later, and don't you dare forget." Kayleigh tapped the soap against Martyn's chest before she returned it to her pocket.

Martyn smiled down at her with such a sappy look in his deep brown eyes one would think Kayleigh had said something romantic instead of threatened him with soap.

Leith shook his head. Martyn and Kayleigh had a unique relationship, that was for sure.

Shad moved to the door and propped it open a crack so they could hear what was happening in the Great Hall.

Leith joined Jamie, Brandi, and Ranson in the far corner of the room. Ranson was pressed against the wall as if trying to become invisible while Jamie had his arms crossed. After Jamie's growth spurt over the winter, Jamie's shoulder was nearly level with Leith's. "Are you sure you want to join the rest of us? You were only a Blade for a few hours."

"Yes, I'm sure." Jamie rubbed at his right shoulder. "I'm

standing with the rest of you. Someday, someone is going to see my mark, and they'll ask. I'll need the evidence from this Gathering to prove that I didn't do anything."

Jamie needed his past erased just as much as Leith, Martyn, and Ranson did. And, perhaps, Jamie's was more complicated. Because he hadn't done anything wrong, yet no one would believe it because of the one mark on his shoulder and his association with Leith.

"Are you disappointed that Ranson and I won't be joining you and Martyn in the Marshals?" Jamie scuffed his boot against the floor.

"No, of course not. You have to follow where God is calling you. If that is to be a minister or..." Leith glanced at Ranson, "a farmer or whatever else, that's where you're supposed to be."

Ranson ducked his head. Leith wasn't sure what Ranson would become. Perhaps a farmer. Maybe something else. But at least he had the chance to choose instead of being forced to kill as he had been in the Blades.

"Good speech. I knew there was a reason you'll be doing most of the talking in there." Martyn's voice had regained its usual tone.

"Besides the fact that I have this Gathering rigged in my favor?" Leith tried his best not to grin as he glanced over his shoulder where Martyn still stood with Kayleigh and Owen.

"As long as you haven't done anything recently to get Renna mad at you." Martyn paused and scratched his chin. "Does Renna ever get mad? Seems I am always doing something to get Kayleigh riled."

Kayleigh swatted his arm. "You deserve it."

Brandi flapped her hand at them and pressed a finger to

her mouth. "Sssh. I think they're starting the interesting part."

They all crowded around the door, peeking out the thin opening into the Great Hall. Two long tables had been set up parallel to each other, the lords and ladies sitting on the outer sides of the tables, facing each other. Keevan sat by himself at a table perpendicular to the others. The middle had been left open. That's where Leith would stand when called in front of the Gathering.

He scrubbed his palms across his black trousers. Soon, he'd have to face his past in front of the whole country.

5

Keevan held his back straight and tried to pretend he wasn't sporting a black eye as they worked through the official business, such as certifying that each of the lords, ladies, and representatives were the legitimate representatives for each town, except for Flayin Falls and Kilm. Since the lord and regent of those towns were under arrest, they lost their voice on the Gathering until the cases were tried.

After an hour of dealing with a few minor matters, it was finally time to present the proposal for the Marshals. He waved to the stack of paper at the corner of his table, and Penelope fetched them and began distributing them to the lords and ladies.

Keevan flattened his own pieces of paper and drew in a deep breath. This was the most ambitious law he'd tried to implement in the less than a year he'd been king. If it was a success, it could define the rest of his reign. If it failed now...his reign would be shaky if he couldn't even get something like this to pass in the Gathering.

Standing, Keevan swept a glance around the nobles at the Gathering, though he didn't look too closely at any one face. "A week ago, all of you were sent a copy of this proposal for your perusal, but my clerk is handing out a copy for your reference for this discussion."

The rustle of paper filled the room along with a few hushed murmurs.

"For generations, Acktar has been plagued by bandits and organized Rovers. The vast stretches of prairie and the deep wilderness of the Sheered Rock Hills are impractical for any town or army contingent to patrol. As we all saw last summer and fall, without a deterrent, bandits will overrun the country." Even with his rasp, Keevan's voice remained strong. Unwavering. "My father did the best he knew how, but he was unable to stop the deprivations. This is one reason many of you supported the traitor Respen. In the Blades, he gave you the needed protection from the bandits."

Some of the Resistance nobles stilled, scowls crossing their faces. But the lord of Deadgrass nodded, along with the lords of Dyman and Mackton.

"But the Blades were also assassins who drenched Acktar in blood. They were the law, judge, and executioner. This is unacceptable. Acktar was founded on the principles of the mercy found in justice." Keevan tapped the papers on the table in front of him. "I don't intend to follow my father's or Respen's mistakes. Instead of a gang of assassins, I propose to found the Marshals, whose sole aim will be to track and apprehend criminals to be turned over to the proper authorities for judgment. They will operate on the prairie and deep in the Hills where the town sheriffs do not have jurisdiction, providing a nationwide, coordinated system of law enforcement that will make Acktar the safest it has ever been."

There. He had stated his case and presented his opening argument. Keevan reclaimed his seat and folded his arms in front of him on the table. "Does anyone have any questions?"

Lord Hartley of Clarbon crossed his arms. "How do you intend to prevent these Marshals from turning into your personal assassins?"

"The Blades were kept isolated from the people here at Nalgar, but the Marshals will live and work among the people where they will form attachments and loyalties. The Blades were stationed at Nalgar Castle under Respen's direct control. The Marshals, instead, will be away from direct royal control." Keevan swept a stern gaze around the tables. "Most of the control will rest in the man appointed as captain over the Marshals. To prevent him from gaining too much power, he will report to the crown and the Gathering each year."

The looks on the faces around the tables mostly seemed considering, even interested. Few showed distaste or downright hostility to this proposal, though some had gleams in their eyes as they recognized Keevan's careful wording. The captain of the Marshals would report to the Gathering, but he wouldn't be answerable to the Gathering, not like he would be to Keevan, since the Marshals would need to report on and even arrest members of the nobility if needed.

Keevan couldn't let himself become too overconfident. Passing this proposal was the easy part. Convincing the nobles to put a former Blade in charge of the Marshals would be harder.

Lord Doughtry of Calloday patted his hands on top of his rotund stomach. "So I guess the only question is, who do you intend to appoint as the captain?"

Now for the moment when the positive feel to the room soured. Keevan cleared his throat, hoping his voice held out for the rest of this discussion after all the speeches he'd been making. "Daniel Grayce, if you would please step forward?"

The door to the side room at the far end of the Great Hall opened, and Leith strolled inside. Dressed in black trousers and with a shirt in the same light green as the Eirdon banner, Leith was a mix between the assassin he'd been and the man he was becoming. At the moment, he wasn't wearing a single knife, and that made him look more the boy and less the man Keevan had fought yesterday morning, even with the yellowness of bruising along his jaw and across one cheek.

Most of the Resistance lords and ladies stared at Leith without recognition, a few with puckered foreheads that probably had more to do with his youth than his past.

But many among the lords who had supported Respen straightened in their seats, their faces whitening.

Lord Chambers of Mackton glanced between Keevan and Leith. "Do you know who that man is, sire?"

Lord Chambers' tone held a sharpness, as if questioning how easily Keevan could be deceived and manipulated. Yes, Keevan knew Leith's past for he was a part of it. He knew who Leith was now. And he knew—or guessed that he knew —who Leith would become. "Yes, Lord Chambers. He is Leith Daniel Grayce Torren, my cousin by marriage and former Blade under Respen Felix."

Now there was the uproar. Keevan leaned back in his

chair as several of the more vocal lords began shouting while many of the Resistance nobles glared and fingered the empty sheaths where their weapons normally hung.

To Keevan's left, Lady Ross of Cornell stared at Leith with a wrinkle creasing her forehead. "But...he's so young."

And that was perhaps the tragedy of the Blades they would all have to face as Leith, Martyn, Ranson, and Jamie told the story of what the Blades had been. It was easy to believe the Blades were full grown men—and some of them had been—but much harder to come to grips with the evil in the heart of humanity that even young boys could kill. How could anyone move on from a tragedy when the perpetrator was barely older than a child?

Across the space, Keevan met Leith's gaze and nodded. Yesterday, he'd fought Leith to the point both of them had been bruised and bloody, but today he was going to fight for him with every scrap of power and respect he had as king.

After all, they were family.

LEITH FORCED HIMSELF TO REMAIN STILL AS THE SHOUTING grew in volume.

Partway down the table to Keevan's right, Renna sat ramrod straight, doing a remarkable job keeping her expression calm despite half the room shouting for his blood. Lord Alistair and Lady Lorraine on either side of her also remained quiet and stoic. Lord Conree sitting along the table to the left also remained more restrained than the others.

When her gaze connected with his, her mouth tipped in a small, tight smile.

Lord Doughtry of Calloday pounded the table with one meaty hand while he flapped the other at Leith. "Did you know about this, Lady Grayce?"

He said it with such derision, as if he believed Renna was such a foolish young girl she could be tricked into marrying a Blade without her knowledge. As if a wife could somehow miss noticing the scars of Leith's marks marching down his right arm. Leith clenched his fists behind his back and did his best not to react. As the lady of Stetterly, this was Renna's battle to win.

"Of course. I have known Leith was a Blade from the day I met him." Renna's voice held a frosty quality Leith had only heard from her twice before, once with Sheriff Allen and once with Respen.

"So what are you? Lady Grayce or Lady Torren?" Lord Doughtry harrumphed, his double chins jiggling, as if any sort of confusion about her name was a personal affront to his dignity.

Renna met Leith's gaze and smiled. "I'm both. We were married with both names."

He couldn't help a smile in return this time. She was both because he was both. And somehow, that felt just right. She'd met him as Leith, gotten to know him as Daniel, and begun to fall in love with him as Leith. He was still Leith, sleeping with a knife strapped to his ankle and the rest of his knives on the table beside their bed. But he was also Daniel, the man who plowed a small vegetable garden behind the cabin he'd built with his own hands.

Renna's posture relaxed somewhat, from stiff to a confident lift to her chin. Leith gave her a small nod. She was ready to handle whatever this Gathering was about to throw at the two of them.

Lord Currin of Aven jumped to his feet, his shout rising above all the others. "You almost had me convinced that the Marshals weren't going to be assassins, but you wish to appoint a Blade to lead it?"

Leith curled his fingers and tried to hide his wince. Yes, that's where he deserved to be.

Keevan didn't flinch. Two nights ago, he'd glared enough daggers and swords at Leith to supply Acktar's army, and the next morning he'd been plenty serious about fighting Leith, but looking at him now, no one would've guessed it. His gaze remained hard and stern, his eyes flashing as if he would be willing to take on all the nobles to prove Leith's worth.

"While Leith Torren will lead the Marshals, it has already been determined that Lord Shadrach Alistair will serve as his second-in-command, keeping a balance between former Blade and former Resistance leading the Marshals. It is Leith's intention—with my approval—to recruit for the Marshals from among qualified soldiers and scouts from both the Resistance and those who supported Respen, thereby keeping the Marshals as balanced and impartial as possible."

Some of the tension left some of the faces around Leith as the lords and ladies glanced between Leith, Lord Alistair, and Keevan. Depending on how they felt about the Alistairs, Shad's position as second-in-command would be either assuring or even more concerning.

Lord Currin remained standing, face reddening. "What is he even doing free? He should be locked in the dungeon and executed!"

Before Leith had a chance to so much as flinch under the words, Keevan's answer came as firm as the castle's foundations. "He has been pardoned and thus no longer deserves to be imprisoned any more than any other free citizen of Acktar."

"But he was a Blade! And you pardoned him? After what the Blades did? What we've suffered?" Lord Currin shook with the force of his words.

Leith turned away. Lord Currin's father had died at Nalgar Castle the night Respen took over, and his oldest son had been killed by Blades a few years later.

"I lost my entire family except for Lady Torren and her sister. Three brothers. My parents. My aunt and uncle. I have lost just as much as anyone sitting here." Keevan leaned forward, the sunlight streaming through the high, upper windows highlighting the scar running across his cheek and down his neck. "After this war, who in Acktar isn't guilty of blood? Those of you who supported Respen, people were murdered in your towns because of their faith. Some of you actively ordered their executions. You turned people over to Respen knowing it would mean their deaths. Should I imprison and execute you for those crimes?"

Some of the nobles who supported Respen squirmed in their seats. Others sat stoically, glared, or stared at their hands.

"Those of you who supported the Resistance, you aren't exempt. During the war, families were driven out if they didn't actively support the Resistance or if they didn't believe as you did, and some of them didn't survive their journey to a friendly town. Who should I punish for those crimes?"

Leith caught glimpses of more lords and ladies shifting

in their seats. Instead of being a hindrance, Keevan's rasp gave his voice an earnest, harsh tone that cut deep as a sword thrust.

Keevan swept his gaze around the room, looking at everyone but Leith. "And what about the men and boys, some as young as fourteen, who died fighting in the war? Should I execute all the soldiers who fought in Respen's army for the blood they spilled, even though many of them fought not for Respen, but out of loyalty to their town and their lord or lady sitting here? What about the husbandless women and fatherless children whose husbands and fathers fought and died for Respen? Who should be punished for those deaths?"

The Great Hall had gone silent as the graveyard on the north hill outside.

"We fought a war, brother against brother, neighbor against neighbor. We are all guilty of blood, and more blood isn't going to take that away. We face the past wherever we turn, including as we sit around these tables. Respen is dead. Let the blood and guilt rest on his head alone. As for the rest of us, the only way we can heal is through forgiveness." Keevan's jaw tightened, stretching the scar taut across his cheek. His blue eyes fixed on Leith for the first time since he'd begun speaking. "I intend to lead Acktar in forgiveness through my example. I am one of Leith Torren's victims. Yet, I have forgiven him, and, as king of Acktar, I have pardoned him."

Leith kept his head held high, his gaze focused on Keevan. Thanks to the grace of God, he didn't have to stand with shame, and thanks to Keevan's pardon, he didn't have to flinch from the consequences.

Lord Doughtry snorted and slapped a palm on the table-top. "That's all well and good, but so far I've heard no compelling reason why you want to appoint a Blade to lead the Marshals. If you're going to pardon the Blade, I say let him slink off to Stetterly and stay there. Let Lord Shadrach lead the Marshals."

Renna stiffened, her lips pressed into a thin line. Leith resisted the urge to smile. She wasn't too happy about any insult to him. Thankfully Lord Doughtry had called him a Blade and not tried for something even more insulting, like mongrel, dog, or mangy cur.

"Because he was a Blade, he's also one of the few men in Acktar with the knowledge and level of training necessary to lead the Marshals. Lord Shadrach's other duties as heir to Walden will eventually interfere with his duties as a Marshal, something that can be worked around for a second-in-command, but not for the overall captain." Keevan's rasp grew worse, as if all the talking he'd done had strained his voice. "This will be a dangerous job. Would you rather volunteer your sons to take it on?"

Leith heard the implication. Better to give it to someone few in Acktar would mourn if he died. Some of the lords who had been shouting the most vocally for Leith's blood a moment ago now looked like they thought giving Leith a job in the Marshals would be a legal way for him to be killed off eventually. Not a pleasant thought. Leith knew the job would be dangerous, but he certainly prayed he'd live to old age.

Keevan gestured to the far side of the great hall. "But I understand that Acktar needs the truth to forgive and heal. Immediately after the war, my first impulse was to move on by hiding his crimes. But that was wrong. Forgiveness and healing can only happen when darkness is brought to the light. True repentance demands a full confession. For that reason, I have asked Leith Torren and the three other remaining Blades to relate the truth of what they've done and answer any questions you might have regarding crimes the Blades committed. But please remember, as you hear their stories, that they have been pardoned and thus nothing they say can legally be held against them."

Leith didn't glance over his shoulder as he heard footsteps behind him. Martyn halted to his right, Ranson and Jamie on his left.

There was something about standing with his brothers on either side of him...he could face anything as long as they had his back.

And then he, Martyn, Ranson, and Jamie told the story of the Blades.

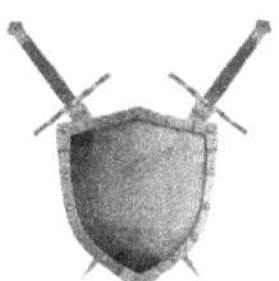

The Great Hall remained silent as Leith, Martyn, Ranson, and Jamie finished. All the nobles gathered there now knew the blood they'd spilled and pained they'd caused. But they also heard how Leith had turned on Respen, given information to the Resistance, and been tortured because of it.

Now more of the lords and ladies regarded Leith with something that might have been speculation, as if he was some new kind of snake they'd discovered in the Waste.

A rattlesnake. That's what he'd probably always be to them. But as long as he could prove he was their rattlesnake, he could live with that.

Leith did his best not to fidget, even though his skin prickled with their stares. He kept his gaze straight ahead rather than glance at Martyn, Ranson, or Jamie beside him, and he definitely didn't look at Renna. He had to concentrate.

Finally, Lady Cecelia Emilin slid to her feet. "I would like to say something."

"The floor is yours, milady." Keevan nodded.

"My husband was killed by a Blade. I have experienced loss like many of you here. But, if this is the Blade that warned about the assassination, then I owe him my life and the life of my son. Even though my husband didn't heed the warning for himself, he made sure my son and I were hidden and were thereby spared the night he was killed." Lady Emilin's voice wavered, but she didn't sit down.

And for the pain in her voice and the steadiness of her stance, the other nobles were listening. Leith could feel it in the hushed breaths and stillness of the room.

"I believe we should see the Blade Leith Torren's appointment to this position, not as a return to the Blades, but as a sign of reconciliation. If King Keevan is willing to put aside his own hurt to forgive this Blade, then will he not also deal fairly and mercifully with those of you who fought against him? And those of us who fought for him, I believe we should extend the same sort of forgiveness to this Blade and to our neighbors." Lady Emilin swept her gaze around the room before facing King Keevan. "No, I don't think we should take this appointment lightly nor should we stop fearing a return of the Blades. For that reason, I would like to make a motion to add a revision to the proposal."

Leith swallowed. What did she want to revise? Perhaps she wanted to accept the proposed Marshals, but without Leith's involvement? He and Keevan had talked about the possibility of that happening, and Leith would accept it if it came.

But leading the Marshals...it felt so right. So like God's

purpose for him. It would be hard to walk away and accept that it wasn't.

Lady Emilin's chin lifted a fraction higher. "I move to change the name of the proposed Marshals to the Blade Marshals to remind them of where they came from and what they are to prevent from ever happening again."

The Blade Marshals.

The Blades as they should've been.

"I second the motion." Lord Farthen of Keestone stated.

The twitch to the corner of Keevan's mouth might've been a smile. "All in favor of the revision to the proposal to change the name to the Blade Marshals, raise your right hands."

Hands shot into the air.

"Motion passed."

Leith breathed a small sigh of relief. If that motion passed so easily, the proposal should pass as well. They only needed a majority for it.

"I move to vote on the proposal to found the Blade Marshals." Lord Alistair's voice boomed in the Great Hall, calling for the vote as agreed.

"I second the motion." Lord Segon of Uster uncrossed his arms and stretched in his chair.

"Very well. Penelope, if you would please hand out the supplies?" Keevan waved to his clerk again before gesturing to Leith, and Martyn, Ranson, and Jamie with him. "You are dismissed."

While the nobles were distracted with receiving paper and pens to vote, Leith spun on his heels and led the way from the Great Hall to the side room. As he stepped inside, Brandi hugged him, then Shad clapped him on the shoulder.

Martyn went straight to Kayleigh and hugged her before Owen slapped his shoulder.

Leith leaned against the wall near the door, listening to the scratching of pens and rustling of paper as the nobles wrote down their votes and passed the paper to the clerks who would count the written votes as a confirmation that they matched what the nobles stated out loud.

As the verbal voting began, Leith counted the votes under his breath, though he kept losing track. But it still seemed like there were more votes for than against.

As what he guessed was the last vote was called out, he glanced around the room, spotting the small smile on Ranson's face.

Ranson ducked his head. "Twenty-nine out of forty. It passed."

It was official. Behind him, Keevan decreed the Blade Marshals officially founded, though Leith only barely heard it.

Martyn met his gaze from where he stood between Kayleigh and Owen. "Looks like we're going to get a second chance to do this right, First Blade."

Leith shook his head. "Not First Blade. Captain. Or, better yet, simply Blade Marshal Torren."

That sounded...right. He had been the first Blade. Now the first Blade Marshal. This time, he was going to make sure the Blade Marshals became what the Blades never could've been.

AFTER A SHORT RECESS FOR A LUNCH EATEN WHERE THEY SAT in the Great Hall, Keevan faced the Gathering once more. Getting the proposal passed had been difficult, but this second half of the Gathering would be perhaps harder.

Lord Norton was marched in between a pair of guards, shackles on his hands and still wearing the same clothes he'd worn when he'd been arrested two months ago. His blond hair straggled long and unkept. Hollows dug into the skin under his eyes and cheekbones, his skin pale after two months of solitary confinement in the near complete darkness of one of the rooms in the Tower.

Still he carried his head high, a smirk forming grooves around his mouth. As if he thought he was still going to gain his victory here. When the guards removed the shackles and retreated to the doors, Lord Norton faced Keevan and crossed his arms.

Keevan met Lord Norton's gaze and held it. "Lord Norton of Kilm, you have been accused of conspiracy to commit treason against your king, colluding with persons rightfully banished from Acktar, and attacking one of your fellow nobles without provocation. How do you wish to plead?"

"Would it do any good to plead not guilty? You have all your witnesses lined up to testify against me. So, yes, I plead guilty. But I would be careful with your accusations, sire, when you are also colluding with Blades." Lord Norton paused, as if waiting for gasps of surprise and an angry uproar.

All he got was silence.

Keevan fought to keep his face impassive, his eyes hard. Exactly as he'd predicted, Lord Norton planned to use Leith, Martyn, and Ranson's pardons to undermine Keevan's authority in this case. Too bad for him Keevan had already countered that argument.

Brow furrowing, Lord Norton gestured to the two tables of nobles on either side of him. "Didn't you hear what I said? Our king has pardoned four Blades."

Technically he'd only pardoned three Blades since Jamie Cavendish had done nothing wrong in the couple of hours he'd officially been a Blade.

Lord Doughtry snorted. "We just spent all morning hearing about those Blades. If your only defense is that a Blade made you do it, then don't bother."

For once, Keevan found himself inwardly cheering for the pompous lord.

"But..." Lord Norton turned in a circle, eyes widening at the scowls and frowns surrounding him.

"Do you plan to attack Keestone next? How about Duelstone? Which of us will be your next target?" Lord Farthen crossed arms stiffened with clenched fists. "Norton, I suggest you get down on your knees and beg for mercy. Again."

"No, I wouldn't...I only..." Lord Norton waved his arms as if pleading for someone to defend him. "I was trying to prevent him from using those Blades to assassinate us."

"By harboring the five Blades he didn't pardon and had banished from the kingdom, as well as attacking an innocent town?" Lady Lorraine raised her eyebrows, her words sharp as the dagger she usually wore at her hip. "And less than a year after King Keevan pardoned you from the first time you committed treason."

Lord Norton focused on the lords from Dyman, Mackton, and Deadgrass. All lords that had supported Respen, but now turned their faces away. "You understand, don't you? Why I had to do it?"

"You aren't our king, Norton." Lord Conree's voice sliced like a sword, not an ounce of pity smoothing the sharp tone. "We have taken matters into our own hands too many times already. How do we know you won't turn on the rest of us the moment you think it is best?"

Lord Norton clenched and unclenched his hands, a wildness gleaming in his eyes. He jabbed a finger toward Lord Beregern of Mountainwood. "I wasn't alone in this. He was going to reinforce me."

Lord Beregern squirmed and glanced around the room. "I didn't know the full scope of the plan, and I returned to Mountainwood as soon as Lord Alistair intercepted me and my men and apprised me of the situation."

Not exactly how things had gone down. Keevan had gotten Lord Alistair's version of the events—one he trusted far more—and Lord Beregern had backed down only once he realized Lord Norton was likely going to lose.

But Keevan was willing to let Lord Beregern save some face here. He'd already, privately, apprised Lord Beregern of exactly what would happen to him if he even thought about rebelling against Keevan again.

Lord Norton spun on his heels again, as if seeking some hint of mercy from any of the nobles sitting around the tables, finding none. The Resistance nobles saw him as a repeat of Respen's violence. The nobles who had supported Respen saw a reminder of the past they would rather forget. It was in everyone's best political interest to leave Lord Norton to his fate.

Keevan waited a few more heartbeats, letting the silence

crumble Lord Norton's arrogance. When he spoke, he forced all traces of mercy out of his voice and off his face. "Lord Norton, the penalty for treason is death. I spared you once already, but this time you put the lives of my wife and son at risk and caused irreparable damage to many families in Stetterly. Worse, you did this in the face of the mercy I had already given you. This is treason I cannot overlook."

Lord Norton paled further, the angles of his face stark.

Keevan had to make sure Lord Norton—and all the nobles sitting around those tables—understood the gravity of this treason. Perhaps they saw him as a weak king after the number of pardons and lack of executions he'd handed out in the wake of the war to regain his throne. This time, he had to make them believe he was willing to order Lord Norton's execution.

Would he, if it came to that? He certainly hoped not. Using the power of the government to end a life wasn't something to do lightly nor something he took pleasure in, as much as he believed it necessary in some cases. It had been necessary for Respen. Depending on how Lord Norton reacted in the next few minutes, it might be necessary for him too.

"While the ax is the traditional execution for nobility, I could have you hung like a common Rover or horse thief. Not a pleasant way to die, I'm told, if you don't break your neck right away." Keevan steeled himself against his churning stomach. "I could make your family—your son and daughter—watch you die in choking agony without any chance to tell you goodbye."

He did his best not to swallow at the bitter taste those words left on his tongue, but he had to say them without pity. Since he wasn't going to break Lord Norton with torture, he would break him with words. Lord Norton had to believe the future Keevan spelled out would be his.

And perhaps the other nobles in the room understood that, since none of them spoke up. Though, Keevan didn't glance at his cousin Renna. He hadn't told her his plan, and he didn't want to see the horror on her face if she believed he would truly go through with forcing Lord Norton's young son and daughter—only eight and six—to watch their father hang.

Lord Norton's hands shook as he crossed his arms, the gesture looking more like he was trying to hold himself together than defiance. When he looked at Keevan, his face was drawn, his eyes shining. "I don't care how you execute me. But please don't make my family...they're just children. Please show them mercy."

"As you showed the children at Stetterly mercy?" Keevan kept the hard edge to his voice. Lord Norton was getting there, but he didn't fully regret what he'd done. Not yet.

Keevan slid a sheet of paper out of his stack of notes. He didn't need to read the numbers. He had them memorized. But the act made what he was about to say seem more official. "Sixteen people died at Stetterly because of your attack. Nine men and seven women. Thirty-two children lost a parent thanks to your actions. Three quarters of those children are younger than fourteen and nearly a third of them lost the only parent they had left. Many of them saw their father or mother die. Tell me, Lord Norton, where was your mercy for those children?"

Lord Norton's shoulders slumped, a tremor coursing

through him as he curled inward and slowly sank to his knees on the floor, head hanging.

Even for a man like Lord Norton, Keevan didn't relish this moment. It wasn't something to rejoice in, reducing a man to shaking through mere words.

When Lord Norton raised his head, his eyes were dull, grooves cutting around his mouth. The face of a man who had resigned himself to death. When he spoke, his voice was hoarse. "I never gave any." His body shuddered as he released a long breath.

He wouldn't say he regretted his actions out loud. He was still too proud to do that. That shudder, that admission, was the best Keevan would get. It was enough.

Keevan let the tension drain out of him. "Too many children in Acktar are already growing up without a father. For the sake of your children, I'm not going to execute you."

"What?" Lord Norton's head snapped up. Some of the other nobles stirred, though no one else spoke.

"But, you will never be a part of this Gathering again. Kilm will lose its seat on the Gathering for the next five years. After that, you may appoint a representative, but you as the lord of Kilm will be banned. You will also be required to pay a lump sum for the damages you and your army inflicted on Stetterly, and you will pay for the raising of the children your actions hurt. If I hear that you raise taxes on the people of Kilm or in any other way make their lives miserable to pay for this, there will be consequences."

A harsh sentence, perhaps, but far less harsh than death by hanging. It would prevent Lord Norton from ever having the prestige among the nobles or the resources to plot rebellion again.

As Keevan called for a vote to confirm the sentence, Lord Norton shakily climbed to his feet. When the votes were called out, many of the nobles stared at Keevan with an odd look. Respect, yes. Perhaps a little fear. Even Renna stared at him round-eyed.

But Lord Stewart gave him a nod, the corners of his mouth tipped into the hint of a smile.

That smile meant more to Keevan than any other praise could have, coming from the man who had done more to shape Keevan into the king he was than anyone else.

Keevan wasn't a weak, indecisive king like his father. He wasn't a tyrant king ruling by fear with little regard for the actual laws of the land like Respen.

But he was going to be a law-abiding and law-wielding king. With the Blade Marshals patrolling the prairie and capturing lawbreakers, he would have to get rather used to handing out sentences. Even if people didn't like him or agree with him, hopefully they would respect him.

The Gathering confirmed the sentence easily, as Keevan had guessed they would. None of them were eager for Lord Norton's execution, except perhaps Lord Beregern who wouldn't want Lord Norton to implicate him any more than he already had.

Keevan motioned toward the guards at the door and met Lord Norton's gaze. "Lord Norton, this sentence is final. You are free to go. I suggest you return to Kilm as soon as possible."

Lord Norton nodded and spun on his heels as the doors opened. Standing in the courtyard outside the doors was a thin woman along with a sandy-haired boy and a girl with white-blond braids. Addie had her arm around the woman's shoulders, as if holding her upright while she waited for news about her husband.

The girl turned first, her eyes locking onto Lord Norton. "Papa!"

Lord Norton took a step toward her, but he was too shaky to hurry. The girl was faster, dashing in a flurry of blond hair and frilly pink skirts. Lord Norton barely had enough time to sink to his knees again before the girl flung herself into his arms.

Moments later, Lady Norton and the boy crashed to their knees, and Lord Norton embraced his son and pressed a kiss to his wife's temple.

Looking away from the reunited family, Keevan glanced toward Addie where she stood outside the Great Hall and gave her a nod. If he had to be the stern words that broke, then she was the touch that healed.

As Lord Norton stood, still holding onto his wife and children, Keevan forced his expression to remain hard for a while longer. "Lord Norton, one more thing before you go."

Lord Norton halted and glanced over his shoulder. "Yes, sire?"

Keevan kept his gaze and voice steely. "Two times have I granted you mercy. There will be no mercy a third time."

"Understood, sire." Lord Norton nodded, then left with his family.

7

Eyes closed, Keevan sprawled on the settee in his and Addie's chamber, the warmth of a heated, damp rag soaking into his aching throat muscles. After all the speeches and talking he'd had to do at the Gathering, his weakened vocal cords were giving out.

Both Lord Norton and Dean Westin had been sentenced and Dean Westin's younger brother had been placed as the new regent of Flayin Falls. And Keevan had somehow survived placing a former Blade in charge of the Blade Marshals without causing another war.

The door opened, and hushed voices spoke from the door, then footsteps approached the settee.

"Queen Adelaide said you needed water."

Leith's voice. Keevan would've groaned if his throat hadn't hurt so much.

"Addie. I told you to call me Addie."

Keevan didn't have to look to know Addie had her

eyebrows arched, the same stern look on her face that she gave her brothers when they annoyed her.

He cracked his eyes open. Leith held a glass of water out to him. "I'm sorry."

An apology. And, somehow, the sound of it soothed the rest of the remaining heat in Keevan's chest. Leith understood Keevan still had to live with the consequences of that night. Leith had momentary memories, but Keevan? Keevan felt that night every time he talked.

Keevan propped himself onto his elbow and reached for the glass. When he spoke, his voice was barely audible. "Good reason not to talk to you."

They were the same words he would've said a week ago, but now he found a smile tugged at his mouth instead of a scowl.

Addie planted her free hand on her hip. "Are you being impolite again?"

Keevan grinned. "Yes."

Addie sighed and shook her head, her mass of brown curls swinging, as she adjusted Duncan on her hip. "I blame my brothers. They think teasing is an art form they were more than happy to teach to Keevan. It's now the only way he knows how to interact with family."

Leith raised his eyebrows and fought a grin. "I see."

He probably did. Keevan sipped the water, handed the glass back to Leith, and swiveled upright. "Is everyone else ready?"

"Yes." Leith held out a hand.

Keevan took it and let Leith pull him to his feet. Might as well get the small ceremony to make Leith a Blade Marshal over with as quickly as possible before Keevan's voice gave out completely.

Addie took Keevan's arm, kissed him on the cheek, and together they followed Leith out the door, down the short hallway, and through the door to what had been the king's chamber.

There, the room was crowded with almost more bustle than it had on the days when it was filled with his father-in-law's workers as they tore down and rebuilt the set of rooms. In one corner, Brandi chatted with Shad's sister Abigail, who held the hand of seven-year-old Esther, the youngest Alistair sibling. Jamie stood near them with Jeremiah Alistair while Ranson Harding leaned against the wall nearby, darting glances as if he wasn't sure where he was supposed to be or what conversation he should join.

Lydia Alistair talked with Jolene, Renna, Kayleigh, and Lady Alistair. After giving Keevan's arm a squeeze, Addie worked her way through the dust, piles of boards, and tools to join them, and Lady Alistair almost instantly claimed Duncan.

Now there was someone more than ready to be a grand-mother. Thanks to his mother-in-law, Keevan could recognize the signs all too well.

Off to one side, Owen, Shad, and Martyn were deep in discussion, and based on Martyn's hand motions, Keevan didn't want to know what sort of gruesome, knife-induced death Martyn was illustrating. Leith joined them.

Lord Alistair and Lady Lorraine stood near the window with Frank, and Frank was nodding along to something Lord Alistair was saying. Tips, perhaps, for organizing protection for Keevan? If there was anyone in Acktar who would know a thing or two about security, it would be Lord Alistair. He was one of the few people in the Resistance who had managed to get his whole family through the war unscathed. Not an easy feat when Respen had known he was a one of the main leaders.

In what would become Keevan's office, Patrick sat on the edge of the makeshift table, grinning and probably doing his best to annoy Penelope as she straightened stacks of papers.

As Keevan swept another glance around the room, a sense of rightness settled in his chest and eased his muscles. He wasn't a carpenter like his father-in-law, much as he loved working with wood when he needed to let his hands move and his mind rest, but he could still build.

What he had here with the Blade Marshals was building Acktar in a way no king had before. Perhaps he was using some of the salvageable pieces that Respen had left him and a vague blueprint of ideas left from King Brian, Acktar's first king.

But the Blade Marshals were going to be something... more. Something that—he hoped and believed—would become part of the lifeblood of the country itself.

And these people in this room were the ones who would make it happen.

LEITH STOOD IN FRONT OF KING KEEVAN WITH SHAD AND Martyn beside him, their families and friends gathered behind them. He tried to keep a straight face, but at that moment, all he could think about was Brandi crossing her arms and telling him a few minutes ago that this ceremony should be held outside where Blizzard could be in attendance because the horse really ought to be there.

Why, when this was such a solemn occasion, was he getting that uncomfortable feeling that he wanted to grin?

Not like the sick churning he'd had when becoming a Blade, his hands still coated with the blood of the fellow trainee he'd killed, his arm bared for Respen to cut that first mark.

That doused any urge to grin. The reminder that he had once been the sort of person he was about to pledge to hunt down and arrest. A murderer many times over.

He didn't deserve to stand here, receiving this responsibility. By all rights he should've joined Respen in losing his head to the ax. Only God's grace had taken him from that life and changed him into the man he was now. And that was a gift he could never stop being thankful for every day of his life.

Keevan halted in front of him, Addie standing to his right holding something small and shining in her hand. Leith would've studied the badge more, but Keevan fixed him with a stern gaze. When he spoke, the rasp nearly overwhelmed his voice, even though his expression didn't betray any of the pain he was in from the strained muscles. "Raise your right hand and repeat after me."

Leith raised his right hand, the arm marked with thirty-seven marks from Respen. His heart thumped so loudly in his ears he could barely hear himself as he repeated the oath. "I, Leith Daniel Grayce Torren, do solemnly swear that I will support and enforce the legally decreed laws of Acktar, and that I will faithfully discharge the duties of my office as Blade Marshal to the best of my skills, abilities, and judgment, so help me God."

Addie handed Keevan one of the shining pieces of metal, and he stepped forward. Leith braced himself, half-expecting Keevan to take the opportunity to draw blood, but Keevan pinned the badge to Leith's shirt without so much as nicking Leith's skin.

With a nod, Keevan shook Leith's hand, and Addie held out the other two badges.

When Keevan and Addie stepped back, Leith took a deep breath and turned so that he faced Shad and Martyn. As the leader of the Blade Marshals, it was Leith's duty to swear in the Blade Marshals under him.

He reached for the layer of command he'd worn as First Blade, yet without some of the cold. A First Blade had to be prepared to kill his fellow Blades if they failed Respen. The captain of the Blade Marshals would discipline those who stepped out of bounds of their oath but would also defend his fellow Blade Marshals with everything in him if necessary. A bond and a brotherhood.

"Raise your right hands and repeat after me."

As first Shad, then Martyn, repeated the oath, Leith pinned each of their badges on their chests, only taking time to really notice the design of the badge once he'd finished pinning on Martyn's.

It was a simple thing. A flat, vaguely shield-shaped piece of metal embossed with the familiar crossed knives symbol of the Blades, yet with an upright sword like the one in King Keevan's standard cutting down between the hilts of the two knives so that the knives and sword formed a single, new symbol. On top of the center point where the knives and sword intersected was the raised badge number. A number three on Martyn's badge, two on Shad's, and a one on Leith's.

Keevan stepped forward, holding a leather pouch that clattered as he handed it to Leith. "I had all of Respen's knives and the knives from the other Blades melted down and turned into those badges. We were able to cast the first fifty badges from them."

Gripping the pouch in one hand, Leith touched the badge on his chest with the other. It was...odd. Uncomfortable, even, wearing metal that had caused so much death and pain and heartache as a badge symbolizing something honorable.

But what else was Keevan supposed to do with the pile of knives left from Respen and the other Blades? Leave them as they were for the next tyrant wannabe to use as a rallying symbol? Melt down and reuse as weapons again?

Perhaps this was the best thing he could've done with them. The metal was only metal, after all, not at fault in itself for the actions of the person who had wielded the knives. Instead, the metal would be a constant reminder of what the wearer was never supposed to become. He was to be a Blade Marshal, upholding the laws of the land, and never to become a Blade who was a weapon wielded as an executioner.

As the congratulations and back slapping and hugs began, Leith threaded his way toward the back of the room. There was only one person he wanted at that moment, and, when he reached her, she wrapped her arms around him and held him. He leaned his chin against her head, knowing that in taking this job, he was sacrificing days and weeks when he would have to be far away from her.

"I'm proud of you." Renna stepped back and kissed his cheek.

"As I am of you." And he meant those words. Yes, he would sacrifice. He would have long days in the saddle and nights on the hard ground and moments of danger when one wrong move could be the difference between returning alive or being carried home dead.

Yet she would sacrifice too. Long days and lonely nights waiting for him to come home, wondering if this was the mission that would cost him his life. Some might dismiss her brand of courage, calling her helpless and weak for sitting at home waiting while he did all the heroics.

But there was something courageous in her act of letting him go. It would hardly be an easy task to keep their home and all of Stetterly running smoothly by herself. To willingly risk losing him each time she let him ride away.

She might never be celebrated for it, but he, at least, would make sure she knew that he saw and understood what she sacrificed.

As he glanced over her head at the rest of the room, he glimpsed Shad with Jolene, Martyn with Kayleigh. They all seemed to understand they could only take on this job because of the support of those closest to them.

That was perhaps the biggest difference between the Blades and the Blade Marshals. As Blades, they'd done what they did because of a cold sense of satisfaction in success and fear of failure, isolated from everything and everyone except their fellow Blades.

But now they took on the responsibility of the Blade Marshals out of love. Love for their friends and family and neighbors and God, a love that drove them to protect, to be the ones standing between others and danger.

By God's grace, he was now the sort of Blade he should have been all along, and with His strength and courage, Leith would become everything a Blade Marshal should be.

THE FIRST MISSION

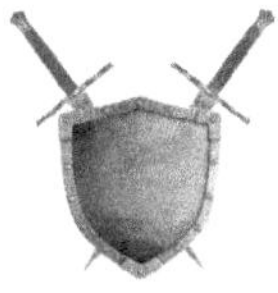

A Novella

1

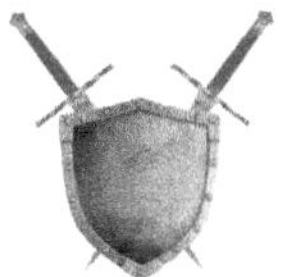

Martyn resisted the urge to cling to the saddlehorn. He shouldn't be this tired after two days of normal riding. But over two months after being burned, he was still struggling to heal and regain his strength. The burns were well on their way to being healed—the skin had mostly grown back in ropy, twisting scars.

But his lungs still occasionally troubled him, and he had the strength of a two-year-old. Then again, based on how King Keevan's eight-month-old could scream with gusto, most toddlers had more strength. No, Martyn was more like a wheezing, doddering eighty-year-old.

He felt the press of his new Blade Marshal badge where he'd tucked it underneath his belt. He probably shouldn't even be an official Blade Marshal yet since he hadn't technically taken the fighting portion of the test.

But Leith said hiring the Blade Marshals was his job, and

he knew Martyn would be capable eventually. If only he could regain strength faster.

"Surgis is just over that hill." Owen pointed to the hill crest less than a mile away silhouetted against the orange, evening sky.

Only his training as a Blade—and what amount of pride he had left—kept Martyn from slumping.

"Good." Kayleigh drew her horse closer to Martyn's. She lowered her voice. "Are you going to make it?"

Martyn gritted his teeth. "It's less than a mile. I'm not about to fall off my horse now."

Especially not when he, Owen, and Kayleigh were surrounded by the guards from Surgis, complete with Lord Conree riding near the front. Martyn wasn't going to pass out in front of so many witnesses.

As they neared the hill, Martyn's stomach knotted tighter and tighter. If only he could blame all the nausea on pain. He was a former Blade. He shouldn't be plagued with nerves.

But he would shortly see the place where his brother had grown up. Where his parents had built a life and died, believing him long dead. Here he would have to face the past and what might have been and somehow figure out a way to handle it.

Kayleigh's eyes—a light brown that paired well with her brown hair highlighted with a hint of auburn—searched his face. "Are you...all right? You don't have to do this now."

Now he did grip the saddlehorn. Part of him wanted to turn Wanderer around and gallop...somewhere. Back to Nalgar, though none of his friends were there at the moment, or perhaps to Stetterly to twiddle his thumbs for a month or more while Leith and Renna enjoyed a wedding trip through the Sheered Rock Hills.

Could he handle facing this now? He'd only known his brother was alive for a little over two months. His faith was still a tenuous thing. Would it survive the next few days?

No, he shouldn't think about faith like that. In terms of survival. Faith was supposed to be—it was—more assured than that. A gift that couldn't—wouldn't—be taken away. He knew it. Mostly.

Perhaps that's why he had to face this part of his past now. Remember who he had been back when he'd had faith and family.

"I'll be fine." Martyn forced himself to sit straighter in the saddle.

"Lying through your teeth already." Kayleigh shook her head, sending the slight curls at the ends of her hair bouncing.

"This will be an interesting few days, I think." Owen huffed out a breath.

Interesting wasn't quite the word Martyn would use. He wasn't sure what word he would use instead—perhaps a few of the swear words he was doing his best not to say these days.

They crested the ridge, and the town of Surgis rose on the next hill, its streets laid out in straight lines stretching from the manor house off to one side and the church with its steeple rising above every building except the manor in the center.

That church was an odd sight these days. Weathered clapboard siding, intricate woodwork around the doors and windows, and even stained glass in a single round window above the double doors. In a word, old.

How many other churches from before Respen's reign were left in Acktar? As far as Martyn knew, this was the only one. Perhaps a few other church buildings had survived by being turned into something else or partially dismantled to look less like a church. But most of the churches in the Resistance towns had been burned, and Surgis was one of the few towns that supported Respen where the lord had protected the Christians living under him.

Still, the sight of the church sent an itchy, squiggly feeling over Martyn's skin. After two months of praying and reading the Bible Leith had given him, shouldn't Martyn be caught in the throes of some return-to-faith excitement?

Yet Martyn was still clawing and fighting for each bit of trust he could manage. So much inside him was still hard. Still bitter. Still...himself. Cynical. Logical. Untrusting.

No, faith was more like tumbling backward off the edge of a cliff, eyes wide open and taking in the full situation, and trusting there would be someone holding the other end of the rope to catch him.

Martyn wasn't good at falling. He was the type to hold onto his life in his own hands and attempt to climb on his own.

Now that Martyn had been pushed over that cliff, he really hoped God had a good grip on that rope.

Lord Conree led the way into the town, his guards surrounding him. People stepped out of their homes or waved from upper story windows, the picture of an idyllic town welcoming their returning soldiers. It was all so perfect that Martyn glanced around trying to detect any hint of some trick. Not that Lord Conree would go to all this trouble to trick the burned former Blade and older brother of one of his guardsmen. Surely Owen didn't rank that high in Lord Conree's esteem.

As they passed one of the prim and proper homes, a girl with blond hair dashed down the front step. "Owen!"

Owen swung down from his horse and halted by the girl. Martyn drew Wanderer off to the side and halted, something in him growing cold.

Owen had a life here. Of course Martyn had known, deep down, that Owen must've had friends and people he cared about in Surgis, but Owen's willingness to drop every-thing and move to Stetterly had fooled Martyn into thinking it couldn't be all that important. But Owen had a *life* here. A home. Friends. Family.

Could Martyn ask Owen to give this all up to move to Stetterly?

Martyn could move to Surgis. He didn't necessarily have to be one of the Blade Marshals stationed in Stetterly, but the thought of letting Leith go off on missions without Martyn there to guard his back didn't sit right either. Leith had no sense of self-preservation, and some green trainee would just get Leith killed.

Kayleigh glanced at Martyn, and Martyn shrugged. He didn't know any more than Kayleigh who the girl was.

"Did you find your brother?" The girl gazed up at Owen's face with such a sappy, heartfelt look Martyn had to choke back his gag reflex. Owen was only seventeen, and that girl couldn't be any older. Probably younger. Weren't they a little young for all that mushy glances stuff?

"Yes." Owen pointed toward Martyn.

Martyn forced on a smile. If he was smiling, hopefully he wouldn't be too Blade-like. He twitched his fingers in a wave. That was friendly enough, right?

"Jaclyn," a woman's voice shouted from inside the house, "is that Owen? Invite him for dinner tomorrow."

"Yes, Mama." The girl, Jaclyn, turned back to Owen with a faint wiggle of her skirts, blinking up at him through her lashes. Not in a seductive way. More shy and proper with a hint of pink on her cheeks. "Well? Can you come?"

Next to Martyn, Kayleigh had her hand pressed over her mouth, her shoulders shaking. She kept the muffled laughter soft enough Martyn didn't think Owen could hear.

Owen glanced over his shoulder, and Martyn did his best to wipe off his grin.

"Oh, your brother can come too." Jaclyn hurried to add. "And..." Her gaze narrowed and the pink flush darkened a hint to red as she focused on Kayleigh.

"That's Martyn's...he's courting her."

Jaclyn's face brightened back to bubbly. "Oh. Then she's invited too, if she wants to come."

"We'll be there." Owen smiled at Jaclyn one more time before he swung back onto his horse and joined Martyn and Kayleigh.

As they set off again, this time at the tail end of the line of guards, Martyn glanced at Owen and kept his voice low. "So...Jaclyn."

Owen sighed and shook his head. "I'll explain later."

All right then. Not that Martyn minded dropping the subject. He wasn't quite ready to confront the thought that, after so recently finding his brother alive, he might have to let him go to stay here in Surgis while Martyn returned to Stetterly.

By the time they reached the cleared, gravel-covered space in front of the wooden manor house, Lord Conree had already dismounted, and Martyn assumed the woman hugging him was his wife. Servants bustled about collecting horses and taking them to the stables while the guards scattered, either to their guard duty or to catch some rest.

Martyn eased from Wanderer's saddle and set his feet on the ground. No shooting pain anymore. His legs wobbled, but he kept a hold of Wanderer's saddle until he could stand steady. Improvement, at least.

Kayleigh touched his arm. "What time do you want me to come by tomorrow morning? I'm sure I can find someone to point me in the right direction to your parent's...Owen's house. Or do you want to meet me somewhere else?"

Martyn closed his eyes and drew in a deep breath. Weight dragged against his eyes, pressed down on his shoulders, ached through his feet. His bones ached to crawl into the nearest bed and pass out for a few hours.

Far too tired for the fight he was bound to have on his hands as soon as he made his request.

"Kayleigh, I would rather have most of the day with just Owen." Martyn didn't look at her. It was probably rude—if not downright ignoble—to drag her to a strange town then dump her on her own among a bunch of strangers on the first day.

"Don't." Kayleigh huffed something between a sigh and a growl. "I know this is hard, and I know you tend to deal with things by shutting everyone out, and I know I can't really talk because I tend to run from my troubles too. But if we're going to make this relationship thing work, we're both going to have to put an effort into opening up and leaning on each other. Don't shut me out."

Her finger poked him in the chest on those last words, as if to remind him to have the decency to look at her when she was angry at him.

Martyn dragged his gaze up. She had one hand planted on her hip next to her sword's hilt. At least she was only jabbing him with a finger. He'd been on the wrong side of her sword once already, and once was more than enough.

"I'm not..." He dragged a hand through his hair. How to explain it? "Every single relationship I have from God on down is a mess at the moment. I just need time tomorrow to try to fix one relationship before I can focus on what we have. Please. Just tomorrow. I promise I'll revisit the house and my parents' graves with you the next day, but I need..."

"Time." Her shoulders relaxed, and she reached for his hands. "All right. I guess I can understand having a lot to sort out."

"I'm sorry to abandon you after you came all the way here with me."

Kayleigh pulled her hands from his, her spine straightening, though a hint of a smile remained. "Do you think I need you at my side every minute of every day? Actually, having a few hours where I'm not stuck with you might be refreshing."

He grinned. "Too much of a good thing?"

"Too much of something, anyway." She kissed his cheek. "I think Lord and Lady Conree are waiting for me. Guess I'll have all tomorrow to enjoy being a guest at a fancy manor house."

"Except for dinner. Apparently we have plans."

"Wouldn't want to miss that. I'll see you then." Kayleigh strode toward the front steps of the manor.

Owen nudged Martyn. "She'll be fine. Lady Conree will look after her."

On the front steps, Kayleigh curtsied, and Lady Conree shook her head and waved, beckoning Kayleigh inside.

"Kayleigh doesn't need looking after." Martyn reached for his saddlebags. A groom waited by Wanderer's head, a bland expression on his face, the reins to Owen's horse in one hand. Martyn forced himself to hand over Wanderer's reins and turn to Owen. "Knowing her, she'll probably attempt to join the guards' morning sword practice."

Owen snorted. "Come on. Let's get home and let the groom take care of the horses."

Martyn fell into step with Owen before he gave in to the urge to turn around to admonish the groom to make sure Wanderer got a good brushing. He'd spent way too much time with Brandi. The girl seemed to think he appreciated it when she gave him an update on Wanderer every single day he'd been laid up in bed recovering from the burns. Which he didn't. He didn't care about his horse all that much.

Owen led the way around the manor house to a narrow side street lined with small homes with barely any space between them. Most didn't have anything for a yard, just patches of dirt and a few weeds. But the clapboard homes were tidy and sturdy, the street clean of refuse. Most of the people walking down this particular street wore the basic leather tunic, brown trousers, and swords that were the guard uniform in Surgis.

Idyllic. Peaceful. Cozy. Everything his mama had always

dreamed of having every time they'd lost everything and had to start over in the rough part of a new town.

He was happy she'd had this for the last few years of her life—of course he was—but sharp stabs lanced through his chest. He hadn't had a chance to share it with them.

Owen stopped in front of one of the houses, nearly identical to the others on the street except that this one's paint was a bit more faded. Owen pulled out a key, unlocked the door, and pushed it open. "Well, this is it."

2

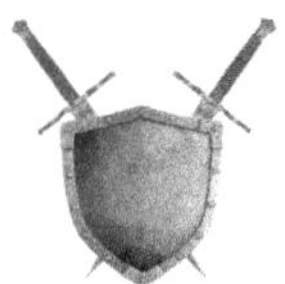

Home. Or, what could've been Martyn's home.

Owen stepped inside, but Martyn couldn't force himself to follow. A lump ached in his throat, his breath lodged in his chest, and a part of him wanted to spin on his heels and dash for Wanderer, leaving all of this behind.

In some ways, Respen's lie that Martyn's parents and brother had died had been less painful than the truth. Papa and Mama had been tricked into thinking Martyn dead. They'd grieved, yes, but they'd still had Owen. They'd moved on, built this house, built a life.

He was coming home, but coming home too late. His parents lay in the graveyard on the outskirts of Surgis, and no matter how much Martyn might want to, he couldn't turn time backwards to join the life that had been built here. This house would never be Martyn's home, not the way he wanted it to be.

Enough dawdling. The past wasn't going to disappear if he stood out there lollygagging.

With a deep breath, Martyn stepped inside and shut the door behind him. He dropped his saddlebags next to the door.

In the light of the lamp Owen had lit and now set on the table—a table with four chairs around it—Martyn took in the house. The floorplan matched nearly every cabin and house in Acktar. Small kitchen along the walls in the main room with a fireplace on one end. Two doors for the two small bedrooms in the back. This particular house was so small it didn't have a loft or a parlor.

A row of knickknacks lined up on the fireplace mantle. Martyn reached out to touch the white, porcelain dog, the one item his mama managed to take with her through all their moves, yet he stopped himself before his fingers so much as grazed the shiny surface. Even after all these years, Mama's admonition never to touch held him back.

He didn't even know why the dog was important to his mama. In some ways, that didn't matter. It was enough that it had been important to her, important enough for her to keep it safe from two little, rambunctious boys and over the miles crossing the rutted prairie in a wagon when they had to move.

A few other items claimed the mantle beside the porcelain dog. The mud-brown pot Martyn had fashioned out of river clay when he was seven contained half a dozen bouquets of dried flowers. A shapeless lump of dried clay sat next to Martyn's pot, a five-year-old Owen's contribution from that same river clay outside of the town of Arroway.

Other craft items made out of sticks, corncobs, bits of string, and fabric filled the rest of the mantle.

Martyn halted at the far end by a painting in a frame, the only thing he didn't recognize since it hadn't graced the fireplace mantle during his childhood. Someone had painted a good likeness of his family, from his mama's soft smile and golden curls to his father's dark brown eyes and gray at the temples. Owen looked younger than he did now, though older than the nine-year-old boy he'd been when Martyn had been abandoned.

And there, in the painting, was a decent likeness of Martyn. He was painted looking the same age as Owen, his features so similar it was as if someone had used Owen as the template and then made a few tweaks from there.

Owen—the real life one—joined Martyn in front of the painting. "Jaclyn painted that. She's an artist, and I asked her to paint it shortly after Papa died."

Martyn swallowed at that nagging lump. There was his family together as it never would be again, if only in a painting. Even after he cleared his throat, his voice still came out annoyingly scratchy. "She did a good job."

Owen nodded, strode across the small room, and pushed open the door to one of the bedrooms. "It's going to be like old times tonight. Just try not to snore too loudly."

Martyn was about to object that he didn't snore but the words caught as he stepped into the bedroom.

Bunk beds.

These weren't a recent addition to the house. No, the wood was weathered, the floor dusty underneath.

Had his parents built this bunk bed when they moved into

this house, hoping for the day when they'd return to Blathe to take Martyn home? Their excitement and preparation to bring their son home turning to mourning as each and every day the empty bed reminded them of the one they'd lost. All those years while killing people for Respen, a bed had been waiting for Martyn here if he ever found his way home.

Owen waved at the bunk bed. Blankets spread over the top bunk, a pillow at one end, while the mattress on the bottom bunk remained empty. "Still prefer the bottom bunk?"

"You slept on the top bunk all these years?" Martyn could barely choke out the words.

Owen crossed his arms, his gaze focused on the beds rather than Martyn. "The bottom bunk has always been yours."

Martyn had been stabbed, burned, beaten, arrowshot, but somehow none of those hurt as deep down as the sight of that empty lower bunk waiting for him. How he ached for the life he could've had here. The one where he shared a room and a few fights with his little brother until his mama grew frazzled with the two of them, yet hugged them anyway. A life filled with love and laughter instead of the blood tainting his hands and heart.

Why? If God was in control and everything happened according to His plan, then why had Martyn been denied this life with his family? Never to feel the strength of his papa's love, his mama's embrace, ever again. He could've grown up with a strong faith like Owen's. Surely it would've been better if he'd had that instead of the years of turning his back on God and the doubting, hardscrabble faith he gripped by the tips of his fingers now.

Instead he'd grown up with a different lower bunk in the far wing of Blathe Manor along with the other boys Respen trained into killers. Except for his brotherhood with Leith, there was very little of that life he didn't regret now.

Martyn sank onto the lower bunk. The upper bunk was so low he had to lean forward to avoid hitting his head.

Owen sat on the floor, one knee drawn up, the other leg stretched as far as he could in the cramped room. "Welcome home."

"But it's not. Not the way it is for you." Martyn buried both hands in his hair. Perhaps someone with a stronger faith wouldn't doubt like this. They'd just accept and move on, not question. "Why did I have to grow up the way I did? Why was this—" Martyn dragged his right sleeve up to show the rows of marks marching down his arm. "Why was all that killing and bloodshed and bitterness and hatred better than me growing up here? Why would God plan things to end up like this?"

The words echoed in the room, and Martyn braced himself for Owen to whip out his Bible and start quoting Scripture and expecting that to solve everything. It should. If Martyn was better at the whole trusting Christian thing perhaps it would. Maybe if God had wanted Martyn to be better at trusting, He shouldn't have let Martyn get so broken in the first place.

And there was the bitterness Martyn had been trying so hard to fight. He rested his head in his hands. Two months of work and he wasn't all that better a person than he had been.

Then again, this could just be his exhaustion talking. All his body wanted to do was collapse onto the bed he sat on, and yet here he was trying to solve all his life's problems.

"I don't know." Owen sighed and shook his head, his gaze focused on the floor. "God's plans tend to be a lot deeper and farther reaching than we can think of. Joseph spent over a decade as a slave and in prison before he was elevated to a position of power and had to wait many more years after that to finally be reunited and reconciled with his family. David spent years and years on the run before he ever became king as promised, and even as king, he had to go back on the run when his own son rebelled against him. Jesus had to suffer torture and death to bring about salvation. The Bible is filled with stories about good coming out of years and years of suffering."

The standard all-things-worked-together-for-good answer. Martyn knew it in his head. But it just wasn't sinking in deeper than that.

Owen shifted and finally glanced up at Martyn. "I can think of a few good things that came out of you being a Blade. You learned skills you couldn't have if you'd been training as a guard at Surgis like I did, skills you'll put to good use in the Blade Marshals. You wouldn't have Leith for a brother. You never would've met Kayleigh, most likely."

Dashed annoying as it was, Owen was right. If Martyn had grown up here, he would've been one of Lord Conree's guards. He still would've fought for Respen like Owen had, since Lord Conree had sided with Respen. As one of the basic infantry soldiers, would Martyn have faced Kayleigh on the battlefield as she fought for the Resistance?

Martyn dropped his hands and sighed. "I get that. The part I don't understand is why God let me turn my back on Him. I'm still struggling to even have the basic amount of trust needed to even count as a Christian. Wouldn't it have been better if I'd been raised with a strong faith like you?"

Owen drew up both legs and leaned his elbows on his knees. "You know it wouldn't have worked like that. Papa and Mama's faith only became deeper after they thought you died because of their actions. My faith grew. It had to. Sure, it might've been easier growing up in this house than what you lived through, but it wasn't easy. I lost my brother. I saw our parents break and learn to pick up the pieces. By fifteen I had to support Mama and me all by myself."

"So how come you turned out the way you did and I'm the way I am?" Martyn shook his head, leaned back, and clunked his head on the bunk. "Am I just..." Broken. "No matter how hard I try, I just can't trust enough."

"The problem is that you keep trying to work hard and build trust, and then go to God. Trying to build trust by yourself is never going to work." Owen leaned back on his hands. "Faith is kneeling in front of God, your hands completely empty. It's knowing you can't bring anything to God. You're too broken. Too weak. It's trusting that the God who brought you to Him will fill you with all the trust and grace and strength you need until He shines through your broken places."

Martyn forced himself to snort. It was better that than getting sappy. "Where did you dig that up? It sounds a little poetic for you."

Owen didn't smirk back as Martyn had hoped. "The minister here in Surgis. It's a paraphrase of what he told our parents when they returned from Blathe after they'd been told you died."

Oh. And there came that pesky lump back into his

throat. Martyn glanced out the open doorway toward where the painting sat on the fireplace mantle. Had he been struggling with faith so much because he was treating faith the same way he'd seen loyalty to Respen? That if he worked hard enough—was loyal enough—then and only then would food and clothes and the basics be provided.

In some ways, serving Respen had been simple. *Do your duty and you'll survive*, as Leith had told him on his first day. Respen would provide food, shelter, and clothing to them as long as they earned those gifts. As long as Martyn obeyed Respen, he never had to fear punishment.

It was harder to figure out how to live when gifts were freely given and obedience was done as a grateful response. Maybe because Martyn wasn't all that great at the whole gratitude thing. Or accepting something he hadn't earned. Usually those types of gifts came with some sort of trap.

But sitting here in this room, confronting what could have been, he was raw, empty, just as Owen said.

All right. I'm empty. Better give me trust because I'm not going to trust on my own.

Did he feel a little better? Maybe? He wasn't sure.

But he was sure that he was wrung out and done with this conversation. "I'm beyond ready for bed, and if I don't lie down soon, I'm going to pass out."

"I'll fetch your bedroll." Owen rolled to his feet and headed for the main room.

Martyn eased his boots and socks off. A few thin scars traced across the top of his feet, not nearly as bad as the scars around his knees thanks to the minor protection his leather boots had provided. The new skin was still tender enough that he didn't wear either of his boot knives strapped to his ankles.

He rolled one of his trouser legs over his knee. The worst of the scars started partway up his shin where the top of his boot had been, ridged across his knee, and halfway up his thigh. A few minor burns traced higher, but those scars weren't as gruesome as the ones on his knees.

"Do they still hurt?" Owen stood in the doorway, Martyn's bedroll in one hand, his saddlebags in the other.

"No." Not much, anyway, and most of the pain was from the fabric of his trousers rubbing against the new skin. Martyn rolled down his trouser leg. He held out his hands and caught his bedroll when Owen tossed it to him.

It only took a few minutes to spread his bedroll on the mattress, tuck most of his knives under his pillow and the rest within easy reach, and settle in for the night. Owen blew out the lamp and scuffed his way to the bunk bed in the dark. The wood creaked as Owen climbed to the top bunk.

Familiar sounds, though it had been the creaking of the bunk he'd shared with Leith that Martyn had spent years hearing. And there had been other creaking bunk beds in that room as well, as Vane, Hess, and the others also settled in for the night. He and Leith used to count the creaking beds, making sure everyone climbed in and no one climbed back out, planning some midnight ambush or prank that would earn Leith or Martyn punishment in the morning.

Martyn rolled onto his back. In the dark, he couldn't even see the bottom of the upper bunk only a few feet above him. "You listed me having Leith as a brother as a good thing. That doesn't...you aren't..."

How could he ask the question without stumbling into feelings and sentimental nonsense?

Owen's snort came from the blackness above Martyn's head. "You're trying to ask if I'm jealous of Leith? Because you now have another little brother? He is younger than you, right?"

"Yes. By about seven months." Martyn laced his hands behind his head. "And, yes, that's what I'm trying to ask."

The silence stretched long enough that, for a moment, Martyn wasn't sure Owen would answer.

"No, I'm not. I'm glad you had him." Owen sighed. "In some ways he's more your brother than I am. He understands the Blade part of you. Besides, he seems to think since I'm your brother, that makes me his brother too."

"Leith was an only child. I think he's making up for it now by continually adopting brothers." Martyn did a quick count in his head. "Counting you, he's up to five. I hope Renna realizes he probably wants a big family."

The bed creaked, probably from Owen shifting. "And what about you and Kayleigh? Does she want a big family?"

Something icy churned in the pit of Martyn's stomach. "How should I know? We've only been courting for two months. It's not like we've talked about kids."

Well, not much anyway. Nothing Martyn was ready to admit to his brother. Marriage. Family. Children. Martyn wasn't ready to start thinking that big and permanent yet, not for the immediate future anyway. He was barely figuring out how to piece something of a life together. Marriage and all the stuff that came with it was a long, long way off.

First he'd have to see if he could even be a decent Blade Marshal. He reached out and found the badge where it nestled in the pile of his gear next to the bed. Could he be a hero? Was this the future he wanted and was called to have?

"Really? Jaclyn and I have talked about dreams about a family someday, and we aren't even courting."

Martyn wasn't about to waste an opportunity like that to change the topic. "You and Jaclyn seem close."

"She's..." Owen trailed off, as if searching for the right word that captured his feelings without actually admitting those feelings out loud. "She was my best friend growing up here."

The dark room filled with all the things Owen wasn't saying. Hopes and dreams and somedays. Martyn couldn't take that away from Owen. "You don't have to return to Stetterly with me, you know. I understand that you have a home and a life here."

The bedposts creaked and popped. "We're young. She's not even seventeen yet. It's not like we'd be getting married tomorrow or anything. I can afford a couple of years at Stetterly making sure you get settled."

"But your job? This house?"

"I'm going to ask Lord Conree to keep me on his list of guards and make me an official guard on loan—or whatever he wants to call it—to Stetterly as a goodwill gesture. Stetterly doesn't have much in the way of trained guardsmen, and you and Leith will be too busy leading and training the Blade Marshals to look after the security of Stetterly. Jaclyn will be happy to help take care of this house while I'm gone, maybe even add some of her own touches to it, and we'll be able to write each other often."

Owen had this all planned out. As if he was the older brother looking out for Martyn and not the other way around. Then again, Martyn hadn't even realized how much Owen truly belonged in Surgis.

Almost Martyn would move to Surgis too. He could volunteer to be one of the Blade Marshals stationed either in Surgis or nearby.

But Owen was right. In some ways the bond of brotherhood Martyn shared with Leith was stronger, forged in blood as it was. They guarded each other's backs, and that didn't change now that they were Blade Marshals instead of Respen's Blades. If anything, that old loyalty between them was even more important now that their goal would be to capture alive instead of kill, putting their lives more at risk than before.

"Thanks for sticking around Stetterly for a few years. But after I'm settled, you'll be free to return here. Don't feel like you have to give up everything on my account."

"All right, it's a deal."

Those words made Martyn think of Kayleigh and a few of the deals he had with her. He closed his eyes and finally let himself relax, even as a smile tugged at his face.

3

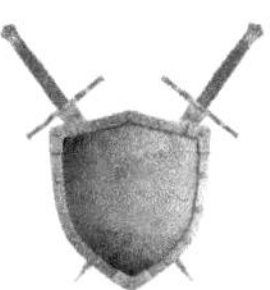

The graveyard sprawled across one of the hills north of the town. After a morning of visiting Owen's favorite places around town, this was the last place they had yet to see. The one Martyn had been dreading all day.

Owen led the way through the gravestones up and over the crest of the hill to the far side. Here the gravestones were smaller, simpler. Some were just wood with the names carved in as if hastily with a knife.

Was that all Martyn's parents had? Or did they have actual headstones?

Owen halted on front of a cluster of three small headstones.

Three? Martyn studied the gravestones. His parents' names and the years of their births and deaths were the only things carved into the stones. But on the stone next to his father's etched the name *Martyn Hamish* with his birth year and the year Respen told them he'd died.

He had a gravestone. That was kind of...creepy. Nice that his parents cared enough to pay for a gravestone for him considering how poor they were, but it was still creepy to see his own grave. Martyn had to clear his throat to keep from sounding choked. "You didn't think to warn me?"

Owen shrugged. "I wasn't sure how to explain."

"Maybe just something like, oh, by the way, you might see your name on one of the stones?" Martyn knelt in front of his parents' graves.

"That would've been the easy part. The hard part is explaining we had a whole funeral and a casket and everything." Owen sank to the ground next to Martyn. "The minister's suggestion. It helped Papa and Mama with their grief."

Martyn hadn't had any such help with his grief. Back then, Respen looked Martyn in the eyes, told him his parents and brother were dead, and ordered him to embrace anger instead of tears. That day he'd lost his entire family, and he never shed a single tear for them. Instead he'd learned to kill and kill again, with a steady ember burning in his chest.

Sitting here, he would give anything to go back in time and feel his papa's clasp on his shoulder, his mama's embrace. If only he could have seen them one last time and told them...what? That he forgave them?

Had he forgiven them? He wasn't sure. After so many years of anger that they'd abandoned him, forgiveness didn't just happen.

Martyn rested his elbows on his knees. "If I could ask them anything, I'd ask why. But I guess we'll never know."

"Actually...I do." Owen's gaze focused on the graves in front of them.

"You do?"

Owen shrugged. "I did a lot of eavesdropping back then. Bad habit, I know."

"I'm not going to judge." Martyn used to eavesdrop for a living, right before he assassinated those he'd been spying on. Not that he wanted to think about that past when sitting in front of his parents' graves. He didn't need any more of a reminder that he was returning as a scarred and broken son with the blood of far too many murders dripping from his hands. Not exactly the godly son they'd believed and hoped him to be.

Not a topic he wanted to dwell on too deeply. Martyn waved at the gravestones in front of them. "I've always wondered why and how they came to the conclusion that abandoning me was the only way to save the family. Were they really so desperate that just one more mouth to feed would make that much difference? I know we hadn't eaten in three days, but surely it would've been worth trying to hold on just a little longer and try to keep both their children."

But Owen was shaking his head even before Martyn finished. "You got it all wrong. They didn't abandon you so that they could survive. They abandoned you so you could survive."

"What?" Martyn twisted to study his brother. Surely that couldn't mean what Martyn thought it meant.

"Papa and Mama didn't think they'd reach the next town, and Respen—then Lord Felix—was kicking them out as vagrants. If not for Lord Conree stumbling across us on his way back to Surgis from a meeting with Respen, then Respen's lies to you would've been true. We would've died in that blizzard, and that's what Papa and Mama knew was most likely going to happen." Owen's deep brown eyes burned with something Martyn couldn't quite name. "They thought about leaving me with you but decided having a little brother to look after would hurt your chances. They chose you to be the son to live, and me to be the son to die with them."

All these years, Martyn had the reasons for his abandonment wrong. He hadn't been left behind to give his family a better chance to survive. Instead, his parents left him to give one of their sons a chance to live.

He glanced back at the headstone with his name on it. "It must have seemed like the cruelest sort of irony when the three of you survived and the son they'd left behind to live died instead."

"That certainly didn't help their guilt any." Owen waved from the gravestone to Martyn. "But they were right, in the end. You did survive, and it was better you did it without a little brother to protect."

If Owen had been abandoned with Martyn and if Respen took both of them...Respen never would've allowed both of them to live. He allowed bonds of brotherhood to form as long as they were formed because of the Blades, like him and Leith and Ranson and Blane. Those bonds kept the Blades loyal to each other.

But a bond between two brothers apart from the Blades? No, he wouldn't have allowed it. Had Martyn and Owen been abandoned together, one of them would've died.

An ache built in his chest, begging for some sort of release. A normal person would probably do something like cry. Perhaps a good release for emotion, but Martyn no longer knew how. Nor did he want to turn into a weak, blubbering mess of a man in front of his brother.

What had he hoped to gain by coming to Surgis? A release of the bitterness? A feeling of finally coming home?

If anything, he'd learned that he couldn't come home. His papa and mama were gone, and he didn't know how to fit into the sort of life Owen had here. Instead of a release, the pressure in his chest, his throat, ached to the point of pain.

There was only one home left he could return to. Maybe he couldn't return to the innocent boy who'd faithfully prayed before bedtime and told his brother Bible stories, but he could trust that eventually God would give him enough trust to be at peace with his past. Maybe not today. Maybe not even tomorrow. But someday.

Footsteps crunched on the dry grass of the graveyard, the rhythm of the stride familiar.

Kayleigh.

She sank to the ground next to him, smelling slightly of sweat and sword polishing oil. "You don't mind if I interrupt your brother time now, do you?"

He held out his hand, inviting her to take it and come closer. He and Owen had paused earlier in the day to watch her join the guards at their sword practice, and she'd appeared happy enough that Martyn didn't feel too guilty about leaving her on her own for the morning. "No. I think your timing is perfect."

She took his hand and leaned against his shoulder. "Did you have a good day?"

He leaned his head on top of hers. "Mostly. Except for

seeing my own grave. That's more than a little disconcerting."

"Yes. I don't want to see your actual grave any time soon."

Considering the way the past year had gone, they might need to keep the gravestone handy. Not that Martyn planned to die but dying was usually an unplanned sort of thing. He shook the thought from his head. "How was sword practice?"

"Apparently I don't push myself hard enough by myself." She gave an exaggerated groan and slumped harder against Martyn. "I'm going to be too sore to move tomorrow."

Owen snorted. "I saw you sparring with our captain. He doesn't believe in going easy."

Not that he should. A real fight was life or death, and practice should take that into account. That was the Blades' way, and probably one of the things Martyn's Blade training had gotten right.

Kayleigh pulled away from him and clambered to her feet. "I know it doesn't take you as long as it does me, but if we're going to look somewhat presentable for Owen's girl's family, we might want to head back toward town."

Martyn held out a hand and let her pull him to his feet. He was going to make a bad enough impression thanks to his past that he wouldn't want to make it worse by arriving late.

It wasn't too late for Martyn to plead some sort of flu or dire illness, was it? Maybe he could come up with a coughing fit and end up too weak to get out of bed.

He tried an experimental cough. Hmm. Somewhat raspy, but not as terrible as it had been.

Kayleigh shot him a look. Not a concerned look, but a I-know-what-you're-thinking-and-you're-not-getting-out-of-this look.

Well, so much for that idea.

MARTYN HAD HIS HAND CLASPED IN KAYLEIGH'S AS THEY strolled past the manor house on their way to the supper at Jaclyn's parents' house.

Not that Martyn was paying too much attention to where they were going. Kayleigh wore the dress made from the green fabric he'd bought at Flayin Falls, the skirt swishing in time with her strides. Every time he saw her in that dress he got this churning in the pit of his stomach that was equal parts an itch to grab his horse and gallop as fast as he could in the other way and a melting mushiness that seemed to damage his brain to the point he struggled to form coherent words.

If romance was this discombobulating, it was downright amazing Leith had managed to spy on and betray the Blades while falling in love with Renna. There were times it was all Martyn could do just to avoid running into walls.

Kayleigh yanked on his arm. He stumbled, and just managed to avoid the hitching rail set along the side of the manor.

She arched an eyebrow at him.

He shrugged. "Sorry. Distracted."

He faced forward again, only to nearly run into Owen, who had halted a step past the manor's corner.

Owen stared at something in front of the manor's main doors. "What is *he* doing here?"

Given the utter loathing in Owen's voice, Martyn dropped Kayleigh's hand, drew his knife, and eased forward to peer around the corner without revealing himself to whatever enemy might be lurking out front.

Four riders had halted their horses on the gravel in front of the manor house. Martyn didn't recognize three of them, but the fourth man with short-cropped blond hair and angular face...him he recognized no problem.

Apparently, Martyn, Owen, and Kayleigh weren't going to make their dinner plans after all.

4

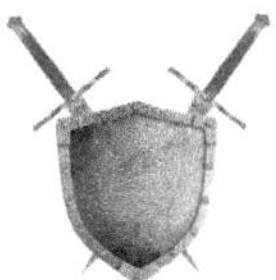

What was Lord Norton—the man who had planned a rebellion, turned Martyn over to the townsfolk in Flayin Falls to be burned, and nearly destroyed Stetterly—doing in Surgis? He would've only been in Kilm a day or two, three at the most, after returning from his trial at Nalgar Castle. Surely he wasn't already trying to recruit Lord Conree into yet another treasonous plan? Not that Lord Conree would go along. He had helped stop Lord Norton's last attempt.

And why did Lord Norton only have three men with him? Yes, King Keevan had put measures into place to reduce the number of guards Lord Norton would be able to raise, but Lord Norton didn't strike Martyn as the type to travel so unguarded, especially if he were planning more treason with King Keevan's promise that he wouldn't be spared a third time still ringing in everyone's ears.

"The filthy, cowardly, murdering..." Kayleigh's mutters trailed off, as if she couldn't think of a suitable insult without delving into the swear words she'd learned from Martyn. "What *is* he doing here?"

"Whatever it is, it has to be trouble. Stay here." Martyn slipped alongside the manor, sticking to the shadows cast by the setting sun behind him. Not that the shadows fully concealed him from the view of those by the manor's main gates, but enough guards and townsfolk were already gathering to mask Martyn's movements.

Gravel clicked behind him. Martyn suppressed a sigh. Of course Owen and Kayleigh hadn't listened and were only steps behind him.

The main doors opened, and Lord Conree strode onto the front step, two guards flanking him. Good. Lord Conree was wary, even if Lord Norton appeared unthreatening with the presence of only three guards.

Lord Conree's gaze swept a glance around the area, much as Martyn would've done in his place. His gaze landed on Martyn—or perhaps on Owen behind him. Still looking in their direction, Lord Conree gave a twitch of his fingers, beckoning them to come closer. Ah, probably a signal for Owen, then, since he was a trusted guard.

In any case, Martyn crept a few feet closer until he, Owen, and Kayleigh were well within hearing distance.

"Lord Norton, what brings you to Surgis so soon after your release? I would've thought you'd remain at Kilm longer to spend time with your wife and children." Lord Conree's tone held such an underlying warning to them that Martyn drew another knife, tensing in case Lord Norton tried something.

Something twisted Lord Norton's face, but the dark circles, his red-rimmed eyes, and the slant to his mouth didn't speak of cunning. No, if Martyn were to guess, the expression was distress. No, more than that. Desperation.

Lord Norton stumbled a few steps forward but halted as Lord Conree's guards tensed. Lord Norton spread his hands, palms up, as if to reassure them he wasn't a threat. "Please, John. I must speak with you. I need your help."

Lord Conree frowned and crossed his arms. "If you're plotting against King Keevan, I told you before. I won't help you again."

"I know. I'm not. I..." Lord Norton gave a shudder as if gripped with some emotion he could barely suppress and drew in a deep breath. "I know I have no right to beg anything of anyone, but please. We were friends once. I have nowhere else to turn. Millie's been kidnapped."

Martyn stiffened. That was a girl's name. Either Lord Norton's wife or, more likely, his daughter, had been kidnapped.

Lord Conree snapped upright, his arms hanging loosely at his sides. "Millie? I..."

As if fearing Lord Conree was about to turn him away, Lord Norton staggered forward, looking about ready to collapse to his knees and beg. "She's only six. Please. They're demanding a ransom, and I no longer have the money. Not after paying that fine to Stetterly."

The daughter, then. Martyn remembered the blond-haired youngster and the doll she'd carted around with her from the time last fall when he'd scouted Kilm Manor. He'd also caught a glimpse of her as he'd watched Lord Norton's trial.

He'd turned away before getting much of a look at the family reunion. King Keevan's sentence had been the right one. Still, that didn't make it easy for Martyn to squash the anger for what had happened.

Lord Conree held up a hand. "Of course I'll provide whatever assistance I can. But, I'm not the person you should ask for help."

When Lord Conree turned and speared Martyn with a look, Martyn froze. What was he...

Oh, right. This was exactly the sort of mission King Keevan had created the Blade Marshals to undertake. And Martyn was a Blade Marshal. Tests passed, sworn in, badged up proper and everything. This kidnapping was his duty.

He released a sigh. So much for learning to forgive slowly. Apparently God wanted him to go about forgiving his parents and Lord Norton all in one day.

Lord Norton spun and searched the gathered guards and townsfolk. His gaze hadn't reached the shadows where Martyn crouched yet, but it was only a matter of time.

Martyn sheathed his knives, pulled his badge from its hidden place beneath his belt, and pinned it to his shirt where no one could miss seeing it. Then, head held high, he stepped between two decorative bushes into the open.

For a moment, Lord Norton's expression froze, as if his brain couldn't comprehend who he was seeing and come up with a response at the same time. Then, his mouth twisted, his eyes hardened, his fists clenched. "If this is some sort of joke or reckoning, I do not have time."

"While you weren't present when the Gathering approved the proposal, I believe you were informed that King Keevan intended to create a well-trained group to enforce the law and deal with problems beyond the skills of your ordinary town sheriff." Lord Conree gestured toward

Martyn. "As one of only three Blade Marshals in the country at the moment, I believe rescuing your daughter would fall under Blade Marshal Hamish's jurisdiction, though I will be happy to provide any assistance he deems necessary."

Lord Norton's shoulders slumped, his eyes dulling. He didn't say it out loud, but the sag in every muscle said he didn't expect Martyn would help.

Martyn swallowed back the churning in his stomach. Memories of wood stacked around his legs, the crackle of the rising flames, the pain of fire eating at his skin...

No, Martyn didn't want to have anything to do with Lord Norton.

But if he turned away now, then he might as well toss away his badge at the same time. Lord Conree was right. This was exactly the sort of mission the Blade Marshals had been designed to take on. This was Martyn's duty, and he had never turned down a mission in his life.

Besides, it was the right thing to do. Somewhere out there was a young six-year-old girl in the hands of kidnappers. It didn't matter who her father was. She needed to be rescued.

If only Leith was here. He was supposed to be the planner of their duo, and Martyn hadn't done so well on his last mission on his own.

Owen and Kayleigh were standing on either side of him now. All right, maybe not quite alone.

Martyn straightened his shoulders. "Lord Conree, if you could have your stablehands ready our horses along with a spare for each of us? I would also appreciate if you and some of your men came along as well."

Lord Conree nodded and started shouting orders for his

men. Something in the pit of Martyn's stomach relaxed. He hadn't liked the thought of taking Owen and Kayleigh with him to Kilm of all places, but they should be safe if Lord Conree came along.

"You're actually going to help me?" Lord Norton was gaping at Martyn.

Did Lord Norton think Martyn was just going to turn his back? The girl was all of six. What else could Martyn do but help?

All right, so jumping into heroics and all that nonsense was more Leith's thing than Martyn's, but Martyn had volunteered for this. He'd studied for hours a day for a whole month to pass that blasted test. Heroics were just going to have to be his thing too from now on.

"I'm not helping you; I'm helping your daughter." Martyn crossed his arms, praying for patience. "You'd best see to it you and your men get ready to ride. I plan to make Kilm by morning."

THEY MADE IT TO KILM AS DAWN BROKE ACROSS THE PRAIRIE, but Martyn was hanging on to his horse by sheer will power. He wasn't about to pass out and fall off his horse on his first official mission as a Blade Marshal, much less in front of Lord Norton.

As they rode down the dirt road between the houses, a shiver ran down Martyn's spine. The last time he'd ridden into Kilm, he had sneaked into the hidden valley, found Owen, gotten captured, and been nearly burned at the stake.

Well, technically it was a lamppost. The town of Flayin Falls had been happy to improvise.

Kilm's manor house lay at the far end of the street, nestled in the foothills of the Sheered Rock Hills. Before they even stopped, a woman with her blond hair streaming loose over her shoulder burst from the main doors and raced for Lord Norton's horse. Lord Norton threw himself from his horse and held his sobbing wife as she sagged against him.

And in that moment, Martyn didn't see the man who'd handed him over to be burned. He saw two hurting parents missing their child. He hadn't been able to return to his own parents, but perhaps he could keep this one little girl from feeling abandoned and this family from being torn apart the way his had.

Martyn eased from Wanderer, holding onto his horse until he steadied his legs underneath him. Riding through the night wasn't going to help him recover his strength.

But he'd have to pull himself together and deal with it. Lord Norton wasn't going to be impressed if the Blade Marshal who was supposedly there to help him was too weak to walk, much less perform any of the heroic stunts needed to rescue his daughter.

"Are you going to need me to prop you upright?" Kayleigh's voice came from beside him.

When had he allowed himself to close his eyes and lean his forehead against Wanderer's saddle? Martyn forced his eyes open and his posture to straighten. "No, but I'd appreciate it if you and Owen stayed nearby to catch me if I pass out."

Kayleigh's mouth twitched as if she was trying not to smile. "I distinctly remember you telling me once you wouldn't catch me if I passed out, so why should I catch you?"

"I did catch you right after that, so you owe me." Martyn rested a hand on his knife, straightened his back, and strode forward. His badge was once again tucked under his belt, hidden in case the kidnapper or any accomplices he might have were watching, but the feel of it lent him strength with the reminder that he had a duty to perform, even if all he wanted to do was collapse on his bedroll or even the nearest chair.

"...Conree will help?" Lady Norton was saying as Martyn approached.

Lord Norton glanced over his shoulder, frowning as his gaze landed on Martyn. At least the frown lacked some of the hostility of earlier. As if Lord Norton only wanted to forcefully escort Martyn off the premises instead of kill him. "Not exactly."

Lady Norton turned to Martyn as well. Her gaze didn't widen, and she didn't stumble back, so she probably didn't recognize him or what he'd been. Instead, her eyebrows scrunched, as if she couldn't figure out what a tottering, pallid man was going to do that Lord Conree and his men couldn't.

Martyn managed a nod, one small enough that it wouldn't send his head reeling. "I'm Blade Marshal Martyn Hamish." That was going to take some getting used to. "I don't know if you've heard about the new Blade Marshals that King Keevan founded at the recent Gathering, but we're a group of highly trained professionals who will handle matters such as this."

He even managed to spout the official rigmarole King

Keevan had used for the Blade Marshals with a straight face. He must be exhausted. Their group of "highly trained professionals" was currently made up of two ex-assassins and a lord's son. Hardly enough to even pretend to cover the whole country.

Lady Norton rushed forward and clasped Martyn's hand with a grip like a bear trap. Martyn barely resisted pulling his hand away. From the look on Lord Norton's face, he was barely resisting yanking his wife away from being so close to an ex-Blade with reasons to want revenge. Lady Norton shook his arm. "Please find our daughter."

Martyn cleared his throat and managed to extricate his hand. "I will, ma'am."

So much for not making promises he couldn't be sure he'd keep. But the woman looked desperate enough to strangle him if he said anything else.

Lord Norton gripped his wife's shoulders and drew her away from Martyn. "Martha, why don't you go inside and check on Nathaniel, all right? I need to brief the Blade Marshal on the situation."

Lady Norton nodded, gripped her skirts, and dashed toward the manor house as if she feared her son had been kidnapped while he'd been out of her sight.

Time to get this back on track. The sooner Martyn got the facts, the sooner he could curl up somewhere and snatch a few minutes of sleep.

Martyn clasped his hands behind his back. "You said your daughter was kidnapped two days ago?"

Lord Norton spun back to Martyn. He glanced to the side as Lord Conree joined them. "Yes. We'd returned late the night before from Nalgar Castle, and my wife and I slept late.

We didn't realize Millie had slipped out of bed early, evaded the maid, and went outside. When we discovered her missing, we assumed she'd wandered off and searched for her, but it wasn't until we found a note partially pinned under a rock in the garden that we knew someone had snatched her."

To time things that precisely... "Someone was watching for you to return from Nalgar. This was planned, not just a random opportunity."

Lord Norton rubbed at his temple, his gaze focused on the horizon instead of Martyn. "That's what I surmised as well. I took what men I have remaining to me and searched the surrounding area, including that hidden valley, with no results."

"Which entrance to the valley did you use?" Martyn was almost impressed by how professional he sounded.

Lord Norton blinked, his eyebrows scrunching. "There's only one entrance to that valley."

His eyes remained on Martyn, too steady to be a lie. Apparently the Blades had been content to keep the secondary way out of that valley to themselves. "Of course. Continue."

Lord Norton's mouth firmed into a hard line. "By the time we returned at nightfall, there was another ransom note waiting. My men and I tried to follow any tracks the kidnapper had left behind but without...well, I don't have anyone skilled at tracking anymore."

Without the Blades, Lord Norton had nearly said. Martyn couldn't let the reminders of two months ago cloud his thinking now. He had to concentrate on this mission.

Whoever had slipped into Kilm twice obviously knew

the town well. Enough to evade Lord Norton and a group of guards who also knew the town well. Perhaps even a man inside Kilm or among Lord Norton's servants was helping?

"Any indications as to how many kidnappers we might be dealing with?"

"The ransom note said *we demand* so there must be at least two, perhaps more, involved."

Multiple kidnappers. That would make things interesting. Without Leith and in his weakened state, Martyn couldn't take on more than one by himself.

Martyn tightened his clasped hands behind his back and tried to ask the next question with a bland expression. "Any enemies you are aware of who have a grudge against you?"

Lord Norton snorted and gestured at him. "Besides you, the entire town of Stetterly, King Keevan, and all the Rovers and ex-soldiers that followed me two months ago and didn't receive what I'd promised them?"

Lord Norton did seem to have a knack for collecting enemies. His tendency to turn traitor to his king, attack innocent towns, and dispose of people in unpleasant manners might have something to do with it.

Martyn met his gaze with a cool one of his own. "I can assure you I have an alibi for two days ago."

Jaw flexing, Lord Norton drew in a deep breath and looked away. "When I realized I wouldn't be able to find her, I left a message under the rock in the garden that I needed to ride to Surgis to borrow the ransom money and left immediately."

With a steadying breath of his own, Martyn glanced in the direction of the manor's garden. It was set off to the back and side of the manor house, tucked almost into the foothills of the mountains themselves. A small creek ran along one side, and stands of saplings and brush grew along the creek and the garden's edges, providing plenty of cover for anyone sneaking into Kilm.

Martyn searched higher into the foothills, spotting the cliff he had used to observe the manor house last fall. He couldn't see anyone up there watching them, but that didn't mean someone wasn't up there. Just meant they were good enough to stay concealed if they were.

"Put a reply under the rock telling them you have the money and ask for instructions on how to make the trade for your daughter. Do whatever it takes to appear as if you are going along with their demands." Martyn tipped his head toward the garden, but not enough that anyone observing would be able to see the movement from the clifftop. "Don't set anyone in the garden to watch or send out your men after them. I don't want the tracks trampled this time. Have someone check once every hour. Once the note is taken, I'll track them back to their hideout and find your daughter."

"Very well." Lord Norton's shoulders slumped, as if he thought leaving his daughter's life in Martyn's hands wasn't going to end well.

Martyn spun on his heel to face Owen and Kayleigh, and he tried not to show how the whole world seemed to spin along with him. "Let's grab our bedrolls and snatch some sleep while we wait."

"Sleep?" From behind Martyn, Lord Norton nearly spat the word. "While my daughter is missing?"

Martyn turned back around, slowly this time, and crossed his arms. "Thanks to your men trampling all the previous tracks, there's nothing I can do now, and if you want me able to do my job when there are fresh tracks, then I need sleep. Send someone to wake us in the stable once the note's been taken."

He marched to the stable without giving Lord Norton a chance to answer. If he stayed standing a moment longer, he really was going to pass out right then and there.

5

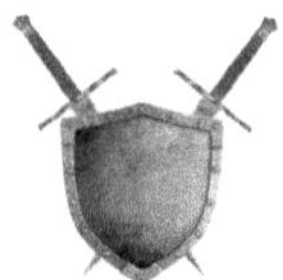

Something was shaking him. Martyn groaned and peeled his eyes open to the sight of hay and the wooden side of a stall.

"Wake up." Kayleigh's voice had a pinched note to it as if she'd been shaking him for several moments. Her hand shook him hard enough to wobble his whole body back and forth. "The note's been taken."

Martyn forced himself upright and ran a hand through his hair. Bits of hay floated down from his head. Sometime while he'd been sleeping, his bedroll had shifted so he'd been sleeping more on the bare straw than the blanket. "How long have I slept?"

"Ten hours." Kayleigh sat back on her heels. Her hair, done in a simple braid down her back, was free of hay while her sword already belted to her waist. She must've been up for some time already.

He rolled to his feet. Owen stood near the stable door, gripping the reins of their three horses.

Martyn strode toward the horses. "The two of you don't have to come along. This is a Blade Marshal mission, and you aren't Blade Marshals."

Kayleigh huffed, as if Martyn had just said something incredibly foolish. A sound it seemed he got from her quite often. "If I understood things right, King Keevan and Leith designed the Blade Marshals to work in pairs. Last I checked, Leith, the person supposed to be watching your back, is still off on his wedding trip with Renna, so you're down one Blade Marshal on this mission. Not to mention you're not at full strength."

Polite way of saying he was probably the weakest fighter of the three of them at the moment.

Owen somehow managed to cross his arms while holding the reins for the horses. "Kayleigh and I aren't Blade Marshals, but we can hold our own in a fight. Between the two of us, we'll make a decent substitute for one Blade Marshal."

He hadn't expected them to stay behind, nor did he really want them to. Well, maybe it would be nice if Kayleigh stayed, but he wasn't about to say that out loud. She wouldn't take kindly to any of his overprotective suggestions. "All right. I'll go to the garden and pick up the trail. I'd like the two of you to circle around and meet me in the foothills. Try to stay out of sight as much as possible. If one of the kidnappers is still watching, I don't want them to know we're tracking them."

Without waiting for their nods, Martyn slipped from the stable door. The sun lowering in the west stretched the shadows along the buildings and down the street, providing some cover from a distant watcher.

He crept along the buildings, eased past the manor house, and worked his way through the tall bushes surrounding the garden to the spot near the center where the note had been left.

A rock lay in the center of the gravel path. Martyn knelt, noting the divots carved in the gravel and sand. Plenty of foot traffic in this area lately made it hard to distinguish the new tracks from the old.

Martyn followed beside a set of hollows where the sand and bigger rocks hadn't started rolling down to the bottom yet. Smaller tracks than he'd been expecting. A woman's or maybe a boy's.

The tracks darted off the path and forged through the brush next to the creek, the undergrowth trampled and shoved aside from the person's passing.

Martyn peered into the stream. Divots marred the sandy bottom of the shallow creek, the rippling water not yet washed the trail away. These tracks were fresh, maybe ten minutes at most since any longer than that and the prints wouldn't be as distinct in the creek's bottom.

He hadn't expected to be quite this close on the heels of the kidnappers. He might have to wait with Owen and Kayleigh a few minutes to make sure the kidnapper or his accomplice had enough of a lead that they wouldn't notice they were being tracked.

The trail followed the creek into the foothills, winding its way into taller stands of willows, birches, and small oaks.

Splashing came from the creek ahead. Martyn eased out of the creek into the underbrush.

Moments later, a boy of about twelve or thirteen dashed

down the creek, hurrying as if worried someone would miss him if he didn't get back soon.

As the boy passed Martyn's hiding spot, Martyn sprang forward, clapped a hand over the boy's mouth, and dragged him to the bank. Less than a second later, he had the boy pinned to the ground. The boy squirmed and tried to buck, but Martyn had too much practice pinning far stronger and bigger opponents than this boy.

"I'm not going to hurt you." Martyn kept his hand firm on the boy's mouth, hard enough to stifle noise, but not so hard he'd hurt him. "Now I'm going to release my hand. If you yell, I might not stay so nice."

When he slowly removed his hand, the boy remained silent, wide eyes staring up at Martyn.

Great. He was scaring the kid. Though, if this boy was involved in helping with the kidnapping of a six-year-old girl, he could use some scaring before he took too many more wrong turns in his life. Otherwise next time Martyn pinned him to the ground, it could be to arrest him.

Martyn kept his hand near the kid's mouth in case he had to stifle a shout. "Have you been carrying messages for the men who kidnapped Lord Norton's daughter?"

The boy nodded.

"Why?" Martyn eased his hand farther from the boy's head. Maybe the boy would get more talkative if he felt less threatened.

"They...they said they'd hurt my mama."

Martyn searched the boy's eyes. Nothing he saw in them indicated that the kid lied. When the boy's eyes remained wide, his cheeks pale, Martyn eased off the boy. "I believe you. I'm going to capture all of them so they won't be able to hurt your mother. Do any of them work at Kilm?"

"No." The boy sat up and wrapped his arms around his stomach.

"Have you ever seen them around Kilm before?"

"Yes."

Not the most helpful of answers. At this boy's age, Martyn would've known to give a full report with specific observations. But this boy hadn't been trained—forced—by Respen to notice everything.

Martyn bit back his sigh. "When?"

The boy squeezed his eyes shut. "A few months ago? Maybe two months? A few times before that?"

Right around the time Lord Norton was planning his takeover of Stetterly. That meant the kidnappers were probably one of the Rovers or ex-soldiers who had worked with Lord Norton and weren't happy that he failed.

The boy was still staring at him as if waiting for permission to breathe, much less move. Martyn pointed downstream. "Return to Kilm and tell Lord Norton and Lord Conree what you told me. They'll protect you and your mama. Let them know I'm going to find the lord's daughter and that they are to wait at the manor for me to return. Got that?"

The boy nodded, then leapt to his feet and took off down the creek as if he didn't want Martyn to change his mind.

Martyn continued upstream until the boy's trail left the stream. He tracked the footprints to behind a boulder. There, the marks from a larger set of feet had disturbed the pine needles. A few yards into the trees, he found where the man's horse had waited..

The clack of a hoof on stone came from the foothills in the direction Martyn expected Owen and Kayleigh. Still, he peeked cautiously around the boulder.

Three horses moved between the trees, two figures leading them. As they drew closer, Martyn picked out Owen and Kayleigh.

He straightened and stepped around the boulder, motioning for them to remain quiet. He didn't speak until he took Wanderer's reins from Kayleigh. "One of the kidnappers is only a few minutes ahead of us, so keep your voices low. The kidnappers were threatening a boy from Kilm to deliver their messages for them. Based on what the boy told me, I believe the kidnappers are a few of the leaders from Lord Norton's army who are disgruntled they didn't get the riches and the better life they were promised. We'll track this kidnapper for a while, but I'm guessing he's headed for the hidden valley."

"But Lord Norton said he and his men searched the valley." Owen stared into the trees as if expecting the kidnappers to leap out at them.

"It would be easy to evade a large patrol of searchers in that valley, especially when they use the main entrance. The kidnappers would've had plenty of time to slip away and hide until Lord Norton and his men left." Martyn shrugged. "We were only caught because the Blades had found the second entrance, the one Lord Norton doesn't know about."

Owen's eyebrows were still scrunched, as if he was still trying to picture it. It was his guard's training showing, the one that dealt with training and patrols and not the shadows and sneaking.

But Kayleigh was nodding. "Do you think these kidnappers know about this second entrance?"

"My guess is no. If the Blades didn't share that information with Lord Norton, I don't think they would have given it to anyone else. They were looking out for their own interests, making sure they would be needed."

Owen shook his head again. "You found that pass with all of one glance around the valley. Surely they've figured it out by now if they are using it for a hideout."

"I found it that quickly because I've been trained to track and scout the land. Based on how little they are able to hide their tracks, I don't think they have much in the way of tracking skills themselves." Martyn gestured in the direction the trail had led off. "Even if they have found it, they've figured out by now that Lord Norton and his men don't know about it. We'll follow the trail for a while, but if it seems like it is heading into the valley, we're going to circle around and enter by the back way in. I don't want the kidnappers moving the girl before we can find her."

Or worse, killing her, but Martyn didn't say that option out loud.

Kayleigh cocked her head, staring at him with a twist to her mouth that was almost a smile. An odd expression considering they were talking about the kidnapping of a little girl.

Martyn eyed her. "Anything to add?"

"No, not really. Just glad to see you more yourself than you've been in two months. You really do love this sort of thing. Tracking, danger, testing your skills against someone else." She shook her head and kissed his cheek. "Now let's stop talking and get moving. Lead the way."

As if he would be able to think after she so thoroughly turned his brain to mush.

Romance. It was going to kill him more surely than an enemy's knife ever would.

BY THE TIME THEY SNEAKED UP AND OVER THE HIDDEN PASS and reached a meadow near the stream cutting through the center of the valley, full darkness had fallen. Crickets chirped in the grass while a whole choir of frogs chirruped from the stream banks and surrounding trees.

It would be nearly impossible to slip any closer to the cluster of cabins with the horses. This side of the stream retained a few trees and underbrush, but the far side was open, especially around the cabins in what had once been the winter camp for Lord Norton's gathering army.

But if they had to make a fast getaway, the horses would be too far away if they left them here.

Then again, if a fast getaway was needed, Martyn would have already failed.

"We'll leave the horses here and sneak the rest of the way on foot." Martyn dropped Wanderer's reins onto the ground. Like many horses in Acktar, he was trained to be ground hitched, treating the trailing reins on the ground as if he was tied to something. With a swish of his tail, Wanderer set to work cropping the grass.

Kayleigh's and Owen's horses followed Wanderer's example moments later. Perhaps all three horses had a sense that they'd better eat while they could. Or maybe the horses simply saw food and were too greedy not to eat it.

Martyn shook himself. He *really* had been spending too much time with Brandi if he was standing here wondering about the motivations behind his horse's eating habits.

Martyn crept into the darkness, Owen and Kayleigh following. Sneaking like this from tree to tree, wading across the stream, its water level low this late in the summer, and hunting potential foes in the darkness thrummed strength into his muscles. Why the darkness should feel so much like home, he didn't know. Perhaps there was something seriously broken and wrong with him.

But this time, he was the rescuer, not an assassin. Of all the people skulking around this valley tonight, he was not the villain to be feared.

How odd to be on this side of that dividing line. Here he was, blood on his hands and all, and somewhere back in Kilm a mother was trusting him to bring her little girl safely home.

Ahead, a glow came from the direction of the abandoned cabins. Martyn reached the outskirts of what had once been an encampment. Once before he'd slipped between these buildings, but back then, they had been filled with people, this place humming with the feel of life even at night.

Now the emptiness tugged at him, prickling along his skin. Most of the cabins and lean-tos were empty, black husks. As he passed a few, animals skittered inside. In one of them, a mouse gnawed at a board. Behind Martyn, Owen's and Kayleigh's footsteps were the barest hint of crackling grass and shushing sand.

Ahead, the light came from what had been the command cabin two months ago. No surprise there.

Martyn scouted around the cabin and the nearby cabins

for a guard but didn't find anyone. Apparently, they were comfortable just having a guard at the entrance. The way the cabin was situated, they probably would have time to douse the lights and move the girl if the guard at the stream entrance signaled someone was coming.

When he was certain it was safe, Martyn crept to the same back window he'd used for eavesdropping last time. He pressed his back to the wall. Owen and Kayleigh eased into the shadows on either side of him.

Martyn tilted his head to peer over the sill while exposing as little of himself as possible to view.

This window looked into a small bedroom in the back of the cabin. The door between the bedroom and the main room stood open, giving Martyn a view of the single lamp burning on the table. Two men sat next to the table, leaning forward as if to discuss their plan. One Martyn didn't recognize, but the other...he fought the urge to draw his dagger. The other was the former general Wentle who had led both Respen's army and Lord Norton's army.

His presence wasn't unexpected. He had escaped at Stetterly, slipping away while Lord Norton surrendered his men, and hadn't been seen since. Until now.

Martyn scanned the bedroom, the lamp casting only a few beams of light past the doorway. In the shadows at the far side of the room, a cot had been set up with a blanket. Someone huddled under the blankets. Asleep or cowering in terror, he couldn't be sure, but it was the right size to be a small child.

It wasn't right, using a child like this. Martyn gripped his knife's hilt and fought to push the heat back into his chest before it addled his thinking. He hadn't realized he had such strong opinions on the subject, but apparently, he did. Children should not be used to fight their parents' battles.

And somehow he was going to have to make sure he got the little girl out of there without her being used in battle any further. This would turn into a disaster if one of the kidnappers got to her first and held a knife to her throat.

6

Martyn eased below the window and whispered. "They have the girl in the bedroom. There's two of them that I can see in the cabin. General Wentle and another man sitting at the table. Probably discussing how they want to collect the ransom without getting caught. With the man guarding the river entrance, that makes three kidnappers."

"Do we take out the man guarding the stream, then the cabin? If he hears noise, it would be uncomfortable to have him show up at our backs." Owen's hand clenched his sword's hilt.

"No." Martyn had already tossed that idea out. "I would rather take the cabin first and make sure we have the girl in our care. We can't risk the guard at the stream shouting a warning before we subdue him. General Wentle wouldn't hesitate to hold a knife to the girl's neck to force us to let him go."

"I agree. That poor girl has been through enough."

Even at a whisper, Kayleigh sounded like she wanted to put a sword through General Wentle. Martyn couldn't blame her.

"I'm glad you think so. I'd like you to slip through the back window and get the girl out of the cabin while Owen and I burst in through the front door." Martyn held up a hand before Kayleigh could object that she could handle fighting just as much as him and Owen. "She's been carted off by strange men enough these past few days. I don't want to scare her more by having Owen or me try to haul her out the window."

"Good point." Kayleigh nodded, and she adjusted her sword so it hung more down her back instead of at her side.

With a quick peek inside to make sure no one had moved and they weren't looking at the window, he wiggled his knife between the panes and lifted the latch. He didn't pull them open. The men would surely notice a cold draft.

He motioned to the window, and Kayleigh took his place under it, poised to yank it open.

Martyn put his mouth close to her ear. "As soon as Owen and I burst through the front door, go for the girl."

Kayleigh nodded, her mouth pressed into a thin line.

Martyn waved to Owen to follow, then crept around the side of the cabin. At the base of the small front porch, Martyn paused. The porch boards could creak, depending on how solidly this cabin had been built. Then again, how much did stealth matter? They planned on busting through the door and confronting General Wentle and his man head on.

Speed mattered more than anything. They had to get inside and keep the men focused on them before either of them thought to dash into the bedroom to use the girl as a shield.

Still, their plans would be all kinds of in trouble if Martyn got to that door, realized it was locked, and struggled to break it down in time.

"Stay here." He motioned to Owen. When Owen gave him a nod, Martyn eased onto the porch, staying in a crouch and near the wall to remain out of sight. He took each step an inch at a time, letting his weight down gently to keep the boards from making noise.

When he arrived at the door, he grasped the handle and lifted it ever so slowly. The door gave a fraction.

Not locked. Good.

Holding the door steady with one hand, Martyn stood and pulled a knife with his free hand. With a nod to Owen, Martyn shoved the door open and stepped inside.

General Wentle scowled. "You shouldn't leave your..." His gaze flicked to the door, and he froze.

As Owen stepped into the room next to him, Martyn gave General Wentle a grin. "I'm Blade Marshal Martyn Hamish, and you are under arrest for the kidnapping of Lord Norton's daughter."

General Wentle shot to his feet, hand dropping to his sword. The other man staggered to his feet as well, but his eyebrows were scrunched. "Blade Marshal?"

Martyn bit back a groan. His first official arrest, and he'd forgotten to pin the badge where it would be visible.

Behind the two men, the bedroom window eased open and Kayleigh's dark shape crawled through. With the door open, they wouldn't notice the addition of yet another cold draft, but he might as well keep them talking and focused in his direction. Martyn fished out his badge and held it out for them to see. "Blade Marshal. By the king's decree, we have authority to hunt down and arrest criminals, such as yourselves."

General Wentle had his sword out, but the way his shoulders tilted away from Martyn, indicated he was thinking about turning around to dash into the bedroom.

Martyn tucked the badge back into his belt since there was no way he could pin it to his shirt one-handed. Instead, he drew another knife. "Now, are you going to come quietly, or will I have to add resisting arrest to your record?"

All that time of studying the official laws and terms was coming in handy. It really did sound more official when Martyn spouted all the correct terminology.

A screech like nothing Martyn had ever heard for sheer ear-splitting power shattered the stillness.

General Wentle spun and took a step toward the bedroom. Martyn lunged forward, one knife raised high, the other sweeping in low. General Wentle had no choice but to turn, barely managing to block Martyn's lower knife with his sword and the raised knife with a forearm.

If anything, the screeching in the next room rose in pitch. Was that the girl? Who knew a child could make such an awful noise. It put a rabid mountain lion to shame.

Behind him, Martyn could barely pick out the scuffing and clashing of Owen fighting the second kidnapper.

Martyn pushed in close, keeping General Wentle from using the full reach of his sword. The general still managed to shove aside Martyn's knife, keeping Martyn from stabbing him in the shoulder, the stomach, his arm. This would be so much easier if he could just kill the man and be done with it, but it probably wouldn't look good if all the criminals died on the very first mission done by a Blade Marshal. Wouldn't that make Lord Norton all smug, as if that would prove Martyn and Leith were nothing but assassins with fancy badges?

The screaming continued from the bedroom. Was the girl even stopping long enough to take a breath? Martyn dodged a swing of General Wentle's sword. "Kayleigh! What's going on over there?"

"Um..." Kayleigh's voice sounded strained. "I think this poor girl is scared of everyone at the moment."

And probably making it difficult to tote her out a window. Martyn shoved aside General Wentle's sword arm and drew in a breath to shout back.

Something tickled in the back of his throat and down in his lungs.

Dust. Clouds of it floated up from their scuffing feet, choking the air even with the door and window standing open. Two months worth of Acktarian summer dust.

Martyn choked and coughed. His lungs—still weak from the lingering effects of smoke inhalation—constricted. He stumbled back against the wall, coughing too hard to even draw in a proper breath.

Through the haze and black spots wavering across his vision, General Wentle's sword flashed in the lamplight, aimed at his head. Martyn tried to raise his knife to block the blow, but he was sinking to his knees, unable to even suck in a breath much less move.

Another sword flashed in front of his eyes, shoving General Wentle's sword aside. A red-brown braid nearly smacked against Martyn's nose as Kayleigh shoved past him, forcing General Wentle back.

She parried another strike. "I got him. You get the girl."

All right. New plan. Hopefully Kayleigh could handle General Wentle. He was better than the untrained bandits she was used to fighting.

But there was nothing Martyn could do, his eyes tearing from the force of his coughs. He had to trust she and Owen could handle General Wentle and his men between the two of them.

Martyn managed to gasp in enough air through his coughing to banish some of the black spots and crawled into the bedroom.

Inside, the screaming pierced loud enough it was amazing the window panes remained intact, but at least the dust stayed on the floor and furniture rather than in the air. After a few more coughs, Martyn managed to drag in a deep breath.

Infuriating weakness. Martyn bit back the swear words that came to mind. He'd known recovering his strength would be slow, but did it have to be this slow? He couldn't even make it through one decent fight without falling to his knees coughing.

The girl was pressed with her back to the wall at the far corner of the bed, gripping the blanket around and in front of her as if it could protect her. At least she'd been too scared to hop off the bed to crawl under it. That would've made things even more difficult.

Though, what Kayleigh expected Martyn to accomplish that she couldn't, he didn't know. It wasn't like he had a whole lot of experience with children.

Not trusting his feet to be steady yet, Martyn crawled over to the bed. As he approached, the girl let out yet another shriek in an octave he hadn't realized a human voice could reach and buried her face in the blanket.

He sat on the floor next to the bed and sheathed his knives. Those probably weren't helping things any.

What would Leith do in this situation? Martyn ran his fingers through his hair and scratched at the back of his neck. Leith seemed to be better at the whole gentle and reassuring thing.

If only the girl would stop screaming for half a minute so Martyn could think. The clashing and thumping of battle from the other room weren't helping him or her.

"Kayleigh! What am I supposed to do?"

"Figure it out!" Kayleigh blocked another strike from General Wentle. Beyond her, Martyn caught a glimpse of Owen charging in for another strike. Kayleigh didn't even glance over her shoulder as she shouted back. "I'm a little busy at the moment."

Ah, yes. Busy saving their lives. Got it. Martyn was on his own.

All this shouting probably wasn't helping to calm the girl. Calm. Quiet. That's probably what she needed. Praying for a dose of whatever gentleness God could spare him, Martyn faced her and said in as quiet a voice as he could manage while still being heard, "Your papa and mama sent me. I'm here to rescue you. I'll keep you safe and take you home."

The screaming was still there, though had it lessened in volume? His ringing ears couldn't be sure. What could he say to prove he was from her parents? What would her parents know that her kidnappers wouldn't?

The girl clutched the blanket to her as she screamed, much as she'd gripped her doll in her sleep when Martyn had scouted Kilm.

Her doll. Martyn forced himself to smile. A small smile, not one that would be so big it would be scary. "You have a doll, don't you? She looks like you. Blond hair, pretty blue eyes. I'm going to get you home to her and to your papa and mama and brother."

Wonders of wonders, her mouth closed, and the screaming halted, even if she still sniffed. Somehow he'd accomplished what Kayleigh had failed to do. He might have to rub that in later. Much later, when she wasn't fighting off General Wentle, and he wasn't one wrong word from setting the girl screaming again. So many tears had poured down the girl's face that her red cheeks shone as much as the badge tucked beneath Martyn's belt.

His badge. That was shiny and distracting. Kids liked shiny things, right? If he could just keep her from screaming again. He tugged out his badge and held it out to her. "See. I'm a Blade Marshal. We rescue people."

Her gaze focused on the badge, shining silver in the lamplight. A thump sounded in the other room. Hopefully one of the kidnappers and not Kayleigh or Owen. He didn't dare break eye contact with the girl to look.

"I'll keep you safe and get you home." Martyn still held out his badge to her. "Would you like to hold it?"

The girl stared at him with huge eyes. As slowly as a deer entering a clearing, the girl eased forward and picked up his badge. Retreating back to her corner, she turned over the badge in her hands, tracing her fingers over the three knives underneath the raised number three.

She wasn't screaming, but now her wide-eyed silence seemed so unnatural it was creepy.

"My name's Martyn. What's your doll's name?" Hopefully asking about the doll would be less scary to her than asking for her own name first thing.

"Sasha." The girl mumbled, her gaze still focused on the badge.

At least she was talking. That was a good thing. "And what's your name?"

"Millie."

"That's a pretty name." Martyn held out his hand again. All sounds of fighting had ceased from the other room. "Can you give me my badge back, then I'll get you out of here, all right?"

Millie crawled across the bed, put the badge in Martyn's hand, and wrapped her arms around his neck.

Um...Martyn froze. That wasn't exactly what he'd been expecting. Maybe hold her hand until she let Kayleigh pick her up, but this?

He fumbled to tuck the badge into his belt with one hand while trying to figure out how to hold Millie with the other. It wasn't like he'd ever held a kid before. Where was he supposed to put his arm? When he gripped her around her back, she felt like she'd just slide out of his grip.

Finally, he tucked his arm under her and stood. Millie had her face buried against the collar of his shirt. "Kayleigh? Everything all right out there? Nothing a little girl shouldn't see?"

"Everything's fine now. Come on out." Kayleigh's voice

sounded almost smug, not like it would if General Wentle had a sword to her neck.

Martyn strode into the next room. Kayleigh stood a yard away from General Wentle, and all three kidnappers lay bound on the floor. Apparently the man guarding the stream heard the noise and came to investigate, only to be captured as well. General Wentle had a scrap of bloody fabric wrapped around his right arm, but that was the only sign of blood. Even Kayleigh's sword was clean as she held it ready.

Owen stood next to the door, peeking through the crack. "No sign of anyone else. What do you want to do with them?"

As much as Martyn wanted to triumphantly march them into Kilm, it would be difficult to control all three of them while they also had Millie with them. "Millie is the important one. I happen to remember there is a really sturdy cabin that can be used as a jail somewhere around here. Let's lock them in there tonight and send Lord Norton's men to retrieve them."

Millie lifted her head, squealed, and buried her face back in Martyn's collar, her legs and arms tightening around Martyn.

Martyn strode across the room to Kayleigh. "Here. Can you take her so I can help Owen?"

Kayleigh sheathed her sword and reached for Millie. "Come here, sweetheart."

Millie's arms squeezed Martyn's neck so tightly he could barely breathe. She squealed something that might have been *no* and clamped her legs firmly around him.

"Um, I guess she stays with me."

Kayleigh smirked. "Apparently I'll help Owen. I captured them, after all."

Martyn made a mental note to make sure to fill out the paperwork properly so that it was listed as a citizen's arrest in aid of a Blade Marshal. It would be a bother if General Wentle escaped justice again thanks to an improper arrest. And after Martyn did all that studying to make sure he knew the proper laws and procedures and everything.

This time, he really wanted to see General Wentle face the full justice allowed by law.

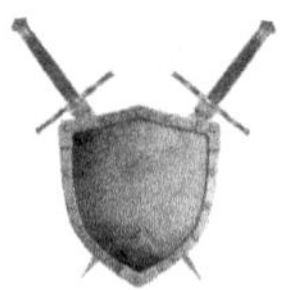

Martyn cradled Millie as he guided Wanderer alongside the stream toward Kilm. Due to the darkness, they traveled slowly, not willing to injure the horses.

Millie's head rested against his shoulder, her breaths long and even. Thankfully she'd finally fallen asleep. At first Millie hadn't wanted to go outside in the dark, even with Martyn carrying her, and it wasn't until Owen fetched the horses that Millie perked up. She'd spent most of the ride chattering in Martyn's ear. And he'd thought Brandi horse-crazy.

The lights of Kilm flickered between the trees. Did Lord and Lady Norton have every lamp in the entire town lit? Did they worry Martyn wouldn't be able to find something as big as a town in the dark?

In his arms, Millie murmured in her sleep, shifting so that her breath tickled Martyn's neck.

There was something...nice about holding a little girl,

her arms around his neck. He'd never thought much about having children...but maybe someday...he glanced over his shoulder at Kayleigh. Maybe eventually.

They neared the town, and Martyn motioned for Owen to lead the way around the manor. By the time they reached the front door, guards had gathered. Lord Norton burst from the front doors, Lady Norton a step behind him.

Martyn shook Millie. "Look who's here."

Millie raised her head and blinked, but it wasn't until Lord Norton skidded to a halt next to Wanderer and reached up, that Millie nearly threw herself from Martyn's arms. "Papa!"

"My Millie girl." Lord Norton sank to the ground, holding his daughter tight. Lady Norton crashed to her knees, and Lord Norton wrapped her into the embrace.

Great. Tears. Martyn glanced away. He had to tell Lord Norton about the kidnappers bound and locked in the cabin in the valley, but that could wait.

Lord Norton lifted his head, his cheeks wet in the lamp-light. When he met Martyn's eyes, his gaze lacked the animosity they had before. "Thank you."

Martyn tipped his head. Something settled into his chest. As if, for the first time in a year—or perhaps for the first time since his parents abandoned him—he was where he belonged. This was right.

He'd become a Blade Marshal because Leith wanted to, and Martyn couldn't let Leith take on that sort of dangerous job without someone to watch his back.

But, perhaps, this was exactly where he needed to be. Wanted to be.

It had been a long journey, and he wasn't sure he would

ever understand why God had planned things to turn out the way they had, but in the end, he would become the godly man his parents believed he would be.

Because faith wasn't founded on feelings. That was the piece he'd been missing. He'd acted like faith depended on his trust. His lack of doubt. His emotions.

But faith was more certain than fickle emotions. Faith was first of all a bond between him and God forged in Jesus' blood and worked by the Holy Spirit. Once established by God, that bond existed when Martyn doubted. When he didn't trust enough. Even when he wandered away, only to be brought back.

That's how Martyn had hope in salvation and love and Heaven even when he doubted. He had forgiveness and could forgive even when he struggled with bitterness.

And, annoyingly reckless and foolish as it was, he might even turn out a tad heroic.

Kayleigh's horse edged next to his, so close Martyn's calf was sandwiched against her horse's round stomach. Kayleigh eyed him. "Are you all right?"

"You know, I think I might be." He glanced at the Nortons, who were still hugging, and nothing but a sense of rightness tugged inside his chest. No more bitterness, at least at the moment. "I think I'm going to like being a Blade Marshal."

"Good." Kayleigh let out a huff so loud even Wanderer turned his head to look at her. "I was afraid you were going to take it into your head to run again, and Owen and I would have to track you down, and I didn't dare accept Renna's job offer until I knew for sure we'd be staying in Stetterly."

Job offer? This was the first Martyn had heard about this.

"What job? For Renna? What does she want you to do? Why didn't you tell me? Not that you need my permission or anything but I kind of thought jobs were the sort of things we were supposed to tell each other about."

He'd thought he'd been getting a hang of this relationship. He'd cleared the whole Blade Marshal thing with Kayleigh first, hadn't he? Talked it over and all that. It had been downright mature of him, actually. So what had he done that she wouldn't feel comfortable sharing the same with him?

Kayleigh fiddled with the ends of the reins. "You've been so...unsettled. You've had a lot to deal with, and I didn't want to add anything that would make you more unsettled before you got things straightened out in your own mind."

That didn't sound exactly flattering. Martyn edged Wanderer farther away from the Nortons. He was nigh on to forgiving the man, but that didn't mean he wanted him listening in on Martyn's rather personal business. At least Owen was getting the right idea and moving away to give them some semblance of privacy. "You can tell me anything, got it?"

"I know." Kayleigh lifted her head, straightened her shoulders, and met his gaze like she expected him to argue. "Renna offered me the position as captain of Stetterly's guards."

"What?" The word burst out before Martyn could stop it. He'd expected Renna to offer Kayleigh a job in the guards, but as captain? *Leading* Stetterly's guards? It wasn't such a big deal in the normal way of things. But if Acktar ever went to war? Stetterly's captain would be expected to lead the town's soldiers into battle.

"I know it's a bit unusual. But Owen and I have the most professional training of anyone in Stetterly besides you and Leith, and Owen has agreed to help me as sort of a second in command since he has actually served as a guard in Surgis."

"Wait, you told my brother? Before me?" Now that was hurtful. Owen wasn't the one courting Kayleigh. Martyn was. Shouldn't Martyn have known first?

"Well, Renna put the offer to both of us, and we all talked it over to come up with the best plan. I think you were studying for the Blade Marshal test with Leith." Kayleigh shrugged. "Normally, a town would have several guards with a large manor to guard. But Renna only has the little cabin, and it would be inappropriate to have a male guard stationed inside the cabin at night when Leith is gone."

Martyn hadn't thought of it, but yes, that could make things uncomfortable. They could station a guard outside on the porches, but it still was a bit close. Not like in the big manor houses such as Walden where the family didn't even have to see the guards.

But Renna was still the lady of Stetterly and King Keevan's cousin so she should be guarded, like any lord or lady.

"But I can easily stay with Renna when you and Leith are called away, while setting up a guard rotation outside the cabin during the day. Renna's planning to train reserve guards who volunteer for duties when they can. It'll be a smaller force, but enough for what she needs." Kayleigh went back to fiddling with the reins. "I'll be off duty—at least mostly—when you're home, because we're assuming Renna won't need guards when Leith is there."

Martyn snorted. No, Renna wouldn't need guarding

then. Any criminal with a grudge against the town of Stetterly or the king or Renna would be downright foolish to attack Renna when Leith was anywhere nearby.

And he kind of liked knowing Kayleigh would be staying with Renna where they could keep an eye on each other while he and Leith were away. The widow and her children that Kayleigh stayed with currently was nice enough, but the house was only as secure as normal houses went. It wasn't the fort that Leith had built his cabin to be. And Kayleigh would have Ranson, Jamie, and Brandi around to help, who were all competent fighters in their own way.

"I...think it's a good plan." Martyn's voice was more strained than he'd meant it to be. Was this what it was like to care about someone? To worry when they could be in danger?

Considering how he would make enemies as a Blade Marshal, Kayleigh could be in danger whether she was the guard captain at Stetterly or not. At least as captain she would keep up her training and have a few volunteers to help guard her back when he wasn't there to do it.

Kayleigh's gaze turned fierce. "I'm not about to sit around however long we're courting twiddling my thumbs. I need to keep busy, and this is...this is everything I've dreamed about. I used to dream about being a guard just like my father, until I realized there was no way a town like Flayin Falls would ever hire a woman as a guard. Few towns in Acktar do."

That explained a few things. It all made so much more sense why Kayleigh disguised herself and joined the Resistance army. It was about more than just winning back the town's good graces, which hadn't happened anyway. It had been her chance to pursue, even for a little while, her dream of following in her father's footsteps.

"Except Stetterly." As Martyn said it, a weight lifted inside his chest. Kayleigh had given up everything—her cabin, the mountains she loved so well, the freedom she'd had in the Sheered Rock Hills—to stay in Stetterly to be with him. That wasn't the kind of sacrifice he'd liked asking of her, especially when he'd done so little to sacrifice for her in return.

But if staying in Stetterly gave Kayleigh a dream she never would've had otherwise? That sat better inside Martyn's chest.

Kayleigh nodded. "Sierra hires women for its archers, and maybe for its guards, but that's the only other town I know that does. I think Renna plans to train most of the town to have some sort of fighting skill. After everything that happened to Stetterly in the past year, I don't think anyone will complain."

No, they wouldn't. As Martyn had heard it, most of the town had already gotten a start on that training, and it had saved them when Lord Norton attacked.

"So...what do you think?" Kayleigh peered up at him, her eyes a rich brown, flashing nearly as much as the reddish tint to her brown hair.

He had to give the right response. He held her gaze. "I'm proud of you. I think you're going to do a great job."

Those were the exact same words she'd said to him after Leith had pinned on Martyn's badge. And Martyn meant them just as much as Kayleigh had.

Yes, Kayleigh would be in danger. Possibly. But Stetterly was a quiet little town, when power-hungry men weren't attacking it. And Martyn would be out there on the prairie, making sure Rovers and horse thieves and other criminal types never reached Stetterly to bother it.

Kayleigh smiled. A warm, bright smile lighting up her eyes and face until Martyn wanted to kiss her. But not there in front of Kilm's guards and Lord Norton standing off to the side as if he was waiting for Martyn's report.

No, kissing would have to wait. It might even have to wait until they returned to Stetterly.

And Martyn might even dare to call that return coming home.

HONEYMOON HOLDUP

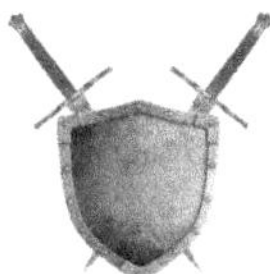

Leith tightened the girth on Valor's saddle. The early morning sun tipped through the trees of the Sheered Rock Hills, bathing the eastern cliffsides with pink.

On the other side of Valor, Big Brown clopped a few steps farther to crop at another stand of grass. Big Brown wore a pack saddle with their things, minus the saddlebag Renna still used as she finished getting ready.

Leith checked Valor's saddle once more before turning. Renna sat with her back to him as she brushed out her long hair, the strands glittering gold in the morning sunlight.

His mouth went dry. Who knew the sight of his wife brushing her hair could be so distracting? But after three and a half months of marriage—the last month of that spent touring the Sheered Rock Hills and Eagle Heights—he found himself more distracted than ever with thoughts of running his fingers through her hair and kissing her.

But they had miles to go today if they were going to reach

the meadow with its small waterfall on one side by nightfall. And that was all right. Having her behind him on the horse, her arms wrapped around him, was nice as they talked and traveled and admired the jagged peaks and splintered canyons around them.

"You're staring again." Renna didn't look his way as her fingers flew through braiding her hair.

"You're distracting."

She laughed and tied the end of the braid. As she stood, her smile froze, her eyes widening.

Only then did the sounds behind Leith register. Valor snorting. The crackle of feet on the dry grass and sand.

The cold steel of a knife rested against his throat, and a deep voice growled near his ear, "Don't move or I'll slit your throat."

The bandit would expect Leith to freeze. But the touch of a blade against his neck, the nick of a sharp edge, was familiar. Respen started training Leith to ignore the panic of a knife to the throat when he was nine. Now, his heart didn't even give an extra thump.

No, instead of racing heart and paralysis, cold settled into Leith's chest.

Four men emerged from the undergrowth, surrounding Renna, but still ten feet away. Another man besides the one holding the knife crunched on the gravel behind Leith and to the right. Valor had trotted a few steps to his left.

Six men. But amateurs. Five of them remained too far back to jump in quickly when Leith made his move, and the sixth man—the one with the knife—hadn't stepped close enough to prevent Leith from moving. The man expected the knife to Leith's throat to be enough.

It wasn't.

Leith stepped back, crunching down on the man's foot and jabbing back with an elbow to send him off balance. Leith grabbed the man's knife hand, pinned it straight over his shoulder, and levered upright while yanking the man's arm down.

A pop, and the man behind him howled as his shoulder dislocated.

The other five men charged, but they'd left too much distance between themselves and Renna to react quickly.

Amateurs. Definitely amateurs.

Before the man finished collapsing to the ground, Leith spun, leapt for Valor, and grabbed the saddle horn and reins. As he turned the horse toward Renna, he pushed off with his foot and swung into the saddle, clinging with his knees rather than try to find the stirrups.

Four of the men snatched at Renna, but Renna—unhesitating—was already lunging toward Leith. Leith reached down, caught her hand, and pulled her behind him even as he kicked Valor into a canter, then a gallop. Renna wrapped her arms around him, clinging to the point of painful around his ribs. Big Brown charged next to them, the horse so used to following at this point that he did so without a lead rope.

Leith let Valor pick the route through a gully and the slope to exit the wash and scramble over sand and rocks. A nudge on the reins sent Valor crashing through a tangled stand of juniper.

Other hoofbeats galloped in their wake. Burdened as Valor was with two people, the bandits would catch up, probably sooner rather than later.

Leith couldn't run, but he couldn't fight either. Not against six men and Renna to protect.

There had to be another option. Something better than going down fighting and leaving Renna at their mercy.

They broke from the juniper into a stand of straggling oaks and pines. Dense enough to provide some cover.

A low-hanging branch dipped into the path ahead. Leith let go of the reins. "Hang on around my neck."

Renna moved her grip around his neck, gripping the leather straps holding his knives across his chest.

The branch loomed in front of them. Instead of ducking, Leith braced himself. The branch slammed into his stomach, jerking both him and Renna from the saddle. Renna gave a small shriek but hung on, pressing her face against his shoulder.

Leith dragged himself onto the branch. "We have to get higher."

Renna swung her legs onto the branch. Together they scrambled higher into the oak.

Hoofbeats clacked on stone. Leith halted and pressed Renna against the trunk of the tree, masking her light blue shirt with the brown of his clothing in case the bandits happened to look up.

Four bandits galloped underneath the tree, and none of them glanced up.

As the hoofbeats faded into the distance and no further bandits appeared, Leith let out a breath. When he raised a hand to touch Renna's cheek, his fingers trembled. He would've kissed her, but he'd gotten in trouble once already by being distracted. Kissing in a tree seemed like a way to get into more trouble.

Renna leaned her cheek against his hand, her fingers relaxing their grip in the front of his shirt. "That was far too close."

Far too close. If they had stayed...if he had been killed... Renna would've been in the hands of six bandits. Alone.

That thought shook through him, turning his stomach. His duty to her came first, even before the duty he'd sworn to Acktar when he'd become the first Blade Marshal. "I have to get you out of here. If we leave now, we should have a large enough headstart we can evade them, even on foot. It'll take a few days to hike to Walden but—"

"No." Renna's fingers tightened in his shirt once again.

"No?" Leith blinked. Was Renna questioning him on strategy? Not that he was angry. He just couldn't remember her ever doing it before.

She met his gaze, steel in her eyes. "No. Thank you for your concern, but you're a Blade Marshal. Would you run off like this if you were by yourself? I know you wouldn't hesitate to take on six men if Martyn or Shad was with you."

Of course she was right. With Martyn or Shad, the odds would've been three to one. Against those amateurs, they would've been easy to apprehend. By himself, with the luxury of time and no one else to worry about, he probably could've taken them on.

But with Renna to protect? If even one bandit got past him, it could be disastrous for her. "No, I wouldn't. But I can't leave you unprotected."

Renna tapped the side of his belt where he'd tucked his Blade Marshal badge to keep it out of sight. "I appreciate and love my gentle husband, but right now you need to be the ice cold, calculating Blade Marshal I know is in there."

This was one of the many reasons he loved her. She kept his priorities straight.

He let out a long breath and drew on the cold that didn't come easily when he was with Renna. Ice settled into his chest, steadying his fingers.

If he was still a Blade, taking on six men wouldn't be a problem. But by the time he was done, five of the bandits—if not all six—would be dead.

Even if he didn't go into this as a Blade, he might be forced to kill. Without someone to watch his back, he would have to be lethal, going for killing blows, to make sure the bandits stayed down. It could be considered self-defense, and perhaps many wouldn't hesitate in his situation.

But with the blood on his hands—the guilt he carried—he hesitated. Not because killing was hard but because it was still all too easy.

Three times Leith had refused to kill when he could have. He could've attacked the former First Blade Vane. He'd had opportunity to try to assassinate Respen. And he could've killed Lord Norton in his sleep.

Some might have considered those assassinations justifiable. It might have spared lives to kill Vane and Respen. Those evil men surely didn't deserve to be spared.

But Leith couldn't. He carried too much guilt, too much blood. More blood, even guilty blood, would stain him further.

Beyond that, the Gathering had voted for the Blade Marshals—and him as its leader—by a narrow margin. It wouldn't look good for his first mission to end with dead bodies. It would prove to all those who had voted against him that he was still the assassin they thought he was.

Killing the bandits was out of the question. He'd have to get sneaky.

And he knew just how he was going to do it.

He met Renna's gaze and grinned. "How are you at acting regal?"

LEITH CROUCHED BEHIND A TANGLE OF JUNIPER GROWING beside a boulder, Renna next to him.

Two bandits had remained behind at what had been Leith and Renna's campsite, the one with the dislocated shoulder and a second, smaller man who appeared to be attempting to help.

"You need to keep the arm straight." The bandit tried to grab the other man's arm, but the bigger bandit yanked his arm out of his grip.

"Do you even know what you're doing?" The bandit pushed him away.

Leith swept a glance over the campsite, the terrain. And his mind laid out a plan. Dart in, stab the smaller bandit in the chest before spinning on his heel and planting a second knife in the larger but wounded bandit. Two seconds. Two dead bandits.

He blew out a long breath and closed his eyes. Still his instincts were that of a Blade. He had to consciously hesitate not to kill someone rather than the hesitation he was supposed to have over killing.

He wasn't sure even Renna knew this about him. She knew his past, but she seemed to think the Blade part of him was completely in the past, not still lurking inside him.

Shad, too, didn't seem to realize how much Leith had to hold himself back at times.

King Keevan knew. And, for some reason, that was comforting. Because King Keevan wouldn't let Leith step over the line.

And Martyn. Martyn understood perhaps better than anyone. He was just as much a Blade as Leith was.

A hand touched his arm. Renna leaned closer. "What's the plan?"

Leith shook himself. Plan B. That's what he should've been thinking about.

Depending on how far Valor and Big Brown ran riderless before the bandits caught them, Leith and Renna didn't have much time, considering how long it had taken to hike back on foot to this campsite.

How was Leith going to take both of these men alive? It took longer to subdue and capture a man than it did to kill him. By the time Leith knocked out one man, the second man would be after him. And, without Martyn, Leith had no one to watch his back.

Or, did he?

Leith turned to Renna and scrunched down farther out of sight. "When I go in there, I'm going to need you to watch my back and shout out warnings, such as 'high left'. They will need to be short and quick, otherwise I won't have time to react. Can you do it?"

Renna stared at her hands twisting in her lap. Finally, she raised her head, her shoulders straightening. "Yes."

"All right." After pinning his badge to his chest, Leith drew a knife. Renna wasn't prone to overestimating her abilities. If she thought she could do it, then she could. Which was good, because he'd be putting his life in her hands. "When I charge them, I'll take on the smaller bandit first. Don't watch me. Watch the other bandit and warn me when he makes his move. I want you to stay by this tree. If I give you the word, make a run for their horses and get out of here. Understand?"

Renna nodded and patted her leg, where she had the knife he'd given her a year ago hidden. "Yes, sir, Blade Marshal."

She might not like fighting, but she'd handle this. Leith fought both his smile and the urge to kiss her temple. He couldn't afford distractions now.

Instead, he reached for the depth of cold inside his chest. With a nod at Renna, he eased around the boulder and through the scrub brush. The two bandits didn't spot him until he was only five feet away from them.

As the bigger bandit's gaze snapped to him, Leith forced himself to remain standing rather crouch to attack. "I'm Blade Marshal Leith Torren, and you are under—"

The smaller bandit whirled, drew a knife, and charged at Leith.

So much for a peaceful surrender. Leith blocked, side-stepping to keep the one bandit between him and the one with the dislocated shoulder.

No need to prolong the fight. As the bandit stabbed at him again, Leith grabbed the man's arm, pinning it across his own body, and bashed the hilt of his knife into the tender spot at the base of the bandit's skull at the back of his neck. The bandit crumpled. Perhaps knocked out. At least stunned.

The bandit with a dislocated shoulder lunged at Leith

with a sword in his good hand. Leith dodged the sword thrust while avoiding the downed bandit at his feet. The swinging sword pushed him back, and Leith gave ground until he found a place with better footing.

Leith ducked below a swing, grabbed the bandit's arm, and swung his elbow back into the man's stomach. As he doubled over, Leith smashed the heel of his hand into the bandit's nose.

The man howled and staggered, nearly hitting himself with his own sword as he tried to reach for his gushing nose with his one working hand.

A snap and the creak of sand beneath leather boots came from behind Leith as Renna shouted, "High right, low left."

Leith ducked as he whirled, avoiding the knife that had been aimed at his chest, and grabbed the bandit's other wrist, stopping the knife headed for his stomach. He planted his foot in front of the bandit and used the bandit's momentum to trip him. Before the bandit could recover, Leith twisted the bandit's arm behind his back and shoved him to the ground.

"Behind you."

Leith glanced up as the larger bandit swung his sword at Leith's head. Leith ducked as best he could. Unless he released the bandit he had on the ground, he wouldn't be able to fight the other.

Too bad he wasn't skilled in throwing knives. Being able to put a knife in the bandit's good shoulder would be handy at the moment.

Though, he didn't necessarily need the knife to go in point first.

As the bandit gathered himself to swing his sword at

Leith's head again, Leith snapped his hand and sent his knife hurtling through the air.

The knife didn't strike point first. It did one better. The hilt smashed into the bandit's lip below his nose. More blood dribbled down the bandit's face as he howled, dropped his sword, and stumbled back.

"Renna, can you search their saddlebags and look for a rope." Leith raised his head and kept both the bandit with the dislocated shoulder and Renna in sight. "And well done, by the way."

Renna flashed a smile as she circled the campsite and approached the horses.

By the time the sound of hoofbeats from the returning four bandits grew closer, Leith had the two bandits hogtied, gagged, and officially arrested.

Renna perched on a boulder, her feet rested on the sword discarded by the bandit with the dislocated shoulder. She'd draped her divided skirt across her legs to give it the appearance of a full skirt. With her back straight, her head angled, her expression blank, she was the image of an aloof, conquering princess.

Leith drew a knife and waited out of sight in the shadows of one of the scrub oaks bordering what had been his and Renna's camp. He adjusted his Blade Marshal badge, now pinned to his chest over his heart.

The four bandits rode into view along the faint trail. Two of them led Valor and Big Brown. As they drew closer, the bandit in the lead—a tall, thin man with a scraggly beard—reined in his horse. His gaze flicked from the bound bandits on the ground to Renna perched on the boulder for all appearances ignoring the bandits as if they were dirt too far beneath her to notice.

Good. Just as he'd asked. Now to play out his bluff and hope it worked. If it didn't, at least four on one was better odds than before.

The thin bandit reached for his sword. "What the—"

Leith stepped into the sunlight. "I suggest you finish that sentence without cursing. There is a lady present."

The bandit glanced between Leith and Renna and back. His hand twitched upward, almost as if to doff the wide-brimmed hat he wore as a gentleman should. Good. This bandit, at least, had been raised with some manners, even if he had decided to ignore them.

One of the other bandits, his left hand gripping Valor's reins, pressed his horse closer. "He's just one man. What are you waiting for?"

Leith tapped his badge with the tip of his knife, leaning back against the tree as if relaxed. "I wouldn't do that if I were you. We're much more trouble than we're worth."

"What's that supposed to mean?" The bandit tried to cross his arms but couldn't while gripping Valor's reins. He settled for bracing his arms on the pommel and leaning forward as if trying to menace Leith.

A good try, but not going to work. Not when the bandit had fallen right into Leith's plan and started asking cliched questions. Leith pointed his knife in Renna's direction. "For one thing, she is King Keevan's cousin. If you hurt her, the king will send his entire army after you."

Renna swept a glance over the bandits, then went back to studying her fingernails as if the bandits were beneath her notice. The picture of a prim lady with all the airs of one closely related to the king.

Three of the bandits shifted uneasily in their saddles. The bandit with Valor snorted. "We can evade an army."

"Perhaps." Leith switched his grip on his knife, holding it by the tip as if he intended to throw it. "But you wouldn't escape me. I am Leith Daniel Grayce Torren, former First Blade and now captain of the Blade Marshals."

Definitely a few swallows and glances between the bandits at the mention of the Blades.

Even the talkative bandit shifted in his saddle now, sitting up and resting a hand on his sword. "Blade Marshals? Never heard of them."

"We're new. King Keevan founded the Blade Marshals to protect law and order in Acktar." Leith tested the knife's weight, as if in preparation to throw it. These bandits didn't know he couldn't throw a knife accurately to save his life. He waved to the two bound and gagged bandits lying on the ground. "Now, here's how this is going to go. I have to arrest those two. That one assaulted an officer of the law and the other was knowingly harboring him. Then they both resisted arrest. But the rest of you don't have to be arrested. Not if you return our horses and ride off."

"And if we don't?"

Leith forced himself to sigh, as if bored by the very idea. "I'm afraid I would have to arrest you as horse thieves. I believe that's a hanging offense. Not a pleasant way to go, I hear."

That sounded like the kind of sarcastic comment Martyn would make if he was here. Just the sort of tone Leith needed at the moment.

Tension curled in his chest, but he didn't let it flood his muscles. Not yet. Nor did he glance at Renna. This was it. Either the bandits rode away or they called his bluff.

The thin bandit's eyes focused on Leith's knife. "You say you were a Blade?"

"First Blade." Leith reached for his right sleeve. "Do you need to see my thirty-seven marks to prove it?"

"No." The thin man doffed his hat and gave something of a bow on horseback. "Sorry to bother you, ma'am, sir."

Renna tilted her chin just enough to give the impression of a regal acknowledgement of the bandit's apology.

As the thin man turned his horse, the argumentative bandit grabbed his arm. "You're just riding away?"

The thin bandit shook off the other bandit's grip. "If you want to fight a First Blade, go ahead. But I'm not staying."

The bandit holding Big Brown dropped the reins, doffed his hat to Renna, and turned his horse to fall into step with the thin bandit's horse.

Soon, only the one bandit was left, still gripping Valor's reins. With a mutter, the bandit released Valor, wheeled his horse around, and set out at a canter after the others.

Leith waited until the hoofbeats faded into the distance, then waited another minute before he finally allowed himself to relax and sheath his knife. "They're gone."

Renna let out a breath in a whoosh. "Good. While I have a high opinion of your skills, I really didn't want to get stuck in the middle of a fight."

Should he be insulted that her tone made it sound like she doubted he could take on those four bandits by himself? Of course, he had entertained his own doubts.

No, not doubts. Contingency plans. He rested his hands on her shoulders. "You doubted I could take them?"

"No. I was more worried about distracting you at the wrong moment." Renna kept her head down, one hand sliding into her pocket as if to check on her hidden knife. "Do you ever wish I was more like Kayleigh or Brandi? That I could defend myself and not be a hinderance or distraction in battle?"

Leith bit his tongue before he blurted out something too quickly. This was the sort of question that needed a careful answer. "Brandi is my sister, and Kayleigh is becoming like a sister. But I didn't marry them. I married you because I love you just how you are. I love that you're gentle. You're a healer. If you ever wanted to learn a few self-defense skills, I would gladly teach you, but don't ever feel forced. You aren't a fighter, and that's all right. You did well calling out instructions for me."

And just to make sure she knew he meant it, he kissed her.

One of the hogtied bandits made a muffled grumbling sound. Leith ignored him. The bandits had the poor sense to barge in on Leith and Renna's wedding trip. They would just have to put up with a little kissing.

Renna pulled back with a sigh. "I guess this means we'll have to cancel our plans to stay at the meadow tonight."

Another annoyance to chalk up to these bandits. "Afraid so. We'll push on to Walden as quickly as we can manage. We'll go back another time. I don't want to risk those bandits circling back and trying to surprise us."

"Then we best get moving." Renna turned as if to fetch

the bandits' horses. "Are you regretting that you let them go? Do you think they'll be a danger to us?"

"I don't think so. If they're smart, they'll avoid us." Leith glanced at the two bandits he had arrested. Both of them glared back at him. "If they're as foolish as I think they are, they'll try robbing someone else, bungle it just as badly, and Martyn and I will track them down then."

"Just you and Martyn? Not Shad too?" Some of the twinkle returned to Renna's eyes as her mouth tipped into a smile.

"All three of us against the four of them? That would be a waste of manpower. Shad's time would be better spent elsewhere." Leith shrugged. "This way, these bandits will spread the word about the Blade Marshals. Maybe next time I won't have to explain what my badge means."

THE WEDDING

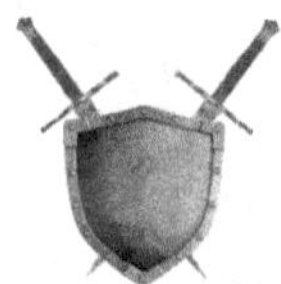

Author's Note: This short story started out as a scene I had to cut from the beginning of Deliver, *and I expanded it from there. I hope you enjoy Shad and Jolene's story.*

Seventeen-year-old Shadrach Alistair leaned against the one scraggly cottonwood next to the graveyard on the outskirts of the town of Sierra, watching the slim, blond haired girl sitting among the headstones. She shouldn't be out there. Not by herself. There might be Blades still in the area. Not to mention, she'd just buried her father after he'd been murdered. No one should be alone after that.

As soon as Lady Lorraine and Shad's father had left the graveyard after the funeral, Jolene Lorraine had slipped away and headed back. Shad had followed.

He couldn't let her grieve alone. It wasn't right, even if Shad wouldn't be able to help much. He had both his parents. He didn't know the grief she felt.

But he could understand. With Lord Lorraine dead,

Shad's parents would be next on Respen's kill list, especially his father. Shad had already lost Lord and Lady Faythe, as close to an aunt and uncle as Shad would ever have. How long would it be before Shad's family was the target? Before his father was the one they buried?

They were already jumping at shadows. Even though Lord Lorraine had been a friend, only Shad and Father had come to the funeral. Mother and the rest of Shad's siblings had remained under heavy guard at Walden.

Shad tiptoed along the worn path between the headstones. Not that he was trying to sneak. But graveyards weren't the place for loud strolling.

Jolene didn't look up as he sank to the ground next to her and rested his arms on his knees. "I didn't think you should be alone."

"Thanks." Jolene still faced forward.

Before them, the fresh-turned dirt of her father's grave marred the prairie even more than the austere gravestone.

Shad didn't break the silence. If Jolene wanted to talk, then she would. If not, Shad was intruding enough without spouting mindless chatter.

Jolene swiped at her face. Her face was even paler against the red rings around her eyes. "I used to come here a lot as a kid."

"The graveyard?" Shad blinked at the hill around them. A few headstones, both old ones and the new one for Lord Lorraine, scattered among the tall prairie grass. Only that one sad-looking cottonwood attempted to add some sort of peace and shade from its place at the graveyard's edge while leftover white cottonwood fluff from that spring still stuck in the long grass at the base of the older gravestones.

"I know it sounds strange. But…" Jolene's voice steadied, and she raised her head as she gestured at a row of stones next to Lord Lorraine. "My brothers and sister are here."

Shad raised his eyebrows but bit his tongue. He'd thought Jolene was an only child.

"Not many people know. I had two brothers and one sister. All stillborn." Jolene rubbed her arms. "They're the reason my mother never laughs. After this, she probably won't even smile anymore. Hard as stone, my mother."

If Jolene had been Renna or one of Shad's sisters, he would've put his arm around her shoulders. "I'm sorry."

Jolene focused on her father's gravestone as if she hadn't heard him. "Whenever it seemed like Mother didn't understand and I needed space, I'd come here. It was the closest I could get to spending time with my siblings." She rested her chin on her knees. "It's something of a comfort to know that Father…Father is with them now. They're all together in Heaven."

Shad stared between the gravestones. What could he say? It wasn't like he could understand. He had four younger siblings. Yes, he'd spent the first five years of his life without a sibling until Lydia was born, but it wasn't like he remembered it well.

He sighed and scrubbed a hand along the back of his neck. "I'm glad you have that comfort, at least. We all need it in these times, I think."

Jolene shot a glance toward him, her eyes watery. "Your father doesn't laugh like he used to either, does he?"

"No. Not since Lord and Lady Faythe were killed." Shad swallowed at the lump forming in his throat. His father used to laugh so heartily, but none of them had heard it in a year. Even Esther, Shad's three-year-old sister, couldn't get much of a laugh out of him. Would she grow up without the memories Shad had? Of Father's chuckle and Mother's giggle? Esther wouldn't even remember Lord and Lady Faythe.

It was all so wrong. And there was nothing Shad could do to fix any of it.

Surely he could do something to help Jolene. He was an older brother to three sisters, and pretty much an adopted older brother to Renna and Brandi. Of all people, he should be well-practiced at fixing problems.

How could he fix death? All the comforting words, prayers, and Scripture verses had already been said, probably more times than Jolene wanted to hear them. Yes, it was a comfort to know the hope of Heaven. To know their loved ones were with Jesus there.

But that didn't fully take away the ache of loss.

Maybe a distraction? It wouldn't do much, not with the pain she had to be feeling. But it might take her mind off it for a while. Shad pushed to his feet and held out his hand. "We probably should head back."

She heaved a final, shuddering breath. "You're right. It isn't proper to be out here like this."

Shad hadn't even thought of that. Sure, two seventeen-year-olds alone would be fodder for talk. What did the gossips matter? Jolene had just lost her father.

But the gossips did matter. To a lord's heir, they always mattered.

As Jolene held out her hand and let Shad pull her to her feet, Shad forced himself to smile. "Actually, I was wondering if you would show me your archery skills. I saw you shooting when Father and I arrived yesterday."

Jolene wrapped her arms around her stomach. "Father, Mother, and I used to do it together."

So much for a distraction. Shad nearly halted, but Jolene kept striding toward Sierra Manor. He hurried to catch up. "I'm sorry. You don't have to, if you don't want to."

"It's all right." Jolene dragged in a deep breath, as if she fought tears again. "It's…calming."

When they reached Sierra Manor, a rectangular brick manor house set on the top of a hill, Jolene pointed toward the back, away from the town of Sierra that stretched down the other side of the hill. "Meet me back there. I need to fetch my bow."

After she'd disappeared inside, Shad strolled around the manor to the open stretch of ground. A target already rested against a stack of hay bales.

After a few minutes, the back door clicked shut, and Jolene strode to Shad's side. A quiver filled with arrows rested against her back, and she carried an unstrung bow in her hand. A leather vambrace covered her left forearm, and she'd even taken the time to tie her long hair back with a leather tie.

"Um, well. This is my bow." Jolene braced one end against her foot, leaned on it, and slipped the string into the notch at the end.

Shad crossed his arms. She'd made that look easy, but he got the feeling it wasn't.

Jolene drew the arrow back, barely seemed to aim, and released. A heartbeat later, the arrow thunked into the center of the target.

"You're very good." Though, he'd already known that. He'd watched her from Sierra Manor yesterday as she'd sent arrow after arrow into the center ring of the target. He hadn't interrupted her then, not when her face had been so hard with concentration and the arrows had flown over and over again as if she'd been trying to shoot grief itself.

"Thanks, but it's all just practice." Jolene held out the bow. "Why don't you take a couple of shots?"

Shad took the bow and the offered arrow. Fitting the arrow as he'd seen her do, he tried to figure out how to place his fingers around the arrow to draw it back. "I've never done this before. Archery isn't something a nobleman is tradition-ally taught. Your father must've been the exception."

"He was." For a moment, Jolene's face crumpled, as if she was about to break down into tears again. But then her shoulders straightened. "You're going to hurt yourself pulling on the string like that. Let me show you."

Jolene stepped closer and showed Shad how to place his fingers on either side of the arrow to draw it back and how to grip the bow with his left hand. She also did her best to fit the leather vambrace to his arm so the bowstring didn't whip against his forearm when he released.

After a few more instructions, Shad drew the arrow back. It kept trying to flop away from the bow. The bowstring cut into his fingers, and the muscles in his back and shoulder strained with the unfamiliar movement. Steadying the arrow, he drew in a deep breath and released.

The arrow flew over the target and disappeared into the shorn grass beyond.

Jolene scowled and crossed her arms. "You just lost my arrow."

"I'll find it." Shad took a step in that direction, but Jolene's short laugh stopped him.

She shook her head. "We'll look for it later after you've taken a few more shots. Though, I wasn't kidding about the losing the arrow part. Arrows tend to bury themselves under the grass, making them hard to find."

She handed Shad another arrow, gave him a few more tips, and he drew the bow again. This time he aimed the arrow lower than before and released. It thumped into the top edge of the target. Only an inch higher, and he would've missed altogether.

"Much better." Jolene handed him another arrow. "Try again."

Shad got off three more shots—two hitting the outside of the target, and another complete miss—before Father's voice called from the manor.

Shad sighed and held out Jolene's bow. "Time to go."

As he set out for the manor and the horse the stablehand had waiting for him, Shad wasn't sure why his feet dragged so much. As if he was reluctant to leave.

Shad swung onto his horse and found himself turning around to wave at Jolene as the guards closed around them. Father gestured, and they set out.

When Sierra Manor disappeared over the horizon, Father swiveled in his saddle. "Don't get any thoughts about courting Lady Jolene."

Shad gritted his teeth, biting off his first impulse of words. Why did his father always have to make his decisions for him? It was Shad's business who he wanted to court or not.

But it wasn't. Shad's life wasn't his own. He was the heir, so his life belonged to Walden.

Years ago, Shad had overheard his father speculating about Shad marrying Renna someday. It had been half a joke at the time, but half serious as well. It seemed to be what everyone had expected including Renna herself...and Shad was always expected to obey.

And, in the end, Shad always did what was expected of him. Yes, a part of him sometimes itched to rebel. To do something reckless for once in his life. But he was his father's heir, and nothing would be gained by rebellion.

Flexing his fingers on the reins, Shad blew out a long breath until he could face his father with a straight face. "I don't have any intention of pursuing her. She just lost her father."

Father rubbed at his face and stared off into the horizon. "What I'm trying to say is, you can't court anyone right now. Especially not Lady Jolene. If Respen sees us trying to deepen ties with anyone, he will send his Blades after us. It will make them a target."

Shad's anger cooled. He'd known that. It was the reason he hadn't seen Renna and Brandi in a year, even after their parents had died.

More than that, the murder of Lord Lorraine had been a warning. Lord Lorraine and Father had gotten too sloppy with planning the Resistance. Now Father would have to back off. Be even more careful.

And Shad would have to be just as careful. Father was right. Anyone Shad courted would be put in danger. Did he really think Respen would overlook the heir of a suspected

Resistance leader courting anyone? It would look like a cover for something else.

How long would this war last? Shad was seventeen now. How many years would he have to sacrifice? Would his siblings Lydia, Jeremiah, and Abigail have to sacrifice as well? Maybe even his youngest sister Esther, little as she was now.

"I see." That's all Shad could say. He knew his duty.

For a few minutes, the only sounds between them were the squeak of the leather saddles and the clump of hooves on the sandy turf.

Father shifted. "When we return, I've arranged for you to train with an old friend of mine. His name is Walter Esroy. He used to be a Rover."

"A Rover?" Shad nearly reined his horse to a stop. Rovers still occasionally raided towns, though less frequently than they used to.

"Like I said, he's a friend." Father kept facing forward. "He will teach you the skills to be able to defend yourself against a Blade. If the worst should happen, I need you to be able to take care of your mother and siblings."

If—no, when—Father was targeted by a Blade, Shad's family would be his responsibility. Shad would have to be capable enough to meet that challenge when it came. No matter what it took.

Father once again had planned out Shad's life, but Shad couldn't argue this time. If he wanted his family to stay safe, he would have to step up and take on this duty.

Even if that meant becoming his father's weapon to counter the Blades.

"All right." Shad tightened his grip on the reins. "But I'd like to learn archery as well."

"Really?" The twitch of a smile broke through the hard lines of Father's face.

Shad forced a nonchalant shrug. "It seems like a good skill to have. It keeps an enemy at a distance, and that seems like a wise move when dealing with Blades."

"I see your point. I'll see to it."

And just like that, Shad's life for the next years was laid out before him.

But that didn't mean he wouldn't slip back to Sierra first chance he got.

NEARLY FOUR YEARS LATER...

Shad clasped his fingers in Jolene's as they strolled down the hill. Behind them, Sierra Manor perched dark and huge in the light of the half moon overhead. After the daytime hubbub of saws and axes echoing from the work being done to rebuild the town, the squeak of crickets and rustle of night-time rodents scurrying through the grass was a lulling hush.

Jolene leaned her head against his arm. "Is the war really over? Sometimes, I dream about another battle, another fight lining up with the other archers, another day worrying you'll be killed out there on the battlefield."

Shad squeezed her fingers tighter. "I wish I could've been in the archers with you."

But he was a lord's son. His place had been at the front lines, leading a division of Riders.

Jolene swatted their clasped hands against his leg. "No, you don't. Not really. You led the Riders that held the gate at Nalgar Castle. You got to be the hero."

"No more than you or your mother or anyone else who fought for King Keevan." Again, Shad saw the bodies piled across the gate into Nalgar, blood pouring across the cobblestones, his own blood pouring down his arm until he was light headed and staggering. No, he didn't deserve to be considered a hero. Not when he was still standing and so many others weren't.

Besides, he'd simply been doing his duty. Exactly what was expected of him. Others, like Jolene, had fought even when it wasn't expected of them. Jolene hadn't had to join the archers. She could've stayed at Eagle Heights.

But she was the heir to Sierra as he was the heir to Walden, and she'd stepped forward to face the same danger and the same fight. That made her far more heroic than Shad could ever be.

Shad settled into the easy stroll as he meandered up the next hill, trying to make it seem like he didn't have a specific destination in mind.

But halfway up the hill, the glow became visible. Little balls of yellow-orange against the gray prairie and black-blue sky.

"Shad? What have you been up to?" Jolene lifted her head, her pace speeding up.

He had to fight his grin as they neared the small graveyard. Candles shone in their carefully cleared patches of dirt at the base of the cottonwood. Even after three years, the tree looked barely taller than it had been, though perhaps a bit broader. A blanket spread on the slight rise underneath the tree overlooking the graveyard below while a vase with the last of the summer wildflowers sat on the center of the blanket.

Pulling Jolene underneath the tree, Shad rested his hands lightly on her waist. "What do you think?"

She wrapped her arms around his neck, tipping her head back to look him in the eye. "Should I be worried? You used to be such a perfect gentleman, before you started skulking around and keeping questionable company. Is this another one of those secrets you're so good at keeping?"

He leaned his forehead against hers. "I told you. Now that the war is over, I don't have any more secrets. You know who the Leader is and who Leith is. That's all I ever kept from you. If anything, you're my biggest secret."

"Oh, really?" Her grin widened. "That's hardly a secret now. Not after you kissed me in front of the entire Resistance army."

"No, but even my father didn't know I was courting you for the past three years. Not until your visit to Walden this spring." Shad didn't let himself wince. He wasn't sure if he regretted all the secrecy or not. His father would've kept his secret, and it wasn't like telling him would've put Jolene and Shad in danger. Honestly, the only reason for secrecy was his own foolish desire to feel like one part of his life wasn't being controlled or planned or manipulated.

Yet the moment he'd seen his father, weak and injured, after the battle for Walden, Shad knew that if he could do it over again, he'd do it differently.

Jolene crooked an eyebrow. "Really? Courtship? That's what you'd call it? I thought you just enjoyed Sierra's food and Mother's company. And sneaking. You adore being sneaky more than you'll ever admit."

"Whatever you want to call it, we've known each other nearly four years. The war is over. All our parents know. There's nothing standing between us anymore. I even talked to your mother."

It wasn't typical to ask a mother for her daughter's hand in marriage, but all Jolene had was her mother. And, honestly, facing her father couldn't have been any scarier. Not when Lady Lorraine had personally killed Second Blade Hess and was the one person to ever capture Leith without him willingly surrendering first. And she'd done it with hair ribbons, of all things.

The grin faded from Jolene's face, replaced with wide blue eyes and slightly parted mouth. "Well, there is one thing you have to do yet."

Yes. Ask. Shad ran his tongue around his dry mouth. His empty stomach clenched so tightly it was a good thing he hadn't been able to eat anything that day.

Why was he even nervous? It wasn't like she was going to say no.

But this moment meant so much. He couldn't ruin it.

He let go of her waist, turned, and sat on the ground facing the graveyard. "Lord Lorraine, I would very much like to marry your daughter, if she says yes and if you give your blessing."

He waited a moment, listening to the crickets and breeze and the faint hiss of burning candles.

Jolene sat next to him. He took her hand again. "I'm going to assume that was a yes. So what about you? Will you marry me?"

She paused, and her gaze swiveled to the gravestones before them.

Shad's heart stopped hammering in his chest. Why was she pausing? What had he done wrong? He'd wanted everything to be perfect.

When she turned back to him, her eyes glittered wet in the combined light of moon and candles. "Yes. Of course, yes."

He breathed out a long sigh. Good. She wasn't as energetic about her response as he'd expected, but maybe that wasn't a bad thing.

She leaned her head against his shoulder. "And thank you for this. You didn't have to do it, you know. I know my father isn't really here and it's probably a bit strange to come out here to feel close to him when he's in Heaven, but... thank you."

Shad disentangled their fingers long enough to wrap his arm around Jolene's shoulders and pull her tighter against him. "My father is going to do his best to welcome you into the family and my siblings will smother you until you will go back to wishing you were an only child, but I know neither of those things will ever fill the hole left by your missing father and siblings. And I'm trying to understand that, even if I haven't had to face a loss like that."

He'd come close in the war, but his family had come out alive and mostly unscathed.

"Well, I do appreciate it." Jolene wrapped her arms around his waist.

Enough morbid thoughts. Shad forced a smile into his voice. "So, when do you want the wedding?"

It would be months away. There were details and planning and invitations and politics to work out. The heirs to two powerful towns couldn't simply get married and be done with it.

After nearly a minute of consideration, Jolene turned her face toward him. Something of a dare hovered in her grin. "How about in three days?"

"Three...days..." Shad couldn't stop his mouth from hanging open. Three days. Surely she didn't mean that. That wasn't how these things were done. Not between noble families.

"Yes, three days. We waited a whole war, after all." Jolene pulled away from him.

"But...the guests and...and..." He wasn't sure why he was protesting. Three days sounded just fine to him.

But the annoying lord's son in him couldn't keep his mouth shut.

Jolene cocked her head. "My family is already here, and your family is only a day away in Walden. Anyone else we would invite is already here, except for all the political guests. And, I don't know about you, but I would rather skip all that. Our parents were leaders in the Resistance. Half the nobles in the country would love nothing better than to assassinate them. Imagine the opportunity they'd see in our wedding."

Shad stilled. He should've thought of that. Half the country had just lost the war, and both sides were bitter. Would someone see their wedding as a chance to get revenge on Shad's father or Jolene's mother?

That wasn't as impossible as it sounded. Years ago, Rovers, the marauding bands of outlaws, made it a point to attack weddings because of the large gathering of guests and rich collection of wedding presents.

"You're right. No one can disrupt our wedding if they don't have time to find out about it or put together a plan." Shad rested a hand on his sword's hilt. Even here, the war won and intending to propose, he hadn't dared take it off.

"Exactly. I've already lost one parent to assassination. I don't want to lose the other." Jolene glanced toward the tall gravestone glowing yellow in the candlelight.

And Shad would do everything in his power to make sure that didn't happen. Besides, the more he thought about it, the more he liked the idea of a small wedding, just family and friends and maybe a few guests from the townsfolk of Sierra and Walden. Nothing too fancy. Just him and Jolene, like it had been during their walks on the journey to Eagle Heights.

He cleared his throat and gripped her hands. "I would like to ask Leith Torren to be a groomsman, maybe even first groomsman. I know it might be painful for you, to have a Blade standing with us at our wedding, so please tell me now and I won't ask him. But I would feel a lot safer if I knew he was the one guarding my back."

Jolene bit her lip, her eyes darting from their clasped hands to the gravestone and finally focusing on the ground. "I know he's your friend and he isn't the one who killed my father and he's been really hurt protecting Renna, but it's hard not to see him as a Blade. I'm trying, but I think, in many ways, he still *is* a Blade. Not the killing part, perhaps, but the instincts are still there."

Shad rubbed his thumb across the back of her hand. Could

he blame her? She was right. For all the progress Leith had made, he still thought and acted like a Blade at times. Like when he put on his knives before his boots in the morning. Or darted a glance around a room before he committed to fully entering it. Or jumped at an unexpected noise and reached for a knife.

But after the war, how many of them did the same things?

Shad held Jolene's gaze. "Am I all that different? Maybe I didn't kill the way he did in the past, but I have killed. I led men into battle. Which of us, do you think, has more blood on our hands? I'm not so sure it isn't me."

"Or me." Jolene looked away. "I don't know how many of my arrows killed and how many only wounded, but with the number of arrows I shot, I had to have killed a fair number of people."

Shad traced his fingers along her jaw. There wasn't anything he could say to make this better. The weight of blood would be a burden both of them would bear for the rest of their lives. That was the cost of war.

"What about your brother Jeremiah? Shouldn't he be your first groomsman?" Jolene pulled back a few inches.

"I talked with him before we left Eagle Heights." Shad couldn't help a grin at Jolene's raised eyebrows. "Yes, I already started planning this back then. Jeremiah took one look at me, shut his book, and said he would be willing to be a groomsman, but not the first groomsman. He barely knows which end of a sword is sharp."

"Shad! That isn't very nice."

"His words, not mine." Shad shook his head. He'd gotten a good laugh out of it when Jeremiah said it. But it didn't seem so funny now. Jeremiah wasn't interested in learning sword-fighting and war. As a lord's son, he had enough trouble making friends, but his disinterest in weapons only made it worse.

Strangely enough, he and Jamie Cavendish, the Blade trainee of Leith's, had started a rather unlikely friendship at Eagle Heights. Perhaps because Jamie, after spending too many years with the Blades, no longer saw the glamor in fighting and weapons the way other boys did.

"Anyway, he also said he didn't want the responsibility for guarding us that day, not when he doesn't know anything about fighting. He's right. He's only thirteen. It's too much responsibility for him."

Jolene cocked her head. "So you want to give it to a former Blade who can barely walk because of his injuries?"

Broken ribs. Lashes. Burns. Torture. Shad worked to steady his breathing. Respen had tortured Leith within an inch of his life. If Respen wasn't already dead and buried...

"Leith might be injured, but as you said, he's still a Blade. He can handle trouble."

Jolene leaned closer. "You really want Leith Torren as your first groomsman, don't you?"

"Yes, I do." Shad clasped her hands. Their faces were now inches apart.

"Then that's settled. We're getting married in three days, and we'll have a Blade guarding us, and we're going to be very happy."

"Yes, we are." Shad kissed her.

Jolene pulled away first, grinning. "I guess the rogue is coming out more than the gentleman tonight? And in front of my father and my most likely overprotective older brothers."

Shad glanced at the gravestones, then back at Jolene. "I'll risk it."

Shad leaned back in his chair as the breakfast table exploded with squeals and chatter at Jolene's announcement. Renna fired off logistical questions while Brandi asked about the dress and flowers. Jolene's smile grew with every question she answered. Lady Lorraine chipped in occasionally.

Lady Lorraine...his future mother-in-law. He wasn't used to thinking of her like that yet, not even after courting Jolene for years. Even now, Shad couldn't be sure she was happy with him as a son-in-law or if she wanted to shoot him full of arrows. He got the feeling both options were still on the table.

Across the table, Leith glanced between Jolene and Renna, his right hand straying to the place on his belt where a knife normally hung. In the weeks since the battle, the bruising on his face had disappeared, though his movements remained stiff with his healing ribs, burns, and injured leg. "That's...great. When's the wedding?"

"Five days." Shad shot a glance at Lady Lorraine, but she was listening to Jolene describe how she planned to decorate Sierra Manor's dining room, the largest room in the manor, for the occasion. Sierra didn't have a church rebuilt yet. "Jolene wanted three, but her mother convinced us that five days would give more time for travel back and forth to Walden."

"Five days. Is that normal?" Leith cocked his head, his eyes narrowed.

Shad nearly laughed but stopped himself. Leith was serious. He truly didn't know how long an engagement normally lasted.

Most of the time, Leith could pass himself off as any other soldier or peasant farmer. But sometimes, like this, he did or said something to remind everyone that he'd grown up locked in a manor and a tower with a few other boys for company, only taught fighting and killing and whatever Respen deemed necessary for an assassin to know, nothing more.

Shad leaned his elbows on either side of his plate of scrambled eggs and beef sausage. "Have you ever been to a wedding?"

Leith hesitated, his gaze fixed on his own, half-eaten plate of food. "Once."

Shad didn't ask. He didn't want to know who at that wedding hadn't lived to see the next morning. Sometimes, it was easier to look Leith in the eyes and see his marks if Shad didn't know what those marks stood for. Because Leith wasn't that person anymore, and Shad didn't ever want to see him that way.

Leith had been a Blade, but he was redeemed, and now he was a friend and like Shad's brother. And that's how Shad would treat him.

"No, five days isn't normal. We just want a small wedding without all the politics."

Leith glanced at Renna, a frown puckering his forehead.

Shad fought his own frown. Now there was a wedding

that could get messy and political. Renna was the lady of Stetterly and King Keevan's cousin. All of the lords and ladies in Acktar would want to show up to her wedding. Yet, Leith was a Blade, and his identity still a secret to most in Acktar. A secret that wouldn't stay hidden long the moment some of the lords who supported Respen caught sight of him.

But that was a problem for another time.

He forced himself to grin and shrug. "We're ready. We would've been married already if it weren't for Respen."

Leith's frown vanished, replaced with his own grin. "Now I know why you were so eager for a quick end to the war."

"It might've been one of my reasons." Shad pushed a bite of his breakfast around on his plate. "We feared Respen would send a Blade to attack us at our wedding or that night. He would've seen it as a strengthening of Sierra and Walden's alliance against him."

Leith stilled, his hand once again clenching at his side. "I might've been the one sent to do it."

Shad didn't want to imagine it. Didn't want to see Leith leaning over him, knife in hand, preparing to slit his throat. Didn't want to imagine Jolene lying in a pool of her own blood.

Instead, he crossed his arms and grinned. "That would've been awkward. Since I want you to be one of my groomsmen."

Leith's eyebrows shot up. "Groomsmen?"

How much should Shad explain to him? The history behind the tradition? That Renna's father had been first groomsman for Shad's father and ended up saving his life?

Best to stick with the simple explanation for now. "The groomsmen guard the bride and groom during the ceremony. It doesn't happen often, but sometimes there's trouble." Shad tipped his head toward Renna and Jolene. "Renna's father saved my father's life at his wedding. There was a Rover attack. You should ask Renna about it sometime. It's how her parents met."

Leith frowned, his gaze fixed on Renna. "I see."

"No, I don't think you do." Shad rested a hand on his sword's hilt, waiting until Leith met his gaze. "I'm asking you because there's no one else I'd rather have guarding my back."

SHAD HAD HIS ARMS CROSSED AND HIS EYES CLOSED AS HE listened to the music filtering through the door to his father's study. The few guests had to be arriving. The minister would be taking his place at the front of the room.

The wedding would start any moment. Shad forced himself to remain lounged in his chair when all his restless legs and body wanted to do was pace. Behind him, the curtains of the alcove rustled. Probably Leith, checking to make sure no one was trying to sneak into the manor from that direction. Near the bookcase, a paper whispered as Jeremiah turned a page in the book he was reading. They, at least, seemed calm.

The door opened. Shad cracked his eyes open as Father stepped inside. Father raised his eyebrows at Leith and Jeremiah. "I think it's just about time."

Jeremiah scrambled to his feet and left. Leith checked his knives one last time and followed him.

Shad eased to his feet and smoothed his white shirt,

black vest, and black trousers. When he faced Father, he wasn't sure what to say. His father wasn't the invincible, strong figure he'd been when Shad had been little. Gray had replaced much of his brown hair. His left arm remained limp in a sling. Shad even stood a few inches taller.

Sure, Shad had swallowed his anger over some of Father's decisions for Shad's future more times than he cared to count, but in the end, that didn't matter.

Father clapped his good hand on Shad's shoulder. "Shadrach, I know I haven't told you this near as often as I should've. But, I'm proud of you. Very proud."

Shad cleared his throat. There wasn't anything he could say to that. Not when he was thankful just to have him here. Jolene didn't have her father at her side.

Father pulled Shad into a one-armed hug, and Shad returned the embrace. Then together, they stepped into the hall.

Mother and Esther waited at the door to the dining room. Shad swung his little sister around until she giggled. "You ready for another sister? Remember, you have to give her a big hug when the wedding is over. Can you do that for me?"

"Yes! Put me down!" Esther squirmed. "You're messing my new dress all up."

He set her down, grinning when she smoothed down her skirt with all the prim properness she could muster at seven years old.

Mother hugged him tightly enough to knock the breath out of him. "I can't believe my boy is all grown up." Letting go of him, she smiled a wobbly, wet sort of smile.

"It isn't like I'm moving out or going very far. Jolene and I will be spending half our time at Walden." Shad shook his head, straightening his vest yet again. He was the heir to Walden, and Jolene was heir to Sierra. They wouldn't be going anywhere.

"I know." Mother hugged him one last time before she and Esther entered the dining room to find their seats.

Leith limped down the hall toward him, Jeremiah trotting at his side. "We scouted the hallways and outside the manor. No signs of trouble."

"Both of you scouted?" Shad crossed his arms.

Jeremiah huffed another panting breath and straightened his hair. At thirteen, he stood nearly as tall as Leith, though he was as thin as a grass blade. "Yes. Both of us. And you'd better appreciate it. I wasn't even able to finish my book before being dragged outside."

Shad patted his brother's shoulder. Scouting and athletic sort of things weren't something Jeremiah enjoyed, but he was putting up with it today for Shad.

Father nudged Jeremiah. "Then we're all set. You'd better let the ladies know we're about to begin."

With a huff, Jeremiah took off down the hallway, poked his head inside one of the rooms, and sped back. "They're ready too."

"Catch your breath, and we'll start." Father opened the door and gestured to someone inside. The music changed to something softer and slower.

Shad drew in a deep breath. Finally. No more waiting.

Leith checked his weapons—two knives in his boots, two knives strapped across his chest, and two knives belted at his waist. With a nod, Leith motioned to Jeremiah and the two of them entered the dining room.

Then it was Shad's turn. He and Father stepped through the door.

Leith stood at the head of the aisle off to one side of the minister, right hand on his knife and eyes scanning the room. Jeremiah stood alongside Leith, hands behind his back, trying to look imposing.

Shad marched down the aisle, Father at his side. Pausing a few yards in front of Leith, Shad spun on his heel to face back the way he'd come. Father did the same next to him.

The music changed again. Abigail, Lydia, and Renna swept into the room and arranged themselves in the front.

Then Jolene glided into the room, wearing a light blue dress that hugged her frame before spreading out in waves of flowing fabric. Her gaze lifted to his, and she smiled.

Shad tried to suck in a breath, but it caught in his throat. He held his breath, fighting the urge to cough.

Jolene's smile widened, as if she could tell he'd nearly choked on air at the sight of her.

Only when Jolene halted in front of him did he finally notice that her mother walked beside her.

Shad held out his hands and Jolene clasped them.

Lady Lorraine rested her hand on top of Shad and Jolene's clasped fingers. "On behalf of her late father and as the lady of Sierra, I bless this union."

Father laid his good hand on top of their hands. "His mother and I give our blessing to this marriage."

Father and Lady Lorraine stepped back and took their seats in the front row.

Squeezing Jolene's fingers, Shad led her to the front of the dining room. Leith and Jeremiah took their places at the front where they could see the whole room. Lydia, Abigail, and Renna stood off to the side.

The minister began speaking about marriage. Shad tried to pay attention, but it was rather difficult with Jolene's hands in his and her smile twitching her mouth and his own heart beating in his throat.

Movement caught Shad's attention. Jamie Cavendish, Leith's trainee, slipped along the edge the room, eased next to Leith, and whispered something in his ear. Leith started, gripped his knives, and whispered something to Jeremiah before he crept along the edge of the room and out the door, Jamie at his heels.

What was going on? Shad pulled his attention back to Jolene. Whatever the problem, Leith was taking care of it, just like he was supposed to. By the time Shad and Jolene said their vows, Leith had retaken his place at the front, looking no worse than he had before.

"You may kiss the bride."

Shad leaned forward and kissed Jolene.

And he would fight the entire war all over again just for that moment.

Partway through the feasting, Shad and Jolene slipped from the room. Shad kissed Jolene's forehead. "I'll be up in a minute. Just checking on security."

Shad found Leith sitting on the manor's front step, his bad leg stretched out in front of him. Leith eyed him. "What are you doing out here?"

Shad leaned against the doorway. "What was all that earlier in the ceremony? Trouble?"

"Nothing to worry about. A few bandits thought the wedding would be a good time to try to steal a few horses. They didn't make it past the stable doors before they got caught." Leith shrugged and cast a glance over the hill, as if checking for any more bandits.

"Make sure you get some rest tonight. With most the guardsmen of both Sierra and Walden on duty tonight, this is about the safest place in all of Acktar." Shad crossed his arms. Leith's dedication was commendable, but he was still healing.

Leith checked his knives. "The hordes of guards you have on patrol are good enough for bandits, but I'm here just in case someone decides to get sneaky. Go on inside. No one will attack anyone in this manor tonight."

With a smile, Shad turned and stepped back inside. He had been right to ask Leith to guard his back tonight. But, then again, Jolene had also been right. In some ways, Leith was still a Blade.

And right now, that was a very good thing.

TO THE FAR GREAT MOUNTAINS

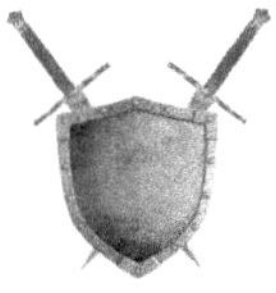

A Novella

1

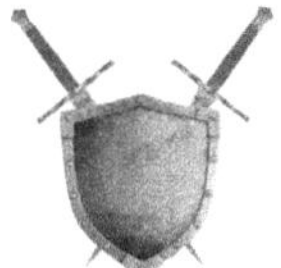

Leith squeezed Renna's shoulders. "We won't be gone long. Maybe a week and a half at the most. Martyn hadn't wanted to go at all, but King Keevan's letter seemed to indicate that he felt it would do both Martyn and the town of Flayin Falls good."

That's what Leith was hoping too, though he was nearly as jittery as Martyn at the thought of getting near that town. He hadn't personally witnessed what had happened to Martyn there, but hearing about it and seeing the burns had been bad enough. Even though two years had passed, the scars were still there.

"I'll be fine. I have Owen, Brandi, and Kayleigh—even if she doesn't know why you and Martyn are going—looking after me. And I'll look after the baby." Renna rested a hand on the bump filling out her dress. "Don't worry. We'll be fine."

Leith rested his hand on top of hers. It was hard not to

worry, not when he had both her and their unborn child to worry about.

His child. Something choking and painful lodged in his throat.

It wasn't, perhaps, the excitement he should be feeling at being a father in a little over two months. More like panic. Or terror. A crush of memory that had him pacing their cabin at night or huddled in the root cellar counting the jars of canned vegetables to convince himself that Renna would never end up like his mother. She was the lady of Stetterly. She was able to provide for herself and a family without him and, if he should ever become like his father, she had the power to have him arrested and locked up for the rest of his life.

Perhaps it shouldn't be a comforting thought. But it was. He'd rather cut off his own right arm than ever hurt Renna.

"Leith." Renna gently rested her hands on his cheeks, forcing him to look at her. Her gaze searched his face, as if she could read each of his thoughts written there. After two years of marriage, she probably could. "Martyn has his own nightmares and shadows to face on this trip, but he isn't the only one with a past that still haunts him. Don't think I don't know how much you've struggled to sleep lately."

He rested his forehead against hers. Why couldn't he let go of this fear? Perhaps because a part of him wondered what would happen if he did. What if that was how his father started? There must have been a moment when his father had started down the path that turned him from a man his mother would marry to a man who only drank, gambled, and took out his frustrations on his wife and son. "I don't want to ever..."

"I know." Renna brushed her thumb over his cheek. "You don't want to become like your father. But, Leith, you aren't your father. Yes, love is a choice, and both you and I have to choose each and every day to love each other and show each other gentleness and kindness. But that doesn't mean you have to live in constant terror of making a wrong choice. Fear will only make you hold yourself distant."

Fear. He wasn't sure how to conquer it once and for all. Not in this. Every time he thought he set this particular fear aside, it came back. On those nights pacing the cabin unable to sleep for the tightness in his chest, he prayed and begged and pleaded that God would keep him from following in his father's footsteps. It was his own weakness that he couldn't rest even then.

He took Renna's hands in his. "I wish I could talk to your father. Whenever you talk about him, I can tell you never had any reason to fear him."

And that was a strange thing to think about. A relationship with a father that didn't include fear. He had a taste of it in the way Lord Alistair had done his best to treat Leith like a son, yet even that hadn't started that way. There had been plenty of fear at the start, when Leith had been a loyal Blade and Lord Alistair a leader in the Resistance.

Renna squeezed his hands, her smile going soft, her eyes distant. "If there is one thing I remember about my father, it's that he always gave us an abundance of love. Hugs. Smiles. Twirling us around the meadow. Laughing. Telling stories. Brandi and I never had to doubt that we had his heart. It never occurred to us that a father could be anything other than kind and loving and gentle. That's what I want for our child. Oh, I know you'll love them, but I don't want you to hold back from giving a hug, a smile, a helping hand, because you're too focused on your worry about that helping hand turning into a hurting hand."

He breathed out a sigh, the tension still aching in his chest. "I know, I know. But that's part of the fear. I fear becoming like my father, but I also fear I won't be enough like your father, and I'll disappoint you."

Renna opened her mouth, paused, and closed her eyes.

His fear was founded, if it was taking Renna this long to come up with an answer for it.

"You're right. I will have to be careful not to constantly compare you with my father. To me, my father is still a perfect father. Perhaps because he was killed when I was still young, before adulthood could show me the imperfect cracks in his shining armor." Renna met his gaze. "While my father is a good example of what it is to be a father, I will do my best not to expect you to be exactly like him. Instead, I'll expect you to be a God-fearing father in your own particular way."

"And I'll strive to be the father God is calling me to be without being crippled by the fear of failing." Leith rested his forehead against Renna's. Talking with her had eased some of the tension. Hopefully by the time the baby was born, he could banish this fear entirely.

He had roughly two months, one week, and five days to make that happen.

As Martyn rode through the scrub junipers and pines in the rocky foothills of the Sheered Rock Hills, he kept the southern horizon in the corner of his eye. There the hills dropped away until the faint hint of the rolling prairie crested the horizon before dropping out of sight.

It was illogical, really, to be so nervous about getting this close to Flayin Falls. It wasn't like the town itself was going to jump the miles to grab him.

Irrational, maybe. But that town didn't exactly hold great memories.

At least Leith, riding on his right, and Shad on his left had the good sense not to ask probing, annoying questions. Owen might have, if he been here, but he'd stayed behind in Stetterly. It would've been harder to pass this off as a secret Blade Marshal mission if Owen had come along. Kayleigh would definitely have been suspicious then, rather than simply worried.

He drew in a deep breath of the cool, spring air, tinged with the spruce and earth scent of the mountains. It had been nearly two years since he'd been this close to Flayin Falls. One year, ten months, two weeks, and three days, to be exact. Not that the day was at all etched into his memory.

Not etched. Burned.

He led the way over a crest of a hill, and there in the hollow was Kayleigh's cabin. At least, what was left of it. The roof and most of the walls were gone, along with the interior walls and the floorboards. All that remained was a two-log high wall and the foundation stones.

Men—and a few women—bustled around the remaining logs, prying the notched and jointed ends apart before lifting and laying the log on a pile, where it was bundled with several other logs behind a team of six oxen. From there, the oxen would haul it down from the mountains where it would be carted from Flayin Falls to Walden before being floated down the Ondieda River to Stetterly.

A pang shot through his chest. He had good memories here. This glade was a beautiful spot, nestled in the trees with the Sheered Rock Hills rising above it and the prairie falling away below, out of side behind the crags of the foothills. And Kayleigh loved this place.

But the neighboring town was something of a downside.

Too bad most of the citizens of that town were in the glade, taking apart Kayleigh's cabin, and Martyn was going to have to face them.

It was time. He'd forgiven everyone else, and now God was calling him to face this part of his past too.

As if sensing his hesitation, both Shad and Leith nudged their horses to lead the way down the slope.

Shad halted his chestnut in front of a young man standing to one side of the workers. The man looked to be about the same age as Shad with brown hair and a wide smile.

Was this the younger brother that had been put in charge of Flayin Falls after Dean Westin had his position as regent revoked for allowing Martyn to be burned?

Martyn drew in a deep breath has he halted Wanderer and swung down. Surely after two years he was healed enough—both body and mind—to be able to handle this.

Shad stepped forward and shook the young man's hand. "Looks like you're almost finished."

"It's been going smoothly. I've made sure they remained motivated." The man glanced between Martyn and Leith, as if trying to figure out which one had requested all this work.

Martyn tried not to shift. Yes, this was a lot of work for

mushy, sentimental nonsense. After all, in the end these were just logs and boards. But these logs and boards had been shaped by Kayleigh's father, the father she'd loved dearly. The least he could do was give back a piece of what she'd given up to move to Stetterly.

Shad gestured at Leith. "This is Leith Torren. You might recognize him from his reports to the Gathering of Nobles. And this," Shad waved at Martyn, "is Martyn Hamish. Martyn, this is Matthias Westin."

Westin stuck out his hand. "It's good to meet you, and I want to offer you my sincere apology for what happened in my town two years ago."

After only a moment's hesitation, Martyn forced himself to shake Westin's hand. It was a firm handshake, but not too firm as if he was trying to prove something.

There was something in Westin's look. If not for Westin's brother, Martyn might almost like him.

"Thanks again for doing this." Martyn nodded toward the disassembled cabin.

Westin shrugged. "It was the least this town could do, considering what happened. It's been good for them. They've experienced good progress in making amends."

Something in the tone of his voice sounded more like an adult talking fondly about the teenagers he was raising than a regent talking about the town under him. Perhaps with a town like Flayin Falls, it wasn't much different than herding a pack of children.

"And it's been good for me too." Westin gave something of a laugh and shook his head. "Growing up, I thought I was going to be a minister. Did a lot of the studying and everything. But then with Respen in power, my brothers sent me to Eagle Heights, and instead of the ministry, I ended up in King Keevan's army. I learned a lot from him. Maybe someday I'll go back into the ministry when I hand this town over to my nephew, but right now, I'm content to be here trying to bring this town past its bitterness."

Martyn eyed Westin. What was he supposed to say after a soul-baring speech like that?

Westin scratched at the back of his neck. "Sorry. I have been told I have a habit of becoming verbose."

"Uh..." Martyn glanced toward Shad. Shad was one of those stuffy lords' sons. Surely he would know what to say.

Shad bobbed his head toward the workers around the cabin. "Shouldn't we get going?"

"Ah, yes." Westin led them closer to the cabin. "Jacob."

One of the men working to remove one of the logs left what he was doing and straightened.

Martyn stiffened. It was the healer from Flayin Falls.

The healer halted in front of Martyn, his gaze darting to the trees, the sky, the grass below their boots. "I..." The man coughed into his hand.

"Jacob." Westin's voice had a stern tone to it.

The healer took a deep breath. "I apologize to you and Kayleigh Ainsley for turning you away that day when you came to me for help. It was my duty as a healer to help and not harm, and instead I harmed by turning you away when she was injured and by turning my back when you were..."

Martyn swallowed. Even after nearly two years, this whole taking apologies and giving forgiveness was only marginally easier. "Thank you for the apology."

Westin patted the healer on the back, then waved to someone else. "Kevin."

The storekeeper from the mercantile. Martyn tried to stay relaxed. This man, at least, hadn't actively done anything to Martyn, at least that Martyn knew about. The storekeeper had overcharged Kayleigh after Respen took over the country and her father was killed.

Unlike the healer, the storekeeper at least met Martyn's gaze. For a moment, anyway. "I guess my apology isn't really for you. If you could pass it along to Miss Ainsley?"

Martyn could only manage to nod.

The storekeeper let out a loud breath. "I wronged Miss Ainsley for months. I have calculated how much I...well, it's more than I can pay back at the moment. I will, if she wishes me to. But if there is anything I can do for you or her, please let me know."

Martyn nodded. "Thank you. I will let you know if I think of anything."

The storekeeper turned to go.

"Wait." Martyn held up a hand. "Actually, there is something you can do for me."

2

Kayleigh parried Eric's blow, using the momentum of her practice sword to throw his sword wide. With a sweep with her other hand, she used her practice knife to slip past his guard and poke him in the rib cage.

"Ouch." Eric Millen, one of the young men of Stetterly who formed part of Stetterly's reserve guards, nearly dropped his sword when he started to press a hand to the spot she'd jabbed.

"You have to keep an eye on both of your opponent's hands." Kayleigh gave him a thwack on the arm with her practice sword for good measure. "Bandits aren't going to fight fair and come at you only one hand at a time."

"But fighting with two hands is *hard*." Eric backed off, rubbing alternately at his arm and ribs.

Yes, it was. It was something Kayleigh hadn't been profi-cient in herself until she'd started courting a former Blade turned Blade Marshal who had insisted that if she was going to be the captain of Stetterly's guards and carry around a sword, then she might as well be as deadly as possible.

Kayleigh swiped sweat from her forehead with her sleeve. "That's enough combat for now. I want you to practice another hour with the post, striking with both your sword and your knife."

"Yes, ma'am." Eric saluted and tromped across the small field Renna had set aside for Kayleigh to use as a practice area until he faced the upright, battered post set into the ground. With a deep breath, Eric started whacking at the post with a steady, if a bit stolid, rhythm.

She was trying, but there was only so much she could do when Eric's heart really wasn't in it. He was a farmer's son through and through, and all he really wanted to do was get back to helping in his father's fields. At least he had volunteered for Stetterly's reserve guards, and he practiced faithfully at whatever task she set him to. That was something.

After setting several more of the men and two of the young women to their practice, Kayleigh headed for the main street of town. It was time she relieved Owen from guard duty, but first she wanted to change into clean clothes.

On one end of the short, gravel road that made up Stetterly's main street, Kayleigh climbed the porch of the small cottage where she rented a room from Lily Stevens, a woman who lost her husband when Respen's army attacked Stetterly.

Kayleigh knocked, then stepped inside. Lily was setting another pot of water to boiling, the steam filling the small kitchen until Kayleigh struggled to breathe in the humidity. One of the children was crying, and the others were playing some raucous game on the other side of the kitchen.

Dodging around the chaos, Kayleigh headed for her tiny bedroom, closed the door, and leaned against it.

What she wouldn't give for a place of her own. She could probably save up the money and have boards shipped down the river from Walden so that she could have a house built. But it seemed wasteful, considering she wouldn't—shouldn't—need it for that much longer.

If a certain Blade Marshal would hurry up and propose.

It made sense to take their relationship slowly. He'd just returned to his faith, and her faith had some rockiness to iron out. They'd needed the time.

But they'd been courting for nearly two years. Two and a half since they'd met. Surely it was about time. She was ready. Ready for her own home with a husband and maybe children, if that was God's will for them. She was ready to spend long evenings with Martyn by the fire, listening to a blizzard howling outside the little cabin nestled in the Spires Canyon.

What if he didn't intend to propose?

She shook that thought away. No, she wasn't going to give in to doubting him. He took loyalty too seriously to have toyed with her affections and his own for the past two years.

Maybe he was waiting for her to give some sort of signal that she was ready for the next step? She thought she'd done some hinting, but maybe she would have to just flat out tell him.

That's what she'd do. Just as soon as he got back from whatever mission had called him and Leith away this time. Hopefully this mission wouldn't take too long and he would be home sooner rather than later.

Shaking her head, she switched into a clean shirt,

buckled her sword sheath to her belt, then donned the protective leather vest. The hardened leather would give some limited protection in slowing a stab and might stop a shallow cut, but it was for looks more than anything. Something to make sure she looked official. Owen had a similar vest that he wore when on duty.

After navigating past the children, Kayleigh left the cottage and strode back the way she'd come, past the training field and over the crest of the hill at the far side of Stetterly. There at the end of a narrow track nestled beside the Spires Canyon stood Renna and Leith's cabin, a partially finished stable rising to one side of it.

That was odd. On a nice day like this, Kayleigh would've expected the workers to be busy raising the last few logs on the walls and beginning on the roof.

As she approached the cabin, Owen strolled from around the far side of the half-finished stable and met her on the track in front of the cabin. She waved at the hills around them. "Everything all quiet?"

"Yep. Like it usually is." Owen grinned and patted his sword hilt. "But that's the lot of a guard's life. Hours of standing around guarding a perfectly peaceful spot until suddenly it isn't so peaceful."

"Exactly." The very reason Martyn never would've made it as a guard. How he managed to find enough patience for staking out a suspected bandit's hideout was beyond her. "How's Renna today?"

"Sick of being pregnant and having to make frequent trips to the outhouse and annoyed that she needs my escort." Owen heaved a huge sigh. "I don't know about you, but I certainly don't want to have to face Leith if something happened to Renna because I wasn't diligent enough in my job."

"Me either." Kayleigh adjusted one of the buckles on her vest where it had been pinching her skin. The joys of guard duty. Keeping a watchful eye on their lady at all times. Wouldn't want her to be surprised by bandits while making a trip to the outhouse, especially not now of all times. And no one wanted to contemplate what Leith would be like if something happened to Renna considering how overprotective he already was. "Anything else to report? Why aren't the workers finishing the stable?"

"Renna gave them the day off. She wanted a little peace and quiet today. I think they might be working on a different project in the canyon." Owen shrugged. "Nothing else to report."

Still odd, but perhaps Renna had decided that work on the new flour mill along the river in the Spires Canyon was more important than finishing the stables. After all, they still had another two months before the baby was due to be born and Jamie and Ranson needed to move into the room that was going to be built for them in the stables' loft.

"All right, then you're dismissed for the rest of the day." As Owen headed for the trail that would lead him down to the cabin he currently shared with Martyn, Kayleigh set out for the surrounding hills. She'd scout the perimeter once before she checked in with Renna. Not that she didn't trust Owen's word that everything was quiet and secure, but it never hurt to check for herself.

As she turned and headed north along the Spires Canyon, she halted. The faint sound of hammering drifted on the breeze, but it seemed to be coming from the north, rather than from the south where the new flour mill was located.

She cocked her head, but the sound was so faint that she couldn't be sure. Why would someone be building something in that direction? Should she investigate?

No. That would leave Renna unguarded. Besides, Owen had set out in that direction. If it was anything to worry about, he would hear and investigate.

As she passed behind the stable beside the large paddock, she waved at Brandi. Brandi was brushing down Ranson's horse Snapper, dodging a nip from the horse's teeth. Brandi just swatted at the horse's nose and kept on brushing. How a sweet boy like Ranson put up with such an ornery horse, she didn't know.

Once she finished scouting the perimeter, Kayleigh headed for the cabin, knocked, and entered at Renna's call.

Renna sat on the bench, a ledger open on the kitchen table in front of her, though she had to sit farther back from the table due to being seven months pregnant. When she glanced up, she smiled and snapped the ledger shut with enough force to cause it to give a sharp thump. "Kayleigh, good. I have a few things to see to in town, and I didn't want to ask Owen to come along when he was nearly off duty. I think Brandi is coming too, as least for part of the way, so she can get in a few hours of practice."

Kayleigh nodded. Until the baby was born, Brandi was technically Renna's heir. With just Kayleigh and Owen as full time guards, they sometimes had to choose between guarding Renna and guarding Brandi, and that meant Brandi remained unguarded rather too often for Kayleigh's taste. Brandi, though, relished every opportunity to run about without a guard hovering.

Not that Kayleigh could blame her. Brandi had spent much of her childhood running free around Stetterly without any guards. Going back to the more rigid procedures of having guards and acting like the heir to Stetterly would be somewhat stifling. At least Brandi was training to be one of the reserve guards, so it wasn't like she was completely defenseless.

Renna pushed away from the table and stood. Small as she was, the baby bump was rather noticeable. "How was training this morning?"

Kayleigh huffed out a breath as she fell into step with Renna. "They're making progress. Slowly."

"You sound like you're trying to convince yourself of that." Renna shut the cabin's door behind them and set out down the dirt track. If she could hear the faint sounds of hammering, she didn't seem to notice. Perhaps that meant it really was nothing to worry about.

"Maybe." Kayleigh shook her head. "They're doing their best. It isn't easy to make progress when they have to train between the long hours of farm life. There's always planting or weeding or harvesting that has to be done. But it was a good idea to go to a more flexible training schedule where they train at whatever point of the day they can be spared. It was too hard to get everyone together at the same time during the day."

"I'm glad it's working." Renna glanced off to the distance. "Perhaps the next time Stetterly is under attack, things won't be as bad."

Next time. That was always the fear. The day they

prepared for. Stetterly remained small, even after two years of some growth thanks to the Blade Marshal headquarters being here. Not that the headquarters were all that much. A small bunkhouse had been built to the north of Renna and Leith's cabin while Leith still ran most of the day-to-day paperwork out of the cabin kitchen.

But two years still wasn't enough time to erase the pain. Women still outnumbered men. Many of the children were fatherless. Half of the men in the town were still boys in their teens doing their best to fill a man's boots to take care of their family.

But Stetterly was determined to become stronger than before. And Kayleigh was going to do her best to make that happen.

Now if only she could have her own cabin so that she felt less like a guest and more like she belonged. Like this was truly her home.

3

"You know, we are putting a lot of effort into helping you propose when you weren't around to help us when we proposed."

Martyn blew out a breath as he hoisted the other end of the log from Shad. "Considering both of you successfully got married, it wasn't like my help was needed."

"He has us there." Leith was perched on the wall perpendicular to the wall that needed the log Martyn and Shad were lifting.

Martyn gave one last shove and set the log in place. Leith was ready with a peg and a hammer to secure it in place.

"Do you think you're going to mess this up so badly that you're going to need this much help?" Owen panted from the corner opposite from Martyn as he heaved a log into place with one of the workers from Stetterly.

Martyn wasn't going to answer that. Proposing involved a lot of gushing mushiness and baring one's heart and soul and uncomfortable stuff like emotions and promising forever. Yes, of course he was going to mess it all up.

And this was one thing he really, really didn't want to bungle. Kayleigh deserved a better proposal than a half-hearted, gruff one. She deserved all the mushiness he could muster. She had moved to Stetterly, left the home where she'd grown up, been patient with him for two years, and hadn't turned her back through all the struggles of those first few months as he'd worked to regain his strength and his faith.

Leith halted his hammering and peered down at Martyn. "Did I really look that...dreamy when I was planning to propose to Renna?"

"Dreamy?" Martyn wasn't even sure how to go about showing how insulted he was over that word choice.

"Oh, you were way worse." Jamie carried one end of the next log over to Martyn. At sixteen, Jamie was all lanky arms and legs. "Martyn at least tries to hide it."

"You still look like that." Ranson brought his end of the next log to Shad. As soon as the words were out of his mouth, Ranson darted a glance to Leith as if worried he'd spoken out of turn.

Leith navigated from his perch on the one wall to a new position on the log Martyn and Shad had just heaved into place. "Shad? Do you have any comments to add about how obviously lovestruck I am over my wife?"

"No. I'd be more worried if you weren't. Especially right now." Something in Shad's expression sobered and reminded Martyn that Shad and Jolene had suffered their own share of both joy and tragedy in the past two years. Jolene had been nearly as far along as Renna when they'd lost the baby. But that sorrow had been tempered with joy a year later, only four months ago, when their daughter Hannah had been born safe and healthy.

Martyn took the end of the log from Jamie and prepared to heave this one into place. At the rate they were going, they should have the cabin completed by tomorrow afternoon.

It wasn't as simple a task as rebuilding the cabin exactly as it had been in the hollow near Flayin Falls, although that task had been made immensely easier thanks to Matthias Westin's wisdom in numbering the logs of each wall and providing a diagram for putting the numbered logs back together.

The tricky part came in joining this cabin with the smaller one that was already in the hidden clearing in the canyon. That cabin, the one he and Owen had been sharing for nearly two years now, was a basic, two-room cabin that worked for two bachelors, but wouldn't be sufficient if children were something in Martyn and Kayleigh's future.

It was kind of hard to picture. Him with grubby, screaming children underfoot? He barely had the patience for helping Leith with training future Blade Marshals, and those were teenage boys nearly full grown.

But maybe it would be different when those grubby, screaming children were his?

No, the difference would be that those children would also be Kayleigh's.

"Uh, Martyn? Are we going to build this cabin or are you just going to stand there staring off into the sky?" Shad shifted the other end of the log that he held.

There wasn't much Martyn could say to that. He heaved up on the end of his log and set it into place.

KAYLEIGH BLINKED AGAINST THE BLINDFOLD OVER HER EYES, peering down at the small patches of light she could see on either side of her nose. Martyn was being awfully cryptic as he led her, blindfolded, down a path that, based on the slope, had to be the trail into the Spires Canyon. "Are you kidnapping me? Because I would've thought kidnapping was a little illegal."

"It's only illegal if you aren't an adult or if you aren't going willingly." Martyn's gentle grip on her arm led her around something in the trail. "You are going willingly, aren't you?"

She smacked his shoulder lightly with the back of her hand. At least, she thought it was his shoulder. "You'd know if I wasn't. There would be a lot of kicking, screaming, and stabbing involved. Still, where are we going?"

"It's a secret. Thus the blindfold."

Kayleigh huffed out a breath. Ever since he'd returned that afternoon, Martyn had been rather mysterious. He and Leith. And Shad, who had apparently decided to tag along to visit Stetterly. As if that wasn't suspicious enough.

She steadied herself as loose gravel slid beneath her boots. Just where it always did on the trail into the canyon, near the base. As she expected, the ground leveled out to rocky gravel.

Why was Martyn leading her blindfolded down this particular trail? And acting...strange. The only reason she could think of that would cause Martyn to go all odd was that he was about to propose.

But she couldn't get her hopes up. Perhaps he just planned to surprise her with a nice picnic next to the river.

The gentle pressure of his hand on her elbow steered her to the left, and she could hear the gurgle of the Ondieda River to her right. This was the same direction as his cabin in the hidden nook.

Sure enough, he turned her left again, and the cool shadows provided by the walls of the narrow opening to the hidden valley washed over her. "Martyn, please tell me you didn't go to all this trouble just to show off the fact that you and Owen actually took the time to clean your cabin."

"Now why would I do that?" Martyn's chuckle came from near her ear. "Besides, I've been gone. You know how neat Owen manages to be on his own."

"So the mess is usually your fault? Remind me, why am I courting you again?"

"I'm gone so often you forget about my bad habits by the time I return." Instead of heading straight across the grassy clearing, Martyn tugged her to the right. "All right. You can take the blindfold off."

Kayleigh pulled it off, wincing when she yanked out several strands of hair that had gotten caught in the knot. She was facing Martyn in the stand of pine trees near the entrance of the hidden clearing, her back to his cabin. As far as she could tell, there wasn't anything different about the trees behind him. When she started to glance around to find something that would be worth blindfolding her to lead her here, Martyn gripped her shoulders to keep her facing him.

She rested a hand on her sword hilt, opening her mouth to make some comment about stabbing him when she noticed the look on his face. Serious. No trace of a smile.

Slightly ill, as if he was concentrating to keep his stomach where it belonged. "Are you all right? Did something happen while you and Leith were on your mission?"

Why lead her all the way out here blindfolded if that was the case? Why not just take her aside and tell her?

Martyn slid his hands down her arms until he held her hands. He swallowed, his right hand twitching in hers as if he wanted to run it through his hair. "Two years ago, we made a deal. If you put up with me, I was going to get around to asking you a certain question."

She swallowed and nodded. Was it a good thing or a bad thing that he was bringing up that deal?

"I also told you I was going to ask Leith how he did it since he obviously got something right." Something of a smile tipped the corner of Martyn's mouth. "As far as Leith—and Renna—remembers, this is about where they were standing when he proposed."

Martyn was proposing. A warmth was spreading in Kayleigh's chest until it took everything in her to stay as serious as he was. "And then what?"

"Then he revealed his deep, dark secrets. Not sure why that worked, and I told you my deep, dark secrets years ago now, so I guess we can skip that part." Martyn stepped closer, close enough for her to see the flecks of colors in his brown eyes. "Although, I do have one, last secret to confess."

"What secret would that be?" She could barely form the words with her tongue sticking to the roof of her dry mouth. Her pulse built in her ears, and she wasn't sure it was excitement or fear or worry over what other secret he had yet to reveal.

He pulled one of his hands free from hers and brushed his fingers across her cheek. "Just that I love you."

"That's no secret." He'd had her all worried for nothing. Still, she savored the words. He said them so little in the past two years. Not that he needed to say them when he showed his love each and every day.

"But it is a secret how much I love you." He squeezed her hands tighter. "It shouldn't be. You deserve all the sappy, mushy stuff I can manage to say out loud, and you deserve to know by every action that I mean what I say."

"Martyn..." She rested a hand on his chest, feeling the steady beat of his heart. She'd known from the day she started courting him that he wasn't the type to spout "romantic nonsense" as he would call it. She didn't need that sort of stuff anyway. She wasn't the type to get all mushy, gushy back. "You don't have to..."

He pressed a finger over her mouth. "You'd better let me finish. It may be the only time you get such a romantic speech out of me. Might as well enjoy it."

She swallowed and forced herself to nod. Her throat was too choked to say anything.

Martyn drew in a deep breath. "Kayleigh, I want to marry you. I promise I will love you. I will love any children God might give us. I promise that while I may ride away for my missions, I will do everything in my power to return and will never, ever abandon you. I may not be able to promise wealth, but I can promise a good, happy life. So? Will you marry me?"

He'd proposed. Finally.

4

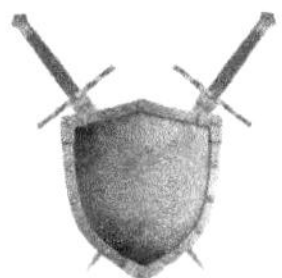

Martyn held his breath. His heart might have even stopped beating. No, that wasn't it. It was beating too hard in his ears. At this rate he wouldn't even be able to hear her answer if she ever managed to give it.

It had probably only been seconds, but minutes could've passed for the ache squeezing his chest.

Kayleigh's shoulders relaxed, and she breathed out, "It's about time."

Wait, what? That was her answer? After he'd bared his heart and spoke all that romantic rot?

Then she wrapped her arms around his neck and kissed him. She spoke between kisses. "Of course. I'll marry you. I'll move into. Your tiny cabin. I don't care."

He could've kept on kissing her, but he had his surprise to show her. There would be plenty of time for kissing later. He pulled back. "Actually, about my cabin. Turn around."

She turned. Her mouth fell open, and she pressed her hands to her face.

Martyn rested his hands on her shoulders as she took in the sight before her.

Her father's cabin now dominated the far end of the valley, recreated nearly exactly how it had been in its hollow near Flayin Falls, except that now the smaller cabin had been joined into it on the left. While they couldn't see it from here, the workers had built a lean-to onto the corner on the back where the two cabins met, providing a sheltered spot for the woodpile that could be accessed easily from the cabin.

"Is this...surely it can't be..." Kayleigh leaned against him.

He wrapped his arms around her. "It's your father's cabin. It turns out the new regent in Flayin Falls was more than happy to help when I approached him with this idea through King Keevan. Both Matthias Westin and King Keevan figured Flayin Falls owed us more than a few favors."

"Really?" Kayleigh glanced over her shoulder. "They really helped with this?"

"Disassembled the whole cabin and hauled it to Walden. Lord Alistair took over after that to get the logs shipped down the river to here." Martyn pulled away from her, took her hand, and tugged her toward the cabin. "That's not the only favor they sent along. Come on."

He led her onto the porch—the one he'd crossed so many times when he'd stayed at Old Man Bendwick's cabin that winter in the Sheered Rock Hills—and held the door open for her to enter.

The kitchen was laid out exactly as it had been, complete

with the stone fireplace set into the wall. On Leith's advice, he'd added a small, brick baking oven into one side of the fireplace, though it was smaller than the one Leith had built since Kayleigh didn't enjoy baking as much as Renna did.

The table—the same one where they'd sat for so many meals before—took up most of the space in the kitchen, except that now there was a large opening in the wall across from the kitchen. This led into what had been the kitchen of the smaller cabin but had been turned into a parlor, complete with a single settee generously provided by Lord Alistair and lacy curtains from several of the ladies in Flayin Falls.

"It's home." Kayleigh traced a finger along the table's top. "I can't believe you did all this, but it's...I can't even begin to thank you."

He took her hand again. "You gave up so much two years ago. I don't want you to marry me like that, having given up your home, the mountains you love so much, the place you grew up. I can't move the mountains to Stetterly, but I can give you back this little piece."

Besides, it seemed right. This cabin was Kayleigh's, its boards soaked with the love she'd had from the father who'd raised her so well. That was the sort of home he wanted for Kayleigh and for his family.

"I love it." Kayleigh glanced at the door to the bedroom that had been hers, her mouth tipping into a smile at one corner. "Makes me want to move in right now, but that's hardly proper."

"Not even close to proper." He grinned back. "Guess you'll have to get started on your wedding dress right away."

He pulled away from her long enough to grab the

saddlebag he'd left by the door. He produced a neatly folded bundle of fabric, much as he had over two years ago, though this fabric was light blue and made of the fine silk that ladies like Renna wore. An expensive fabric, but the storekeeper hadn't blinked considering how much he owed Kayleigh.

Kayleigh took it, stroking it with her fingertips. But when she glanced up at him, her eyes had that twinkle and her mouth quirked. "Will you stick around long enough to see me wear it this time?"

And there, standing in the doorway where he once turned and ran, Martyn grinned back. "I promise. I'm done running away."

He leaned in to kiss her, but a knock sounded on the door.

What was someone doing here? Leith, Owen, and Shad knew Martyn was busy proposing and wouldn't interrupt. At least, he didn't think they would.

With a sigh, he stepped away from Kayleigh and opened the door.

Leith stood on the porch, a piece of paper in his hand. There was something in his eyes and the hard line of his mouth. "Sorry to interrupt, but..." he held up the paper, "I got a message from the town of Ably. Blade Marshal Adam Sullivan was killed there three nights ago."

Ice flowed from Martyn's fingers, down into his toes, freezing him to the floor. Adam Sullivan was one of the two Blade Marshals assigned to patrol the middle section of Acktar's southern border, especially the prairie around the towns of Ably and Dyman. In the two years since the Blade Marshals were founded, they hadn't had one of their number killed. Hurt, of course. Injured to the point they had to retire from the Blade Marshals, yes. But this was the first death.

Worse, Sullivan had a wife and two young children.

Martyn swallowed. "His killer?"

"Escaped."

In that one word, Martyn knew, even without the steel in Leith's eyes and the cold in his voice.

Martyn wasn't going to be here with Kayleigh planning a wedding. He was going to be with Leith, tracking a killer to the ends of Acktar if necessary.

And it might be necessary. By the time he and Leith could reach Ably, Sullivan's killer would have a six-day head start.

It wouldn't matter. A Blade Marshal had been killed. His killer would not—could not—be allowed to escape. He would be brought to justice no matter how long and far Leith and Martyn had to track him.

"I'll grab my pack. Will Shad be coming with us?"

"No. As my second-in-command, he's going to be staying here to see to covering the gap left by the two of us and Sullivan. Blade Marshal Nolan was injured and won't be in much shape to patrol for a while." Leith glanced over Martyn's shoulder, nodded toward Kayleigh, and turned to go. "I'll be with the horses when you're ready."

With that, Leith left, shutting the door behind him. Giving Martyn a few more minutes to say goodbye to Kayleigh.

When Martyn turned to Kayleigh, she was holding the saddlebag he always kept packed and the two additional knives he wasn't wearing since he'd been expecting to spend the afternoon with Kayleigh.

Not even a full day with her before he had to leave again, this time for who knew how long.

"Kayleigh, I..." What could he say when he had to leave only minutes after proposing?

She held out the saddlebag. "I know. You have to go. I've had two years of courting you to get used to you leaving. You have to go, so go. I'll be here keeping Renna safe, my wedding dress ready, when you return."

This was his Kayleigh. No fuss. No tears. Strong enough to look after herself and guard Renna while she was at it.

Yet, somehow, he was the person she'd chosen to let catch her when she needed catching. And she was that person for him. The person with whom he could be vulnerable and broken, knowing she would be strength for him when he needed it.

He took the knives and saddlebag from her, then leaned in to give her a lingering kiss. "I'll write as often as I can. Stay safe."

"You, too." Kayleigh gripped his free hand. "I'll walk with you to the horses."

Once they hiked out of the canyon and reached the horses where Brandi and Jamie had them waiting, saddled, by the half-finished stables, there was no more time for mushy goodbyes or long kisses.

Only one more short kiss. A promise to write. A whispered *I love you.*

Then there was the familiar saddle, the easy movement of Wanderer's muscles beneath him, and the horizon before them.

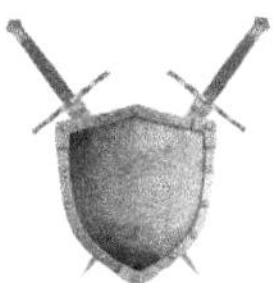

The town of Ably perched on a hill straddling the crossroads of the main trade route from the nations to the south of Acktar up to Nalgar and the dirt road running east-west that connected most of the southern towns in Acktar together. Thanks to this position along two major trading routes, the main street choked with wagons filled with goods as men and women bustled along actual boardwalks between the many shops.

All that trade meant that Ably had more wealth in hand —and thus more to steal—than many towns.

As Leith drew Valor to a halt in the valley in front of the town, Martyn halted Wanderer next to him. "What's the plan?"

Leith grimaced and pointed at the squat, stone manor sitting at the northwest corner of the crossroads. "I guess I'd better stop at the manor to introduce myself to Lord Spencer. Hopefully he doesn't toss me out on sight. Since his parents were killed by Blades, he might not be so eager to talk if he realizes who I am. While I'm doing that, I'd like you to find the healer's and talk to Nolan. See what information he can tell us about the man we'll be hunting."

Martyn scowled at the hustle and bustle before them. Already he itched to turn Wanderer around and hightail it back to the open prairie. He already didn't do so well with towns, but this town made Nalgar Castle look like a small, rustic village. "I don't have a good experience with talking to random healers. I was tossed out last time I tried."

Leith raised his eyebrows. "I'll trade you. You can talk to Lord Spencer."

"And probably have to deal with all the political posturing and that sort of rot." That would be worse than braving the town. Martyn didn't have the patience for fancy, smooth talking.

"That's what I thought." Leith dug his badge from its hidden pocket in his belt and pinned it to the front of his shirt. "No reason to hide our badges here. The more we flash them and look official, the more cooperative everyone will be."

Martyn fished out his own badge and pinned it on. Something about having that badge boldly displayed on his shirt made him sit up straighter. "Where should we meet afterwards? Looking at that helter-skelter town, I don't want to have to try to hunt you up there."

"We'll meet here in two hours. If you finish before then, get a list of witnesses and track them down to interview. Once I'm done with Lord Spencer, I'm going to give my condolences to Adam Sullivan's wife." Leith's shoulders hunched, as if already burdened with the weight of having to face the widow and the children of one of his Blade Marshals.

It was not a task Martyn envied. Perhaps he should offer to go along, but he wouldn't be anything other than a silent moral support, and he could do that role just as well from a distance. He would be more helpful interviewing those who witnessed Sullivan's death, getting a description and name of the killer, and finding a trail he and Leith could follow.

Leith nudged Valor into a walk, and Wanderer followed without Martyn's urging. They threaded their way through the riders and wagons clogging the streets, though people made an effort to make room for them as soon as they caught sight of the badges.

Even though only two years had passed since the Blade Marshals had been founded, people at least recognized the badge on sight, and many respected what it meant. Much of that respect was due to men like Adam Sullivan who had worn the badge and done his duty with integrity.

As Leith turned Valor into the gravel path leading up to the manor house, Martyn found the sign inscribed with the word *Healer* in black letters across the street. Guess it made sense to have the healer's office centrally located in a town like this.

After swinging down and tying Wanderer to the hitching rail, Martyn stepped inside, accompanied by the sound of a bell tinkling. The small entry room was small, barely holding the three chairs stationed along the portions of the wall not taken with doors.

"I'll be right with you." A man's deep voice called from

somewhere in the back rooms. Footsteps pounded on floor-boards a moment before a large man, taller and broader than Martyn stepped from the door facing Martyn. The man's gaze flicked up and down Martyn before focusing on his badge. "You must be the Blade Marshal sent to investigate."

"One of them. I'm Blade Marshal Hamish." Even after two years, saying his new title still sounded odd to his own ears, but in a good sort of way.

"I'm Nate Harvey, the healer." The big man jabbed a thumb back the way he'd come. "Are you here to see Blade Marshal Nolan?"

Martyn did his best not to stare at the man's muscled forearms. Healer and town wrestling champion perhaps? Guess one could never judge a man's occupation by his appearance, but this healer looked more like he spent his nights breaking up the tavern brawls rather than patching the men up afterwards. Maybe he did both. "Yes. Is he awake and able to have visitors?"

"Yep, and maybe telling you what happened will put him at ease enough so he can actually rest. He's been grouchier than a trapped bear." The man bobbed his head toward the door he'd just left. "He's in the back room. Last door on the left."

Heading in that direction, Martyn tipped Harvey a polite nod as he passed. As he stepped through the doorway, Martyn found himself in a short hallway with doors on either side. He strode to the last door on the left and knocked.

"Harvey, if that's you, go away. I don't want any more tonic and my bandages don't need changing and I'm about ready to hobble on out of here, see if I don't!" The voice was a tenor, one Martyn vaguely recognized from the few times he'd met Arthur Nolan. He and Adam Sullivan had spent a few months at Stetterly shortly after the Blade Marshals had been founded turning the skills they'd learned as scouts for the Resistance into the training they needed as Blade Marshals.

Martyn pushed the door open. "Not the healer. Blade Marshal Martyn Hamish."

Nolan lay propped up on the bed, the blanket only partially covering the bandages wrapped around his chest and one of his shoulders. His wiry, gray-brown hair frizzed out in all directions while a scruffy beard covered most of his face. But his eyes were still an alert, clear blue. He struggled to sit farther upright as he gaze flicked to Martyn, and he raised a stiff hand to his forehead in a military-style salute. "About time help arrived. I've been stuck in this blasted bed for nigh on six days and all the while that cur has been getting farther and farther away."

The way Nolan spat out that last sentence, he was working hard to hold back the harsher swear words that were springing to mind. As someone who had to fight the same impulse, Martyn could recognize the struggle.

Martyn sat in the one chair, pulled out a folded piece of paper, and one of the new-fangled pencils that a trader had brought into the country a year ago. So much handier than a quill for carrying around in a pocket, and they could be sharpened with one of Martyn's knives. Just about the best invention since the cookie. "Blade Marshal Torren and I intend to track down Sullivan's killer. What happened?"

Nolan sank back onto the pillow, lines cutting into his

face around his eyes. "Adam and I tracked down these three men that had been attacking trading wagons as they left the towns loaded with gold and coins after successfully trading goods. The gang was led by a man named Sean Grier. We caught up with them outside of Ably here, but when we tried to ambush them, we were ambushed instead. We got two of them, but Grier killed Adam, left me for dead, and hightailed it off south. He's probably close to the border by now."

Martyn tried not to let a hint of his thoughts show on his face. Grier would probably be well into Verden, the country to the south of Acktar, by the time Leith and Martyn could even reach the border.

But a Blade Marshal had died. Martyn didn't intend to let a little thing like a border and jurisdiction stop him this time, and he didn't think Leith did either. "What does Grier look like?"

After a few more minutes, Martyn had a description of Grier, the horse he'd been riding, and any recognizable stolen goods he'd had that could be used to track him.

As Nolan finished, he collapsed deeper into the pillows, looking worn beyond even the weakness of his wounds. "It should've been me that bought it, not Adam. I'm the dyed in the wool bachelor. No family who'd mourn my death. But Adam? He has that wife and those two kids. They shouldn't have lost him. It should've been me. I tried to make sure it was me, but..."

Nolan trailed off, squeezing his eyes shut.

There wasn't anything Martyn could say to undo that guilt. Not really. He could remind Nolan that Sullivan's death was Grier's fault. But the Blade Marshals were a brotherhood, and partners became as close as brothers due to the way they had to depend on each for their very lives. At least, that was the case for the six pairs of men that made up the Blade Marshals currently.

Well, five pairs and just Nolan now.

Martyn gave an awkward pat to Nolan's shoulder. "I know you'll do your best to look after his widow and children. And King Keevan has promised that the family of a fallen Blade Marshal will never go hungry."

"You can bet your last pair of boots I'll take care of them. Adam would've wanted that." Nolan shook his head and squinted up at Martyn. "But that hardly makes it better, does it?"

Martyn grimaced. He was right. Nothing would or could make this hurt any less.

This was the life Martyn was asking Kayleigh to join. It very well could be Kayleigh widowed someday with children to raise on her own.

Could he ask her to marry into this kind of life? Was it better to be like Arthur Nolan and never marry when doing a job like this?

LEITH PERCHED ON THE EDGE OF THE HARD-BACKED CHAIR IN the small parlor. Maisie Sullivan hunched on the settee across from him, her arms around her two children, a twelve-year-old boy and ten-year-old girl. All three had red rimmed eyes and hollow, shattered looks that tore at him. In the kitchen, family and friends bustled about making food.

"I'm so sorry for your loss, ma'am." It was such a small,

empty thing to say even if he meant it. But there was nothing more he could say at a time like this.

He'd had to face grief before when tracking down killers and bandits. But this time it was one of his men that had been killed.

It had been years since he'd felt this deep-down cold in his chest. There was barely any room to miss Renna with the ice running through his veins that ached to run this killer to the ground no matter how long it took.

The widow sniffed, nodded, and pressed another kiss into her daughter's hair. "You're going to catch my husband's killer?"

"I'm going to do my best. You have my word on that." Justice was a cold relief at a time like this, but it was all Leith could give her. He stood to leave. He'd already taken up too much of her time. "I'll be praying for you and your family."

None of them looked up as he left. Outside, he stood next to Valor for a minute, letting the horse's warmth soak into his fingers.

That could be Renna someday. Huddled in the parlor with their children, grieving over his sudden loss to a sword thrust, a knife in the dark, an arrow in the back.

What kind of husband was he that he didn't want to quit this job? What made him ride away when he had a wife and soon a family that needed him back at Stetterly?

He shook those thoughts away and swung onto Valor. Now wasn't the time for doubts. Not until after he'd caught Sullivan's killer.

When he returned to the spot on the hill outside of town, Martyn was already waiting. Martyn pointed toward the road south out of town. "Our killer's name is Sean Grier. I have a decent description of him, and the sheriff led me to the spot where they found Art Nolan wounded. I scouted around, and I think I found a set of tracks that belong to Grier's horse."

"Then let's go." Leith turned Valor to the south. They had a killer to catch.

6

Leith halted Valor and eased upright in the saddle, stretching his legs and knees. Four days of hard riding had brought them here, farther south than he'd ever traveled before.

Prairie surrounded them into the far distance, rolling hills in all directions, broken only by the occasional ranch house and herds of cattle or farmland. Behind them, a few buildings dotted the horizon. In the couple of years that the Blade Marshals had spent patrolling Acktar, the rougher element had been somewhat driven out, causing the rowdier drinking and gambling establishments to build just across the border into Verden.

At least, what everyone guessed was the border between Acktar and Verden. The border wasn't marked nor were there any distinguishing landmarks to show where one country ended and the other began, leaving a sort of gray area that both countries left alone. Keevan had been trying for years to get the Verdenish king to agree to a treaty to define and mark the border, but so far the Verdenish king had been unwilling to open negotiations.

Martyn stretched in the saddle as well, gazing around them. "We are definitely in Verden now, aren't we?"

Yes, they were, as best as anyone could guess. Even if they managed to find Grier, they didn't have jurisdiction here. They couldn't arrest him.

Beyond that, he and Martyn shouldn't even be here. As law enforcement officers from Acktar, it was an encroachment into Verden if they were caught here, causing an international incident that would have King Keevan tied up for weeks trying to calm.

Leith settled back into the saddle, focusing on the road disappearing into the far southern distance before them. While Martyn could only rarely pick out Grier's tracks from the muddle of hoofprints on the road, they hadn't seen any signs that Grier had left the road. At the tavern and small store they'd stopped at to resupply, the owner remembered Grier passing through four and a half days ago.

The smart thing to do was turn around. Give up. Admit that Grier had too much of a head start for them to catch.

But the ice was still in Leith's veins. Cold. Calculating. And those calculations told him that a Blade Marshal's killer could not be allowed to ride free. Word would spread that it was possible to kill a Blade Marshal and get away with it, and that would place him, Martyn, Shad, and the eight other Blade Marshals in Acktar at an even greater risk than the one they already took.

No, Sean Grier needed to be brought to justice to send a message to every bandit and half-baked schemer in Acktar that anyone who killed a Blade Marshal would be ruthlessly, relentlessly tracked down to the very ends of the earth if necessary.

"I don't know. The border isn't marked. For all I know, we're still in Acktar. What about you?" Leith glanced at Martyn.

"I see what you mean." Martyn's voice took on that knowing tone. "It's not like I can be sure we've crossed the border. Until we cross some sort of border marker, I'm going to assume we're still in Acktar."

It was a poor excuse when they both knew the truth, but this would be the official story. No markers, no border, and thus they were still in Acktar as far as their reports would show.

"Then let's keep moving." Leith nudged Valor forward. "Grier will think he's lost any pursuers since he's now this deep south *in Acktar*. He will be slowing down, and that will give us a chance to catch him."

Martyn gave a tight grin. "You know, I've always wanted to explore this far south *in Acktar*."

THE STARS WINKED WHITE AGAINST THE DARK BLUE-BLACK OF the night sky, so clear that a strip of wispy, almost cloudlike brightness sparkled in a strip across the sky, something visible only on moonless nights. In the distance came the gurgle and rush of the Lissri River they'd crossed before setting up camp.

Martyn lay on his back, staring upward. He was supposed to be sleeping while Leith took the first watch, but a thought kept itching at him, as it had each of the six nights since they'd left Ably. "Leith. Do you think there's something wrong with us?"

Grass rustled nearby, and Leith crawled closer, avoiding raising himself too far above the grass where he'd concealed himself to watch their camp. While only starlight lit the surrounding prairie since they hadn't dared light a fire, that was still bright enough for an enemy nearby to locate him if he stood upright.

There was nothing they could do about their horses, standing tall and dark against the lighter silver of the star-slicked grass, but enemies weren't likely to shoot the horses full of arrows. Horses were too valuable.

"What do you mean?" Leith's voice was low to avoid carrying far on the still night.

"There must be something wrong with us, I think. I could be getting married right about now, spending tonight with my bride, and you have your first child on the way, yet we're both here, somewhere in the middle of nowhere hunting a killer we may never be able to track down." Martyn sighed and stared up at the glittering sky above. "Surely there must be something wrong with us that we would willingly choose this kind of life even with the good lives we have waiting for us back home. What makes us do this, you think, when any sane man would have quit long ago?"

Leith was quiet for a long moment. "You aren't thinking of quitting, are you? Now that you're going to be marrying Kayleigh?"

"No." The ease of that answer surprised Martyn, though it sat right in his chest. No, unless Kayleigh begged him to quit, he had no intention to. "What about you?

Having second thoughts now that you're going to be a father?"

"Second thoughts, yes. But not about being a Blade Marshal." Leith huffed out a breath, and it puffed silver briefly against the night sky, the only momentary giveaway to Leith's position. "I used to think our pasts—the weight of the blood we carry—still drove us to repay that guilt despite of the forgiveness we have been given by King Keevan and more importantly from God. But that can't be all of it, because none of the other Blade Marshals have our past and many of them are married and are just as dedicated to the job as we are, like Shad. He certainly doesn't do the job out of a sense of guilt for his past."

No, Shad grew up the perfect lord's son. Whatever drove him to join the Blade Marshals, it wasn't guilt. At least, not a guilt that was known beyond him and God. "Shad has an overabundant sense of justice and adventure fever."

"And that's just it. I think we all do." Grass rustled again, and Leith's form materialized out of the darkness. Leith sat, and only his profile against the sky showed Martyn that Leith was still alert and scanning their surroundings even as he spoke. "Someone has to do this job. There is too much evil in this world for there to be peace and safety without someone actively fighting and protecting others. God has called some to peaceful lives, but He has called others like us to be the protectors."

Too much evil. Martyn knew that all too well. He and Leith had both been a part of that evil.

"As much as I would like to never ride away from Renna, I can't expect someone else to take on this job if I won't do it." Leith tipped his head toward the sky. "I guess if that means there's something wrong with me that I can handle the long weeks away from my wife and seeing the bloodshed and facing the danger, then so be it. I love my family and my neighbors too much to sit back and do nothing when I have the skills to protect them."

"Glad to see you actually believe the speech you give all the trainees." Martyn puffed out a breath, watching it collect in a vaporous cloud before wisping away into nothing.

"You mean my love the neighbor speech?" Leith's voice had a hint of a laugh to it. "Only two years into training Blade Marshals, and I already have an infamous speech."

Martyn gave in to a soft chuckle of his own. He'd listened to Leith give the speech often enough to have it memorized. Some loved their neighbor by baking good loaves of bread or weaving good cloth. Blade Marshals loved their neighbor by facing danger each day. If they didn't do the job out of love for their neighbor, then they shouldn't wear the badge. "You're going to be a legend before you know it."

"I don't know about that." The sand whispered as Leith shifted position. He was silent for a long moment before he added, "But I'm forever grateful to God for the women He's given us and the special sort of courage He gives them to let us go."

Martyn thought about Kayleigh and what should have been a romantic moment for her to savor, broken by word of a mission calling him away. Yet there had been no tears. No pleas for him to stay. She'd simply handed him his pack and knives, kissed him, and asked him to do his best to return.

How many times had he seen Renna do the exact same thing for Leith? She and Kayleigh, they were women strong enough to stand on their own two feet.

For the first time since he'd left Kayleigh next to the stable in Stetterly, a knot in Martyn's stomach loosened. This was Kayleigh. He could trust her to take care of herself whenever he rode away, just as she trusted that he could take care of himself when he was gone.

And just as soon as they tracked down Sean Grier and dragged his sorry rear end to Nalgar Castle for King Keevan to deal with, Martyn was going to ride straight back to Kayleigh and marry her. He didn't care if her wedding dress was half-finished and held together with pins. His heart was all hers.

Perhaps Kayleigh's answer to his proposal had been exactly right. It was about time.

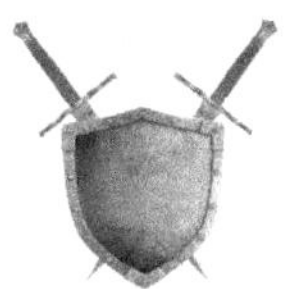

Kayleigh slid the needle through the silk fabric, relishing the way the fabric glided against her skin even if it was a pain to work with. She'd never dreamed she'd have a dress made of such silk.

A light breeze wafted up from the Spires Canyon, carrying with it the faint wet smell of the river down below. The afternoon sunlight baked the prairie before her, though the porch of Leith and Renna's cabin shaded Kayleigh where she sat on a chair she'd hauled onto the porch.

Renna sat in a chair next to her, stitching at another section of the skirt to Kayleigh's wedding dress. "At this rate, we'll have this dress done in a matter of days. You'll be ready as soon as Martyn returns."

Kayleigh smiled, casting one more glance around the prairie, before she added another stitch. She and Martyn hadn't talked about it, but she didn't figure they'd have a long engagement. All of their immediate family was already in

Stetterly. It would be nice if Shad and Jolene could make it. Maybe even King Keevan and Lord Conree.

But they weren't necessary. Kayleigh would be just fine if they stood out under a pine tree somewhere just the two of them, the minister, and Leith, Renna, and Owen to witness. At this point, she didn't even care if she wore her trousers, though she did have the green dress she'd made two years ago that was still more than serviceable.

Kayleigh caught Renna's gaze flicking toward her. Renna smiled. "Are you excited yet?"

"Maybe. Hard to get too excited when I don't know when the wedding will happen." Or if it would happen.

No, she couldn't think like that. Yes, Leith and Martyn were hunting a man who had already killed a Blade Marshal. But they outnumbered him, and they had taken on far harder opponents than one ham-fisted criminal.

A drumming sounded in the distance. Was that horses?

"We can at least—"

Kayleigh held up her hand for silence. Renna snapped her mouth shut and tensed. She didn't even ask what was going on.

Was that Martyn and Leith on the way home?

But her heart pounded, some sense telling her there were more horses than just Leith and Martyn. Something wasn't right.

She set her sewing aside and stood. Owen was somewhere out there keeping watch. He should—

Owen popped up just below the crest of the hill to the north, pointing north and waving four fingers.

Four riders. Probably not friendly.

She and Owen might be able to handle them on their own, but she didn't want to take any chances. Brandi was near the stables, and Jamie was inside his room. They would be able to help, but Kayleigh didn't want either of them getting hurt. Ranson was in one of the far fields helping a farmer.

Kayleigh pointed toward Owen, then waved in the direction of Stetterly. Owen nodded and disappeared from sight. Hopefully that meant Owen had gotten the message to get help from some of the guard reserves from town.

The riders crested the hill and poured into the yard before the cabin as Kayleigh reached for her sword.

The lead rider yanked his horse to a halt. The horse tossed its head, its ears pressing back against its skull.

Definitely not friends. At least, Kayleigh wasn't going to be friends with someone who was so rough on his horse's mouth.

"I wouldn't bother with that sword, lady." The lead rider leaned on the pommel of his saddle, the grimy billows of his shirt tucked beneath a weathered sword belt. "We heard the Blade Marshal was called away, so don't try to bluff. Just hand over your valuables quiet-like, starting with that dress, and we'll be on our way."

It was unreasonable, really. She had just been thinking that she didn't really need this fancy dress to have the perfect wedding.

But the moment this grubby bandit mentioned the fabric, Kayleigh tightened her grip on her sword hilt with no intention of handing it over. Martyn had given her this fabric. She would be married in it, see if she wasn't.

Behind the four bandits, Brandi sneaked along the edge

of the stables and slipped inside. Fetching Jamie. Help would be coming.

Renna set her portion of the sewing aside and pushed to her feet, no easy task with how pregnant she was. "We don't have anything worth stealing."

The bandit leader snorted. "You're the lady of Stetterly. Do you expect me to believe that?"

Renna gestured at the cabin behind her. "Look around you. Stetterly was razed to the ground during the war. I've put everything into rebuilding the town, not building wealth for myself."

The bandit leader pointed at the fabric. "You really are terrible at lying."

Renna huffed, as if offended that this bandit would question her word.

Behind the bandits, Jamie and Brandi crouched near the stables. A rustle stirred the grass on the hill in the direction of town. Hopefully that was Owen and the rest of the guards and not just the wind.

Kayleigh drew her sword and stepped in front of Renna. As she did, Jamie and Brandi started working their way closer. Owen and two of the reserve guards popped into view. Kayleigh faced the bandits. "As captain of Stetterly's guards, I order you to surrender."

"You're the captain of...oh, that's a joke." The bandit leader burst into laughter, slapping his knee.

He was still laughing when Kayleigh grabbed him by his belt and yanked him from the saddle. Landing hard on his face in the dirt knocked the laughter right out of him.

Owen, Eric, and a third guard Sam Nelson charged down

the hill with swords drawn. Brandi and Jamie dashed forward from the stables.

Kayleigh dodged a sword's thrust from one of the other bandits and jumped back when the bandit leader on the ground tried to stab up at her. She smacked his sword hand with the flat of her sword. He kept his grip on his sword, but he was grimacing and rubbing at his wrist with his free hand instead of taking another swing at her.

Jamie pounced on one of the bandits, getting him halfway out of the saddle before Brandi also jumped him. Together, Brandi and Jamie landed on the man, pinning him to the ground. With how tall both Brandi and Jamie had become at sixteen, almost seventeen, the man wasn't going anywhere. Owen traded blows with the third bandit while Eric blocked a thrust from the fourth bandit.

"Use both hands!" Kayleigh kicked the sword out of the bandit leader's grasp and shoved the tip of her sword against his neck when he reached for a knife.

"Oh, right!" Eric drew his knife and jabbed it into the bandit's leg. The bandit howled and was quickly toppled from the saddle by Sam.

Within a minute, they had all the bandits tied hand and foot and all their weapons confiscated.

Kayleigh sheathed her sword and glanced over the bandits before focusing on Owen and the other reserve guards. "Well done. We had them all apprehended in less than two minutes. Less than five minutes after Owen spotted them. Eric, next time I expect you to remember you have two hands before I have to remind you. Sam, please jump in quicker if you see a fellow guard could use the help. It's all right to fight two against one when apprehending criminals.

Still, you all did well, and your training showed. Brandi, Jamie. Great teamwork.”

Eric and Sam exchanged grins. Owen tipped a nod in her direction. Brandi grinned at Jamie, and Jamie grinned in return, though there was something in his grin and a faint tinge of red to his ears.

“Owen, could you, Eric, and Sam see to hauling these men in to Sheriff Allen and writing up the charges? I’ll stay here to guard Renna. Brandi, could you stand watch on the hill while Owen’s gone?”

“I’ll go with her.” Jamie said a little too quickly. He cleared his throat. “I need a break from studying anyway.”

As Owen, Eric, and Sam hauled the bandits to their feet and heaved them across their horses’ backs for an uncomfortable ride to town, Kayleigh returned to her seat and reached for her sewing.

Only then did she notice Renna sliding a knife back into her pocket. Renna set a heavy, cast iron skillet on the floor beside her and returned to her seat. As if noticing Kayleigh’s look, Renna shrugged. “I wasn’t going to step in and get in the way, but I also wasn’t about to stand idly by if one of the bandits did manage to get past you. I may not be good at fighting, but there isn’t much anyone can do against a frying pan to the face. And I figured if a bandit should manage to catch the frying pan, he’d have his hands too full to notice my knife.”

“You have been spending way too much time with Leith if you’re starting to think in terms of fighting tactics.” Kayleigh made another small, neat stitch in the fabric, tugging the needle through.

“I’m a Blade Marshal’s wife and best friends with the

captain of my guards. It's to be expected." Renna took up her section of the wedding dress's skirt. "Are you planning to remain the captain of my guards once you're married?"

Kayleigh halted halfway through a stitch. For some reason, she hadn't really thought about it. Would Martyn expect her to quit once they were married?

No, this was Martyn. Besides this fabric, the other gifts he'd given her had been a new dagger and a nicer sharpening stone. It wasn't like the job of captain of Stetterly's guards was that intense a job. She had to train the reserve guards and stick near Renna, which she would do anyway since Renna was a friend.

Besides, it was a job better suited to a female guard. It wasn't like a male guard could camp out in Renna's parlor when Leith was gone. This cabin wasn't like the large, many roomed manor houses of much of the nobility.

"I haven't talked it over with Martyn yet, but I don't think so. Once I move into his cabin, I'll actually be closer to you than I am living in town. His cabin is the place of last resort if for security reasons you can't stay here." Kayleigh returned to her stitching. "Besides, I'd probably be here almost every day anyway so our children can play together and we can talk while we do our mending or other handwork. I might as well guard you while I'm at it."

"I'm glad. I know Owen intends to return to Surgis, and I'd hate to lose both of my experienced guards." Renna's smile told Kayleigh that losing her experienced guards was the least of Renna's concerns, even if it was the one she said out loud.

Kayleigh grinned back. "We Blade Marshal wives need to look after each other."

Renna's smile grew as she turned back to her stitching.

Even as she sent another glance around the area, Kayleigh felt something inside her shift. Yes, there were times she still missed the cool nights of her mountain home surrounded by the smell of pine and juniper.

But she had so much more here than she'd had there. She had friends who understood and encouraged her. A new home. A church community that, while it still had its faults, wasn't as troubled as the one she'd left behind at Flayin Falls.

And she had Martyn, a man who loved her as she was and yet managed to encourage her to continue to grow, whether that encouragement took the form of giving her a new sharpening stone for her sword or a long afternoon discussion on some point of doctrine that sharpened both her faith and his.

Yes, God had brought her to exactly where she belonged.

And she prayed God would bring Martyn back home safely so she could share this happiness with him.

8

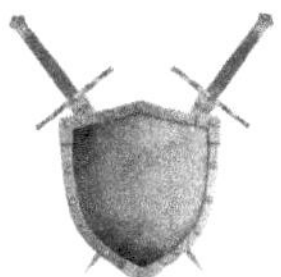

Leith leaned against Valor's saddlehorn as Martyn swung down from Wanderer to inspect the bent grass in front of them, parting it to peer at the hoofprints left in the soil. Two days ago, Grier had left the main trail and struck out to the southwest. As long as the rain held off, they had a clear trail to follow.

In the distance, scrub-covered foothills taller than some of the peaks in the Sheered Rock Hills rose against the sky, and above them, loomed the gray, snow-covered crags and peaks of the largest mountains Leith had ever seen. When they'd turned off the main road, the mountains had been nothing but a smudge in the distance, but now they were distinct peaks stretching for as far as he could see along the southwestern horizon.

He'd heard of the Great Mountains, but to see them jabbing at the sky...he finally understood why the person who'd named them hadn't gone for a more creative name and had simply called them great.

"We're gaining on him. If we push hard today, we might even be able to catch him at nightfall." Martyn swung back into the saddle and tipped his head at the mountains. "The closer we get to them, the harder it will be to plead ignorance that we didn't realize we'd wandered so far out of Acktar."

"Apparently we are really bad at geography and navigating." Leith urged Valor forward. The horse gamely walked onward, uncomplaining even after the miles and miles of country they'd covered. Both his and Martyn's horses were originally mountain bred horses from the Sheered Rock Hills. They had a streak of grit in them, that was for sure.

"Yes, we are terrible at finding our location on the prairie, yet we tracked a single man and horse hundreds of miles." Martyn huffed out a breath. "We'd better hope we continue to avoid the Verdenish authorities. They'll throw us in their darkest, dirtiest prison for sure with a story like that, if we're lucky. What are the odds that King Keevan will actually negotiate to have us returned to Acktar if we aren't killed on sight as spies?"

"We really need to get you back home to Kayleigh before you completely lose all sense of optimism." Leith nudged Valor into a steady lope. While the trail was this plain, they might as well cover some ground.

"Who said I had any optimism to begin with?" Martyn shot back as he urged Wanderer to keep pace.

As the day wore on, the mountains continued to draw closer until they blotted out any sense of a horizon beyond their hulking, soaring heights. The sunset flamed from somewhere behind the mountains, washing the peaks in light golds and pinks.

Martyn stared up at them, and Leith caught a glimpse of something in Martyn's eyes, something he'd seen before in their early days as Blades when they'd been sent to explore the Sheered Rock Hills and track down bands of Rovers. "You want to explore them, don't you."

"Yes. There's just something about a new horizon, a new peak." Martyn heaved a sigh and tore his gaze away from the snow-filled peaks high above. "Perhaps I will someday. Perhaps never. I'm not going to abandon Kayleigh to run off to the far great mountains."

Leith felt it too. Perhaps not as strongly as Martyn, but there was the stir in his own chest.

Yes, they were Blade Marshals out of love and justice and duty. But there was also this. A good horse underneath them, a good friend beside them, and a new horizon before them. Few other thrills could compare to that of the unknown spreading before them, the sweet taste of adventure luring them onward.

By the time gray twilight wrapped the landscape with a hush of impending night, they had worked their way up steep, pine-covered slopes into the foothills.

Leith was about to call a halt, unwilling to continue riding in treacherous, unfamiliar territory such as this, when something caught his eye. He halted Valor, scanning the foothills and mountains around them.

There. A flicker, then a flare. A growing campfire. A grin tugged at his mouth, even if Martyn wouldn't be able to see it clearly in the gathering dusk. "Unless someone else has wandered into this section of mountains, our friend Grier has decided it's safe to light a fire tonight."

"Our friend, huh?" Martyn gathered up Wanderer's reins.

"Then I say let's pay him a visit. It wouldn't be proper to pass by a friend's campfire without dropping by."

Leith kept the fire in the corner of his eye as he worked his way toward it, but he made sure not to focus too hard on it. It would be too easy to be lured in by the campfire and miss an ambush.

When they were within a hundred yards, he dropped Valor's reins and crouched. When Martyn crouched next to him, he pointed to the left and whispered, "You take the left, and I'll circle in from the right. Give a screech owl's call when it's clear."

With a nod, Martyn disappeared into the darkness.

Leith worked his way in a circle to the right, taking his time picking his way over the dry pine twigs and sprigs of crackling grass. The muted gray-green of his trousers and gray-brown shirt blended into the night better than the black he'd worn as a Blade, a color Respen had chosen less for its practicality and more for intimidation.

One man sat near a crackling fire, setting a pot onto the coals. When the man looked up to sweep a glance at the surrounding area, Leith froze where he was, trusting his stillness to keep him hidden in the darkness.

The firelight gave him a good look at the man's face. Thin eyebrows framed wide eyes above a slim nose and firm jaw. Some might call it a handsome face, something that had deceived many a traveler who had been held up by Grier's three-man gang of thieves. The man matched Grier's description all the way down to the fancy stitching of the leather boots he wore, a stiffer sort with a larger heel preferred by men in countries to the far south of Verden rather than the soft leather boots Leith and Martyn wore.

This was a man who liked the figure he cut when gussied up. Still, Leith couldn't let that fool him into thinking this man would be easy prey. Even now as Grier settled back into a comfortable seat, he glanced around him rather than staring at the fire in a way that would ruin his night vision.

Cautious, but overconfident. If Grier had done a halfway decent job of checking his back trail, he would've been able to spot them following him when he'd started his ascent into the foothills. And he never would've lit this fire.

Leith eased through the brush on his side of Grier's camp until he was certain no one lurked out here guarding the camp.

From the darkness on the other side of Grier, there came a low hoot ending in a sort of chuckling sound.

Grier straightened, cocking an ear as if uncertain of what he'd heard.

Leith would've given the call in return, but Grier was already too alert.

Instead, Leith stood and strode toward into the firelight before Grier had a chance to draw his sword. "Hello, traveler. I saw your fire and thought I'd drop in."

"What are you...who are you?" Grier gripped his sword's hilt but didn't draw it. Not yet, anyway.

Leith forced himself to relax as he dropped onto a seat on the ground. He pulled his badge from its hidden slot in his belt. "I'm Blade Marshal Leith Torren."

Grier stumbled back a step, his arm poised to draw his sword. "You can't arrest me here. You don't have the authority."

"No, I can't arrest you." Leith pasted on a smile, though it was hardly cheerful. "But there's nothing that says I can't join up with you and ride alongside you. Fellow Acktarians far from home and all that. So where are we going? I've always heard the Great Mountains are a sight to behold."

"What makes you think I won't just kill you and leave your body to rot right here?" Grier began to draw his sword.

"I wouldn't do that if I were you." Martyn's voice cut the air only a few feet away from Grier. "Actually, please do. I'd love an excuse to gut you right here and be able to return to Acktar with our mission complete."

Leith couldn't see Martyn from where he was sitting, but he didn't have to. Martyn had his back.

Grier stiffened and let his sword slid back into its sheath. "I should've known. Blade Marshals always come in pairs."

"That's right. And the two of us are your new saddle partners." Leith lay back and stretched out on the ground, hands behind his head, eyes closed. "You'd best get to sleep. Don't worry. Martyn has the first watch so pesky bandits won't trouble us in our sleep."

"Why, I should—"

Grier's boots crunched a step closer, his sword whispering against its sheath. But Leith kept his eyes closed, forcing his muscles to remain relaxed in spite of his vulnerable position.

"Take another step, and it will be your last." Martyn's voice again. "I'm not fooling. I'd love to kill you and get this mission over with. All the way out here in Verden, no one would even have to know I slit your throat."

It might have been a bluff, but Martyn's voice was cold. The voice of a remorseless, heartless Blade.

Grass crunched, and sand squeaked as Grier plopped to the ground with curses muttered under his breath.

Leith tried to relax, telling himself he should sleep. But he wouldn't be able to with Grier only a few feet away.

What would tomorrow bring? He and Martyn had caught up with Grier, but their hands were tied. They couldn't so much as lay a finger on him here without compromising whatever trial he might have in Acktar if they got him back alive.

Killing him would be easiest, but Leith wasn't going to resort to that unless forced. He'd rather bring Grier back for a trial and king's sentence. That was his job, not assassinating criminals outside of Acktar's borders.

They couldn't force Grier to return to Acktar, yet they couldn't continue to wander the Great Mountains with him forever. The longer they were with him, the more chances he'd have to put a knife in one or both of them in a moment of exhaustion or inattentiveness.

Besides, Leith wanted to return home. His first child was due to be born in a little over a month, and he needed to be there. And each day they were gone delayed Martyn's wedding to Kayleigh.

Leith had to figure out some way to trick Grier to return to Acktar. Even if, right now, that looked impossible. How could he possibly convince someone to willingly return to a country where he would most likely be hanged for his crimes?

THE NEXT MORNING, GRIER LED THEM DEEPER INTO THE GREAT Mountains. Martyn would've enjoyed it, except for the fact that they were tagging along with a man who'd killed a Blade Marshal.

The air was growing colder, the scrub brush thinner as they pushed past the foothills into the mountains themselves. Somewhere up ahead had to be some sort of valley or pass.

Grier kicked his horse into a gallop. Ahead of him, the valley they were following narrowed and curved, obstructing their view.

Another attempt to get away. If Grier managed to outrun them around that blind corner, who knew where he could scurry off to. Martyn urged Wanderer into a gallop. He'd tracked Grier too far to let the man get away now.

Behind him, he vaguely heard Valor's hooves pound into a gallop as well. Martyn didn't glance over his shoulder. He kept his gaze focused on Grier as Grier swept around the bend and disappeared.

Moments later, Wanderer pounded through the narrow corner, Martyn hunched low over the horse's neck. He wasn't going to let Grier get away.

The valley began to open up again, the crags of the mountains rising far above him.

And there, filling the pass in front of them, sat squat, stone castle, guarding the road through the mountains. Turrets spired into the sky, though remained below the surrounding jagged peaks as if the castle wished to remain inconspicuous. Grier was riding full tilt toward it, waving his arm and pointing back at them.

Of all the...Martyn bit off the swear words before he said them out loud though he would have to give his tongue a good soap scrubbing for still thinking them. He tugged

Wanderer to a halt, the horse's hooves skidding as he went from a gallop to a stop.

The castle's gates opened, and mounted men wearing the dull brown and white uniforms of Verden poured outside, surrounding Grier within moments.

Leith reined in Valor next to Martyn. "Probably wouldn't be a good idea to charge in there."

That was about the closest Leith would get to reprimanding Martyn for charging ahead like that. It had been foolish. Reckless. He'd gotten too focused on Grier.

A mistake. And one that could cost him dearly.

"Shouldn't we be turning around and charging the other way?" Martyn's knuckles tightened around Wanderer's reins. "I really, really don't want to spend the rest of my natural life in some Verdenish prison."

No, he wanted to return to Acktar, get married, maybe even have a passel of kids. Exploring the mountains no longer had the lure it had yesterday.

"Neither do I. That's why we're going to ride right up there and introduce ourselves. Might as well make our visit official." Leith nudged Valor forward. "There's nothing else we can do. Considering they know the territory better than we do, I doubt we'd escape if we tried to run."

Just ride up and be surrounded? Martyn's right hand itched to reach for his knife. Yet what other choice did they have?

The Verdenish soldiers surrounded them, pointing long spears. The soldiers had more of a mix of skin tones than in Acktar, probably due to Verden's place serving as a crossroads in the trade routes between several countries.

At least Grier was also similarly surrounded and

menaced with spears near the castle. Martyn could keep an eye on him while they all got thrown into some Verdenish dungeon together.

Leith eased his badge out of its hidden pocket and held it out to the soldier in front of him. "We're Blade Marshals from Acktar. We'd like to speak with whoever is in charge of this castle."

The soldier in front of Leith leaned forward and took the badge from Leith's hand, the soldiers around him tensing with their iron-tipped spears aimed at Leith's chest. The soldier who appeared to be somewhat in charge turned the badge over in his hands. "Very well. Drop your weapons."

His voice had an accent to it, the words drawling thick and smooth to Martyn's ears. But at least Martyn could understand them just fine, a benefit to Acktar and Verden still speaking the same language, mostly, since they'd had common ancestors. Just one of those semi-helpful history facts Martyn had studied up on for that test to become a Blade Marshal a couple of years ago.

"Do as he says." Leith slowly unclipped the buckles holding his knives to his belt and the leather straps across his chest.

Martyn hesitated. Surrendering grated against every shade of instinct in his body.

The Verdenish soldier thrust his spear at Martyn. "Now."

With a sigh, Martyn eased the buckle free on his knife belt and let it fall to the ground. Leith was right. They didn't have a choice.

9

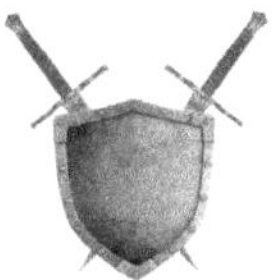

Martyn paced across the cell where he and Leith had been thrown. Well, not really thrown. They had been politely escorted and told to wait here for the captain to see them. They hadn't even had their hands tied, though they'd been searched.

The cell was roughly eight foot by eight foot with a stone floor, walls, and ceiling. The wooden door and one of the walls had barred windows that looked into the castle court-yard, which bustled with drilling Verdenish soldiers. A single cot stretched most of the length of one wall.

Leith sprawled on the cot, hands behind his head. "At least they put us in what appears to be the guardhouse. They wouldn't keep us here if they intended to hold us for long. There has to be some other dungeon or tower cells for that."

"Maybe." Martyn glanced out the window again. "This isn't a regular castle. There aren't any women or even men not wearing a uniform bustling around. I think this is more of an army fort."

Martyn inspected the door. He might be able to reach the lock on the outside if he stretched, and he probably could pick the lock one-handed from that position if he had to. But that was assuming that none of the guards pacing outside the door or drilling in the courtyard noticed. Maybe at night the guards would fall asleep or something.

He and Leith might be able to escape. Maybe. Assuming they could sneak their horses out of the castle, since they'd never make it back to Acktar on foot.

But that would mean leaving Sean Grier behind because there was no way they could sneak him out of this border castle with them.

Martyn spun away from the window and paced to the other side of the cell. "What do you think Grier is telling them?"

Grier had been led away by the soldiers as soon as they were all hauled through the castle gates. Martyn could only assume Grier had been given a chance to talk to the captain first.

"Probably telling him we are dangerous spies or something like that." Leith didn't even tense as he sprawled on the cot.

Martyn dragged a hand through his hair. "How are you so relaxed?"

Leith rolled upright and swung his feet to the floor. "Believe me, I don't want to find out what Verden does to spies any more than you do. But there's nothing to be gained by worrying, and I'd rather spend the time thinking about what I'm going to say to sway the captain to our side."

"And if you don't?" Martyn faced Leith. He forced

himself to remain relaxed, his arms at his side. No need to start arguing with Leith. This was Martyn's fault, after all.

"Then we're going to be in big trouble." Now tension stiffened Leith's muscles, the easy tilt gone from his mouth.

Martyn clenched his fists. They could be thrown into some Verdenish dungeon or hauled to Lorado, Verden's capital, and spend years in a stinking, rat-infested prison while King Keevan tried to negotiate their release. Or, worse yet, hanged or stabbed or beheaded or whatever means of execution Verden practiced for disposing of enemy spies.

All Martyn wanted to do was return to Acktar, marry Kayleigh, and hold her tight. Why had he thought seeing new territory and exploring the mountains was thrilling?

The lock grated, and the door creaked open. Two guards stepped inside. They weren't carrying their spears, but instead had short swords strapped to their sides. They rested their hands on the hilts but didn't draw their weapons. "Come with us."

Leith slid to his feet and headed for the guards, his hands loose at his sides.

Martyn swallowed and fell into step behind Leith. As they stepped through the doorway, the two guards fell in behind them while four more soldiers closed around them.

Off to one side, three more soldiers held Grier, probably waiting to shove him into the cell. Grier smirked as Leith and Martyn were marched by.

That probably wasn't a good sign.

THE VERDENISH SOLDIERS LED THEM ACROSS THE COURTYARD toward the square, two-story building in the center of the castle's walls. Leith scanned his surroundings, noting the locations of what looked like barracks along several of the walls, at least one of the castle's wells, the height of the walls and towers, and anything that could be useful to know in the future.

Two guards stood by the double doors for what appeared to be more a military headquarters than a traditional castle keep. Inside the large front doors, a hallway stretched down the center of the building with doors on each side. Probably office rooms and sleeping quarters for the commanders of the various units stationed here.

The soldiers halted in front of the first door on the right, and one of them knocked on the door.

"Send them in."

The soldier opened the door and gestured. "Enter."

Leith stepped inside, and Martyn followed, the door clicking shut behind him.

The Verdenish captain must be a confident sort of man if he didn't fear being alone with two possible enemies, though he did have six soldiers on hand just outside the door if he needed them.

The captain sat behind a large, plain desk with two wooden chairs in front of it. The stone floor was bare, the walls bare. It was a stark room, but in a starched and professional sort of way. The captain's hair was a dark brown, his skin a shade or two darker than Leith's or Martyn's, even with their tans. He wasn't much older than them, maybe in his late twenties or early thirties. He wasn't looking at them, but instead was studying something he held in his hands. "Please, have a seat."

Leith claimed one of the chairs, and after a moment's hesitation, Martyn took the other.

There wasn't much else they could do but continue to cooperate, and Leith needed to buy time and gather information before he planned their next move.

Light glinted as the captain turned something over in his fingers. Leith's badge. Finally, the captain raised his head and swept a calculating glance over them. "I'm Captain Jim Wyeth, commander of Fort Peak. Who are you and what are you doing in Verden?"

What had Grier told the captain and how much had the captain believed Grier's version of events? Leith didn't like going into this not knowing how much of a hole Grier had already dug for them.

In the end, it probably didn't matter. His and Martyn's greatest defense was the truth and hope that Captain Jim Wyeth was the sort of captain to give respect to fellow law enforcement officers, even if they belonged to another country.

Leith gestured to the badge Captain Wyeth held. "As you can see by our badges, we are Blade Marshals from Acktar. He's Blade Marshal Hamish, and I'm Blade Marshal Torren. The other man you captured is Sean Grier. He ran an outlaw gang in Acktar robbing trade wagons until three weeks ago when he and his men ambushed two of my fellow Blade Marshals. One was killed, the other injured. We have tracked him since and plan to bring him to justice for his crimes."

"I see." Captain Wyeth's expression remained impassive.

He tapped the front of the badge. "Is this a random number or does it have special meaning?"

Leith could tell him it was random. For the most part, the badge number was randomly handed out as the Blade Marshals were sworn in. But his, Martyn's, and Shad's badges were very purposefully the first three. "I'm the captain of the Blade Marshals."

That sparked something in Captain Wyeth's dark eyes, but other than that his mouth remained a flat, neutral line. "Why would the captain of the Blade Marshals assign himself the duty of tracking this petty criminal down? It was a mission you could delegate to someone else. Makes me wonder what other motives you might have had."

"Grier killed one of my men." Leith kept his tone flat. Hard. "I am the sort of captain who takes a hands-on approach to leadership."

As he suspected Captain Wyeth did as well. Beneath the blank expression, there was intelligence. A sharpness. This man was calculating. Yet, without pretention. A no nonsense, practical sort of man who ran an efficient fort.

"Still. This was a long way to go after one man, especially when you don't have the jurisdiction to arrest him, unless Acktar thinks it now has rights in Verden." Captain Wyeth tossed Leith's badge onto his desk. The metal tapped against the wood before coming to rest in the center of the desk between Leith and Captain Wyeth.

"That's where you can help me." Leith didn't take the badge. Not yet. He met Captain Wyeth's gaze. "I don't have the jurisdiction to arrest Grier, but you do."

Captain Wyeth leaned back in his chair and crossed his

arms. "Why should I help you? Acktar and Verden has no treaty specifying how we should handle extraditing criminals. In fact, we have no treaty at all to clarify how my country feels toward yours. Why should I not have you all detained and brought before my king? Or I could have you hanged as spies. We both know Verden is too strong for your king to even threaten war over two foolish Blade Marshals."

Captain Wyeth was right. As much as Keevan may or may not want to send a strong message to Verden, he wouldn't threaten war. Verden had a strong, numerous, and well-trained army, along with being the bigger country with more resources. And nearly all of the goods that couldn't be made in Acktar came from trade routes from Verden. Perhaps King Keevan could threaten to establish trade routes to the northeast to bypass Verden, but the disruption to trade would hurt Acktar just as much as it did Verden.

"Yes, Verden is too strong for Acktar, but Acktar is also too strong for Verden." Leith folded his arms loosely. He couldn't appear tense, not if he wanted to talk his way out of their predicament. "We both know the moment Verden gets caught up in a long, grueling war in Acktar, the Surrana Empire is going to sweep over your western border and attack you as they've longed to do for years. It is, I believe, the whole reason you have this fort with all these men stationed here."

"So we've established that you aren't important enough for either of our countries to go to war over." Captain Wyeth tipped his chair back. "But that doesn't tell me why I shouldn't ship you off to Lorado and let our kings figure this out."

"Because I'd really rather not waste away in some Verdenish prison." Martyn muttered under his breath. When Leith glanced over at him, Martyn had his arms tightly crossed. "Can we stop talking far-reaching politics and start talking about how we avoid a Verdenish prison?"

Leith suppressed a grin. Martyn never had been one for political maneuvering. And he had a point. It was time to lay out the issue plainly. "I have my first child on the way, and Martyn there is supposed to be getting married. Both of us would rather not spend any more time in Verden than we have to. Nor, I think, do you want us staying in Verden longer than necessary either. We didn't come here to be spies, but we can't help but see a great deal of your country and its defenses if you take us to Lorado. That might be information your king would rather we didn't have."

"And what do you suggest I do instead? I'm assuming you aren't suggesting I hang the two of you." Captain Wyeth sat forward, his posture and twitch to his mouth that of a man who already had an idea of the answer but wanted Leith to say it out loud anyway.

"Escort us—all of us—to the border into Acktar. After all, Grier is a known thief willing to kill law enforcement officers and not someone you want to linger in your country, and we are Blade Marshals you would rather get out of your country as quickly as possible." Leith picked up his badge and tucked it into its pocket in his belt. "Let our kings deal with the official complaints, negotiations, and paperwork once no one's lives are hanging in the balance."

"I would have to take men away from my defenses here at Fort Peak for a long round trip. That's a lot of hassle for three men." Captain Wyeth's expression held a hint of a smile, as if he'd already made his decision in Leith's favor but just needed the right excuse to write down in the official reports.

"A small sacrifice to keep good relations with Acktar. Who knows? It might even be a good opportunity to strengthen an alliance between our countries."

A broad grin spread across Captain Wyeth's face, crinkling the laugh lines around his eyes. "I knew I was going to like the two of you."

"Well that made one of us." Martyn slouched against the back of his chair.

Leith let out a long breath, though if anything his stomach knotted more than it had during the negotiation. His instincts told him he could trust Captain Wyeth, but what if he was wrong? In the end, nothing he or Martyn did or said would make a difference. Captain Wyeth had their weapons, their horses, the man they set out to apprehend, and the power in this situation. Leith was helpless to make sure Captain Wyeth kept his word and took them to Acktar.

And Leith ached to return to Acktar. To stand next to Martyn while Martyn married Kayleigh. To hold his newborn son or daughter. To at least have the chance to give everything in him to be the kind of father he should be.

"Lieutenant!" Captain Wyeth sat forward in his chair.

The door opened, and Leith glanced over his shoulder as one of the soldiers stepped inside. "Sir?"

"Prepare ten men and horses for a patrol north to Acktar. I would like to investigate that area to make sure Surrana hasn't been using our fluid border with Acktar to infiltrate Verden." Captain Wyeth shoved stacks of paperwork together. "You'll be in charge of Fort Peak while I'm gone."

"Yes, sir." The lieutenant turned on his heels and called out orders even as he shut the door behind him.

Captain Wyeth planned to go himself? Was that a good thing or not?

Leith couldn't be sure. He only hoped Captain Wyeth proved to be as honorable as he was efficient.

10

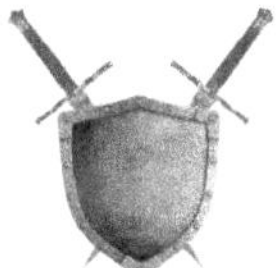

"I believe we should be in Acktar now." Captain Wyeth drew his horse to a halt. "Is that what you figure?"

Leith glanced over his shoulder at the tavern buildings to their south. Rolling prairie hills spread as far as he could see in every direction. Home. "Yes. I believe we should be well and truly in Acktar now."

"In that case..." Captain Wyeth gestured to his men.

Leith held out his hands as one of the Verdenish soldiers untied his hands. Beside him, Martyn's hands were also loosed. They'd been tied as part of the whole forcefully-escorted-to-Acktar part of the bargain. Captain Wyeth wasn't about to fully trust them, even if they were on friendly terms. Leith probably would've done the same thing in Captain Wyeth's place.

A soldier also untied Grier's hands. Grier gathered his horse's reins as if he intended to make a break for it, but a row of spears halted him.

Captain Wyeth gestured at Grier. "I believe he's yours now."

Leith grinned, pulled out his badge, and faced Grier. "Since we are now officially back on Acktar's soil, Sean Grier, you are under arrest. Martyn, care to do the honors?"

"My pleasure." Martyn steered Wanderer over to Grier and held out a hand to the Verdenish soldier who still had the rope he'd taken from Grier's hands only moments before. "Could I borrow a rope?"

The soldier grinned and held it out to Martyn.

While Martyn tied Grier, Leith turned to Captain Wyeth. "Thank you for your escort to the border."

"As you said, it was informative." Captain Wyeth held out Leith's weapons. "If you are ever in my country again, I'd say you are welcome at my fort, but I fear I wouldn't like the reason you would be so far into Verden. I'd rather you stay far away and remain someone else's problem."

Leith couldn't argue with that. He buckled on his knives, breathing out a sigh as their weight settled against his chest. It hadn't felt right to travel for the past week with near strangers and yet not have a single knife on him.

Captain Wyeth started to turn his horse, but Leith held up his hand. "One more thing, captain."

Captain Wyeth halted and turned in his saddle to face Leith.

Leith did his best to look serious. "It could be worthwhile if a complaint about our excursion into Verden made its way to your king. It might make him see fit to approach my king about a treaty regarding the border. Something like that would go a long ways to making sure there are no more... misunderstandings in the future."

"Ah, yes." Captain Wyeth nodded, that gleam back in his eyes. "Especially if a loyal captain reported that he was convinced the Acktarian Blade Marshals wouldn't hesitate to ride into Verden again if they were after a similarly dastardly man."

Leith couldn't deny it. "I see we understand each other."

"Perfectly." Captain Wyeth raised his hand in salute. Then he turned his horse, and his men followed him as they cantered south toward the border.

"Well, now that we got him, what do we do with him? Head for Ably?" Martyn gripped the reins to Grier's horse and glared.

Grier was once again tied hand and foot onto his saddle. A gag kept him from shouting protests. But that didn't stop him from glaring back.

"Not Ably." As much as Leith wanted to head straight for Stetterly, he had one more stop to make before he could complete this mission. "We're going to head straight for Nalgar Castle. Grier killed a Blade Marshal, a king's officer. Only the king can properly pass sentence on him."

Another four, almost five days to Nalgar. Then they could turn this criminal over to Keevan for the due process of the law. Another five days to Stetterly, and then, finally, they would be home.

LEITH STOOD IN THE COURTYARD, WATCHING, UNTIL MARTYN and four of the guards at Nalgar escorted Grier across the bridge and disappeared into the Tower. Only then did Leith stroll in the other direction, heading for the stairs to Keevan's office.

The guards at the base of the stairs glanced from his badge to his face, then waved him to go on up.

While the stairs were in the same place they had been back in Respen's time as king, a carpet had been run down the center to make them less slippery. More wall sconces burned along the narrow passageway so there was no danger of tripping or running into someone.

At the top of the stairs, another set of guards met him, and once again they let him pass.

Leith wound his way past the rows of desks that filled the room, dodging around clerks as they bustled back and forth carrying the paperwork that kept the country running. In the far corner, he finally reached Keevan's private office chamber.

The door was shut, but Leith didn't bother knocking. He pushed it open and stepped inside.

Keevan bent over a stack of paperwork, pen scratching furiously. Behind him, his brother-in-law Frank leaned against the wall, hand on his sword. Frank met Leith's gaze and nodded, though Keevan never looked up.

"If that's a protest from Lord Doughtry about the discrepancy in his taxes, then tell him that if he reworks his sums on page six, he'll find our numbers are indeed correct and his calculations are in error." Keevan flipped the page he had been working on and dipped his pen into the ink to begin on another page.

"Ah. Taxes. I see I'm interrupting terribly important business." Leith reached for the door behind him, trying to fight his grin. "I can always come back later."

Keevan's head snapped up, and he almost grinned. "Leith. The fact that I'm almost glad to see you tells me I've been spending too long double checking these figures. Though, I have yet to see Stetterly's tax forms on my desk. It would be a shame if I had to send the captain of my Blade Marshals to investigate his wife's tax evasion."

"Stetterly's taxes aren't due for another three months yet. She's hardly overdue." Leith strode to the desk and dropped a stack of paper in front of Keevan, ignoring Keevan's scowl at having his careful organization disrupted. "I wanted to personally deliver your copy of my report of my recent mission. I fear some parts might be a tad messy. I was writing it by firelight on our way here while trying to keep an eye on Sean Grier. He has the escape instincts of a rat."

"You caught him?" Keevan picked up the stack of papers and did his best to tap them into a neat stack, a difficult task considering how bent and crinkled some of the papers were from being roughly set aside to stop a few escape attempts.

"Martyn and I were gone for a month. Do you really think we would've pursued him that long without catching him?" Leith grinned, but the grin was all cold and no humor. Grier's crime was nothing to joke about. "He's being locked in the Tower dungeon as we speak."

"Excellent. Any complications with his trial that I should be aware of?" Keevan's eyes were scanning Leith's report even as he asked the question. "I would hate for Grier to escape his sentence because of some legal technicality."

"No. He was legally and rightfully arrested in Acktar, and I have eleven witnesses besides Martyn who can testify to that, though getting a hold of them on short notice might be difficult." Leith headed for the door but halted as if just remembering one last thing. "Oh, and by the way. You might receive an angry visit from an ambassador from Verden about the little matter of me and Martyn being found wandering deep into their territory."

"Leith." Keevan looked up from his paperwork then. "Please tell me you didn't."

"You know I'd never lie to you like that." Leith turned back around and plopped into one of the two hard backed chairs facing Keevan's desk. "It's all in the report, but we were apprehended in a valley in the Great Mountains along with Grier, who we happened to be traveling with as fellow Acktarians without any duress involved whatsoever, and a squad of Verdenish soldiers nicely provided us an escort all the way out of their country."

Keevan heaved a sigh. "You just have to make my job harder, don't you?"

"I don't see why. This is exactly the sort of international incident you were hoping for." Leith resisted the urge to prop his boots on Keevan's desk. That would take the whole annoying cousin thing a step too far.

"Yes, but I didn't want us to be the ones to cause it." Keevan crossed his arms and leaned back in his chair. "It means they have the initial advantage, being the injured and innocent party, while I have to make an official apology without actually apologizing for anything, and that's all before I can even begin negotiating from that weakened position."

"Just admit it. You'll have the Verdenish ambassador talked around and agreeing to a treaty on your terms within an hour." Leith pushed to his feet, giving in to his grin. "You can thank me later."

"Not a chance." Keevan muttered the words through a smile. Then the smile dropped from his face. "Since you're here, I might as well pass this information along in person. Kane Rivers ran away from the family in Dently who took him in."

Kane Rivers. Leith let out a long breath. The boy had been eleven last time Leith had seen him. The one loyal Blade trainee who had refused to leave Nalgar Castle with Leith and Jamie. Kane would be about thirteen, almost fourteen now. "Have Blade Marshals Dillon and Chester searched for him?"

Covering most of the central part of Acktar, those Blade Marshals would be the closest to Dently.

"Yes. Couldn't find a trace of him. I'm sure that report is already headed for your desk as we speak." King Keevan traced a finger along the scar on his neck. "I only heard first because I asked the family to keep me informed. They tried their best, but he never wanted to be there."

"All he wanted was to be a Blade." That ached inside Leith. He'd wanted to help all the trainees escape Respen's hold. But there was nothing he, Keevan, the adopting family, Jamie, or any of them could do if Kane refused to be helped. "I'll put out the word to all the Blade Marshals to watch for him."

"That's all we can do at this point." Keevan shook his head, as if dismissing what he couldn't fix, and the smile returned to his face. He waved at the wall that separated his office from the family wing of the castle. "Will you be staying for supper? Addie would love to see you and show off Aileen. Duncan will probably chatter your ear off, though you'll be doing better than me if you can understand half of what he's saying."

Something warmed inside Leith at the thought of Prince Duncan and Princess Aileen. They were almost like a niece and a nephew. But he shook his head. "I've been gone long enough as it is. I don't want to delay even another night."

"I understand."

He probably did. Keevan had left for war against Respen when Addie was seven months along with Duncan. He knew exactly what it was like to worry about the wife he'd left behind.

Keevan nodded toward the door. "I won't keep you any longer, then. I pray the next report I receive from you will have good news."

"So do I." With one last nod in Keevan's direction, Leith left.

It was beyond time to return home.

KAYLEIGH PARRIED BRANDI'S THRUST AND TURNED THE momentum to a side cut of her own with her practice sword. Brandi side-stepped and blocked, lashing out with a kick that would've taken Kayleigh down if she hadn't jumped back.

On the cabin's porch, Renna's knitting needles clicked. When Kayleigh risked a glance, Renna still had Leith's letter in her lap, re-reading it yet again, as she worked on yet another pair of socks for the baby.

Not that Kayleigh could blame her. She had Martyn's letter tucked into a pocket. They had gone over two weeks without a single letter to let them know if Leith and Martyn were still alive. When letters finally came, they were short, saying they'd captured Adam Sullivan's killer and would be home as soon as they saw him properly locked up in Nalgar.

Something slapped into Kayleigh's thigh. "You aren't paying attention."

Kayleigh turned back to Brandi in time to block a second strike, spin, and let loose with a quick succession of strikes and counterstrikes.

"Leith!"

Renna's shriek nearly caused Kayleigh to drop her practice sword. She turned in time to see Renna wiggle and rock her way out her seat, moving faster than Kayleigh thought possible considering Renna was eight months pregnant.

Kayleigh whirled, and then she did drop her practice sword.

Riders crested the hill on two dust-colored horses. The sunlight glinted on one of the riders' blond hair.

Renna was already partway down the road. How she was managing to run when she normally could do nothing more than waddle, Kayleigh didn't know.

But then her own feet were skimming the ground, even as Martyn and Leith urged their horses down the hill toward them.

Leith practically threw himself from his horse as he reached Renna, and there was laughing and kissing as Leith held Renna close.

Then Martyn was jumping down from his still moving horse and wrapped Kayleigh in his arms, and she didn't care about Leith and Renna's reunion anymore. She hugged him back, burying her face against his neck and shoulder. He was warm and solid against her. Strong. Smelling a little rank after so many days in the saddle. Strange how she didn't care. Not too much, anyway.

"How I missed you." He mumbled before he kissed her. "Especially during those tense moments when I was certain we were either going to be killed on sight or arrested and have to depend on King Keevan to eventually negotiate our release."

"What?" Kayleigh pulled back enough to glare up at him. "What did you do?"

"We went all the way to the Great Mountains. They're amazing, just as grand as the stories you hear about them. I'd take you someday, but depending on how King Keevan manages to smooth over the incident we caused, Leith and I may be banned from Verden for life." Martyn shrugged, his hands resting lightly on her waist. "It was my fault, really. I got too focused on Grier and charged on ahead without a good look around first. Got ourselves captured by a passel of Verdenish soldiers, but then Leith put it in their commander's head that it would be in everyone's best interest if he simply escorted us to the border."

And that was why Kayleigh would never insist on moving away from Stetterly. Because no one made quite as good a team as Martyn and Leith, unless it was Leith and Shad.

"And I'm very thankful he did." Kayleigh tightened her grip around Martyn. It had been bad enough to have no word from him for two weeks while he had been apparently deep inside Verden. But it would've been so much worse if, instead of the short note that he was coming home, she had received an official message from King Keevan that Martyn had been captured or killed. "I finished my wedding dress. It would've been horrible if I'd gone through all the work of making it and then couldn't use it."

"That would have been tragic. Knowing your skill with needle and thread, it will be stunning." Martyn's voice softened on the last word, a smile touching the corners of his mouth. "It must've been quiet here if you had enough time to finish it already."

"Nothing too exciting." That bandit raid hardly counted.

Something must've shown in her eyes or come across in her voice because Martyn's smile faded. "What happened?"

"Just four bandits who thought it would be a good idea to rob the lady of Stetterly while the infamous Blade Marshals were away." Kayleigh focused on Martyn's shirt rather than look at his face. She didn't want to see him go all overprotective over something that hadn't truly put her life in danger. "It honestly isn't anything to worry about. We had them subdued in less than five minutes."

She braced herself, feeling the tension in Martyn's hands from his grip on her waist.

"Really? I'm sorry I missed it. I so love standing back and watching you take down smug bandits." Martyn planted a quick kiss on her forehead. "You'll have to tell me all the details over a celebratory dinner tonight."

She met his gaze then, searching his face. "You really want to hear about it? You aren't going to go all overprotective on me?"

Martyn sighed and cupped her cheek. "Being overprotective is more Leith's thing than mine, you know that, and somehow Renna has the patience to put up with it and the glare to make sure he backs off when he's too overprotective.

That's how they work. But we have our own thing. I tell you about the bad guys I've taken out, and you tell me about the miscreants you've beaten up. That's how we work."

"I know, it's just..." Kayleigh trailed off. She wasn't even sure what she'd been about to say. Why was she getting all these doubts and worries? She'd been courting Martyn for two years now. Only weeks ago she'd been impatient to marry him.

This doubt wasn't about Martyn, exactly. She knew his heart, everything from his sarcastic grouchiness to his kindness to the layers of pain.

But marriage was going to change things, wasn't it? After all, she'd been essentially independent and answering to no one but God for most of her life. Yes, she'd had her father, but he'd been gone for long hours, and he'd raised her to be independent, trusting that she would make good decisions. Because she loved him and valued that trust, she'd never let him down.

And then she'd been on her own. Even while courting Martyn, she'd remained independent. Yes, she'd asked his advice on a few things. But it wasn't like she'd needed his permission, nor had he needed hers.

But marriage was different, wasn't it? It came with its own expectations and demands and as the reality loomed, she wasn't sure she was as ready as she'd thought.

"It's just what, Kayleigh?" Martyn's voice had a hint of strain to it, like it did when he was trying hard not to run his fingers through his hair.

"It's just..." Why was she biting her tongue with this anyway? This was Martyn. Maybe he'd get mad. Maybe not. But it wasn't going to do either of them any good keeping these doubts all bottled up when it did far more to talk them over. "I know I'm not your typical wife material. Yes, I enjoy sewing and cooking and even cleaning occasionally, but I also enjoy sword practice and I love my job as the captain of Stetterly's guards, and I'm just...I don't know...worried that you'll—"

Martyn pulled away from her, ran a hand through his hair, and huffed out a breath, the muscle at the corner of his jaw knotting as if it physically pained him to hold back his muttering. When he inhaled deeply, he pulled a bar of soap out of his pocket, swiped it over his tongue, grimaced, and jammed the soap back into his pocket. For the words he'd been thinking, apparently, since he hadn't said them out loud.

When he turned to face her, his hand on her cheek was gentle, even if his eyes had his stubborn, tight look to them. "Saying you are or aren't a *typical* anything is a bad road to travel. It just means you're too busy comparing yourself to others to see the logical truth setting out in front of you. God created us all to be unique men and women. You're going to be your own version of a God-fearing wife, just like Renna is her version and Jolene is hers."

As he said it, the churn in her chest eased. Perhaps she hadn't been doubting. Not exactly. But she'd still needed to hear him say this out loud.

"Whoever said you couldn't enjoy cooking and sewing *and* whacking people with a sword? I happen to love that you're skilled with various pointy objects ranging from a needle to a butcher knife to a sword." Martyn placed his hands on her waist, tugging her closer. "I fell in love with you because you are you."

When put that way, her doubts did look rather superficial after all. Then again, Martyn's ability to bluntly cut to the heart of things was one of the reasons why she fell in love with him. Kayleigh stood on her tiptoes and kissed his cheek. "And I love you because you don't put up with any nonsense. Even nonsense like worries that really shouldn't be worries."

"Happy to be of service, my lady captain." Martyn bent down to kiss her.

Kayleigh held up a hand. "No kissing after washing your mouth out with soap."

Martyn grimaced. "Forgot about that. So how does three weeks sound for the wedding?"

"Three weeks?" Kayleigh shook her head. Here she had been all filled with doubts a moment ago, and now three weeks sounded too long.

Ugh. Wedding jitters. She could really do without them.

"Too short? I thought you had the dress finished? But I guess maybe you need some more time to plan all the fancy rigmarole." Martyn's grin faltered, like he was trying hard not to scowl.

"No. Too long."

Martyn grinned. "Ah. While I share your impatience, we can't get married any sooner. We have to wait for the circuit-riding minister to make his swing through Stetterly, and he won't be back for three weeks. And that will give Shad and Jolene a chance to come."

"It would be nice to have them there. They are the only friends who aren't already in Stetterly." Kayleigh cocked her head. "How could you possibly know the minister won't be back for another three weeks? You just returned minutes ago."

"We ran into Owen on our way here." Martyn smirked. "I always scout first."

"Except for when you charge in and get yourself captured by Verdenish soldiers."

"Except then." Martyn rested his forehead against hers. "Three weeks."

They were going to be three rather long weeks.

11

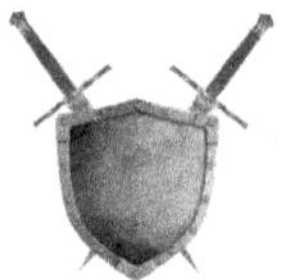

Martyn paced in front of the fireplace in the cabin that had once been Kayleigh's and soon would be theirs. Apparently his nerves were bad enough that Leith, Shad, and Owen abandoned him.

Oh, they had all come up with good excuses. Owen, as first groomsman, was checking to make sure Kayleigh and her bridesmaids were ready. Shad was making sure all the guests—the few of them that weren't a part of the wedding—were settled in the church and that the minister was ready. Leith was scouting the trail from Martyn's cabin out of the canyon, as if any bandits would dare invade Stetterly today with three Blade Marshals here.

A knock sounded on the door.

Hopefully it was Owen coming to say the wedding was finally going to start.

"Come in." Martyn kept pacing. He might as well get all his energy out now. He wouldn't want to get shifty feet while standing there in the church, not after he'd promised Kayleigh he wasn't going to run.

The door creaked open, but it wasn't Owen's boots on the floorboards. Instead, footsteps shuffled across the floor.

Martyn turned in time to see Renna, wearing a fancy blue dress for the wedding, sink into the nearest chair. She grimaced and rubbed at her back. "That was way more work than I expected, especially for a tradition that you probably don't even consider a tradition."

"How did you even get down here?" Martyn gripped his wrist behind his back to stop himself from running his hand through his hair and messing it up. "And what tradition?"

"I rode, and Leith led the horse." Renna huffed and leaned back in the chair in a very unladylike fashion. It seemed that being eight months and two weeks pregnant made Renna unconcerned about proper posture. "And Leith said you probably hadn't even noticed. Oh, well. It wouldn't have felt right if I hadn't come. You were there at both of my weddings."

Martyn stifled a chuckle and sat backwards on the chair facing Renna. "God willing, this will be the only wedding I ever have to endure. I don't want to go through this hassle again."

"No running?" Renna smiled.

"No running. And I'm counting on you to drag me down the aisle if you have to." Martyn couldn't help but grin back. For some reason, it did feel right to have Renna here right now. She was his sister, after all.

"I'm not sure if I'm able to drag anybody at the moment. You're going to be lucky if I don't have this baby right in the middle of the ceremony." Renna rubbed her side. When she glanced up, she laughed, perhaps at the sheer horror that must have been etched across his face. "Don't worry. I doubt it will happen. I have two whole weeks yet, and if the ride down here didn't do it, then standing a few minutes for the ceremony certainly won't."

The door opened again, and this time Leith stepped inside. "Owen's back. Says everyone's ready when you are."

Renna held out a hand. "Help me up."

Leith took her hand and hauled Renna to her feet. "We'll scout the trail on our way up. You and Owen can follow in a few minutes."

Renna grimaced. "I am so ready not to be pregnant. Let's go."

As Leith and Renna left, Owen stepped inside, his mouth tipped in a smile. He held out a flat, fabric-wrapped package. "This is for you."

What sort of gift would Owen give to Martyn moments before the wedding? Martyn pulled off the fabric wrapping and froze. He held a small painting in his hands. A painting of his family.

Yet it was his family as they never would be on this earth. He and Martyn stood in the back, both of them fully grown and looking as they did now. Mama and Papa sat in front, smiling.

His family as they should've been. Happy. Whole.

"Papa and Mama would've been proud today." Owen stood next to him, also looking at the painting.

He was...a good man. That was a strange thought. A man his parents could've been proud of.

Yet there was an ache too that, now that he was finally

the man they had always believed he would become, they weren't there to see it. But they were in Heaven, and Martyn had Owen.

And Martyn was thankful for the life God had given him, even with its heartaches.

After setting the painting on the table, Martyn hugged his brother. "I'm so glad you managed to track me down two years ago."

Owen patted his back and pulled away. "So am I, but please don't go all sentimental on me. I really don't know how to handle that kind of nonsense."

And there was his brother keeping Martyn's priorities straight. "I'm supposed to be sentimental today of all days, right? Beam with sheer joy at the sight of my bride walking down the aisle, choke up when hugging my brother, maybe even shed a tear at the wonder of pledging my life to hers..."

"You do that, and Kayleigh is going to hold you at sword point to demand who you are and what you've done with her husband-to-be." Owen grinned. "Honestly, I'm going to be surprised at your willpower if you manage to get through the entire ceremony without demanding the minister skip to the vows and get it over with."

Martyn opened his mouth but paused. Leith and Renna's wedding had been forever long with all sorts of symbolic rigmarole that probably served some sort of purpose to someone. The ceremony could be over in five minutes if the bride and groom just said their vows and were done with it. Maybe it would be different this time because it was Martyn's own wedding and he wasn't about to pass out from recent burns but...no. It would probably seem more interminable.

He was doing this for Kayleigh. He had to remember that. She deserved her wedding to be everything she wanted it to be.

"You're probably right." Martyn fell into step with Owen as they left the cabin and started the hike toward the top of the canyon. Martyn kept his gaze focused on the trail, trying to hide how his throat tightened. Annoying emotions. "I'm going to be settled, you know, after today. You've stuck around, just as you promised, but now it's time for me to let you move on with your life like I promised."

"I can stay longer if you need me to."

Martyn shot a glance at Owen, but Owen's jaw was tight, his head down. Was Owen offering because he didn't really want to return to Surgis or because he thought it was the right thing to say? "You have a home in Surgis. A girl who has been waiting for you and writing you letters all this time. I'm going to miss you, but I always knew you would return there sooner rather than later. Besides, it's not like Surgis is that far away."

"I'll stick around here a week or two yet. Long enough to make sure my guard duties here are properly handed off. But..."

"It's time you went home. I understand." Martyn clapped Owen on the shoulder. "Now let's get me all properly married off and settled before Kayleigh starts to wonder if I really have run off."

HER STOMACH HAD BEEN ONE BIG CHURNING, TIGHT KNOT ALL morning. She'd barely managed to nibble on the bread Renna insisted she eat so she didn't pass out from hunger.

But the moment Kayleigh stepped into Stetterly's church and saw Martyn standing there at the end of the aisle, dressed in simple black trousers and a white shirt along with knives in his boots and strapped to his waist, all the flutters and churning and knots faded away.

Behind Martyn were his groomsmen, Owen, Leith, and Shad, and off to the side stood her bridesmaids Renna, Brandi, and Jolene, but if she hadn't seen them earlier in the day, she wouldn't have been able to say at that moment what they were wearing.

Her light blue, silk dress swirled around her. She'd done without the usual train since it had seemed like more hassle than it would be worth to remove it afterwards if she wanted to wear the dress for special occasions later. Instead, she used the extra fabric to add pleats to the skirt so it was more full and twirly around her ankles.

It had taken some doing, but she'd worked the skirt on the right side so that it draped nicely underneath the sword she wore buckled at her side. After all, she was the captain of Stetterly's guards, and if Martyn was going to wear his weapons at their wedding, then she would too.

Martyn smiled, and, gripped by an impulse, she stopped right there in the church aisle and spun, much as she had that day over two years ago when she'd worn the dress made from the green fabric he'd traded for in Flayin Falls. Some of the more staid matrons of Stetterly were probably scandalized, but Kayleigh didn't care.

All that mattered was, when she faced forward again,

Martyn's smile widened, and he was as close to beaming as she'd ever seen him.

She walked down the aisle by herself. Sheriff Allen, Lord Alistair, Lord Conree of Surgis, and even Matthias Westin had offered, but it hadn't seemed right to find a substitute for what should've been her father's role.

But then she reached the end of the aisle and clasped Martyn's hands, and she wasn't thinking about those who were missing because her chest filled with the warmth of everyone who was here.

Two and a half years ago, isolated in her little cabin in the Sheered Rock Hills, she never would've guessed how God would use a sarcastic, annoying, highly improper former Blade to bring her into the family and community she had now.

The pews behind her were filled with the citizens of Stetterly, Lord Alistair and his family, Lord Conree of Surgis, and even Matthias Westin. It had seemed right to invite him after everything he'd done to help move her father's cabin to Stetterly, and he'd said he was honored to attend in memory of Kayleigh's father.

For two people who thought they had no one when they met, the church was remarkably full.

THE CEREMONY WAS NOT INTERMINABLE. IT COULDN'T BE WITH Kayleigh smirking at him, making it awfully hard to remain suitably solemn.

But soon enough Martyn slipped from the feasting and out the church's front door with Kayleigh's hand in his.

No sooner had they stepped outside than Owen appeared leading Wanderer. "Shad is scouting the area from here to the canyon and Leith is scouting the canyon trail."

"Thanks." Martyn turned to help Kayleigh mount, but she was already clambering up behind the saddle. As she settled into place, she had to adjust her sword and the voluminous folds of her skirt.

When she was settled, Martyn swung into the saddle, taking extra care not to kick her in the stomach. If she noticed, she didn't say anything about it. He didn't expect her to.

Kayleigh's arms wrapped around his waist, and she leaned against his back. He rested his hand over hers clasped around him.

"What are you thinking about?" Kayleigh whispered in his ear.

He patted her hands. "How things have changed. To think I grumped at you the first time we did this."

Shad appeared out of the darkness. "It's safe between here and the canyon."

With a nod to Shad and Owen, Martyn nudged Wanderer into a trot, then an easy canter. They passed Leith and Renna's cabin at a distance, the candlelight shining through the windows. Lights also shone in the finished stables.

At the top of the trail, Leith stepped from the darkness. "I scouted the trail. No signs of trouble."

In the darkness, Martyn met Leith's gaze as best he could. A little under two years ago, their roles had been reversed, but now Martyn understood better what it was to know tonight, at least, he didn't have to worry about a knife in the back. And for a man who'd lived the life he had, that wasn't the sort of safety he experienced often. "Thanks."

Martyn directed Wanderer down the trail, and both he and Kayleigh leaned back during the steep sections of the trail. At the bottom, they rode along the rippling, moon-flecked Ondieda River before they turned into the winding entrance into the hidden valley where their cabin lay.

As they turned the final corner, a cheery glow lit up the hidden clearing. Lamplight welcoming them home.

In front of the cabin, Martyn dropped to the ground and reached for Kayleigh before she had a chance to scramble down by herself. "You can let me help you down. Just this once."

Kayleigh rested her hands on his shoulders as he swung her down, and she didn't step away when he set her feet on the ground. "In this dress, I probably would've fallen off anyway. I got a little carried away when making the skirt nice and full and swirly."

"It looks...nice."

Kayleigh kissed his cheek. "I know."

He pulled her closer. "You know, last time I spent a night with you in this cabin, you threatened me with a frying pan. I'm not going to get tossed out on my ear this time, am I?"

"Nope. We're entirely proper this time. Said the vows and everything." Kayleigh's arms wrapped around his neck. "Now are we going to stand in the dark all night or are we going to go inside our cabin?"

"The bugs are biting tonight, aren't they?" He swept her up into her arms, wincing when her sword swung around and smacked his knee.

She huffed out a breath. "Would it do any good to tell you to put me down?"

"Nope. Though I'd appreciate it if you got the door. Considering how much we reinforced it, I doubt I can kick it in." Martyn kissed her as she opened the door. "Welcome home, Kayleigh Hamish."

ONE AND A HALF WEEKS LATER...

The early dawn light filtered through the windows. Not that Leith was paying too much attention to the pink sunrise outside as he perched at the edge of the bed beside Renna.

His son was a tiny, warm bundle in his arms, breathing in and out slowly in sleep. Leith eased a finger over the wisps of dark hair covering the baby's head.

Dark hair. Like his own. For some reason that fact, more than anything, struck him. It was as if, subconsciously, he'd always expected their child to look just like Renna and only Renna.

Perhaps because Renna's family and Renna's father was the legacy he'd imagined passed down. Maybe because he'd spent most of his life hating the features that marked him as his father's son when he would've preferred not to share any blood with the man.

It hadn't occurred to him how precious it would be to see his dark hair on his son. The sight sent something hot and fierce through him, burning away in a part of his heart that had still been ice until that moment.

And he wasn't afraid. It would probably hit him later. The absolute terror would probably send him to his knees in prayer many a dark night. But at that moment, holding his newborn son in his arms, what burned in his chest left no room for anything else.

Renna leaned against his shoulder, her eyes half-closed.

He leaned his head against hers. "You probably should rest. It was a long night."

She yawned but struggled to sit upright. "It was. But I've already had a nap, and I'll sleep more later. I can tell you are bursting to show David off and I don't want to miss the looks on everyone's faces—or the look on your face—when they see him the first time."

Leith kissed her forehead. "All right." If she asked for a pot of gold and the moon at that moment, he would've gladly trotted off to fetch them.

"Does my hair look all right?" Renna patted down a few stray wisps that had come out of her braid. Dark circles shadowed under her eyes, but at least her cheeks had more color in them than they had a couple of hours ago after David's birth. "And if you say I look like I just gave birth…"

He nearly said *No one will care*, but his better sense caught up with him just in time. "You look beautiful."

"No, I don't, but thanks for saying it."

"I'm not lying." With her tired, but beaming smile, how could she be anything but beautiful? Leith eased off the bed while still cradling David in his arms. "Do you want everyone all at once or a few at a time?"

"It's going to be crowded in here, but might as well let them in all at once." Renna settled back against the pillows propping her upright and adjusted the bedcovers.

Leith crossed the room and opened the door to the kitchen.

Michelle and the older woman from Stetterly who was the unofficial midwife for the town bustled about the kitchen. They'd stuck around in case of complications.

Leith smiled before either of them asked him if something was wrong. "Renna says she's up for visitors. Could one of you fetch them? I'm sure Brandi at least is getting rather impatient."

Michelle stood, then paused. "All of them?"

"Yes, it's only nine people. I think we can fit them all inside." Leith left the door open a crack and returned to Renna's side.

Brandi was the first one to burst inside. "Renna! You're all right? We were told the baby was born and you were both healthy. Boy or girl? What's the name?"

She skidded to a halt next to Leith, and Leith cradled David so she could better see the baby's face peeking from the blanket. "Brandi, meet your nephew, David Grayce Torren."

Brandi's mouth widened, caught somewhere between a grin and a gasp. She reached out as if she was going to touch the baby, then halted, as if she didn't dare. "David. A man after God's own heart."

Trust Brandi to pick out the reason behind David's name. It was Leith's deepest prayer for his son. More than health. More than safety. More even than that his son would never have a cause to doubt Leith's love.

"Do you want to hold him?" Renna leaned forward.

Brandi nodded yes, but her eyes were wide as she sat on the chair next to the bed and held out her arms.

Not that Leith could blame her. His own heart was thumping in his throat as he maneuvered through safely transferring David from his arms into Brandi's. David was so tiny and delicate and his head had to be supported, and Leith really didn't want to drop him.

More footsteps scuffed, and Leith looked up in time to see everyone else file into the room. Martyn and Kayleigh with hands clasped. Shad and Jolene with Hannah, their dark-haired six-month-old propped against Shad's shoulder. Lord Alistair with a smile on his face and Lady Alistair, who breezed to Renna's side to check on her first. And, finally, Jamie and Ranson crept into the far corner, eyes wide.

Martyn peered over Brandi's shoulder, then glanced up at Leith. "He looks like you."

Kayleigh huffed. "Of course, he looks like Leith. He also looks like Renna. He is their son."

"Yes, but..." Martyn shook his head, as if he was just as mystified as Leith was over David's dark hair.

Kayleigh shot Martyn a *look*. "If you say another non-helpful comment, I might just threaten you into holding him."

Martyn's eyes widened, and he stared from Kayleigh to David in Brandi's arms. "Please, no. I don't want to break the baby on the first day."

Kayleigh muttered something that sounded like Martyn was going to have to learn eventually, but then she was pulling Martyn around the bed so they could talk to Renna.

While Jolene joined Martyn and Kayleigh by Renna, Shad knelt in front of Brandi, putting Hannah's face level with David. "This is..." Shad glanced up at Leith. "What are we going to tell them they are to each other?"

Lord Alistair halted next to Leith. "Cousins, I believe.

Unless you don't intend to have Hannah call them Uncle Leith and Aunt Renna."

"I just wanted to be sure. That makes David our first nephew." Shad grinned at Leith before turning back to David. "Hannah, meet your cousin David."

Hannah blinked dark brown eyes at the baby, then stuck her fist in her mouth and chewed. A line of drool worked its way down her chin.

Lady Alistair joined them and held her arms out to the baby. Brandi frowned but passed David over. Lady Alistair traced a finger over the dark hair. "I've already told Renna, but please know David will never lack for grandparents, if you don't mind us taking on the role."

"I'd be honored." It was a good thought—if strange one—that David would grow up surrounded by so much family. Shad, Martyn, Ranson, and Jamie for uncles. Kayleigh, Jolene, and Brandi for aunts. Lord and Lady Alistair for grandparents. Hopefully many cousins and a few siblings. Keevan and Addie and their children for even more cousins.

After David had been passed from Lady Alistair to Jolene to Kayleigh, Leith reclaimed him and headed for the corner where Ranson and Jamie stood, glancing around as if they didn't think they should be there.

Leith held David so both Ranson and Jamie could see him. "Your nephew."

"Nephew?" Ranson asked, peering down at David as if a baby was a puzzle Ranson couldn't figure out.

"I said you are both my brothers. That makes David your nephew just as much as he's Brandi's nephew." Leith stared at Ranson until Ranson looked up. "You're family."

Jamie stepped closer. "May I hold him?"

Handing David over this time wasn't as nerve-wracking. Perhaps Leith had grown numb to the panic after watching David being passed from person to person.

It was so *right* having them all gathered here. Leith had traveled to the far Great Mountains and back, yet this was the best sight he'd ever seen.

THE HEALER AND THE CLERK

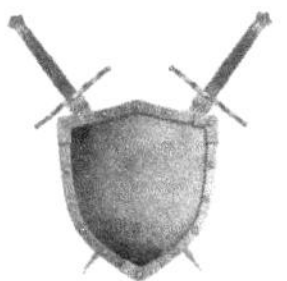

1

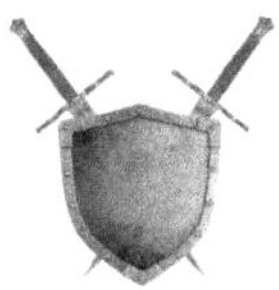

Michelle Allen adjusted her drab, brown dress. It sufficiently hid her curves, didn't it? It had better, considering how it hung boxy and tent-like around her.

For two years, she had been training to be Stetterly's healer, only asking for Renna's assistance when it was something more than a simple broken bone or gashes caused by a farming accident.

And for two years, she'd been doing everything in her power to erase the reputation of town flirt she'd gained as a fifteen and sixteen-year-old. Too bad she was now more a woman at eighteen than she'd been when she'd flaunted herself at sixteen.

Even wearing drab and unflattering clothing didn't stop the assumptions and accusations. If she so much as smiled at a man, she was accused of flirting. She'd had some of the young women refuse to let her stitch up their husbands because they thought she'd act inappropriately.

Two years apparently wasn't enough time to erase that sort of tainted reputation, no matter how many tents she wore for dresses and how many smiles she kept from crossing her face. Never mind that she'd never done anything more than flirting.

She glanced one last time at the mirror. Her dark brown hair pulled back into a tight bun. No powder hid the smattering of red bumps on her chin and nose. Surely she was sufficiently unbeautiful for the day.

Grabbing her leather bag that held her healing supplies, she stepped from her room.

The main room was empty, her papa having left over an hour ago to begin his rounds of the town.

Good. No disproving frowns to welcome her day. Her papa loved her, she knew. But there was always that frown. The one that said, she suspected, that she was turning out too much like her mama. Too beautiful. Too flirtatious. Too likely to get herself into the same trouble her mama had.

After grabbing a piece of bread, Michelle strode down the outdoor stairs from the upstairs rooms above the jail that served as their home along the main street of Stetterly, if one could call the dirt track that ran between the houses and businesses a road.

As she set off down the street, she concentrated on walking without her hips swaying. Not an easy task, and she nearly ran into someone because she was concentrating so hard. Only a voice saying her name and the vague impression of some figure standing before her halted her steps in time.

She looked up to find herself barely a foot away from Ranson Harding. He was slim and small, barely taller than he'd been at sixteen when she'd met him. His face was level with hers, and his brown eyes—more a chestnut than dark brown—kept flicking from the street to her face and back down again.

"Ranson." She smiled, remembered she wasn't supposed to smile that wide or brightly or she'd be accused of flirting, and tempered her smile into something respectable. "Did you need something? Are Renna and David all right?"

Renna and Leith's newborn was only three weeks old. Still a dangerous time for a baby.

"Um, I..." Ranson clasped his hands behind his back, rocking back and forth on his heels. "I wanted to...to ask..." Ranson swallowed. When he managed to get the words out, they came in a rush. "Could I court you?"

Michelle stepped back, her breath catching in her throat. That was...unexpected. Yes, she'd kissed him and flirted with him. Once. Two years ago. Before she'd resolved to stop flirting and not encourage anyone. Since then she'd done her best to just be friends.

She liked Ranson. He was nice. Sweet, in an adorable sort of way.

But he wasn't the kind of man she needed. He was someone it would be too easy for her to manipulate with a smile and a bat of her eyelashes. No, she needed someone with a strong personality. Someone who could resist her charms and keep her in check. Someone who would control her rather than be controlled by her.

What was she supposed to tell Ranson? There was no good way to tell him no without hurting his feelings. And Ranson deserved so much better than having his feelings hurt by the likes of her. He needed a sweet, quiet girl who would appreciate him for how kind and gentle he was.

"Ranson, you're a nice guy, but..." How she hated having to say it. "I like you as a friend."

He still blinked at her, as if he wasn't quite sure what she meant.

Was she going to have to hurt him worse by saying it plainly?

"Sorry, I just don't see you as more than a friend."

"So you don't want to court me?" Ranson's smile faltered.

"No, sorry."

She couldn't look at the hurt melting those liquid brown eyes of his. She spun and strode off as quickly as she could manage without her hips swaying.

THAT...HADN'T GONE WELL. RANSON KICKED AT ONE OF THE pebbles in the dirt road but missed and sent up a cloud of dust instead. A lump formed in his throat, and he blinked back tears.

Tears. As if he was an emotional little boy instead of the tough, eighteen-year-old grown man he was supposed to be. Why couldn't he hold back his tears and control his emotions? A man didn't cry. A Blade didn't cry.

Had he done something wrong? He'd remembered to keep his smile in check instead of grinning too wide and awkwardly. He'd thought he'd stayed a proper distance away since standing too close apparently made other people uncomfortable, but he had been standing closer than the three feet away he normally stood when talking to other people. His hands had remained clasped behind his back so he wouldn't fidget in a way that made other people edge away from him.

He'd forgotten to make eye contact. Was that it? He hadn't managed to be normal, and she could tell he was faking it so she'd run.

Had it been approaching her there in the street? Was there a proper, expected way a boy was supposed to ask to court a girl? He should've asked Leith before he'd set out today, but Leith had been distracted lately with the new baby. Maybe Jamie would know. Jamie knew a lot of stuff like that.

Or maybe Ranson was just too awkward. He did his best to act like everyone else. Some days it felt like he had a stack of paper in his head where he stored all his memorized patterns for how to pretend to act during social situations. Every time he talked to people, he had to frantically shuffle through that mental stack of paper until he found the proper response.

Mostly he could pretend to fit in all right. Unless he accidentally grabbed the wrong paper for that social situation or didn't find it fast enough or didn't have a set of memorized steps for that particular setting.

Other people just seemed to know—as if by instinct— how big their smile should be and how loud their voice should sound and how close to stand. When to shake hands or speak or nod or stay silent.

Whatever that instinct was, Ranson's was broken. Or missing.

A horse pulling a farmer's wagon rumbled down the street. Somewhere behind him, a shop door creaked open and a bell shrieked. People talking. The scent of dust and horse choked the air.

Too much. Too much noise. Too many people. His breath caught in his throat, jamming with the tears until he couldn't breathe.

He hurried out of the town as quickly as he could manage without drawing too much attention to himself. He probably should find one of the farmers he worked for occasionally and see if they needed any help, but...not right now. Not when he was still trying to blink away tears.

As he crested the ridge to the east of town, Leith and Renna's cabin came into sight near the rim of the Spires Canyon. Off to one side, the new stables rose against the prairie, a corral connected to one side where Blizzard, Valor, Big Brown, Buster, and Snapper grazed.

Ranson paused by the fence and leaned against it. He might as well spend some time with the horses until he could wrestle the tears back under control.

Blizzard and Buster trotted right up to the fence, Big Brown and Valor not far behind.

Ranson lifted the lid from the barrel where they kept apples too worm-eaten or bruised for humans to eat. He fed apples to the pack of friendlier horses, holding out the last apple to Snapper.

Finally Snapper clopped to the fence, his ears flicking back and forth. He bared his teeth and stretched out his neck.

Ranson dodged the horse's bite that had been aimed at his shoulder. He held out the apple and, eyeing him, Snapper took it. Ranson barely managed to snatch his fingers away before Snapper chomped on those too.

The others didn't understand why he liked this horse so much. There had been a time the stablehands at Nalgar would've put Snapper down if he hadn't been a Blade's horse.

But Ranson understood Snapper. Snapper just didn't know how to interact with people the way he should, just like Ranson.

Patting the horse one last time and evading another bite, Ranson headed for the stable. Inside, a staircase led to the attic room Ranson shared with Jamie. The room was big enough for each of them to have a bed and a trunk of clothes each while Jamie had even squished in a small table he used as a desk. Windows in each of the peaked ends provided light. Quilts covered their beds, a rug on the floor.

Home. So much better than what he'd had in the Blades. It felt more like the little room of his childhood with Nana Harding.

Nana. She wasn't his real grandmother. To this day he didn't even know who his real parents were or if Ranson was his real name.

But Nana was better than any family he could've had. She'd taken in a skinny, abandoned three-year-old who could barely talk and raised him as her own. She'd given him her last name, and he'd been the son she'd never had until the day she'd died when he was twelve.

As Ranson entered their room, Jamie remained hunched at his desk, studying a book on some dead language, not even looking up. How things had changed. There was a time when neither Jamie nor Ranson would've sat with their back to a room or ignored the sounds of footsteps behind them.

Over the past year, Jamie had grown, passing Ranson by

an inch or two and well on his way to catching Leith. At sixteen, Jamie's voice had deepened, heading for a baritone. Unlike Ranson's voice, which had remained a higher tenor.

Ranson shifted but he wasn't going to find company here. Did he want company or solitude? He wasn't sure.

Either way, Jamie was busy. Ranson turned and hiked back down the stairs and across the eight paces from the stable to the cabin. He tiptoed onto the porch and cracked the door open as quietly as possible in case David was taking a nap. Being yelled at once by a sleep-deprived Renna had been one time too many.

Leith and Renna sat at the opposite sides of the kitchen table, stacks of papers covering the whole tabletop. Renna had her head on her hand, eyes scrunched and mouth moving as she worked sums in Stetterly's ledger, comparing them with a sheet next to the ledger. Probably Stetterly's tax assessment. Leith frowned as he compared two sheets of paper and made notes on a third.

David wasn't anywhere in sight so it was just as well Ranson had been quiet. Must be nap time.

"If a bushel of corn equals five percent of a gold coin and each head of cattle equals half a gold coin, and Stetterly's yield is fifteen thousand bushels of corn and five hundred head of cattle, and our taxes owed is thirty percent of the yield, minus the three percent school credit, two percent road credit, and the Blade Marshal expenses incurred, then how much does Stetterly owe for taxes? Have you figured out which of your expenses I can count as tax deductible?"

"It should be sixty-two gold coins, but I'm double checking. Something isn't adding up right." Leith rubbed at the back of his neck.

"Well, I can't finish these calculations until you finish your calculations." Renna's voice had an edge to it.

Ranson shifted. Could he slip out the door without either of them noticing?

A cry pierced from the second bedroom, the one that had been Ranson's and Jamie's until the stable was finished a little over a month ago.

Renna groaned, letting her head fall onto her arms, muttering something under her breath.

The baby's cries hurt against Ranson's ears. Smells choked his nose. Sour milk and dirty diaper. Bread and sausage from breakfast. The woodsy scent of the cabin walls.

Too much sound. Too many smells. Ranson clasped his hands behind his back so tightly they hurt. His breath ached inside his chest. There were those pesky tears again threatening to spill over.

Numbers. Counting. He focused on the far wall. Ten logs to the ceiling. Forty-eight bricks across the width of the kitchen. Fifty-one bricks deep for a total of two thousand four hundred and forty-eight bricks in the floor.

Leith stood, walked around the table, and knelt beside Renna, resting a hand on her back. "I'll get him." He pressed a kiss to Renna's temple and murmured something in her ear that brought a tired smile to her face before he stood.

Heading for the bedroom, Leith hopped the one step to the parlor and entered the bedroom. The crying went from a shriek to a whimper.

Leith returned carrying three-week year-old David cradled against his chest. Tufts of dark hair stood out from around David's head, his face a strawberry red from crying.

The baby was still giving hiccupping sobs in between softer whimpers as Leith rubbed his back.

As Leith handed David to Renna, the baby snuggled against Renna, making some sort of whining, whimpering cry.

Leith glanced at Ranson. "Was there something you needed?"

Yes. No. How could he explain that he simply didn't want to be alone at the moment? Ranson's feet were stuck to the floor, even if his skin crawled with the urge to bolt out the door. His chest was tight, his mind spinning.

"A hundred eighty-eight." The words burst from him before he could control it. He clamped his jaws shut.

"What?" Leith raised his eyebrows.

"A hundred and eighty-eight gold coins. That's how much Stetterly owes in taxes if your estimate of Blade Marshal expenses is correct." Ranson shifted his clasped hands behind his back.

If only he kept his mouth shut. He wasn't supposed to ever tell people about the numbers and the counting. It never ended well, except for that one time when Leith had figured it out years ago when training Ranson in the Blades.

Renna gaped at him as she patted David's back.

Ranson forced his clasped hands to remain behind his back. He must not fidget. A Blade didn't fidget. How many times had King Respen or Harrison Vane shouted those words at him?

"I'd forgotten how good you are with numbers." Leith eyed Ranson, and his gaze took on a look Ranson didn't have a hope of deciphering. Leith turned to Renna. "I saw him first."

"Think we can share?" Renna's smile was back on her face.

"Well, since we're so good at sharing..." A dimple appeared in Leith's cheek as he and Renna shared another one of those looks, the kind that held paragraphs of words without a single sound.

David gave another cry and fisted his hands into Renna's dress.

Renna sighed and patted David's back. "He's hungry again."

"Feed him and take a nap. The paperwork can wait." Leith rested a hand on Renna's shoulder.

"It can't wait too much longer. Keevan is already grumbling because we've waited this close to the deadline as it is." Renna leaned against Leith and mumbled something too softly for Ranson to hear.

After a murmured reply to Renna, Leith brushed his finger over David's wispy, dark hair, then straightened and strode to Ranson. "Let's step outside for a while."

Why? What was...

Oh, right. Ranson stumbled as Leith steered him out the door. As Leith had explained before, Renna appreciated a few minutes of peace and quiet. Something that was apparently hard to come by with five of them in and out of the cabin all the time and the new baby.

Leith led the way to the small garden to one side of the cabin. At this point in early summer, the corn was knee-high and a dark, rich green. "Might as well weed while we talk. You seem like you have something on your mind."

He did? Ranson trailed after Leith. Maybe he did. He wasn't sure how much he wanted to tell Leith. Or anyone. At least talking would be easier when his hands were kept busy.

Ranson settled into weeding one of the ten rows of corn, mentally counting the number of weeds he pulled.

Leith pulled out three weeds and tossed them to the side. "I know Renna and I said it as something of a joke inside, but I was serious."

"About what?" What was Leith talking about? Ranson had apparently missed something. Again.

Leith yanked out two more weeds. "I need a clerk. I've been thinking about it for a while. There's too much paperwork involved with running the Blade Marshals for one man to do it all, especially when I also have my duties as a Blade Marshal. But I'd need someone who understood the job and the dangers and who could assess reports and spot patterns more than simply transcribing and filing reports."

Now that Leith mentioned it, he had been doing a lot of paperwork lately.

Leith stopped weeding long enough to glance at Ranson. "I think you would be good for the job, if you're interested."

"Me?" Ranson halted mid-weed pull. Leith thought he would make a good clerk?

"You have neat handwriting—much better than mine—and you're good with numbers." Leith turned back to his weeding. "But only if you want the job. I don't want you to feel obligated because I'm the one asking. If you'd rather have a plot of land to farm, then I'll be just as proud. There's no shame—and a great deal of worth—in a life spent tending the ground. A quiet life that doesn't look like much to others can be just as glorifying to God, perhaps maybe more so, than a life that looks more honorable to other people."

Ranson thought he understood what Leith was saying. But Ranson didn't want to farm. Not really. He'd tried it, helping out with Stetterly's farmers, and it was all right. But not for him.

Not that he should be picky. At eighteen, almost nineteen, he was well past the age when he should've settled into some kind of job. Michelle had probably been right to reject him, considering he didn't even have the means to support himself at the moment.

He swallowed back the lump in his throat at the thought of Michelle's rejection. No, he wasn't going to think about it right now. Concentrate on what Leith was saying.

Ranson wasn't afraid of hard work or of doing things he didn't enjoy. He'd survived the Blades, and there hadn't been much that was enjoyable about that life.

But now another option was spread out before him. Work with Leith in the Blade Marshals, but without the fighting and killing Ranson couldn't stomach? He could spend his time with paper and numbers and no one would yell at him because he wasn't strong enough or tough enough. "Are you sure?"

"You understand what it's like to be a Blade Marshal, at least somewhat. Better than someone who has never had to fight for his life." Leith yanked out the last weed in his row and started on another row of corn. "But I would like you to take the tests and officially become a Blade Marshal, even if you never serve in the field."

"Why?" Ranson's stomach churned. Could he handle fighting even if it was only a test?

"You shouldn't be in danger as a clerk, but I can't guarantee you will never become a target." Leith stared at the weed in his hand. "With all the Blade Marshal reports I'm collecting and will keep receiving, there's going to be a lot of information that will need to be guarded from falling into the wrong hands. And, considering the confidential information we handle, I would rather set the precedent that the information is kept solely within the Blade Marshals. And, finally, I want you to have the confidence that you are a part of the Blade Marshals, not just an outsider temporarily handling the paperwork."

There would be a possibility of danger. Of having to fight again. Ranson sat right there in the dirt between the cornstalks and drew his knees up. "Do you think I can? I know I wasn't a very good Blade."

Leith stopped weeding. "That's not a bad thing."

No, it wasn't. But that wasn't what Ranson meant. Not entirely, anyway. Ranson drew in deep breath, but the words poured out of him anyway, as if he'd been holding them back for two years and they wouldn't stay inside any longer. "It would've been better if Blane had lived instead of me. He could've been a Blade Marshal like you, and he would've been good at it. I know Respen only kept me alive because it helped him control Blane."

Ranson's throat closed. Blane Altin had been as close as a brother from the moment they'd found each other on the streets when they were both twelve. And, in the end, Blane had died for Ranson. And what had Ranson done in the past two years with the life Blane had died to give him? Nothing besides odd jobs and bumbling around in Leith's footsteps.

He couldn't even ask a girl to court him without getting rejected. Nothing that was worth Blane's sacrifice.

Ranson never could do anything right. He'd fought as a Blade. Killed. Only to sink to his knees, vomiting and crying afterwards. Not what a Blade was supposed to be.

He hadn't even managed to lose his faith. Even as hard as he'd tried not to, he'd found himself praying even after blood stained his hands and the other Blades said God didn't exist. The other Blades stood on their own, but Ranson had been too weak to walk away from God even temporarily.

Leith sat back and blew out a long breath. "Yes, Respen let you live so he could manipulate Blane. He was good at that, letting us make friends then using those friends as weapons to keep us obedient to him. In the end, Martyn and I turned on each other because of it, but not you and Blane."

Maybe not, but only because Blane and Ranson bowed to Respen's control. So many times Respen sent Blane out to kill while keeping Ranson behind to make sure Blane killed and returned as he was supposed to. Even when Blane failed for the third time, he'd returned to Nalgar Castle to face a quick death rather than attempt to run and leave Ranson behind alone.

And Ranson had done the same thing when Leith had given Ranson a chance to escape to Eagle Heights. How Ranson had wanted to leave Acktar far behind. No more killing. No more Respen.

But he couldn't leave Blane behind to face Respen alone. So he'd returned, and Blane had died anyway.

"But I think Respen let you live for more than just manipulating Blane." Leith paused, his eyes steady on Ranson as if waiting for something. "You were the one Blade he never managed to break. He could make you kill, but he couldn't make you a killer like the rest of us. That baffled him."

Ranson had baffled Respen? Somehow Ranson couldn't picture King Respen ever being baffled by anything. If Ranson had failed to be broken, it was only because he was too odd and broken already to crumble any more. What more could Respen do to him when he was already too weak to hold back his tears or his churning stomach over the blood and the death? "I just couldn't manage to be strong like you or Blane."

"You had and still have a heart, Ranson. That's strength." Leith's gaze was focused on him.

Only after Leith looked away to yank out another weed did Ranson realize Leith had probably been waiting for him to make eye contact. Why could he never remember to make proper eye contact?

Ranson sat straighter. Leith thought Ranson had strength? That his weaknesses weren't such a bad thing?

He could handle this job. It would mean he could work with Leith, and he'd be doing something important. "I think...I think I'd like to be your clerk."

Leith grinned but kept weeding. Maybe he'd figured out Ranson wasn't going to make eye contact. "I'll be proud to work with you. Maybe now I can justify building that separate office. It isn't working to run both the town of Stetterly and the Blade Marshals from our kitchen table. Renna will be happy to have her table back."

"She'll probably be excited about the tax credit Stetterly will get." Ranson's mind raced with the calculations of what it would cost to build a small office for the Blade Marshals.

"She is rather bound and determined to get Stetterly's taxes owed down to zero. Of course, Keevan's clerks are just as determined to make sure Stetterly pays as much as possible." Leith tossed a few more weeds to the side. "Depending on how busy I keep you with the Blade Marshals, I'm sure Renna wouldn't mind if you helped her occasionally with Stetterly's accounts."

It wouldn't take more than a few minutes to tally up Stetterly's ledgers. Ranson picked at the dirt wedged under his fingernails. "Would I have my own office? Somewhere quiet?"

"I'll work it into the plans when I draw them up. I'll need to think about a place for records storage too." Leith's eyes got a faraway look in them that Ranson had learned from past experience meant that Leith was planning something.

Ranson nodded, even if Leith didn't seem to notice. Maybe he had found his place and purpose after all.

2

TWO YEARS LATER...

Ranson tapped the stacks of papers on his desk into neat piles. One stack for the reports from Blade Marshals from around Acktar that he still needed to sort through. One stack for the reports he needed to file. Another stack for the ones to be brought to Leith's attention beyond the quick scan Leith did of all the reports.

The quiet of the office filled Ranson's head and chest, the air soothing with the smells of ink and paper and the lingering cut wood smell that the office still hadn't lost even after a year and nine months.

Across the room, the window splashed early morning sunlight in patches on the floor, the view outside showing only sky from Ranson's angle. If he stood up, he would see empty prairie and the line of the Spires Canyon nearby. Nothing distracting, not like the window beside the door in the outer office that faced the training ground.

Shelves along the wall held ledgers bound together containing the most recent Blade Marshal reports. Past years were kept in the dry cellar lined with stone beneath the office building where they wouldn't burn if the rest of the building caught fire.

This was Ranson's space. The one place where he was sure of himself. Here there were numbers to figure out and patterns to decipher in the movements of bandits from one section of Acktar to the next. In the past two years, he'd even begun to relax under the weight of how much Leith trusted him to find important details in the reports.

A knock sounded on the door before Leith stepped inside. "Do you have the papers I need to take along?"

Ranson picked up a packet of papers he'd tied with a string. "There are two copies of the proposal for the fast message riders. One for you to keep so you have an original copy and one to go over with King Keevan before you present it to the Gathering. I also have three copies of your annual report and our spare copies of the longer, more concerning reports in case the nobles ask for clarification on anything."

"Thanks. I knew you'd have everything ready for me." Leith took the packet of papers. "Coming to see us off?"

Ranson trailed Leith from the back office into the main room of the building. There Leith's desk sat along the wall next to the door to Ranson's office, facing the door. It was unusual, perhaps, for the leader to have the front desk while the clerk had the back office, but it worked. Leith needed to be easily accessible in case of emergencies.

Another few paces and they stepped from the office building and onto the porch. In front of the building, a flat training ground spread out. On the other side, the barracks building was being expanded to accommodate more trainees and Blade Marshal Nolan after he'd retired from active duty and came to Stetterly to assist Leith with training the new recruits. At this time of morning, Nolan was just finishing up the trainees' five-mile morning run.

"Art is going to be here so you shouldn't have to take over any of the training while I'm gone." Leith didn't break his stride or glance at Ranson. "But I'd appreciate it if you kept an eye on Thomas Chambers. He's trouble. I'm going to dismiss him from training, but his father is lord of Mackton and I can't dismiss him until I have a solid reason complete with proof instead of just my instinct that he doesn't have what I'm looking for in a Blade Marshal."

Ranson grimaced. He'd learned enough in the past couple of years working with Leith that politics could mess a lot of things up, even something as simple as deciding who wasn't fit to be a Blade Marshal.

Thankfully Ranson didn't have to deal with that part. He was just numbers and reports. Anything political landed on Leith's desk.

It was only a short hike over a small hill to Leith and Renna's cabin. When they arrived, Brandi already had Big Brown and Valor saddled and waiting in front of the cabin. She was still by the stable, saddling Blizzard.

As they approached, the door to the cabin burst open and two-year-old David dashed outside, Renna only a step behind him snatching at his shirt to pull him back. She missed by inches. "Don't run by the horses."

David kept running, his black hair flying around his head.

Leith shook his head. "David, listen to your mother. Don't run by the horses. You'll startle them, and they'll kick."

David slowed and circled wide around the horses. "Papa!"

Leith lengthened his stride and swept David up with his free arm. David squealed and babbled something Ranson couldn't understand. Apparently parents were given internal translators for their toddlers because Leith and Renna always seemed to know what David was saying.

Renna stepped from the cabin, hitching five-month-old LeeAnna higher on her hip. "He gets faster every day."

"We'll have to keep a close eye on him." Leith stepped closer to Ranson. "Here, can you hold him for a minute?"

Hold him? What—Ranson barely reacted in time to catch David as Leith handed him over. David squirmed in Ranson's grip, pushing his small hands against Ranson's chest.

Ranson grimaced. He wasn't David's favorite uncle. Not by a long shot. He didn't have the instincts on how to make the toddler laugh or smile. Not like Jamie or Brandi did. Even Martyn managed to somehow make David like him while acting completely grumpy about whole the thing.

"You'd better hurry." Ranson adjusted his grip on the squirming, wiggling David. Amazing how slippery a toddler could be.

Leith picked up the saddlebags and strapped them to the horses while Renna shrugged into a cloth carrying sling and wedged LeeAnna into it. When she was finished, she strode to Big Brown, and Leith boosted her into the saddle.

As Brandi rode toward them on Blizzard, Martyn and Kayleigh crested the ridge on the trail from their cabin in the canyon. Kayleigh's horse was a pale palomino with a white mane and tail. The mare had been a six-month-anniversary gift from Martyn to Kayleigh, and Kayleigh had named the horse Sandy.

Kayleigh wore a pack on her back, carrying her and Martyn's year-old-daughter Molly. Molly had so many flyaway, blond curls that her face was barely visible. Molly waved her arms and kicked her legs, grinning as if excited to be going on an adventure.

Leith swung onto Valor, and Ranson hurried to Leith's side. He was beyond ready to hand over David. The toddler's face was going red. Any longer and he was going to start screaming. David lunged out of Ranson's grasp, and only Leith's quick reflexes saved David from falling to the ground. Leith set David on the saddle in front of him, one arm firmly wrapped around David's chest.

David started chattering again, something that had Leith's mouth tipping into a smile. Leith turned to Ranson. "We'll be back in a few weeks. We might swing through Walden on our way home to visit Jamie and the Alistairs. Please forward anything on to Nalgar Castle that's needs immediate attention."

Ranson grinned. "That would be easier if we had fast message riders. We could have a message to Nalgar in a little over a day instead of five days."

"That's the plan." Leith gave Ranson a nod and nudged Valor into a trot.

Ranson watched them leave before he turned and strolled to the office. He had stacks of paperwork to file.

"Keep the gash damp so that it doesn't scab over. I'll come back tomorrow and check on it." Michelle tied of the bandage around the trainee's calf. The eighteen-year-old first year Blade Marshal trainee had managed to cut himself on one of the dulled training swords. How he'd managed that, she didn't know. But she'd learned not to be surprised at the ways the trainees managed to hurt themselves.

Michelle picked up her things as the trainee limped out of the room. She exited the small storage room at the end of the barracks, and halted next to Blade Marshal Nolan who was waiting for her in the hallway. "Any more injuries that need tending?"

"Not at the moment." Blade Marshal Nolan nodded. "Thanks for taking time out of your normal routine. I can walk you back to town."

"No need." Michelle waved him away. No reason to inconvenience him. "I know you have a lot of work to do."

After strolling out the door, Michelle walked around the corner of the building to head for town.

A young man stepped in front of her. His light brown hair was cropped short while his face had the angular, high-cheekboned good looks that turned heads. He smirked and leaned against the wall in front of her. "Leaving so soon?"

Thomas Chambers. Michelle forced a polite smile to her face. He was a second-year Blade Marshal trainee and a younger son of Lord Chambers of Mackton. Without an inheritance, he apparently had decided to try being a Blade

Marshal instead. He had also decided his looks were a gift and he planned to use them to his advantage.

She knew his type. She'd been just like him a few years ago.

"I finished my work here." Michelle tried to step around Thomas, but he blocked her path. "I need to return to town."

"You can spare a few minutes for me." Thomas rested a hand against the wall of the barracks, closing her in. His face drew closer to hers. "I'll make it worth your while."

"No, not interested." She tried to duck around his arm, but he shifted to keep her in place. Her breath hitched in her chest. This had just escalated from slightly annoying to buzzing a warning down her spine. "Please, I need to get back to work."

"Come now. I've heard around town about you." Thomas leaned even closer. "You like this sort of thing."

She squeezed her eyes shut to take a breath. Her reputation—the one she was trying so hard to change—wasn't her. Wasn't what she wanted. But that was the problem with living in a small town. Rumors and gossip never truly died.

Nearly five years ago now she had been foolish. She had been wild. And she'd nearly paid for it during a blizzard when a Blade snatched her. Only Leith's intervention, even if he'd been a loyal Blade at that point, and her father's arrival had saved her.

Leith wasn't here to rescue her this time. Father was in town, too far away to realize she was in trouble.

Should Michelle try to shove Thomas away? Or would he turn violent if she tried? He was training to be a Blade Marshal. She wouldn't be able to fight him off.

She gritted her teeth and met his gaze, curling her

fingers into fist. If this turned bad, she would go down fighting, even if she wouldn't have a chance of winning. "You've heard wrong. I don't. Now let me pass so I can get back to work."

"Why, you—"

"You heard Michelle. She needs to get back to work." Ranson's voice was surprisingly hard, even if it had a shake to it.

Michelle leaned to the side to see around Thomas's arm. Ranson stood with his legs braced, a hand on his knife. He even had his badge pinned to his shirt, flashing in the morning sunlight.

Thomas snorted and stepped back from Michelle. "If it isn't the bean counter. What do you plan to do? You can't make me step away from her."

Ranson swallowed, but his grip tightened on his knife. "Let her go."

"Fine. If you want to make a big deal about it. I didn't do anything." Thomas sauntered away from Michelle and rammed his shoulder into Ranson. When Ranson stumbled, Thomas slammed a fist into Ranson's stomach. As Ranson doubled over, Thomas huffed and kept walking. "That's what I thought. To think you were a Blade. It's pathetic."

Michelle let out a breath, both hands shaking. That had been too close.

"Are you all right?" Ranson tottered toward her, an arm around his stomach.

She had to pull herself together. She forced herself to smile. "I should be asking you that. How bad?"

Ranson drew in a shaky breath and stood somewhat

straighter. "I'm fine. I'll probably be bruised, but nothing's broken. I know what that feels like."

The way he said it...Michelle wasn't sure she wanted to know what had happened in the Blades that Ranson could so easily judge how hurt he was from a punch. "If you start coughing up blood or notice your stomach is swelling, then you might want to see me."

"I'll do that." Ranson's hands shook, waving in the air for a moment before he tucked them behind his back. "Do you want me to walk you to town? I'm going that way anyway so it isn't any trouble. If you'd like me to. I mean, I understand if you don't. I..."

"Thanks. I'd love to walk to town with you." Michelle gave him a carefully measured smile. She didn't want to accidentally lead him on, not when her normal defenses were down.

When Ranson didn't move, she started for town, and Ranson fell into step beside her.

"We...probably should report Thomas to your father. Or Blade Marshal Nolan. With Leith gone, they're the only two left in town who could deal with him." Ranson had his hands clasped behind his back as he walked, his gaze focused away from her.

"No! Don't..." Michelle let out a long breath to steady herself. "No, we can't tell my father."

Her stomach churned at the thought. She'd have to endure his disappointed frown, again. He'd look at her like she'd failed yet again to be better, even though this time wasn't in any way her fault. This was Stetterly. She'd never needed an escort around town in the years she'd been the healer.

"Are you sure? He probably should be told. Thomas might bother you again." Ranson's gaze flicked to her so quickly she would've missed it if she hadn't already been looking at him.

"I'll be careful. My father can't do much more than you did and warn Thomas to stay away from me. He didn't outright break any laws." Michelle rubbed her arms. It wasn't like he could be arrested for just being a jerk who didn't back off when he was told.

"I still don't like it." Ranson scuffed his boot against the gravel of the track as they neared the town. "Leith warned me about him. Said he'd be trouble. So come to me or Blade Marshal Nolan if he bothers you again. We might not be able to officially dismiss him from the Blade Marshals until Leith returns, but we both outrank him."

"I'll do that. Thanks, Ranson." Michelle turned to him, and her heart beat faster in her chest. Not the way it had when Thomas hadn't let her leave. This was a steady, thrilling pulse.

She shouldn't be attracted to Ranson. She wasn't the right type of girl for a sweet, unassertive man like Ranson. She'd end up walking all over him, and he deserved so much more than that.

"I...guess I'll..." Ranson trailed off, gave a random sort of wave, and spun on his heels without finishing his farewell.

Just as well. Michelle hadn't been able to think of what to say either.

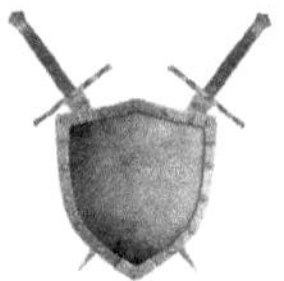

3

Ranson finished up the last of the stacks of paperwork on his desk. Outside, long rays of the setting sun left orange streaks across the prairie.

About time he headed back to his room above the stable, though with Renna gone, there wouldn't be any supper waiting for him keeping warm at the edge of the fire.

Ranson cleaned his desk, made sure all the windows were locked, and finally locked the outer door behind him.

He took a few steps toward the south before he paused and changed directions to head for the barracks. Stepping inside, he found Blade Marshal Nolan in his office finishing his supper.

Blade Marshal Nolan looked up. "Did you need something?"

Ranson clasped his hands behind his back. Should he say something? Michelle hadn't wanted him to, but a knot in Ranson's stomach told him that wasn't right. "Thomas Chambers cornered Michelle Allen outside the barracks today. Hassled her, and I'm not sure what he would have done if I hadn't stepped in." Ranson wasn't going to mention the bruise he had forming over his ribs. "I think we need to keep a closer eye on him until Leith returns."

Blade Marshal Nolan nodded. "Yes, Leith asked me to watch him. This could be the incident Leith was looking for to dismiss him. I was just about to make sure all the trainees are in the barracks, if you want to come along."

Ranson followed Blade Marshal Nolan from the room and into the hall. A waft of a breeze blew across Ranson's neck. Probably from one of the windows, left open to let the cooling night air freshen the barracks after they'd been baking in the sun all day.

After a short walk down the hall, they climbed the flight of stairs to the second floor barracks room that housed the trainees. At a glance, Ranson counted the beds and the trainees in the room.

Fourteen beds. Thirteen trainees.

One was missing.

That knot in his stomach twisted tighter, hurting underneath the bruise. Thomas Chambers wasn't in the Blade Marshals' barracks where he was supposed to be at this time of night.

Ranson spun on his heels and dashed back down the stairway even as Blade Marshal Nolan began questioning the other trainees about Thomas's whereabouts. Ranson didn't care where Thomas was at the moment as long as Ranson reached Michelle first.

He sprinted up the rise between the Blade Marshal's office and the town of Stetterly. His breaths whooshed through his chest. His muscles surged. Dust flew from his feet. He'd kept up the practice of running each morning, and now he couldn't be more thankful.

The town appeared over the horizon, then he was careening toward it, coming at it at a right angle to the single street running down its center. He dashed into the alley between the sheriff's office and the store next to it.

Something slammed into Ranson's stomach. He crumpled to his knees, arms over his stomach.

"Well, Bean Counter." Thomas' voice rang in the darkness. "I knew you'd come looking for Michelle. All honorable, aren't you? Making sure she's all right."

Ranson tried to suck in a breath. He couldn't draw in enough air to call for help. Not that it would do much good if he did. At this time of night, few people were about, leaving the boardwalks and the street nearly deserted except for a single wagon rattling out of town to the north and a few men talking as they strode from the blacksmith's shop at the far southern end of town. With as thick and solid as the jail was, Sheriff Allen probably wouldn't hear anything amiss.

People's voices drifted down from opened windows in their homes above their shops. Pans clattered. A child giggled. Dogs barked. The smells of stew and frying bacon and something spicy from too many different suppers lingered in the street, merging with the smoke from the blacksmith's fire and the ever-present odors of sunbaked dust and horse manure.

Ranson tried to ignore all the noises and smells pounding into his head in time with the pain throbbing through his stomach.

A boot crunched into Ranson's side, and he collapsed onto the dirt. Pain hitched deep inside. A broken rib.

Another kick. Ranson groaned.

"You are so pathetic. Why are you a Blade Marshal and not me?" Thomas stepped around Ranson so that the light from the upper story of the sheriff's office slanted across his face. "I heard you and Blade Marshal Nolan talking. I know Leith plans to dismiss me. Why he's so eager to get rid of me when I'm so much more skilled than you is beyond me."

"That's Blade Marshal Torren to you." Ranson winced, and not all the wince was due to the pain. That had sounded childish out loud. He'd risen to Thomas's prodding, something Leith never would've done. Then again, Leith probably could've said those exact same words and they would've come out menacing. "Your father is the only reason you stayed in training this long."

"My father had nothing to do with this!" Thomas's boots crunched on the gravel. "I did this on my own."

Ranson fumbled for his knife. He'd heard Leith and Blane say this was the moment they went cold, the world stilling.

But Ranson shook and fought for breath as he curled on the ground, noise and smell whirling through his head to the thunder of his heart. Bile rose in his throat, and he worked to fight it back down.

Gravel bit into Ranson's cheek, an interesting gray pebble with a line of quartz resting near Ranson's nose. No, this wasn't the time to be distracted by a pebble. He had to concentrate.

"How you ever managed to pass the Blade Marshal test is beyond me." Thomas kicked Ranson's stomach again.

Ranson wasn't sure how he'd passed either. He apparently couldn't even fend off a second-year trainee.

But Leith had believed in Ranson. And Ranson had passed. He'd survived the Blades.

You're good with numbers. So make fighting about the numbers.

Blane had told him that back when Ranson was struggling to learn to fight. Turn it into a numbers problem.

Something burned deep in Ranson's chest, crackling into his fingers, his toes. Blane had believed Ranson could make something of himself. Leith believed it too. Ranson wasn't just the weak bean counter Thomas thought he was.

He was a Blade Marshal. The badge pinned to his chest said so. That meant he was supposed to be able to fight when he had to.

It also meant he had the authority to arrest Thomas.

Ranson lifted his head so he could face Thomas. "Thomas Chambers, you are under arrest for assaulting an officer."

Thomas snorted. "Wait, you're arresting me? You're on the ground, unable to fight back. Though, knowing you, you're going to tattle this to Leith the moment he returns."

Make it an arithmetic problem. Take him out in five.

That's how Ranson had learned to fight. Assigning each move a number and have his opponent on the ground or dead when his moves added up to five.

The calculation laid out in Ranson's head. His focus sharpened as Thomas drew back his foot for another kick.

One. Ranson kicked, and his heel connected with Thomas's kneecap on the leg he balanced on.

Thomas stumbled, nearly going down before he caught himself. He hunched as he gripped the knee Ranson had kicked.

Two. Ranson rolled to his feet, using his momentum to put weight and power behind his blow. The heel of his hand connected with Thomas's nose with a solid crack.

Thomas howled as blood gushed down his face. He dropped his knife as he tried to staunch the blood pouring from his nose and grip his injured knee at the same time.

Three. Ranson pivoted, gripped Thomas's right wrist, and yanked the arm behind his back.

Four. Ranson kicked the backside of Thomas's good leg. Thomas plunged onto his knees.

Five. Ranson shoved Thomas's lower back with a foot, and Thomas sprawled face-first on the ground. Ranson followed the motion, keeping his grip on Thomas's arm. He braced his legs on either side of Thomas's torso, grabbed his free hand, and pinned both hands behind his back with enough downward pressure to keep him from getting up or rolling.

"I guess we'll add resisting arrest to the charges." Ranson let out a long breath and tried to hold on to his focus. His fingers were threatening to shake, pain stabbed through his chest with each breath, and the alley was clogging with the stench of blood. A puddle of blood was forming by Thomas's nose on the ground, washing over the pebble Ranson had noticed earlier.

Ranson's stomach heaved at the sight. Best not to stand here looking at it, or he'd lose what little he'd eaten that day, not to mention he was about ready to collapse again from the pain of his broken rib. He hauled Thomas to his feet. Well, he started hauling him and Thomas did the rest by stumbling upright.

The door to the sheriff's office was only a few steps away.

Ranson shoved Thomas against the door, unlatched it, and both of them more fell into the room than walked.

Sheriff Allen bolted to his feet so fast he knocked his chair over and probably would've toppled his whole desk if it hadn't been a large, sturdy table. His hand went for his sword, but he stilled as he swung toward the door. "Ranson. What is it? What happened?"

Ranson couldn't put the buzzing in his head into words. He tried to speak, but he just couldn't. He shook his head and multiplied the number of floorboards by the logs in the wall. That settled his head long enough for him to blurt, "Lock him up."

Sheriff Allen took Thomas from Ranson. While Sheriff Allen hauled Thomas into the jail cells in the back, Ranson managed to stumble the three steps to the chairs in front of Sheriff Allen's desk and sank into one.

His stomach, his chest, even his arms cramped with pain. More pain than he'd felt in five years.

The door at the far end of the room creaked, and then the floorboards popped and squeaked as Sheriff Allen crossed the room.

"What happened?" Sheriff Allen's voice was close, and when Ranson managed to raise his head, he found the sheriff was standing in front of him. "Where are you hurt?"

"Thomas overheard Blade Marshal Nolan and I talking and found out Leith planned to dismiss him, and Leith would for sure now that Thomas hassled Michelle. I was coming to check on her when he cornered me in the alley." Ranson drew in a breath past the ache. "I cracked a rib."

"Let me fetch Michelle."

"No. It's just a broken rib." Ranson braced himself

against the arms of the chair. All Michelle could do was check to make sure his lung hadn't been punctured, and he knew that much already since he wasn't coughing up blood. No reason to bother her. "I need to head back to the office and write up my report."

He shoved to his feet. Everything tilted. Gold spots, then black crowded his vision.

Then he was on the floor, blinking, as Sheriff Allen's face hovered in a haze above him.

4

ichelle wasn't fine. She should be. Nothing
permanently scarring happened, right?

But here was she huddled under a blanket on the settee in their rooms above the jail, jumping at every sound. Voices, too indistinct for her to pick out words, echoed up from below.

The voices died away, then boots scuffed on the stairs outside.

Michelle tensed and gripped the hilt of the knife she'd taken out of a drawer. Her skin crawled as she stared at the unlocked door. The door she hadn't locked because she was waiting for her father.

This was Stetterly. Safe, calm Stetterly. That was most likely her father trudging up the stairs.

Yet a part of her didn't feel safe. Like nothing and nowhere would ever feel completely safe again.

Everything in her wished she could undo tonight and go back to the innocence of a few hours ago. The girl who thought she could take care of herself. Who thought she'd changed enough and done enough that something like this wouldn't happen again.

Still it had happened. Even when she'd never flirted with Thomas Chambers. She'd been wearing her most unflattering dress. She'd been in broad daylight on the Blade Marshal training field walking home from calling on a patient just like she did so many times without incident.

Nothing all that bad had happened. He'd crowded her space. He'd even backed off when Ranson came along and told him to leave.

Yet there had been that one moment when she hadn't been sure he'd back down. When she hadn't known how far he'd go and how much she'd be hurt before he was finished. And it was that feeling plaguing her now, shaking through her fingers, into her bones.

The door creaked open, and her father hurried inside. "Ranson is downstairs. He's been beaten. He thinks he only cracked a rib, but he just passed out a moment ago."

Ranson. Something cold plunged through her. She threw the blanket off and dashed for her medical bag. "Thomas Chambers did it to him, didn't he?"

"Yes." When her father looked at her, lines etched across his face, as if tonight had aged him. Only two other times had she seen him age like that. The night her mother died and the night she was kidnapped by a Blade.

She looked away, unable to hold his gaze. He knew. Ranson must have told him. She would've been angry he'd gone behind her back, except that he was lying downstairs, injured.

Michelle raced out the door and took the stairs as quickly as she could, her father only a few steps behind her.

When she entered the ground floor sheriff's office, Ranson was lying on the floor in front of the desk with her father's spare cloak pillowed under his head. But at least he was breathing, in and out in a rhythm too steady to be anything but forced.

"Ranson." She knelt next to him. His face was pale, making his brown hair look darker. But at least she couldn't see any bruising on his face, and there didn't seem to be any bleeding on his scalp, so she could rule out a head injury.

He cracked his eyes open and peered at her. "Fourteen."

"Fourteen?" What did that mean? Was Ranson delirious?

"Fourteen boards across the ceiling." Ranson lifted one hand long enough to point at the ceiling above them. "I was counting them to distract myself."

From the pain. Michelle reached for Ranson's shirt, then halted, something in her hesitating.

Why? She dealt with wounds and bruises all the time. Awkwardness never bothered her, not when she kept things impassive and clinical.

But it was different with Ranson. She couldn't think of him clinically, not when her heart was still thumping too hard at seeing him hurt. She felt more for him than she'd ever felt for any of the boys she'd flirted with growing up.

"Do you need my help?" Her father was still behind her. Was she embarrassed or grateful that he was there?

"Yes, please." There, that tone in her voice sounded official. Like she was the healer and he was just her patient.

And she was grateful for her father's help as they

propped Ranson upright and maneuvered his shirt off while hurting him as little as possible.

When her father helped Ranson lay back down, Michelle got her first good look at the bruises. Dark and purple, covering Ranson's stomach and chest all along his side with a lump forming over the cracked rib.

Something burned deep inside her chest, and she found herself clenching her fists as if she intended to storm out of there, find Thomas Chambers, and repay him bruise for bruise. "Father, you need to find Thomas Chambers and arrest him for this."

"He's already locked in a cell in back. Ranson brought him in."

He had? After taking this beating? Michelle glanced at her father, and he nodded, as if to confirm that she'd heard correctly.

"I'm a Blade Marshal." Ranson's words held a confidence to them, even between his increasingly ragged breathing.

"And you've taken a Blade Marshal's injuries to prove it." Leith and Martyn occasionally returned from missions with bruises or wounds, though Michelle never saw those injuries herself since Renna tended them.

After giving him a small dose of painkiller, Michelle tried to be gentle as she probed Ranson's wounds. Just the one cracked rib that had thankfully remained in position instead of puncturing anything. None of his internal organs felt overly swollen for the amount of bruising.

Still, it would be best if someone kept an eye on Ranson through the night. He'd most likely passed out because of pain and lightheadedness from lack of food, knowing how he tended to skip lunch and probably hadn't eaten supper before he was attacked.

"We'll need to set up a pallet for him here so we can keep an eye on him tonight." With one of the cells occupied, her father would've slept down there anyway. "We should also ice those bruises to bring some of the swelling down."

Her father stood. "I'll fetch ice from the icehouse while you set up the pallet in here. I can help you move him when I return."

"I can get up." Ranson started to roll upright.

Michelle placed a hand on his shoulder and pushed him back to the floor. "Maybe, but let's not risk it tonight."

Ranson flopped back to the floor. "Leith usually doesn't listen when Renna says stuff like that."

"Ignoring his healer—who also happens to be his wife—probably isn't his wisest decision." Michelle stood to fetch her father's pallet mattress from the side room next to the jail cells and raised her voice to keep talking while she dragged the mattress through the doorway. "You don't have to push yourself to get up just to prove you're tough. It's all right to admit when you can't get up or don't want to get up because it hurts too much."

She dropped the mattress in the far corner where someone sitting at her father's desk could keep an eye on Ranson while watching the door to the cells for trouble.

When she returned to Ranson's side, his dark brown eyes had a pain in them that didn't seem to be all from his bruises. "Bad habit from the Blades, I guess. If we didn't get back up, we'd probably be killed."

"Well, you aren't in the Blades anymore. It's all right to rest." Michelle should try to get him to eat something, but his stomach probably hurt too much for him to feel hunger at the moment. "And I know Leith means a lot to you—the big brother that you want to be like. But you can be yourself. You don't have to be exactly like him to be a good man."

And that's what Ranson was. A very good man. Kind. Gentle. Humble. She squeezed her eyes shut. Why did she have to like him so much?

By the time her father returned with the ice, Ranson had fallen asleep. Michelle helped her father carry Ranson and set him on the pallet. Then she sat next to him and placed towel-wrapped bundles of ice on the worst of the bruising.

"You should head for bed. I can take over from here."

She shook her head. "I'm not tired yet. Maybe in a little while." She wasn't ready yet to leave Ranson. She had to be absolutely sure he would be all right before she could sleep.

Her father sank into the chair behind his desk, leaning his elbows onto the tabletop. The silence grew heavy, as if filled with the questions her father was figuring out how to ask. "Why didn't you tell me Thomas Chambers gave you trouble?"

Why hadn't she? Maybe because it had seemed like nothing more than him cornering her and being rude. Maybe because a part of her wanted to believe she could handle it by herself. Telling anyone felt like she was weak. Unable to take care of herself. But most of all...she couldn't look at her father. "I didn't want you to be disappointed."

She wasn't sure why she felt like the one who'd failed. As if being cornered by Thomas had been her fault. Maybe she should've taken up Blade Marshal Nolan's offer to walk her back to town, but she'd never needed an escort to walk from the Blade Marshal training field to the town before. They were within sight of each other. In broad daylight. And Stetterly was reputably the safest town in Acktar.

"Michelle." He said her name with a sigh.

Just like she'd expected. He was disappointed. She concentrated on shifting the ice to another bruise on Ranson's chest.

"I could never be disappointed in you. Not over something like this."

Michelle risked glancing up at him. Did he mean that? "I know I disappoint you. I'm too flirtatious like Mama."

She winced. She shouldn't have said that. It was unspoken for a reason, much as most things about her mother were.

"Whatever made you think your mother was the flirtatious one?" Her father shook his head. Gray hairs caught the lamplight at his temples. "Your mother was the sweetest, kindest woman I have ever known. No, I was the flirtatious one."

"What?" Michelle stilled as the words settled into her. Why had she always assumed she had inherited her scandal-causing nature from her mother? Her mother had been so kind. Gentle. Quiet. And Michelle had assumed she had been quiet because she'd conquered her flirtatious side. By becoming its opposite.

Yet, it was her father who was good with people. That's what made him an excellent sheriff. Had he been much like her when he was younger?

"I'm not proud of some of the things I've done. I've made mistakes. And, yes, I was disappointed—afraid even—when I saw you becoming too much like me." Her father leaned forward. "But you have so much of your mother in you. And it makes me so proud."

Proud. Not disappointed?

For the first time that evening, she wasn't shaky. A warmth settled in her, despite her fingers growing numb from handling the ice.

Yes, she would be fine. It might take a while before she'd go to bed without checking three or four times that the door was locked, but, eventually, she would be fine.

"You are beautiful, just like your mother." Father stared at the wall as if not really seeing it. "There's nothing wrong with that. Yes, there are ways to make mistakes. I've done them. But you are beautiful inside and out, and there's absolutely nothing you need to be ashamed of in that."

It was all right to be beautiful. Michelle breathed out a long breath. She'd flaunted her beauty, and, yes, she had motivations in her heart that had been wrong.

But she'd gone too far in the opposite direction. She'd tried to dress in a way that was taking responsibility for the hearts of others.

All she could do was take responsibility for herself and her own actions. That was all anyone could do.

What did that mean for how she would dress and act? What was the balance?

In the Bible, the church was often is described as a bride. A beautiful bride. Yes, with inner beauty. But with outward beauty too. The temple in the Old Testament was built to be stunningly beautiful.

God loved and enjoyed beauty. He'd created the world beautiful. He'd created Michelle to be beautiful. She was to be like the temple, shining her inward beauty through the outward for God's glory.

She couldn't control how others looked at her or the thoughts in their heart. But she could control the thoughts in her own. But controlling herself didn't mean trying desperately to hide the beauty God had given her. There was no shame in finding a balance between flaunting beauty and hiding it.

Tomorrow, she would pull out her favorite dress. She would smile a genuine smile.

And she would feel free for the first time in years.

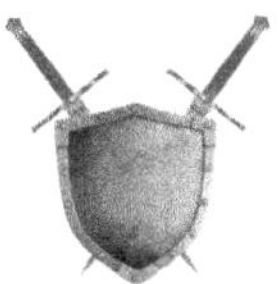

fter two weeks, Ranson's bruises had faded into yellow and brown instead of purple, but his cracked rib still stabbed his side as he hurried to keep up with Leith as Leith strode into the sheriff's office. Leith had barely stayed still long enough in the office to hear Ranson's report before he'd marched out the door.

Sheriff Allen stood, but Leith only spared a nod in his direction as he strode straight on past, headed for the jail cells in the back of the building.

Sagging into a chair sounded promising, but Ranson wasn't about to miss this.

Leith shoved open the door that separated the main office from the jail cells. As Ranson trotted inside on Leith's heels, Thomas swung to his feet. His gaze darted from Leith, to Ranson, then back to Leith, and his face whitened.

He should be scared. Ranson found a place in the corner. Leith's anger wasn't something easily roused.

Leith crossed his arms. "Thomas Chambers, you have

violated the code of conduct and integrity expected of a Blade Marshal trainee. You are hereby dismissed from your training and will be escorted home to your father as soon as possible."

Thomas stepped forward, crossing his arms. "My father will...I'm the third son. I don't have anything else."

Leith's gaze didn't waver. "You should have thought of that before you harassed the town's healer and ambushed my clerk and fellow Blade Marshal in an alley. What makes you think I would ever trust you with Acktar's people after that?"

"But I...my father..."

Leith stepped right up to the bars, and when his spoke, his voice was low and cold as a blizzard wind. "I will alert the Blade Marshals near Mackton to keep an eye on you. If you ever harass anyone again, I will personally hunt you down, and there will be nowhere you'll be able to hide. Not when I have Ranson on my side to track every move you make through every report across Acktar. If I can't find you, I can guarantee he will."

Really? Ranson tried to keep his expression dangerous and Blade Marshal-like and definitely not surprised.

Leith spun on his heels and strode from the room.

Ranson glanced at Thomas, then left. He found Leith waiting for him on the boardwalk outside of the sheriff's office. Leith's face had warmed from the ice it had been a few moments ago, but he still wore his hard edges. "I'm sorry for what happened. I never should've let politics or any sort of pressure stop me from dismissing Thomas from training, but without any evidence besides my instincts..."

Ranson shrugged, then flinched when the movement

shot pain through his chest. "It's not your fault. You can't arrest someone merely because you're suspicious of them. You can only arrest them after they've broken a law and committed a crime."

"There are times I wish I didn't have to wait for someone to be hurt before I can officially act, and I'm especially sorry that person was you this time." Leith shook his head, a hand resting on one of his knives buckled to his waist. "I meant what I said back there. If Thomas causes trouble in the future, you're the one who will spot his patterns first in the reports."

Ranson wasn't so sure. Yes, he'd pointed out a horse thieving gang here, a thief traveling between the towns there. But Leith and the other Blade Marshals were the ones who went out and arrested the criminals.

Still, Leith had trusted Ranson enough to ask him to keep a watch on Thomas. Ranson glanced at Leith before he returned his gaze to the boardwalk below his feet. A nail was sticking up from one of the boards. Someone was going to trip on that if it wasn't pounded back in. "You asked me to watch Thomas before you left. Why did you trust me with a job like that? Did you know I could beat him in a fight?"

"Yes." Leith's answer was so firm, Ranson had no choice but to look up to try to read Leith's expression. But with the hard edges still there, Ranson could decipher even less than normal.

Ranson looked away and nudged the nail sticking up from the boards with a toe. It wasn't loose. Just working its way out of the board with the swelling and shrinking the wood did during the summer and winter. "But how did you know? I mean, you taught us both. We both know all the same things, don't we?"

"You may have had the same teacher, but you were taught in the harder school."

Um, what? Ranson eyed Leith, trying to piece together the meaning of the words.

The corner of Leith's mouth twisted upward. "What I mean is that yes, I taught you both. But all Thomas had is the training. He's never fought for real, not the way you have. It's a different feeling, fighting when you know you could die rather than fighting a practice battle where the worst thing that could happen is your teacher gives you a reprimand and maybe extra work. As hard and as cruel as the training was in the Blades, I'm never going to get the same results with the sort of training I'm willing to do here."

Ranson thought he understood. Things had been different in the Blades, and Leith wasn't going to capture that for the Blade Marshals. That was good in some ways, because the Blades had been evil, many of them relishing the pain and suffering they caused.

But that could also be a bad thing. The first time a Blade Marshal trainee faced a real fight, it would be in the field where their reactions could get them or their partner killed.

Not much Leith could do about that besides push the trainees hard and give them the skills to react the way they should when a fight came. After all, it was better to be honorable than ruthless.

Ranson had fought. When pressed, he'd pulled himself together and took down his opponent. And that made him worthy of the badge he wore even if many dismissed him as merely the Blade Marshal bean counter. Maybe he wasn't normal. But God had given him his own kind of strength. And that was enough.

When Ranson looked up again, Michelle was walking toward them. She wore a red dress Ranson hadn't seen her wear in years. Not since that first year he'd come to Stetterly, now that he thought about it.

It fit her nicely. Better than the baggy brown dresses that she had been wearing that looked like she'd dragged them out of someone's discarded rags. But in the past two weeks, she'd been wearing a lot of nicer dresses.

She halted in front of them. Ranson blinked, then stared at his feet. He'd seen her a lot lately while she kept an eye on his broken rib and bruises. And something had been different, even if he couldn't figure out what it was. What was he supposed to say to her?

Leith gestured from her to the sheriff's office. "I'm sorry for the way Thomas Chambers treated you. He won't bother you again."

"Thank you." Michelle smiled, but even Ranson could tell the smile didn't look quite the way a smile should. Not that he could tell exactly what was wrong with it.

Leith nodded to Michelle, then glanced at Ranson. "I'm heading back for the office. Come when you can. You don't have to rush."

As Leith strode off, Ranson would've followed right then, but Michelle was still standing there. Looking at him.

Did she expect him to say something? "How are you?"

"I think I should be asking you that. You're the one with the broken rib." She stared at the ground. "I've been wanting to talk to you about something."

She wanted to talk to him? Ranson's heart beat harder in

his chest. No, he shouldn't get his hopes up. She probably didn't mean anything like what he was hoping she'd meant. "Uh, all right."

She squared her shoulders and faced him. "I've always been safe with you. It took me far longer than it should have to realize how important that is and how wrong I was to turn you down two years ago. I was looking for all the wrong things, and I'm sorry. If you'd still...that is, I'd like...I'd be happy to say yes this time."

What? Ranson stared. Was she saying what he thought she was saying? He wasn't misreading her words at all? "No, you were right. Two years ago. Neither of us was ready. I didn't even have a job yet, and it wouldn't have worked, and..." And why was he babbling about this?

She looked away, her shoulders hunching. "Oh, I see. I should've realized you would've moved on after two years. Sorry. I'll just go."

No, that wasn't what he meant. Why couldn't his words work like they were supposed to?

She turned to leave.

"Wait!" Too loud. Too frantic. Ranson clasped his hands behind his back. "Yes. I'd like that. Courting you."

She spun back to him. "You would?"

He could only nod. Nodding was a lot safer than trying to talk. And he even knew that nodding was the right response in this case, so that made it even better.

She stepped closer, halted, and cocked her head at him. Then she held out a hand.

He stared. Did she want to shake his hand? For some reason, that didn't seem to be the correct response. Then again, Ranson wasn't sure what the correct response was.

He'd only ever asked Michelle, and she'd said no before. He wasn't sure what to do with a yes.

"You're supposed to hold my hand, Ranson. If you want to." Her smile was broad, too wide to be anything but genuine.

Hold her hand. Right. Ranson stuck out his own hand, only to realize four seconds too late that it was the wrong one for walking side-by-side. He switched hands, then it took another few seconds to figure out how to twine his fingers with her.

By the time their hands were firmly together, his face was as hot as a sunburn. He couldn't even hold hands without being awkward. And, honestly, he wasn't sure what the big deal was. Her hand was warm. Kind of clammy, unless that was his hand causing the damp feeling. Strange to hold someone's hand, like he was a little boy again walking to the general store with Nana Harding. But it was Michelle's hand, so that made it kind of nice.

She was smiling at him again. So, of course, he blurted the first thing that popped into his head. "Ranson Harding isn't my real name."

"What?" She stepped back, as if she was about to pull her hand away.

Considering how awkward it had been a moment ago, he oddly enough didn't want her to let go. And that started him babbling. "Well, it is. Sort of. I don't really know my name. I was three when Nana Harding took me in, and I couldn't talk very well. When she asked my name, all I would say was something that sounded sort of like Ranson to her, so that's what she called me. And she gave me her family name since I couldn't remember mine."

"And you don't know your real parents?"

Ranson shook his head. "Leith asked the Blade Marshal near Dymon to search the town records to see what he could find. He couldn't find anything in the records, nor could anyone remember anything. Best guess is that I was abandoned for one reason or another. But it's all right. Nana Harding was the best family I could've had, besides Blane. She took me in, raised me when no one else would, and taught me the Bible. So I'm happy to carry her name."

"It's a nice name." Michelle's hand remained in his.

And it was...nice. He might be awkward around people, but as long as Michelle understood him, then everything would be all right.

THE PERFECT PLAN

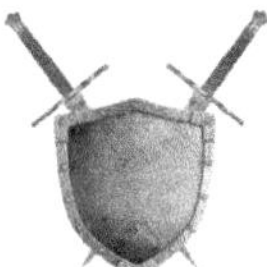

Author's Note: Since this story occurs many years before Respen took over Acktar, Lord Alistair is still merely Lord Henry, heir to Walden, while his father is the Lord Alistair. This is Acktar before Respen. One where Rovers terrorize the towns and a princess definitely does not like the stuffy lord of Stetterly...

Princess Annita Eirdon swayed in time with her horse's stride. The spring breeze whipped through her long, golden curls. If only she could laugh, dig her heels into Horse's sides, and lean into a full tilt gallop.

But she was a princess, and after her father's death by Rovers a year ago, she needed to act more dignified for her brother's sake.

Besides, Horse wouldn't be up to a full tilt gallop. Not at his age. She'd been two when she'd named him and now, at twenty-three, the horse was white-whiskered and grumpy. If Walden had been any farther than a leisurely two and a half day ride, she would've taken a different horse.

She probably should have anyway. It was hard to be dignified while explaining to the stablehands that her horse was named Horse. Next time she named a horse, she'd think up something a bit more creative.

Beside her, her brother King Leon slumped, sitting heavy in the saddle. "Would you at least think about what I said? Father wanted nothing more to see you married, and I'd like the same. Would you at least try at this wedding? Surely you can find someone to take you."

Annita gritted her teeth. How many times had she heard versions of this lecture over the years? First from her father, now her brother. She understood. They had enough to worry about with the burden of the country. All they wanted was her to be safely married off.

But did they have to use the same lecture? Stop being so wild. Start acting like a lady. Bat her eyes and pretend to be helpless until some guy up and decided to marry her.

Blegh.

No. Annita wouldn't stoop to that. Not for anyone. She'd rather stay unmarried.

But Leon had enough to worry about. After a year, he still struggled with the demands of being king while finding time to spend with his wife Deirdre and his son Aengus. Though how Leon managed to get any work done with little baby Aengus around to be distracting, Annita didn't know.

Annita forced herself to smile. "I'll try."

"What about Lord Henry Alistair's friend? What's his name? Lord Laurence Faythe. Stetterly is a small town and not ideal, but there aren't that many unmarried lords around your age." Leon scratched behind his ear.

Annita grimaced. She should've kicked Horse into a

gallop when she'd had the chance. "No, not him. He's...boring."

Stuffier than a scarecrow, more like. He was probably all traditional like her brother. He had certainly seemed like it the times she'd seen him at Nalgar Castle when he'd come for the Gatherings.

She shouldn't judge him too harshly. He'd lost both his parents to the fever that had swept across Acktar a number of years back, the same fever that had taken her mother. A loss like that would make anyone a bit...humorless.

Or maybe it was just his family's temperament. Both he and his older sister were still unmarried. If Leon worried about Annita becoming an old maid, then Lady Mara Faythe was in even more danger of that.

Annita would do her best to enjoy the wedding, even if she and Lord Laurence Faythe would be spending far too much time together since she was Eve Hannoran's first bridesmaid and Laurence was Lord Henry's first groomsman.

Eve was too dear a friend for Annita to do anything to mess up her wedding.

Laurence Faythe escorted his sister Mara to the front steps of Walden Manor, where their carriage waited to shuttle her the short distance from the manor to Walden's white clapboard church at the other end of town.

"I'm sorry I'm not going with you." Laurence helped Mara ease her skirts into the carriage.

"I'm fine. I'm used to sitting alone." Mara smiled and

smoothed her green skirts.

Yes, she was far too used to it. Sometimes, Laurence wanted to pound sense into the young nobles who hadn't thought to look twice at his sister. She was short and slightly on the plump side. Her blue eyes and straight, brown-blond hair were unremarkable. But she had the gentlest smile and a heart filled with compassion for others.

And she had been ignored.

It wasn't right, but at least Mara seemed content to train with Stetterly's healer and remain unattached. Even if Laurence would've liked something else for her.

"Now go on." Mara flapped her hands at him. "You have your own duties to attend to."

Laurence shut the carriage door and motioned to the driver. Once the carriage was safely trundling down the street, he turned and strode back into the manor.

Inside, he had to dodge through the bustle as servants prepared food and decorations for the reception banquet to be held in Walden's gardens after the ceremony. Other guests tromped down the stairs, also on their way to the church.

Laurence ducked down the hall and into Lord Farley Alistair's study, which had temporarily been turned into the dressing room for the groom and his men.

"There you are. Is my necktie straight?" Henry adjusted the necktie again and peered into the small mirror that had been propped against the map of Acktar behind the lord's desk.

"It looks fine. Stop fidgeting with it." Laurence shook his head and plopped into one of the chairs on the other side of the desk. "It's a ridiculous fashion anyway, tying a piece of fabric around your throat in a fancy knot."

"But it *is* the fashion." Henry sank into his father's leather chair. "But if you think it's so ridiculous, how come your necktie is so pristine?"

"Skills, my friend." Laurence grinned and smoothed a hand over his necktie's perfect double twist knot. He wasn't going to mention the skills were Mara's, not his.

Henry leaned back in the chair and propped his feet on the desk. "Seems a bit unfair, though, strangling a man half to death on his wedding day. Fashion could be more considerate of comfort."

"That's your own nerves doing that, not the necktie." Laurence stretched out his legs. He couldn't help his grin as Henry checked the necktie again.

"I should've grown a beard." Henry rubbed his chin.

"I don't think a beard would make a difference one way or the other. Eve already said yes, and I don't think she'd walk out on the wedding just because you don't have enough facial hair." Laurence shook his head. Wedding day jitters. If he ever got married, hopefully he would remain calm.

The door opened, and Lord Farley Alistair marched inside. He glanced at Henry, who immediately dropped his feet back to the floor and straightened.

"Most of the guests have left, and the last are fetching their carriages now. Eve's mother was escorted to the church." Lord Alistair strode toward the desk, his voice booming with the same deep timbre as Henry's.

Laurence got to his feet and headed for the door. That was his cue to leave. Lord Alistair and Henry need a few quiet moments before the wedding to remember those who weren't there. Henry's mother, taken by pneumonia years ago. The little brother who had died shortly after birth.

Laurence's parents, who'd been like an aunt and uncle to Henry.

Someday, if Laurence ever married and had children, hopefully he would live to see them married. Between Rovers, the harsh winters, and sickness, not many fathers and mothers did.

Climbing the stairs, Laurence knocked on the door to the rose room, which had been set aside for Eve Hannoran to get ready.

When the door opened, Princess Annita glided out, her pale green dress swishing about her ankles. Her wavy curls had been tamed and pinned at the back of her head, a few curls left to frame her face.

Laurence sucked in a breath and tried to keep his heartbeat steady. He could never admit he found the princess attractive. She barely found him tolerable, and Stetterly wasn't prosperous enough to make her look twice or convince her brother to condone the match.

Instead, Laurence forced a polite smile to his face. "Is the bride ready?"

"Nearly. Her father is with her." Princess Annita's posture remained stiff. "You might as well start the groom on his way to the church."

"Very well." Laurence strode back the way he'd come and entered the study.

Lord Alistair now lounged in his large, leather chair while Henry paced by the bookshelves. Not surprisingly, the heart-to-heart, father-son talk was already over. It only would've taken a few sentences, at most.

"The ladies are almost ready, so we might as well head to the church."

"Finally." Henry straightened.

Henry was halfway to the door before Laurence stopped him. "Wait. Let me go first."

Henry crossed his arms and sighed. "Fine. We have half of Acktar's army here. Nothing's going to happen."

"But it's my duty as first groomsman." Laurence checked that the hall was clear before he led Henry and his father through the entry hall and out the front door.

Two divisions of soldiers waited outside, as well as horses for Lord Alistair, Henry, and Laurence. The bride's carriage waited a few yards away, the white horses hitched to it stomping to get moving.

As Henry and his father swung on their horses, Laurence checked with the division captains, making sure they were clear on their orders.

Then, finally, Laurence swung onto his horse, one of the divisions closed around them, and they set off for the wedding.

ANNITA KEPT HER GAZE FOCUSED ON THE BRIDE AND GROOM, not the stiff, far-too-proper man standing to her left. Lord Laurence Faythe was every bit as boring and uptight as she remembered. His necktie was even neater and straighter than the groom's.

Slightly mussed necktie or not, Henry and Eve were an adorable couple. Henry's brown eyes warmed to gooey chocolate cake when he looked at Eve. Not that Annita would've stood for anything less for her best friend.

As the minister declared them married and they kissed,

Annita swallowed a lump in her throat. She'd miss Eve at Nalgar. Eve always knew when to be proper, even if she'd been raised as the daughter of an army commander only distantly related to the Segon family of Uster. She was one of the few people who put up with Annita's chatter.

But Annita would never hold Eve back from this happiness. Eve should have a loving husband, a home, and maybe children, Lord willing. Annita would just have to make sure she didn't visit Walden when Henry's friend Laurence was also visiting.

LAURENCE TRAILED BEHIND THE NEWLYWEDS, A GLASS OF APPLE cider in his left hand and his right resting on his sword's hilt. Not that he expected trouble. But it was his duty as first groomsman to be watchful, just in case.

Henry and Eve greeted Lord and Lady Lorraine. Lady Paula Lorraine's face was pale and drawn.

Henry shook Lord Lorraine's hand. "Thanks so much for coming."

Eve gave Lady Lorraine a gentle hug. "I know this is a difficult time for the two of you."

"Thank you for your condolences." A smile broke across Lady Lorraine's face, though lines creased around her eyes.

"It is good to leave the memories behind for a little while." Lord Lorraine wrapped an arm around his wife's waist.

Laurence stepped closer. Lady Lorraine had been several months along when she'd lost the baby. A boy. He would've been their first.

"And thank you, Laurence, for the kind words you and your sister sent. They were much appreciated." Lady Lorraine turned toward him.

"I only wish we could've done more." Laurence meant every word. He understood the pain of loss. He and Mara had lost their parents within a few days of each other. But losing a child even before he was born? That was a loss Laurence couldn't comprehend and hopefully would never experience himself.

The distant sound of thunder rumbled in the distance. Was it going to rain? Laurence peered at the sky. Nothing but a few wispy clouds.

Whatever it was, the thunder wasn't stopping, but getting nearer.

A mass of charging riders, maybe thirty or so, charged over the southern hill and barreled toward Walden.

"Rovers!"

The shout echoed through the garden. Ladies screamed. Men yanked out their swords. The soldiers that had remained mounted after the ceremony, only about ten in all, wheeled their horses to face the oncoming riders.

Laurence drew his sword and placed himself between Henry and Eve and the riders. "Henry, get her inside."

Drawing his sword, Henry nodded and gripped Eve's arm.

Laurence and Henry made it halfway to the door when the riders slammed into the garden. Horses leapt over the hedge and trampled the flower beds. They surged through the stand of trees at the far side of the gardens.

Soldiers clustered around King Leon while other guards tried to organize some sort of defense.

A Rover charged at Laurence, Henry, and Eve. Henry pulled Eve out of the way while Laurence stepped forward. He ducked under the Rover's swinging sword and grabbed one of the horse's reins. The horse's momentum lifted Laurence off his feet a moment before it skidded to a halt. The Rover stabbed at him past the horse's head, and Laurence lost his footing avoiding the thrust.

With his awkward position and the horse's head in the way, Laurence couldn't use his own sword. Letting go of the rein, he rolled out of the way and sprang to his feet.

In the time it had taken him to roll free, the Rover had wheeled and charged at Henry and Eve again. Henry side-stepped and raised his sword, but the horse's shoulder and leg rammed into him, sending him stumbling.

The Rover raised his sword. Laurence's heart caught in his mouth. Henry wouldn't regain his balance and raise his sword in time.

Laurence lunged forward and stabbed his sword into the Rover's thigh. It wasn't a deep wound, since it had been dealt at the end of the Laurence's reach, but the Rover cried out and halted his swing, clapping a hand to the wound.

Without a guiding hand on the reins, the horse veered away from them.

Laurence gripped Henry's arm. "We have to get to the manor. Now."

A knot of soldiers and Rovers fought by an overturned table, the wedding gifts strewn on the ground. A mob of wedding guests surged toward Walden's main door.

Was Mara among them? Laurence couldn't pick out any faces in the chaos.

But Henry and Eve came first. They were the bride and

groom, and it was Laurence's duty to make sure they weren't killed on their wedding day.

They would never be able to force their way through the mob by the front door. Even if they were the bride and groom.

"Come on." Laurence waved in the opposite direction.

It took Henry only a moment to recognize Laurence's plan. With Henry pulling Eve with him, they sprinted under the arbor, around the kitchen vegetable garden, and reached the kitchen door.

Laurence ushered them inside and shut the door after them. When he turned, he came nose to point with a large butcher knife.

The cook coughed and lowered the knife. "Sorry, sir."

The rest of the kitchen staff peered around him, several of the scullery maids and assistant cooks also brandishing knives and other cooking utensils.

"Carry on." Henry nodded at them as he hurried Eve across the room and into the hallway beyond. Laurence followed him a moment later.

People jostled and screamed as they poured through the front door into the entry hall. The jumble of panicked voices filled the room, turning into a solid roar of noise.

Henry opened the dining room door. "Barricade yourself inside. Laurence and I have to get back out there."

Laurence caught Henry's arm. "You're staying here. You aren't allowed to get yourself killed on your wedding day. Your bride needs you."

"Don't worry about me." Eve gathered her skirts, her face smooth and focused. "I'll stay here to calm down these people. You can go if you have to."

"It will take two of you to calm this lot." Laurence kept his gaze focused on Henry. "And someone should stay here in case a Rover gets inside."

"Fine." Henry turned to the crowd of people. "Women and children into the dining room. Don't panic. Single file."

Laurence didn't wait any longer. He gripped his sword and sprinted for the kitchen door to rejoin the fight.

ANNITA SEARCHED FOR A WEAPON, BUT A GROUP OF EIGHT Rovers had her and a few others cornered next to the water fountain.

A few feet away, Lady Felix of Blathe pressed her hands to her face and keened hysterically.

"Can't you get her quiet?" A Rover jabbed his sword at Lord Felix.

Lord Felix grasped his wife's shoulders and shook her roughly. "Stop wailing! Can't you pull yourself together for once!"

She only wailed louder, screeching an even higher pitch.

Another Rover grumbled under his breath, nocked an arrow to his bow, and released.

Lady Felix's wail cut off in a choked whine. She crumpled to the ground.

Annita gasped. This...this couldn't be happening.

"What? Why you—" Lord Felix lunged at the Rover, but a second arrow caught him in the chest before he'd gone two paces. He fell only a few steps away from his wife.

"Anyone else?" The Rover leveled another arrow at them.

Annita glanced over her shoulder. The elderly Lord and

Lady Spencer huddled behind her, as well as Lord and Lady Dawson with their infant daughter.

She clenched her trembling fingers into fists. She was the princess. She had to do something before anyone else was killed.

She stepped forward and addressed the Rover who had first complained about Lady Felix. "Sir."

He and Bow Rover turned to her. "Don't take another step."

She raised her hands. "I'm not going to attack you. I'm not armed."

Something she regretted now. If only her parents and brother hadn't been so traditional. Then she might know how to defend herself and these people.

If she couldn't fight with a sword, she'd have to fight with her wits.

"There are more soldiers here than you thought, aren't there?" She eyed the Rover. His attention was split between her and a group of soldiers advancing on them. "You aren't going to get out of here alive."

"Shut your mouth, or I'll have him put an arrow in you too." Bossy Rover's gaze flicked between her and the lead soldier.

The soldiers were hanging back, not wanting to rush the Rovers with their princess caught in the middle.

That gave Annita an idea.

"I wouldn't do that if I were you. I'm your only way out of here."

Bossy Rover's gaze focused solely on her. Good. She'd gotten his attention.

"I'm Princess Annita Eirdon. If you hold me hostage,

you'll be able to get away. The soldiers wouldn't attack you."

Bossy Rover grabbed her arm and pulled her against him. "You're right. I don't want to kill you. You're coming with me."

He pressed a knife to her neck and motioned for his men to fall in behind him.

Annita had to stifle a smile. Her plan was working. The Rovers were letting the others go.

"Step back. Lower your weapons, or your princess gets hurt!" Bossy Rover's voice bellowed right in Annita's ear.

She shuffled along with the Rover as he and his men trudged past the soldiers. The edge of the knife shifted against her skin, slicing like a paper cut under her chin. The least he could've done was use the flat of the blade.

The Rovers caught a few horses. Three other Rovers joined them, swinging onto their horses.

They were leaving. No one else would get hurt. Her plan was working perfectly.

No, not perfectly. A Rover reached down and pulled her onto his horse in front of him, pinning her arms to her sides.

Not good. Not good at all.

Her plan had worked perfectly, but she'd forgotten one small detail.

They weren't going to let her go.

Laurence sheathed his sword as the soldiers rounded up the last of the Rovers.

Trampled flowers, overturned tables, and discarded plates and glasses littered the ground. A few bodies lay still and motionless. Laurence checked a few of them. One soldier, the rest were Rovers. Some of the soldiers and wedding guests staggered with hands clutched to wounds.

Mara. Laurence hurried through the garden, searching for her short frame.

"Mother!" The cry was half a scream, half a yell.

Laurence dashed toward the sound, skirting around a hedge until the opening by the water fountain came in sight.

Thirteen-year-old Respen Felix knelt on the ground, gripping his mother's limp body. Her head lolled, an arrow stuck in a gaping wound in her throat.

Laurence knelt next to Respen and laid a hand on his shoulder. "I'm sorry."

Respen knocked his hand away. "Don't touch me."

Laurence withdrew his hand, trying to find the words he should say. He knew the raw edge of this moment. He'd held his mother's hand as she slipped from this world into the next. But hers had been a quiet death. Peaceful, almost. Nothing compared to the sudden horror that had happened to Lady Felix.

"They killed her." Respen's voice edged higher. His fingers tightened into claws around his mother's body. "They had no reason to kill her."

"No, they didn't." Laurence swallowed. As far as he knew, Lord and Lady Felix had attended the church in Blathe. "But she is at peace in heaven now." He rested his hand on Respen's shoulder once again.

Respen lashed out, striking Laurence's cheek with the back of his fist. "I said, don't touch me! Leave me alone!"

Laurence tumbled to the ground. When he touched a

hand to his mouth, his fingers came away with a dot of blood. His lip throbbed.

Some of the nearby soldiers dashed forward and grabbed Respen's arms, dragging him to his feet. Respen struggled, kicking and punching at them.

Laurence clambered to his feet. What had caused such a reaction in Respen? And why was he only mourning his mother when his father also lay dead a few feet away?

Laurence wasn't sure he wanted to know the answer.

Respen shouldn't have to take anything more. Laurence brushed himself off. "Let him go. His parents just died. Give him space."

The soldiers let Respen go. As soon as he was free, Respen dropped to his knees next to his mother's body.

Laurence finally spotted Mara as she bent to check Lord Felix's pulse. As she straightened, Laurence gripped her shoulders and hugged her. "You're safe. I'm so sorry I didn't go to find you during the attack. I had to get Henry and Eve to safety, and by the time I did, I couldn't find you."

"I'm fine. Better than they are." Mara gestured to the bodies of Lord and Lady Felix. "Laurence, the Rovers took Princess Annita."

"What?" Laurence stumbled back a step, ice in his stomach.

"I was hiding back there and saw them take her away with them." Mara pointed toward the north where the Sheered Rock Hills rose into the sky. She pulled away. "There are people injured. I need to help."

Laurence let her go. Everyone with healing skills would be needed.

He had to find Henry and organize a party to go after

Princess Annita. Dashing toward the manor, Laurence shoved through the crowd by the door and into the entry hall. Inside the dining room, he found King Leon leaning against the table, his face white.

"...my sister. Will they hurt her? Maybe they'll ask for a ransom. Yes, a ransom. I'll have to pay it. That's...that's what..." King Leon gripped the table, his hands shaking.

"We have to go after them. We have enough soldiers here." Henry gripped the hilt of his sheathed sword as if thinking about drawing it again. "Witnesses said only eleven or twelve Rovers got away with Princess Annita."

"But...but if they hurt her out of fear...wouldn't it be better to wait for a ransom demand?" King Leon glanced between those assembled in the dining room, as if looking for someone to tell him what to do.

"I agree with Henry. Send men after them. It's the quickest way to rescue her. They don't have that big of a head start." Lord Farley Alistair crossed his arms.

"But I...I can't go. I'm king. There's..." King Leon rubbed his hands down the front of his shirt, as if trying to dry them.

"No, you're right. You should stay here. Lord and Lady Felix were killed today, and the country will need its king to be here to deal with the ramifications." Lord Alistair nodded sharply. "And I'll help with the organization and clean up here."

"I'll go." Henry stepped forward, hand flexing on his sword's hilt.

"No, I'll go." Laurence shook his head. "You were married today. You need to stay with your new bride and help your father. I'll get the princess back."

With a sigh, Henry nodded.

Within an hour, Laurence, fifteen men, and an army tracker set off after the Rovers and the captured Princess Annita.

THIS WAS A FINE BARREL OF PICKLES SHE'D GOTTEN HERSELF IN.

Annita tugged on the rope tying her wrists to the saddlehorn. At least she now rode a horse by herself, not stuffed on some Rover's lap.

But she wasn't going anywhere. Not with her hands tied to the saddlehorn and a Rover gripping the horse's reins.

As surreptitiously as possible, she pulled up part of her skirt and tried to rip it. It wouldn't so much as tear. Of course not. Fabric wasn't as easy to tear as the stories made it sound.

Instead, she kicked at any trees or undergrowth they passed as the Rovers took her farther and deeper into the Sheered Rock Hills. The more of a trail she left, the easier it would be for someone to find her.

Would anyone even come after her? Leon was many things, but decisive wasn't one of them. Would he dither so long they'd lose the trail? What would become of her then?

At least, if this ended badly, she would be the only one hurt. If she hadn't talked the Rovers into leaving, how many others might have been hurt?

Darkness came hard and fast. The Rovers finally called a halt at the base of a cliff. They built several fires, picketed their horses, and started cooking some sort of meat.

Several of the Rovers sent glances her way. The Bow Rover leered at her. "Well, we got away. What are we going to do with her now?"

Uh, oh. That was a direction of thought she had to stop immediately.

"You have to keep me for ransom, that's what you have to do." She kept her back straight, her voice even. She couldn't appear afraid.

"Really? Ransom, huh?" Bossy Rover sauntered closer.

"Yes." She held his gaze without flinching. "My brother will pay handsomely to get me back. You'll make more through the ransom than you would've with a few paltry jewels from the wedding."

Bow Rover smirked. "Doesn't mean we can't have some fun with you while we wait for ransom."

Oh. She hadn't thought of that.

"Actually, you can't." She tried to appear calm while her brain and heart was racing. "I'm worthless to my brother if I'm ruined. I'm a princess. I'm only good as a marriage bargaining piece. He won't pay nearly as much for me, if anything at all, if he loses that."

She held her breath, her heart thumping in her ears.

Bossy Rover grimaced. "Fine. Hands off, men. Got it?"

Annita breathed out a long sigh. Hopefully Bossy Rover had a good handle on his men.

"Walter, she's your problem."

A Rover who looked to be in his thirties with long, brown hair tied back with a leather string stood and walked toward her. Annita searched his lined face. She didn't see the same leer in his eyes as some of the others. Maybe she could work with this one.

She put on her very best smile. "Walter, is it? What's your family name?"

"Esroy. I'm Walter Esroy." He held out a plate with a

piece of meat on it. "You'd better eat. We'll have a long day tomorrow."

As he began to retreat, she waved her bound hands at the ground in front of her. "Why don't you stay? I haven't had someone to talk to all day. And you can guard me better while you're talking to me."

Walter hesitated. After she gave him another smile, he sank to the ground.

All right. She had his attention. How was she going to talk him over to her side? A story was always a good choice. Maybe a Bible story. She took a bite of meat, chewed, and smiled. "Once there was a boy named Joseph. He was his father's favorite son, and his brothers were really jealous."

Walter's brow furrowed. He crossed his arms. "Are you going to tell me a Bible story?"

Shoot, he'd recognized it. Oh, well. A person could never hear Bible stories too often.

After eating another bite, she grinned. "Hush. I'm telling a story."

Amazingly, he listened. Maybe there was hope for him yet.

A HAND SHOOK HER ROUGHLY. ANNITA BLINKED AND PEERED into the gray haze of morning. Surely it wasn't time to get up and riding already. Didn't these Rovers ever sleep?

Apparently, they didn't eat breakfast either. They threw their saddles onto their horses and scrambled on.

As the Rover Walter motioned for her to get on, she got another idea. She messed with the ruffles and mounds of her skirt, exaggerating how difficult it was to arrange the layers of her fancy dress, which hadn't been meant for riding.

"What's taking so long? Get her tied and let's get moving." Bossy Rover wheeled his horse, scowling.

Annita sighed. "I think you'd better cut the skirts."

After a moment's hesitation, Walter sliced long slits down either side of her dress as best he could while she sat on a horse and he stood on the ground. Her skirts flopped to either side, freeing the space around her in the saddle.

Without a word, Walter tied her hands to the saddle, grabbed the reins, and clambered onto his own horse.

Annita stifled her smile as they set off at a trot. She hadn't been able to tear her dress herself, but convincing a Rover to cut it for her worked even better.

"Where were we in the story of Joseph?" Annita kept her tone light. Empty-headed. The more foolish they believed her to be, the less attention they'd spend on her. "Oh, yes. Joseph's brothers had sold him into slavery in a far off kingdom. Well, Joseph was purchased by a man named Potiphar."

As she talked, Annita drew her knee up, grasped the fabric with her bound hands, and shifted it until her fingers reached a sliced edge. Without pausing in her story or even looking to see what she was doing, she pried fingerfulls of thread loose and dropped them to the ground.

Hopefully it would be enough for whoever was following them.

LAURENCE LEANED AGAINST HIS SADDLEHORN. THREE DAYS AND nights of grueling travel ached in his back, legs, and rear end.

How was Princess Annita holding up? Had the Rovers hurt her? She would be enduring the same sort of hard travel, made worse by her captivity.

Surely they would catch up soon. The Rovers couldn't keep up this pace.

No matter what, Laurence couldn't lose them. Princess Annita depended on them.

The tracker straightened, a tuft of light green fabric pinched in his fingers. "They kept on this way. Would've lost them over these rocks if not for Princess Annita. She's leaving a trail even you could follow, sir."

Laurence could only shake his head. The Rovers were doing everything possible to lose them, but somehow Princess Annita was leaving such a path of destruction—broken branches, scraped bark, and scraps of fabric—that the tracker followed without trouble.

As if Laurence needed another reason to admire her. Captured by eleven Rovers, dragged into the Sheered Rock Hills, and Princess Annita still thought to leave a trail for them to follow. And she'd been getting away with it for three days.

"Let's keep moving." Laurence nudged his horse.

The Rovers had stayed one step ahead of them for days. It was time to cross that step and rescue the princess.

"THEY'RE CATCHING UP." ONE OF THE ROVERS GRIPPED HIS horse's reins, staring back the way they'd come. A group of fifteen riders were visible picking their way along the base of the far mountain.

"Why won't they give up?" Bossy Rover growled. After four days, he was becoming even more grouchy. He'd even called Annita's storytelling "chatter" earlier in the day. "We should've lost them by now."

And after four days, it was clear Annita would have to do the rescuing herself. Her rescuers weren't catching up fast enough, as much as Annita had been helping them.

Who was leading those fifteen men? It wasn't her brother. He would've given up already. The man back there, he was tenacious.

Annita couldn't help but let herself dream a little. After all, stories told about romantic, dramatic rescues with handsome, brave rescuers. No, Annita wasn't going to sit by and scream and sob while waiting for someone to rescue her. She planned to rescue herself. Still, it would be nice to have the handsome rescuer part.

"We should fight it out." Bow Rover fiddled with an arrow.

"They outnumber us. We'd probably all get killed." Another Rover glanced back toward their pursuers.

This could be her chance. Annita put on a wide-eyed, innocent look. "You could leave me here and keep on riding. They will stop pursuing you if you don't have me."

"But we'd lose the ransom!" Bow Rover scowled.

Annita shrugged. "Seems I was wrong. Looks like my brother doesn't intend to pay a ransom. He'd rather kill you all and be done with it. If you want to live, leave me here. I'll make sure they stop chasing you. There will be other stuff to steal later, but you can't do it if you're dead."

The Rovers looked at each other.

"She's right." Bossy Rover straightened.

"But the ransom!"

"We can't collect a ransom if we're dead. Let's get out of here while we can. Walter, get her down from the horse."

Walter dismounted, strode to Annita, and untied her hands. As she swung to the ground, he pressed something into her hands. His canteen. And a hunk of dried meat. "In case it takes them a while to find you."

"Thank you." Annita caught his arm. "If you ever want to leave the Rovers, come to Nalgar. I'll help."

He met her gaze and gave her a small nod.

Maybe something good had come out of all this mess. Hopefully Annita would see Walter Esroy again.

LAURENCE'S HORSE LUNGED UP A HILL. THEY WERE CATCHING up. If he pressed his horse just a little harder...

They trotted around a dense stand of juniper, and he pulled up short.

Princess Annita perched on a boulder, torn skirts draped around her as primly as if she were sitting in Walden's parlor. Her eyes widened, and she blinked at him for a moment before her expression smoothed into a pert smile. "Ah, good. You're here. It took you a little longer than I expected, but you finally arrived."

Laurence gaped. What was she doing here? All alone? Where were the Rovers? Had she managed to escape?

He threw himself from his horse as the rest of his men arrived and stumbled toward her. "Princess Annita, are you all right? Did they hurt you? How did you escape?"

"I'm fine. They didn't hurt me a bit." Princess Annita gathered her torn skirts and hopped down from the boulder. "And I didn't escape. I rescued myself. I talked them into leaving me behind."

"Sir, should we go after them?" One of the soldiers halted his horse next to Laurence.

Princess Annita huffed and shook her head. "I told them I'd talk you out of going after them. Besides, you'll probably have a chance to capture them again. They aren't the brightest candles in the room."

Laurence was beginning to doubt his own intelligence. He'd gone all this way to rescue the princess, only to have her rescue herself first.

The soldier was still staring, waiting for Laurence's response.

Laurence cleared his throat. "No, we'll let them go. The king has waited long enough to see his sister safe."

Princess Annita tromped toward the horses. "Did you bring an extra horse for me?"

Laurence shook his head. "No, we planned to get a horse when we rescued you from the Rovers."

"Sorry, I couldn't communicate my plan. Guess I'll have to ride double." Princess Annita shrugged and marched toward his horse.

Laurence swallowed and forced himself to follow her. He could manage to be polite and distant while she rode double with him. He wouldn't let a hint of his admiration for her show. She was his princess.

Annita swung up behind Laurence and wrapped an arm around his waist. Perhaps he wasn't quite the stuffed scarecrow she'd thought him to be. After four days on the trail, blond scruff covered his chin and cheeks. Dust covered his rumpled clothes.

But he sat straight in the saddle, relaxed and confident in the movement of the horse beneath him. Not like her brother, who sat on his horse with all the grace of a dead fish.

As they set off back down the trail, she patted Laurence Faythe's shoulder. "Thank you for coming when you did. It would've been a long walk back to Walden."

He glanced over his shoulder. "You're welcome. Glad I could assist you in your rescue."

He didn't seem too disappointed that she'd rescued herself before he could. What, no lectures on being proper? And, was that something like respect in his eyes?

Sure, some of this plan had been reckless. But at least she'd gotten the Rovers away from Walden and the wedding guests. Someday, she might do something so reckless she got herself killed. But she wouldn't worry about that now.

Annita stifled a grin. With the horses tired and one carrying double, it would take them five or more days to get back to Walden. Five days where she'd have to ride double with Laurence Faythe. Five days for her to talk him into asking to court her.

Actually, this plan was turning out to be pretty near perfect.

THE TREATY

Blade Marshal Leith Torren lay on his stomach in the deep grass at the crest of the hill. On the hill opposite him, a tavern spilled light, music, and noise into the night. Though, *tavern* probably wasn't the right name to call it. That made the place sound respectable.

Next to him, Martyn propped himself onto his elbows. "Figures he'd end up here."

"It is the sort of place where he could boast about robbing women and get a round of applause." Leith eased his knife in its sheath.

Max Arnold, the man they were hunting, had a habit of waiting until a man left for the fields or for his business in town, then in daylight while the wife and children were home alone, Arnold would break in, hold the wife at knifepoint, and take whatever coin and goods he could carry.

"Makes me wish he'd tried his shenanigans in Stetterly. I would've loved to see the look on his face when Kayleigh took him out. Would've saved us so much trouble." Martyn eased one of his knives out of its sheath. Like Leith, he kept his voice low.

Not that anyone would hear them past the shouts, laughter, and worst music playing Leith had ever heard blasting from the tavern.

Leith's stomach knotted. Not that he doubted Kayleigh's skills. But the thought of Arnold getting that close to Renna and the children...Leith shook his head. He couldn't let himself imagine. And he couldn't let Arnold get away to terrorize Renna or any other woman home alone. "I'll settle for arresting him here."

"What's the plan?" Martyn waved his knife in the direction of the tavern, though he kept it below the crest of the hill where it wouldn't be seen.

Leith studied the tavern once again. The sprawling building and its accompanying stable sat alone on the hill, nothing but prairie around for miles and miles. In the years since the Blade Marshals had cleaned up Acktar's prairies, taverns like this had sprung up just across what everyone was guessing was the border into Verden to harbor criminals out of the Blade Marshals' reach.

"It's going to be tricky. We technically don't have jurisdiction here." Leith fingered the hilt of his knife. He wasn't going to let this one get away that easily. Rustlers and horse thieves were one thing. But this man—someone who terrified women and children—he had to be brought to ground.

Martyn flexed his fingers on his knife's hilt. "That didn't stop us last time."

"We can't. Keevan was adamant that we abide by the new treaty even if the official border markers haven't gone in yet." Leith resisted the urge to draw his own knife. He said the right words. He was the leader here, after all. But he couldn't help agreeing with Martyn. It would be so easy to ignore all the jurisdiction issues and grab their quarry.

But it would do no good to capture Max Arnold only to have him escape justice on a technicality. And jeopardizing relations with Verden would only make capturing future criminals that much harder.

Leith sighed. "All we are supposed to do on Verdenish soil is contact their authorities, wait for them to apprehend him, and hope our new treaty with them works as it is supposed to and they hand him over to us."

"Please tell me that's not what we're actually going to do." Martyn's jaw tightened. "Because if it is, I'm going to slip across the border, quietly bash Max Arnold on the head, and hope that when we get him back to Nalgar, I hit him hard enough that he won't remember which side of the border he was on when snatched."

"Don't worry. I'm not leaving here without him, one way or another." Leith gritted his teeth. Now he just had to come up with a plan to make that happen. Legally.

Something down below caught his eye, and a slow grin spread across his face. Now that might work. He pointed. "Tell me if I'm wrong, but does that look like one of the survey stakes over there?"

Martyn peered in the direction he was pointing and grinned. "Yes, I believe it is."

"Here's what we're going to do. While I wait in the stable, you march into the tavern, announce you're a Blade Marshal, and demand that Arnold be turned over to you immediately. Be as angry and noisy as possible." Leith felt his grin turn into a smirk. "You should be good at that."

Martyn tapped his knife's tip against the ground. "And if the tavern owner objects? He'll have his henchmen toss me out on my face while hollering about me violating the treaty."

"Then holler back. Demand to talk to the local authorities like the treaty says. Just do it loudly. Doesn't matter if they cooperate or not. As long as Arnold hears the commotion." Leith shrugged.

"Think it'll work?" Martyn slid back from the crest of the hill and brushed off his trousers.

Leith eased to his feet as well. "We've hounded his footsteps for a hundred miles. That'd make anyone jumpy, and he doesn't know if they might turn him over to us. It'll work."

Martyn sighed and ran his hand through his hair. "Why do I have to be the one to go in? Why don't you go into the tavern, and I wait in the stables?"

"Because you're taller, bigger, and look more convincing as an angry, dangerous Blade Marshal. That's how we work. You take care of the tavern brawls, and I do all the victim comforting." Ice settled into Leith's hands and chest. They would get him. Tonight. Forcing himself to grin, Leith slapped Martyn's shoulder. "Just don't start too much trouble. My cousin won't be happy if I mess up his shiny new treaty, not after it took him six years to negotiate for it. Especially since we're the reason he had to make it in the first place."

For some reason, the Verdenish hadn't been happy when they'd stumbled across Leith and Martyn deep in their country after trailing a man to the Great Mountains and innocently claiming that, since the border wasn't marked, they couldn't be sure they were in Verden and not Acktar.

Hence the treaty.

"Fine, I'll be careful. But you know King Keevan is happiest when he has some major diplomatic crisis to brilliantly solve by signing treaties to get what he wanted all along. Ruling is all boring taxes and paperwork otherwise." Still grinning, Martyn straightened his knives and strode down the hill.

Leith slipped through the grass after him, veering to the right toward the stable. Easing the door open, he crept between the rows of stalls until he found Arnold's horse. He crouched in the shadows near the floor and waited.

The music screeched to a halt. Shouting came from the direction of the tavern, and Martyn's voice was audible even through the stable's wall.

If Leith had guessed right, then right about now…

The stable door crashed open. Max Arnold dashed inside, blond hair shining dirty and greasy even in the faint moonlight from outside.

As Arnold reached the stall and scrambled to open the latch, Leith slid to his feet and drew a knife. "Max Arnold, you are under arrest."

Arnold pawed at his belt for his own knife.

"I wouldn't do that if I were you." Leith eased a step forward, drawing a second knife. He probably shouldn't be hoping Arnold was foolish enough to draw that knife.

Arnold raised his hands, but his flabby face cracked with a smirk. "What are you doing, Blade Marshal? You can't arrest me here."

"Actually, I can." Leith allowed himself an answering smirk. This man deserved a little gloating. "As you probably know, until the treaty, no one knew exactly where the border was. But, thanks to the recent treaty, a joint Acktarian-Verdenish survey team is marking out the official border. While the men haven't installed the stone markers yet, the surveyors already marked this section of border."

"So?" Arnold crossed his arms.

"So if you'd being paying attention, you would've noticed that, while the tavern falls on the Verdenish side of the border, this stable is in Acktar. That means I have the authority to arrest you here."

Arnold's eyes widened. He whirled, as if intending to make a dash for the door and the border.

Leith stepped forward, hooked a boot around Arnold's ankle, and twisted Arnold's arm. Arnold's momentum sent him sprawling to the stable floor as Martyn strolled inside.

Arnold glanced up at Martyn and swore.

Martyn snorted. "I think we're going to have to use soap on this one. Though I'm afraid the soap in my pocket is coated with dirt and lint. I haven't had to use it in a while."

"Let's get him tied first." Leith put a knee into Arnold's back, pulled out a slim cord, and yanked it tight around Arnold's wrists.

Once tied, Leith hauled Arnold to his feet and shoved him at Martyn. "Watch him while I saddle his horse."

Martyn gave Arnold a cold glare. "Don't even think of trying anything."

Locating the saddle, Leith swung it onto Arnold's horse. After the horse was saddled and bridled, Leith led it from the stall. "Let's get him mounted up and head for Nalgar."

"Nalgar? But I didn't do anything in Nalgar." Arnold stumbled as Martyn dragged him from the stable.

"No, but to ensure you receive the harshest sentence

possible, the towns agreed to send your case to Nalgar rather than give you several smaller punishments." Leith couldn't help another smirk. "And King Keevan isn't known for his leniency in cases like yours."

As Martyn dragged a swearing Arnold outside, Leith patted the horse's nose and followed. A few days' ride to Nalgar, a day to file the proper paperwork, then it was home to Renna and the children.

Finally.

THE SUN HAD LONG SINCE SET WHEN THE TOWN OF STETTERLY came into view, a black silhouette against the gray twilight sky. Leith nudged Valor to circle the town. Martyn on Wanderer kept pace beside him.

The lights of the Leith's cabin came into view, spreading gold into the surrounding prairie.

Leith lifted a hand in a wave as Martyn urged Wanderer into a trot. Martyn waved in return, but his gaze was focused ahead as he headed for the trail that would take him home. Leith didn't blame him. Martyn had Kayleigh, Molly, Lila, and Kalissa who he was just as eager to see as Leith was to return to his family.

He drew rein outside of the stable and swung down. The stable was quiet. Almost achingly so. It had been two years since Ranson had moved to his own small cabin near the Blade Marshals' office when he married Michelle and three years since Jamie moved first to Walden, then various towns in Acktar to begin his formal training as a minister. Last Leith had heard, Jamie was all the way across the country in the town of Hendor near Acktar's western border with the Surrana Empire.

Of course they were all moving out, starting their own lives. But was it so wrong that Leith missed the little family they'd built those first few years?

But that was the way of life. Changes. Growth. Jamie and Ranson couldn't stay the same any more than he could.

After unsaddling Valor, Leith turned him into the corral where the horse was greeted by Blizzard, Big Brown, and Snapper. At least Ranson's horse was still there, since wood was too expensive to build a stable for a single horse near Ranson's cabin.

Slinging his saddlebags over his shoulder, Leith headed for the cabin. Halting on the porch, he unstrapped his boot knives and held them in one hand while he reached for the hidden string in the eaves that would unlock the door. When he felt the bar inside lift, he pushed the door open.

The warmth of the lamplight and the fire's heat washed against his face, the air filled with the smell of freshly baked maple sugar cookies.

Renna was by the fireplace, pulling a tray of cookies from the brick oven with one hand while she balanced their one-year-old daughter Amara on her hip.

In the parlor, Brandi sat in the middle of the settee with six-year-old David leaning against one shoulder and four-year-old LeeAnna against the other shoulder. They looked like they were dozing, or had been dozing, for in that moment both children bolted upright. "Papa!"

Leith barely had time to get the door closed and barred behind him before David and LeeAnna slammed into him, one to a leg. He pretended to stagger under their onslaught, and they clung to him, giggling, with arms and legs wrapped around his legs.

He dropped his saddlebags onto the floor by the door and hung the sheaths with his boot knives on their peg by the door, a peg well out of reach of all the children except David, who knew better than to touch Leith's knives.

Leith unbuckled the knives strapped across his chest and the knife belt around his waist and hung those on pegs as well. And, with that action, it was if he'd hung up the Blade Marshal part of himself—the cold, hard part that could look a bandit in the eye and make him believe Leith could kill him without blinking, much less hesitating—and now Leith wasn't Blade Marshal Torren. He was Leith. Papa. Husband.

He'd had to learn this routine. The leaving of all the cares and worries of his job at the doorstep so he could smile and laugh with his children. They didn't need him bringing home the burdens of the country.

Renna reached his side, and Amara just about threw herself from Renna's arms. Leith caught her and tucked her against his shoulder.

"Welcome home." Renna tipped her face toward him.

He kissed her, ignoring the howls of "Eww!" coming from David and LeeAnna as they still hung around his legs.

Hopefully they'd never know how good they had it. It would be so expected that their parents loved each other and them that it wouldn't even cross their minds that there could be any other kind of parent.

"I love you." Leith whispered into Renna's ear before he kissed her cheek.

"Of course you do." Renna's smile had a tilt to it, a spark

in her eyes. She held up one of the maple sugar cookies. "And you'll love me more once you taste this."

"My favorite." He took the cookie. It was still warm, flopping in his hand, and he quickly stuffed most of it into his mouth before it broke off. He'd hate to lose the cookie to the floor. He chewed and swallowed. "Guess this explains why the children are so giggly tonight."

David and LeeAnna were giggling nearly uncontrollably, sitting on top of Leith's feet. He shifted, and their arms tightened around his calves, the giggles increasing.

"They may have eaten a few more cookies than normal." Renna shrugged. "They weren't going to sleep anyway, not when your letter said you'd be home tonight."

Very true.

"Come on, Papa!" David wiggled on Leith's leg.

Leith grinned and lumbered toward the parlor as best as he could with a child on each leg.

At the step from the kitchen's brick floor to the parlor's smooth wood, Brandi met him and gave him a side hug to avoid squishing Amara. She was nearly as tall as he was, and even though she'd been that tall for years, it sometimes still surprised him on returning. "Welcome back."

"Do you have a message run tomorrow?" Leith eased onto the step one leg at the time since he couldn't bend his knees well with David and LeeAnna clinging to him.

"Yep, and I'll probably regret staying up this late when I get up tomorrow." Brandi's mouth twisted like she was trying to scowl but couldn't.

Brandi had joined the message riders three years ago, carrying messages from Stetterly to the nearest outpost and back. Leith shuffled out of her way. "Then you'd better head for bed. I'll try to keep the noise down."

"No, you won't. Let them giggle all they want." Brandi grinned and headed for the ladder to her loft bedroom. "I'll probably fall asleep even with the ruckus."

Smiling, Leith eased onto the floor on his back. He had just enough time to set Amara safely to the side before David and LeeAnna pounced and general rough-housing and chaos ensued. Lots of giggling and children bouncing on Leith's stomach. Even Amara was giggling as she fell-tackled Leith's face.

After a few minutes, Leith could tell by the pitch of the giggles that he was needed to calm the children down before someone got hurt. He managed to roll into a sitting position. "You want a story?"

"Did you get the bad man, Papa?" David plopped onto Leith's knee.

LeeAnna clambered onto his other knee. Amara toddled over, and Leith wedged her between LeeAnna and David on his lap. "Yes, I did. He was a very bad man. He took things that weren't his. I'll tell you the rest of the story once you're in bed."

"Awww…" LeeAnna and David both groaned, but they jumped to their feet.

After all three children were in bed, the story—a highly edited version—told, he told them a Bible story and listened while they said their prayers. Then he tucked each of them in. Amara in the trundle bed on the floor. LeeAnna on the bed above her. David across the room, which was divided by a curtain to give him some privacy from his little sisters. Before too long Leith would need to turn half of Brandi's loft into a room for David. But he wasn't going to ask Brandi to give up some of her space any sooner than he had to.

If there was one thing he wished he could tell his younger self, it would be this. That it did get better. All the doubts he'd had. All the times he'd worried he'd never be the man Renna needed him to be. He'd been so unsure of himself back then.

But now? Something inside him was settled in a way he hadn't been years ago. As if he was finally comfortable in his own skin, knowing his own limits and strengths in a way he hadn't before.

And life was good. Yes, there were still struggles. Times he stayed awake burdened by the people who'd been hurt because of his failures as a Blade Marshal. But there was joy. So much joy. A joy he never would've thought possible as that eighteen-year-old Blade that had slipped into Lord Alistair's study yearning for something more. He hadn't even known what he'd wanted. Just something free from the Blades.

But God had blessed him with so much more than he'd dared ask for.

"Are you all right?" Renna touched his arm.

Leith started, realizing he was still standing in the doorway to his children's room. He eased the door closed, then turned to Renna, pulling her into his arms. As she tucked her head against him, he pressed a kiss into her hair. "I'm fine. Just...thankful."

FREE STORY!

Deal

A Blades of Acktar Short Story

Once there was a nine-year-old boy Leith Torren who only wanted to bring food home to his mother...and was noticed by Lord Respen Felix of Blathe.

Free for newsletter subscribers. Sign up at https://triciamingerink.com/my-newsletter/

DAGGER'S SLEEP

A prince cursed to sleep.
A princess destined to wake him.
A kingdom determined to stop them.

High Prince Alexander has been cursed to a sleep like unto death, a curse that will end the line of the high kings and send the Seven Kingdoms of Tallahatchia into chaos. With his manservant to carry his luggage and his own superior intelligence to aid him, Alex sets off to find one of the Fae and end his curse one way or another.

A hundred years later, Princess Rosanna learns she is the princess destined by the Highest King to wake the legendary sleeping prince. With the help of the mysterious Daemyn Rand, can she find the courage to finish the quest as Tallahatchia wavers on the edge of war?

One curse connects them. A hundred years separate them. From the rushing rivers of Tallahatchia's mountains to the hall of the Highest King himself, their quests will demand greater sacrifice than either of them could imagine.

For readers of adventure, fairy tales, and stirring allegories comes this fresh imagining of the classic Sleeping Beauty tale, the first book in a new YA fantasy series from Tricia Mingerink

Buy Now!

BOOKS BY TRICIA MINGERINK

The Blades of Acktar

Dare

Deny

Defy

Destroy: A novella

Deliver

Decree

Beyond the Tales

Dagger's Sleep

Midnight's Curse

Poison's Dance

ACKNOWLEDGMENTS

Thank you to all of those who have stuck through yet another "Surprise! There's another book!" Apparently I was no more ready to let go of *The Blades of Acktar* than any of you. I hope you enjoyed *Decree*, the fifth and final book in the series. This time, it really is the end and time to let the characters live their happily ever afters.

Thanks to my parents, my brothers, my sisters-in-law, my friends Jill, Paula, and Bri, and everyone else who puts up with my crazy as I write these books. I don't know what I'd do without you!

Thanks to Nadine, Katie, Ashley, Jaye, the Mitchtam crew, and all my other writer friends who encourage me through the ups and downs of writing.

To Sierra, who once again stepped up as critique partner to both encourage me to keep writing and help polish this book.

To Karis, who managed to beta read this book on a tight deadline and was so amazingly helpful!

A huge thank you to Mindy Bergman and Kara Grant for proofreading this book.

But most of all, all glory belongs to my Heavenly Father who sustains and strengthens me.